JUSTICE DENIED

Also by the author

Material Witness
Reversible Error
Immoral Certainty
Depraved Indifference
The Piano Teacher
No Lesser Plea
Badge of the Assassin

ROBERT K. TANENBAUM

JUSTICE DENIED

A DUTTON BOOK

DUTTON

Published by the Penguin Group
Penguin Books USA Inc., 375 Hudson Street, New York, New York 10014, U.S.A.
Penguin Books Ltd, 27 Wrights Lane, London W8 5TZ, England
Penguin Books Australia Ltd, Ringwood, Victoria, Australia
Penguin Books Canada Ltd, 10 Alcorn Avenue, Toronto, Ontario, Canada M4V 3B2
Penguin Books (N.Z.) Ltd, 182–190 Wairau Road, Auckland 10, New Zealand

Penguin Books Ltd, Registered Offices:
Harmondsworth, Middlesex, England

First published by Dutton, an imprint of Dutton Signet,
a division of Penguin Books USA Inc.
Distributed in Canada by McClelland & Stewart Inc.

First Printing, September, 1994
1 3 5 7 9 10 8 6 4 2

REGISTERED TRADEMARK—MARCA REGISTRADA

Tanenbaum, Robert K.
    Justice denied : a novel / by Robert K. Tanenbaum
        p.   cm.
    ISBN 0-525-93814-1
    1. Assassination—New York (N.Y.)—Fiction. 2. Police—New York
(N.Y.)—Fiction. I. Title.
PS3570.A52J8   1994
813'.54—dc20   93-47605
                                                                CIP

Printed in the United States of America
Set in Garamond No. 3 and Latin Elongated

Designed by Steven N. Stathakis

For those most special:
Patti, Rachael,
Roger, and Billy

Acknowledgments

WITH UTMOST RESPECT, TO MY PARTNER AND COLLABORATOR, MICHAEL Gruber, whose genius flows throughout this book, and who is primarily responsible for this manuscript.

Special appreciation must be extended to my friends Archie Dickranian, Archbishop Vatche Hovsepian and Wally Karabian, for their wise counsel, particularly for vital historical background regarding the birth of the Armenian nation and the nightmarish 1915 Turkish genocide of 1.5 million Armenians; and to their colleagues on the Truth Squad,* who, together with Archie, Wally, and the Archbishop, struggle for justice for Hampig Sasoonian and fight for official Turkish acknowledgment of the genocide.

*Alex R. Baghdassarian, Paul Krekorian, Jacob Adajian, Stephen Saroian, Sally Cotrel, William Paparian, Paul Geragos, and George Garikian

With heartfelt gratitude to Mel Glass, Bob Lehner, and John Keenan for their friendship, guidance, and passion for justice during my years at the Manhattan D.A.'s office.

JUSTICE DENIED

1

A FAT MAN WITH A JAUNTY AIR AND FIVE MINUTES LEFT TO LIVE WALKED out of the Izmir Restaurant on Third Avenue and 46th Street on the island of Manhattan and turned east. He moved with the twinkle-footed gait adopted by many of the stout, but his progress would have been faster had he not, at nearly every convenient window, slowed to check his image in the reflecting glass. He saw a bland moonlike face, neatly mustached in the manner of the late King Farouk, a face that demanded topping with a fez but which at the moment supported a smoke-colored homburg. Below the man's several chins there lay a heavy silk rolled collar, a large-knotted Sulka tie in burgundy, and a dark double-breasted pinstripe suit of a beautiful, if antique, cut. Small oxblood cordovan shoes were on his feet, kid gloves were on his hands, and he had a fawn cashmere topcoat resting on his shoulders, in the manner of Italian filmmakers of the fifties.

It was a Sunday morning, and though few of the other strollers were as formally dressed as the fat man, he did not draw unusual attention, not in that neighborhood. The United Nations, whose headquarters stands on First Avenue between 48th and 42nd streets, employs thousands of diplomats, most of whom live in the immediate area, and many of whom are peculiar in their dress. The fat man was, in fact, a diplomat, but his mission this morning, as every Sunday morning, was personal.

He was a man of fixed habits. Each morning save for the holy day of Friday, he arrived at the Izmir at eight and ate Turkish pastries and drank thick, sweet coffee, while he perused the *New York Times* and *Washington Post,* together with the previous day's editions of an Istanbul and an Ankara newspaper that had come by air. This occupied no more than ninety minutes.

Then, on the four weekdays and Saturday, he would walk down 46th Street to the tall slab of One U.N. Plaza, where he had his office. On Sunday, he would instead turn south on First to the Tudor City apartment block, where he had his mistress.

He had reached the intersection of Second and 46th. Traffic was light, but there were a number of pedestrians about, enjoying the late winter sunshine. A young woman in a stocking cap walked a blond afghan hound. A couple in Norwegian sweaters pushed a stroller containing a well-bundled toddler. A blue-black man in a Burberry loden coat and an African cap spoke in French to a like-colored woman wearing a turban. Across the street, the proprietor of a northern Italian restaurant unrolled his awning. It was a peaceful Sunday in one of the more peaceful and pleasant New York neighborhoods, a district that was exotic without being dangerous and policed like the Kremlin because of all the diplomats.

The light changed, and the fat man twinkled across the broad avenue, casting an interested glance at the girl with the afghan. As he mounted the curb, he heard a car door open, and a figure moved into his path. The morning sun pouring westward formed a corona around the shape of a man. The fat man smiled and politely moved to his right, but the shape moved to block his way. The fat man looked more closely at the person before him, squinting hard against the light. There was something wrong about the man's head: it was bright blue, he was wearing a ski mask.

The fat man turned sharply, alarm flooding his body, and saw that there was another man blocking his path to the west. He had no difficulty seeing that this man wore a ski mask and a blue parka, and that there was an automatic pistol in his hand.

The fat man was frightened, but he was not a coward. He was a Turk, and Turks are tenacious in defense. He grabbed the lapel of his slung topcoat, whipped it out at the face of the man in front of him, and took three rapid steps toward Second Avenue. He heard a woman scream, and shots, many shots, and felt them strike his body, and saw the white, distorted face of the girl with the afghan whirling across the sky as he fell.

The police were there in four minutes, a sergeant and a patrolman from the permanent mobile post set up at the U.N. to control the almost perpetual political demonstrations. They secured the crime scene, rounded up a group of stunned witnesses, and made the necessary calls. They prevailed on the proprietor of the Villa d'Este Restaurant to make a room available for processing these.

Shortly thereafter came the meat wagon from the medical examiner and the car from the crime-scene unit and an unmarked Plymouth Fury containing two homicide detectives out of Midtown South. The two detectives were a Mutt and Jeff act: one tall, angular, watery-eyed, with a lugubrious tan fringe hanging below his bony nose—Barney Wayne; the other shorter, younger by a dozen years, stockier, darker, a feisty man and a cigar chomper—Joe Frangi.

Both of them bore the rank of detective second grade. Wayne thought that being a detective second grade was pretty good going. He was not the sort of Wayne who gets called "Duke" in the NYPD. Frangi thought the same but also thought that he himself was good enough for a gold hat and meant to get one. Frangi thought Wayne was a good guy but a little too cautious. Wayne thought Frangi was a good guy but a little too reckless. They were a reasonably good team: neither the flawless heroes of the TV shows nor the corrupt villains of the hard-hitting investigative reports. Like most NYPD detectives, they were somewhat heroic and somewhat corrupt.

Wayne and Frangi introduced themselves to the sergeant. The sergeant was glad to see them, and to turn over possession of the crime scene. The sergeant was a detective from Brooklyn who had been placed back in uniform on a series of crummy details, of which this U.N. thing was one. Placing detectives "back in the bag," as the saying went, usually for crowd control duties, is a means of petty discipline or harassment in the NYPD, and is one reason why crowd control in the City is often unpleasant for the crowd.

"What do we got, Sarge?" asked Frangi.

The sergeant gestured at the prostrate corpse. "They hit him at ten past eleven. It's a fresh one. The owner of that Italian restaurant called it in."

Frangi said, " 'They'? We have witnesses?"

The sergeant nodded. "Yeah, at least half a dozen. I put them over in the restaurant. Two guys in ski masks did it and got out in a blue car." He pointed at crime-scene technicians photographing the tire marks left by the putative blue car.

"They hauled ass down Forty-sixth. They must have come right by me."

"You didn't spot the car?"

The sergeant shrugged, then laughed. "Hey, I got my hands full with the fuckin' Palestinians or Pakistanis or whatever the fuck they are."

The sergeant was about to get himself in trouble trying to think of a way to explain how a blue car with two assassins in it driving like a bat out of hell away from a place where moments before at least ten shots had been fired, that place being not a hundred yards from the sergeant's own command post, had escaped all notice. Embarrassed for the man, Frangi forestalled any further lies by asking the sergeant to show him the witnesses. They walked off toward the restaurant.

Wayne approached the corpse. As usual at such moments, he let his mind go blank, to convert it into a receptive sponge for any clues that might be invisible to the willing intellect. As usual, his mind remained blank, except for a vague sadness about the finality of death. The murdered man was not wearing two different shoes or unmatched socks. He did not have in his mouth, which was open and full of congealing blood, a mysterious signet ring, and Wayne, sighing, did not believe that he would find in the man's pocket a torn matchbook with the killer's name written on it.

Wayne moved away to let the crime-scene man put plastic bags over the victim's hands, a routine procedure, and then, stepping carefully to avoid soaking his shoes in the thick blood, he went through pockets.

Frangi, meanwhile, was getting names and addresses of the eyewitnesses and writing down where they had been at the time and place of the crime and whether they had seen anything. He decided to start with the young dog walker, who was apparently the witness closest to the crime. She had by this time recovered from her hysterics and was sipping coffee. Her afghan was quivering at her feet, chewing on a beef knuckle supplied by the proprietor.

Frangi established the basic facts: two shooters, both had shot. There was no talking from either the shooters or the victim. The victim had tried to get away by flinging his coat. The shooters had not taken anything from the victim. They had reentered their car and driven off.

No, she hadn't taken down the license plate number. No, she hadn't recognized the make of car. Yes, she would be available to look at different pictures of cars. No, she hadn't noticed anything peculiar about the shooters. They were average. She couldn't tell their race because they had been wearing ski masks and gloves.

The other witnesses added little to this except that, by a miracle, the restaurant proprietor had spotted the car for a '77 or '78 Ford Fairlane two-door. His sister had one just like it.

Wayne watched the body being bagged and loaded into the waiting M.E. wagon, and he then put the evidence bags with the pocket contents into a cheap plastic briefcase and walked over to the restaurant.

The press had picked up the scent already, and the sergeant had called in a few more troops to handle the growing crowd of journalists and photographers. People shouted questions at Wayne and poked microphone tubes at him and held up recorders in the din to catch some marketable vibrations from his lips. He waved them off and pushed past into the restaurant along a path kept clear by the uniformed men.

Wayne put his briefcase on the table where Frangi was sitting and sat down himself.

"Have some coffee," said Frangi. "It's the first time I ever got good coffee on a crime scene. Probably the last too. I hear the jackals make it for a terrorist attack."

Wayne raised an eyebrow. "We're always the last to know. The target's right, anyway." He removed a clear plastic evidence bag from his briefcase. It had in it a long European-style notecase that had once been tan but was now almost entirely covered with red-brown stains. It had a rough half-inch wide hole punched through it.

"Got one right through the passport. The vic's name is Mehmet Ersoy. He's the cultural attaché at the Turkish embassy to the U.N."

"Holy Christ! Ah, crap! The slicks'll be all over us on this one."

"Yep. I'm surprised they're not here already. Uh-oh, I spoke too soon. They're playing our song."

The sound of sirens coming closer could be heard. "Hey, I just remembered," said Wayne. "Did you call D.A. Homicide?"

This was new. An instruction had been passed down from the chief of detectives that the detective in charge of a crime scene in a suspected homicide was to call the newly reconstituted homicide bureau of the New York D.A.'s office immediately upon arrival at the crime scene.

Frangi said, "Yeah, I made the call. Our luck, we'll get a fourteen-year-old girl just out of law school."

Now the little restaurant's window reflected the beams of a half-dozen red lights as the slicks arrived, in increasing order of rank, for it would never do for a superior officer to arrive on a scene without his inferiors stacked up to show that they too were on top of things. An elaborate system of delays and phone calls built into the vitals of the NYPD insured that this would ever be the case.

Thus Wayne and Frangi had to tell their story to the lieutenant in charge of their precinct squad, who told it to the duty captain, who informed the deputy chief in charge of Manhattan, who told the deputy commissioner, who told the deputy mayor. It was somewhat unusual to have a deputy mayor on a slick, but the mayor knew that the U.N. brought forty thousand jobs to New York, and he was determined to let the world know that whether or not lesser New Yorkers fell like flies, the flesh of the international community was as sacred to him as that of his sainted mom.

After the word had gone down and the deputy mayor had posed gravely before the cameras to ritually renew the City's marriage to the World Body and its every minion; and after the man from the P.C.'s office had come out strongly against terrorism in general and especially in New York (not forgetting to boast about the matchless anti-terrorism capacity of the NYPD); and after each level of command had left in decreasing order of rank, each one telling the next one down that there better not be a fuck-up on this one, they wanted clearance *yesterday,* and whosoever got the blame if there *were* to be a fuck-up (and it would certainly not be *himself*) would spend the rest of their career in a blue bag guarding a motor pool in the South Bronx; after all that, when there was no one left in the restaurant but the lieutenant, the two detectives, a half-dozen irritable witnesses, a restaurateur wondering whether a story he would tell for years was worth losing a Sunday lunch hour, and a dog who had to pee, Wayne said, "Hey, Lou, could you tell us one thing? What's all this horseshit about terrorists? We don't know zip yet. The guy's old lady could've had him whacked for the insurance or something."

The lieutenant stared at him. He motioned the two detectives to follow him into the restaurant's small bar.

"Nobody told you?"

"Naw," said Frangi. "I mean, what the fuck, we're just the detectives on the case, why give us any information? It'd be like cheating—"

"A guy called the *Post* and CBS. He gave the time and place and the name of the vic and said he was the Armenian Secret Army, and then a lot of political horseshit. We got a transcript back at the house."

"Armenians, huh?" said Wayne. "You think it's legit, Lou?"

The lieutenant rolled his eyes. "The fuck I know. The brass wants a terrorist. If it turns out the guy was dorking some big *gaupo's* kid sister, well, we'll have to work around it. But, guys, I need speed on this one. Whatever you need—cars, radios, stealers up the ying-yang, whatever. Red ball, all right?"

Wayne and Frangi exchanged a look. Wayne said, "We'll toss his place, see if he's into anything naughty. His office too, maybe—"

"Uh-uh, the office is out. It's foreign territory," said the lieutenant. "The guy's a dip; we're gonna move like silk around most of the people he knows. You understand the drill."

"It's like parking tickets," said Wayne.

The lieutenant shaped his face into a false smile. "You got it. No leaning. Please, thank you, yessir, nosir. Any intrusion on U.N. mission property, and that includes motor vehicles, has to be cleared up the chain to the P.C. After you've made your calls and figured out who you need to talk to at the mission, if anyone, I need to clear it in writing. There's a form." The lieutenant paused and lit a cigarette from the butt of his old one. He asked, "You run the car yet? No? Well, get on it, and when you get the printout, check it for Armenian names."

"Armenian names?" asked Frangi wonderingly. "You think these big-time terrorists used their own car on a hit?"

"It shows movement, dammit," snapped the lieutenant. "And

call B.S.S.I. too. There's a guy there, Flanagan, he's waiting for your call."

Frangi made a sour face. The Bureau of Strategic Services and Intelligence, the former Red Squad, was not popular with street detectives, who considered politically motivated crime of such trivial concern that it was not worth the time and money expended on it. Besides that, B.S.S.I. did not put people on the pavement, which meant they were kibbitzers rather than helpers.

The lieutenant caught the look. "Just do it!" he said. "Okay, you got the word. I want to be kept up on this on a daily basis, follow?"

Frangi let his head loll and dangled his arms at shoulder height, miming a marionette. In a squeaky voice he said, "Hi, kids! I'm a detective. Want to play with me?"

The lieutenant shook his head and allowed himself a sour grin as he left.

Wayne said, "Movement, huh? Tell me, you think this case is gonna be a serious pain in the ass or what?"

"Well, the first movement I'm gonna make is my bowels," replied his partner. "And after that I think we should movement the witnesses out of here before they all starve to death."

"Yeah," Wayne agreed, "and speaking of which, we could make a movement toward getting some lunch. Maybe the guy here could give us some veal scallopini on the arm, seeing how we brightened up his day so much. Hello, Roland."

This last was directed toward a man who had just entered the restaurant. Both detectives smiled and greeted him warmly, because he was evidence that they would not, amid their other troubles, have to put up with a fourteen-year-old girl assistant D.A.

"You on this case, Roland? You poor bastard!" said Frangi with feeling.

Roland Hrcany, assistant D.A. in the homicide bureau, sat deliberately down on a chair and regarded the two detectives balefully. "You know what I was doing when you guys' call came in? Do you know? I was in my bed and I was chewing on a buttock the size and firmness of a ripe cantaloupe melon and letting the juice drip into my mouth."

"Not a voter, hey, Roland?" said Wayne.

"Correct in your surmise, Detective," said Hrcany. "Twenty is plenty. Okay, what do we have on this abortion?"

They discussed the case, easily and humorously. They were all pros and had worked together many times before. Besides that, Roland was the most popular with the police of all the A.D.A.'s in Manhattan. It was his stock in trade, and he worked at it. He was arrogantly male in the way most cops conceived maleness: profane, violent, and a tremendous drinker. He knew hundreds of available women and had made dates for hundreds of cops, not that cops need help in that area, but the thought counted. He would also do favors for cops in line of duty, save them from embarrassment in court when they had screwed up the evidence, or make a cop look particularly good, or help cops stack up overtime for court appearances around the holidays when they needed extra cash.

But most of all there was the body. Roland Hrcany was a committed bodybuilder and weight lifter. He had twenty-five-inch biceps and a forty-four-inch chest and a nineteen-inch neck. Cops are physical people. They believe they have to dominate physically to survive. Roland was physically dominating. That he was also a very smart, aggressive lawyer, capable of grinding mutts and their candy-ass lawyers to powder in court, was just the cherry on top.

They laid out the case, respectfully, knowing that Roland would understand the fix they were in with the slicks and sympathize, and he did. Roland interviewed the witnesses and dismissed them. Frangi went to the bathroom. The patrolmen stopped guarding the entrance, and the Villa D'Este opened for business.

Frangi came back. The proprietor walked over and, smiling, offered lunch, which they accepted. His place was going to be on television, and he was happy with the world. When they had been given a huge bread basket and a round of drinks, Wayne said, "So, Roland, what do you think? A ball breaker, right?"

"Not really, Barney. I got a good feeling about this one. I think it's gonna play right for us." The two detectives made skeptical noises, but Roland advanced his case with undiminished confidence. "No, look: they were waiting for the guy, this Ersoy. They were parked where they knew he was going to pass at that particular time. So they knew him—"

"Not necessarily," Frangi interrupted. "They could've been pros, casing him for weeks."

"Okay, or they knew his habits, but no way they were pros. A pro who knew as much about the vic as these guys did would've waited by his apartment and given him three in the head from a small-caliber gun."

"How can you say that, Roland? It's on TV all the time: the terrorists in Europe and the Middle East hit these politicians like a fucking army: machine guns, rockets—"

"Yeah, but those people are covered by heavy security. You can't get to them unless you blast your way through. Our guy was naked. He didn't feel threatened at all. So, of all the times to hit someone, why pick broad daylight on a Sunday, with your car pointed down a one-way street whose only outlet is through U.N. Plaza, which practically every other weekend is loaded with cops and demonstrators. It doesn't make sense unless it's amateur hour."

"He's got a point, Joe," said Wayne.

Frangi replied, "Okay, fine, say I buy that, what does that give us?"

"It means," said Roland, "that either the killing comes out of his life, as usual, and the Armenian Army thing is horseshit, a dodge, or that you're looking for a bunch of Armenian assholes sitting around a kitchen table in Brooklyn. I mean, it's not gonna be Carlos the Jackal."

Wayne sighed. "Yeah, well, nothing against the Armenians, but that would suit me fine. We have to start tracing through this dude's life, we're talking weeks, swimming upstream against this diplomat shit all the way. So I guess we have to start with the blue car and the printouts and the Armenian names. And if you're right, they *might* have used their own car."

"They might have," Roland agreed. "But we still have to check out the vic. Did I see a safety-deposit key on that case you took off him? Yeah? People with boxes usually have more interesting lives than most. You're going to toss his place today?"

The detectives looked nervously at each other. "Well, that's what I meant about swimming upstream. We got a lecture about being diplomatic," said Wayne. "The brass wants us to go through the embassy on everything."

"Yeah, well, that's fine for the embassy personnel and the office, but his personal place is our meat. It's a felony investigation, not a parking ticket. If you get any heat there, call me. I'll take it all the way up the line if I have to, and—"

He looked up, aware of a presence looming over him. It was a very tall, very black man wearing a Burberry over a gray suit and a brightly colored pillbox hat on his head. He had gold-rimmed spectacles. They all stared. The man smiled and reached into his coat. They all tensed, but he brought out only a leather card case.

"Excuse me," the man said. "I understand you are of the police?"

"Yeah," said Frangi. "Who're you?"

The man passed each a large, stiff engraved card declaring him to be M. Etienne Mbor Sekoué of the Senegalese mission to the U.N. He said, "I extremely regret not coming before this, but I felt it proper to escort my sister home. She was entirely devastated by the lamentable events of this morning. It is her first visit to New York and—"

"Wait a minute, you're a *witness*?" Frangi exclaimed.

"Yes, I approached one of the officers on the street, and they directed me here."

"Please sit down, Mr. Sekoué," said Roland. "Tell us what you saw." Wayne brought out his notebook and said, "Where were you when the shooting took place?"

The African settled himself at the table's fourth seat. "I . . . we, that is, my sister and myself, were on point of crossing Second Avenue. We were perhaps in the center of the street when we heard the shots commence—a fusillade."

Wayne frowned. The man had been farther away from the action than some of the other witnesses. He asked a few more questions about the movements of the killers and their victim, but this merely confirmed what they already had. "Anything else, Mr. Sekoué? Did you notice anything unusual about the killers? Or their car?"

"Of the assassins? No, no one could see anything of them. Their masks, their gloves. As to the car," he smiled self-deprecatingly, "it was a large American car, new, of the color dark blue. I am not familiar with the American marques." He paused. "Surely, however, you will be able to search it, having the license number, no?"

Frangi said, "Sure, if we had the number, but we don't."

M. Sekoué's spectacles glittered when he smiled. "Ah, but I have written it down, you see."

And he had. Before their amazed faces he produced a tiny leather address book with a gold pencil attached. A license number had been neatly written inside the back cover. Wayne wrote it down in his notebook. The three men thanked the diplomat profusely, and he departed.

"That's the kind of brother we need more of in this town," said Frangi with feeling. "Now, five bucks says it's ripped off and we're back to zero. You want to make the call, Barney?"

Wayne nodded and walked over to the pay phone in the bar. He dialed and had a brief conversation. Roland and Frangi sat waiting, not speaking. Wayne came back to the table and sat down. "It's not on the latest hot sheet. The next one's not due for a couple of hours, so it could have been boosted this morning and the guy hasn't missed it yet . . ."

"Barney, for chrissake, who owns the fucking vehicle?" cried Frangi.

Wayne smiled broadly. "How do you like Aram Tomasian? A local boy. Lives in Murray Hill."

Roland Hrcany laughed out loud. Frangi raised his eyes to the ceiling and said, "Thank you, Jesus!"

2

THEY LOOKED HIM OVER. A COMPACT, SHORT, OLIVE-SKINNED MAN IN his late twenties, Aram Tomasian stood in the doorway of his apartment and returned their look out of deep-set brown eyes. He didn't seem surprised to see two cops at his door at eight of a Sunday evening, which was itself surprising. What was more surprising, he didn't say, "What's this all about?" or "What's wrong?" or give them the phony smile that most people kept in stock for a visit from the police, but gravely ushered them into his home and said, "I've been expecting you."

Frangi and Wayne walked into the place and absorbed it in a glance, as cops do. Upscale but not ostentatious: white carpeting, beige Haitian cotton sofa and armchairs, an expensive stereo system and a large television mounted in a long teak wall unit, a glass and chrome coffee table. There was a large framed color poster of what looked like some old ruins on the wall and a dozen or so family pictures in silver or leather frames placed on various shelves of the wall unit, together with a substantial library.

Wayne looked at Tomasian and once again tried to make his mind blank, hoping for a telling illumination. A regular guy, was all he got, a little cocky, in control. Wayne didn't care for that. "Why were you expecting the police, Mr. Tomasian?" he asked, making his voice a little flatter and louder than necessary.

Tomasian gestured at the TV. "The Turk who got shot today. I figured you'd be around." He sat down on his sofa and crossed his legs.

Frangi sat down opposite. Wayne paced around the room, looking at the books, photographs, and jacketed LPs stored neatly in the wall unit. One shelf, behind clear glass, was devoted to a collection of some kind: four pieces of old-looking jewelry with bright enamel insets, some dull gems deeply engraved with designs, and several small panels of gray or whitish stone incised with carvings of saints.

Frangi said, "Why did you figure that, Mr. Tomasian?"

The man shrugged. "That call to the papers. It was on TV. They blamed it on Armenian nationalists. I'm an Armenian nationalist . . ." He made a flowing gesture with his hand indicating the obviousness of it all.

"And you know something about this Armenian Secret Army that claimed credit for the killing?"

Tomasian allowed himself a faint smile. "If I told you that, it wouldn't be much of a secret, would it?"

From behind the couch Wayne said, "Withholding information about a murder investigation is a serious crime, Mr. Tomasian." Wayne liked to get physically behind the subject during interrogations. He found it got them off balance. Then he and Frangi could shoot questions at the subject alternately, and have the pleasure of seeing the guy's head whip back and forth as he tried to face his questioners.

This pleasure Tomasian denied them, however. Keeping still, he said to Frangi, as if he had made the statement, "In that case, let me say that I have absolutely no knowledge of this murder, either the planning of it or the execution, and don't know anyone who did. I am not aware that the Armenian Secret Army or any other Armenian organization had any part in it. I am not going to discuss the Armenian Secret Army with you in any way, or reveal its plans, its organization, its activities, or its membership."

Frangi said, "Okay, Mr. Tomasian, if that's the way you want to play it, fine. Let's talk about you personally, then. This morning between eight and eleven—you were where?"

"Right here. I had a late night last night and I slept in, until about noon."

"Alone, right?" asked Wayne, still behind the sofa.

Tomasian smiled again. "No, I was with my girlfriend. In bed. She left about one-thirty."

"We'll need her name, then," said Frangi.

Tomasian paused and then said, "I guess there's no way around it. This is all going to come out in the papers, right? The thing is, her family will have a shit fit. There's no way to, um, keep this private."

Frangi stared at him blankly, his pencil poised above his pad.

"Her name's Gaby Avanian, Gabrielle." He added an address on St. Marks Place in the East Village.

"You own a car, Mr. Tomasian?" asked Frangi.

"Yes, why?"

Frangi ignored the question. "Make and model?"

"It's a 1977 Ford Polara."

"Is that a blue car, sir?" asked Wayne, and when told that it was in fact that color he and Frangi exchanged a significant look. "Where do you keep it?" Wayne asked.

"In the garage in the building."

"Did you use it today at all?" asked Frangi.

"No. I don't ever use it much, as a matter of fact. I can walk to work. Sometimes I drive out of town on weekends or visit relatives in the boroughs, Westchester, like that. And sometimes I pick up supplies for my business."

"What business is that?" asked Wayne.

"I'm a jeweler. My dad owns Metropolitan Jewelry. It's a chain. I run the store at Lex and Forty-first, and I also do a lot of our original designs."

The detectives exchanged another look and Frangi rose. "Thanks for your time, Mr. Tomasian," he said, and offered a business card. "If you think of anything that might be helpful, give us a call."

Tomasian glanced at the card and placed it on the coffee table. Again he smiled faintly. "But meantime, don't try to leave town?"

Frangi said, "That would be considerate, Mr. Tomasian, but in any case, if we decide we want you, we'll find you."

Tomasian didn't offer to see them to the door, and they let themselves out. In the elevator, Wayne said, "So. You like him. I could tell."

"Like him? I *love* him. I want to marry him and have his babies. It's the guy, Barney. This is a twenty-four-hour clearance. The fucking fans will go wild."

"Yeah? I hope."

"Why? You don't like him?"

Wayne did not want to dispel his partner's enthusiasm, but he had seen better suspects than this one go glimmering. He said, "Well, I'll like him better after we talk to the girl, and after we get a couple of pieces of physical evidence."

Frangi gave him a look. "Partner, if by some chance our boy was not the trigger, he knows who it was. Count on it! Fucking cute asshole! 'It wouldn't be a secret.' Hey, I got an idea. Let's take a look at the car." He pressed the *G* button.

"Look at that," said Frangi with satisfaction when, after ten minutes of searching, they stood behind the blue Polara. Wayne looked and then after a moment knelt down and examined the bolts that held the license plate into its frame. He rose, rubbing his fingers together under his nose.

"That settles it," said Frangi.

"Hmmm," said Wayne.

"What, what do you want, a signed confession? It's the right plate on his car. He's our guy, for cryin' out loud."

"Well, we can get a warrant with this, but I don't know . . . he could have an alibi. Somebody could've boosted this car, and besides, the car they used was a Fairlane. This is a Polara."

"Hey, let the D.A. worry about that shit."

"I will. But I'll tell you, even Roland'll be happier if those ski masks and parkas show up in his closet, or the guns. And another thing. How do you figure a guy sloppy enough to use his own car for a hit in broad daylight is careful enough to clean the rust off his license-plate bolts and keep them oiled up?"

"We're doing good," said Roland Hrcany, concluding his tale of what the detectives had learned. "I'm almost amazed." He was sitting across the desk from his boss, the bureau chief of the Homicide Bureau of the New York County D.A., on the Monday following the murder of Mehmet Ersoy.

The bureau chief said, "It *is* amazing. The stupidity of criminals has no known limit. And speaking of stupidity, the district attorney will be pleased. I know that's important to you, Roland."

Hrcany laughed obligingly. It had been a private joke between them for years that Roland was trying to curry favor with the exiguous Sanford Bloom, the D.A. In fact, Hrcany had as little respect for the D.A. as his chief, but his ferocious ambition showed itself as a desire to impress. The bureau chief was, in contrast, long past caring what anyone thought of him.

The bureau chief's name was Roger Karp. Now he stood up and stretched and paced back and forth behind his desk. He was a very tall, lanky man, with close-cut light brown hair and a bony face. He moved stiffly, with a slight limp. At the age of four he had decided that he would be called Roger no longer, but Butch instead, a decision he had enforced by ceasing to answer to any other name. It was a stubbornness he had retained in adulthood.

Karp said, "They talk to this alibi yet, this girlfriend?"

"No, they haven't turned her up yet. There's nobody home at her place, and her parents don't know where she is."

"That could be a problem, if she comes out of nowhere later and confirms his story. However . . ."

"However, we've got way enough for a warrant," said Hrcany.

"No question," Karp agreed. "Let's do it, and let me know as soon as you get anything. Bloom's already been on my ass about it."

Hrcany scooped up his papers and left. Karp walked over to his window and looked out. Six floors below he could see Leonard Street, a patch of blacktop that, at that point, was largely devoted to the parking of judges' cars, while directly across Leonard was the New York State Office building, where he could actually observe an army of slow-moving clerks making it difficult for the citizens of New York to get license plates.

The license plate was the odd thing about Roland's case. Simple carelessness and stupidity or a sophisticated bluff? Karp could imagine a defense lawyer saying to a jury, "Ladies and gentlemen: can you really believe that this intelligent, successful businessman would use his own car, bearing his own license, to commit an assassination in broad daylight?"

Well, yes, Karp could believe it. In his twelve years with the D.A. he had seen acts of egregious stupidity on the part of defendants that made this license-plate business look like the special theory of relativity. Still, the defense always used the "can you believe?" argument. And sometimes it worked.

Karp was not as sanguine as Roland about the lock they supposedly had on Mehmet Ersoy's purported killer. On the other hand, Roland knew what he was doing. He was the best of Karp's twenty-nine prosecutors, a man with a record in homicide prosecutions nearly as good as Karp's own, which was the best ever. But had he been the worst, Karp still would not have interfered, except to correct some obvious legal or procedural boner. Karp could cajole, criticize, even humiliate his minions, but the A.D.A. in charge of a case was in charge of the case. To behave otherwise, to second guess, to countermand decisions, was to court chaos. Karp could not supervise the prosecution of all the thousand-odd murder cases that Manhattan produced each year. A thousand and climbing.

This rule, of course, did not apply to the D.A. himself, who felt free to intrude in any case that took his fancy. What took his fancy were the cases with high political profiles. Rich people or famous people getting killed. The bizarre ones that stuck to the front pages and appeared on the nightly news. Cases involving the interests of his friends, or acquaintances, or anyone with a nice suit who could grab him for fifteen minutes.

Karp was often able to ignore these intrusions or confound them. The D.A. was not a trial lawyer and never had been. If it was up to him, there wouldn't be any trials at all, just gentlemanly discussions between defense and prosecution leading to a plea bargain and another cleared case.

Unfortunately for the D.A., without the capacity to go to trial and win an overwhelming proportion of the time, the plea-bargaining system would not work. The defendants would laugh in your face. Karp won trials, murder trials especially, which was why he was able to get away with what he got away with.

Karp moved closer to the window, resting his forehead against the cool glass. From this angle he could see the green street sign that dedicated the foot of Leonard Street to the former D.A., the legendary Francis P. Garrahy. Garrahy had died six years ago, an act for which Karp had just begun to forgive him. Karp's heart still lived in the D.A.'s office that Garrahy had created and run for three decades: an organization of uncompromising legal probity, dominated by men whose natural home was the courtroom. In that organization the cream had risen to the old homicide bureau, of which Karp had briefly been a part.

When Bloom had got in, the first thing he had done was to dissolve the homicide bureau and assign homicide cases at random to a series of identical Criminal Courts bureaus. It made more sense administratively, went the argument, which meant it made sense to a man who had never tried a murder case and saw no difference between murder and any other crime.

But murder *was* different. The emotional currents and the legal intricacies that surrounded murder cases were unique, even in a state, like New York at the time, which had no death penalty. A homicide bureau had to be a special sort of place.

Karp had recently been given a recreated homicide bureau, not because Bloom had seen the light but because Karp had caught him at so much chicanery, malfeasance, and blundering so often that, although Karp had never even hinted at a quid pro quo, Bloom's politician's soul had cried out that Karp must be given something big and substantial, that by such a gift his fate might be more closely tied to Bloom's own. Besides which there was the chance that, in the dangerous world of murder trials, Karp might one day screw up so badly that Bloom could dump him publicly, and with the approbation of the vulgar herd.

Past the foot of Leonard Street, and barely in Karp's field of view, was a small park called Columbus Park. At this moment a dozen or so elderly Chinese had gathered on the new grass to do their morning t'ai chi. Karp admired their movements for a few minutes and then, as he turned away from the window to get back to work, imitated one of the positions, holding his hands high, balancing on his left foot, and sweeping his right foot across to the left.

Karp was a naturally graceful man, and the movement might have even pleased the Chinese had not Karp's left knee collapsed, sending him crashing into a couple of conference table chairs and to the floor.

He lay there cursing and gritting his teeth against the fierce pain jabbing up from his bad knee. A dark, worried face appeared upside down over the edge of the conference table.

"Are you all right?" asked Connie Trask, his secretary.

Karp flushed and managed to get his good leg under him. Trask rushed around the table to give him a hand, but he waved her off and, groaning, struggled to his feet.

"You ought to see a doctor," said the secretary.

"I don't need a doctor, Connie. I'm fine. I just tripped."

She looked at him doubtfully. "Hmmph. Tell it to the marines!

You've been shuffling around here like the wreck of the *Hesperus* for weeks. You and that leg—"

"It's the weather changing . . ."

"I thought that was when it got cold. It's getting warm now."

Karp moved around to his desk and sat down heavily in his chair, elevating the left leg on the edge of a desk drawer permanently pulled out for that purpose. He scowled and snapped, "Connie, we know you're a grandmother, but you're not my grandmother, okay?"

"Lucky for you," she replied. "Meanwhile, you got an appointment waiting. Guy wants to work here, don't ask me why. You want me to send him in?"

"Give me a couple of minutes."

She nodded and left. Karp massaged his knee and flexed it gingerly. It felt like bits of pea gravel were trapped under the cartilage. It was nearly twenty years gone since a big USC guard had come crashing down on that joint, ending Karp's basketball career at Berkeley and the possibility of a bid from the pros. The memory of that moment of pain could still nauseate him.

And as it had turned out, Karp had gotten to play for the pros, a brief debut the past winter on a New York team as part of a murder investigation. His knee had sufficed for six weeks of not very strenuous play, but had not been the same since. For now, however, Karp's will was as strong as his knee was shaky. He willed the pain away and looked up brightly as his appointment walked in.

The branch of Metropolitan Jewelers run by Aram Tomasian was located on 42nd just west of Lexington. There, at ten on the Monday after, appeared the two detectives, Frangi and Wayne. They had with them the search warrant hastily but perfectly drafted by Roland Hrcany, ordering them to search for a list of specific items, including weapons and clothing and "any other articles and instruments used in the commission of the said crime."

There was a clerk in attendance at the glassed counter, and when the two officers identified themselves, she brought Tomasian out from the back of the shop. Tomasian was wearing an old-fashioned tan work smock and a loupe attached to an elastic band. It stuck up from his forehead like a stumpy horn.

Tomasian seemed anxious, and again he surprised them. He asked, "Are you here about Gaby?"

They had to think a moment. Frangi said, "Gaby. You mean your girlfriend."

"Yes," said Tomasian. "I called her after I talked to you yesterday and I couldn't reach her. I tried her half a dozen times and then I gave up and went over to her place. I have a key. She wasn't there. I called her work and a couple of her friends, and nobody seems to know where she is."

Tomasian seemed genuinely worried, but, on the other hand, Wayne, for one, thought that Tomasian might turn out to be a considerable actor. He had been too cool on the day of the murder, and too cute.

Wayne said, "Why were you so interested in reaching her?"

Tomasian uttered a sound of annoyance and exasperation. "Why? She's my girlfriend. I wanted to talk to her. I knew you guys would be coming to see her and—"

"You wanted to get your story straight. Your alibi," Frangi interrupted.

"It's not a 'story,' " snapped Tomasian. "I was concerned. She's not the kind of person that police visit. I wanted to talk to her. Is that a crime?"

Wayne removed a paper from his coat pocket and smoothed it out on the glass counter. "This is a search warrant, Mr. Tomasian. It gives us authority to search your business premises and your home."

Tomasian looked briefly at the document. A flush appeared along his cheekbones, and he licked his lips. The sight of this discomfort brought a surge of gladness to the heart of Detective Wayne. Tomasian said hesitantly, "Look, my apartment, fine, but this store— it's not my property. It belongs to my father; I just manage it for him."

"It's your place of business, Mr. Tomasian," said Wayne, "and it's described in the warrant."

Tomasian sighed and told his clerk to pull down the shades and lock the front door. The two detectives began to search.

There was nothing in the display cases out front except jewelry and the accoutrements of the jewelry trade. The back of the store looked more promising. It held a substantial jeweler's workshop: a long, scarred wooden table covered with tools and bits of shining wire, a high stool before it, and the wall it faced was lined with cabinets and boxes full of tiny drawers. A small desk was placed at one end of the room, and this held a phone, a Rolodex, and assorted papers. It was flanked by a tan four-drawer filing cabinet. And then there was the safe.

It was a green steel room the size of an apartment bathroom, its two thick doors hanging open invitingly. Wayne and Frangi moved toward it instinctively: if a suspect owns a safe, of course that's the first place you look for the good stuff. The safe was lined floor to ceiling with metal shelves, upon which were stacked long, flat steel boxes and open bins. The bins, they found, contained gold and silver wires of different gauges and in sheets, as well as various semiprecious stones and jewelers' findings. The boxes held gems and finished pieces. Under one of the lower shelves there was a steel-bound footlocker, painted olive drab and locked with a heavy hasp and padlock.

The detectives pulled the locker out into the center of the safe. Tomasian was sitting on his stool, watching them. Wordlessly he held out a key ring, holding it up by a small brass key. Wayne took the key and opened the footlocker.

Three hours later, the detectives were in Roland Hrcany's office, sucking on illicit cans of beer and feeling pleased with what had gone down.

"He give you any grief?" asked their host.

"No, he went like a lamb," answered Frangi. "Same thing at his apartment. We checked the closet, and there was the red and blue parka, just like the witness described. We also picked up a lot of paper—stuff about this Armenian Secret Army—leaflets, posters. We even got carbons of a couple letters he sent to the Turkish embassy at the U.N."

"Threats?"

"You could say that, but it's kind of vague what he was gonna do if they didn't come across. But they weren't love notes."

"But you didn't find the ski mask?"

"No," said Frangi, "but that don't mean much. It's the kind of thing that's easy to trash."

"I presume he's still denying the whole thing?"

Wayne said, "Yep. We read him his rights and he clammed up. He sticks to the line he was with his girlfriend, who's still among the missing, and he didn't know who the other guy at the shooting was because he wasn't at any shooting."

"So what do you think? He'll keep sticking to it?" asked Roland.

Wayne said, "Yeah. This boy's no scuzzball off the block; you're gonna have to take it the distance, Roland, unless we turn up the partner."

"Any leads on that?"

"Nothing so far, but we haven't been through his papers completely yet. We'll find him."

Roland nodded and picked up a piece of paper on which Wayne had written an inventory of the items seized from Tomasian's home and business.

"Okay, what about these guns?"

Wayne said, "He had a damn armory in that footlocker. The pistols are new, some of them still in boxes, but a couple could have been fired. Walther P5's, 9mm. Then we got two H&K 54 submachine guns, also 9mm, also new, with the packing grease still on them, plus about three thousand rounds of 9mm. Parabellum."

"That's what the vic was shot with, right?"

"Right. And illegal as hell, the bunch of it."

"What's his story? You ask him?"

"A shooting club. Self-protection for Armenian businessmen. He picked the stuff up in Germany, he says. Goes over a couple times a year to buy gems. He doesn't deny he smuggled the weapons in. Says he got a good deal, he didn't think it was any big thing."

"How wrong he was," said Roland. "Meanwhile, we'll do the ballistics on all the weapons, just to make sure he didn't use them and then clean them up and rebox them. Now what about this assassination gun?"

Frangi smiled. "Uh-huh. You don't see many like that. In fact, there weren't that many to begin with. It's an old World War II, what they call a grease gun, an M3 submachine gun chambered for the 9mm. Parabellum, but this one's modified with a built-in silencer in the barrel. They made about a thousand of them for the OSS during the war. Shoot thirty rounds out of that thing, it'd make no more noise than a wet fart in an elevator."

Hrcany seemed about to say something but didn't. Instead he let out a hard laugh. "Also for protection and sport, no doubt?"

"I don't know; that one he wouldn't talk about," said Frangi.

Hrcany picked a heavy spring-type hand exerciser from his desk and began to squeeze the handles without apparent effort. The muscles in his forearms flexed dramatically. He thought for a minute in silence as he pumped.

"Okay, like you said, do the papers. Find the other guy. Do the ballistics. Get the witnesses in to look at the car and Tomasian—I know he was masked, but let's go through the drill."

"They got a rubber print off the car at the scene," offered Wayne.

"Yeah, that too," said Roland. "Every little bit helps." He looked at his watch. "Okay, let's see this bozo now. I got a full day."

The initial Q. & A. with Aram Tomasian did not in any way diminish Hrcany's belief that he had in custody the murderer of Mehmet Ersoy. Tomasian had a lawyer present, so Roland could not get away with his famous screaming wildman act, but he was able to confront the suspect with: his hatred of Turks; his possession of the requisite hardware and the right car; his inability to account for his whereabouts at the time of the crime and for hours on either side of it.

Tomasian's response to all this was weak. The alibi was a joke. Even if the girlfriend showed up, her testimony was hardly gilt-edged. Tomasian admitted the letters but denied the license plate. His plate had been stolen ten days before the crime. He had reported it to the police. He had not used his car in the interim, while he waited for a replacement plate to be issued. Or so he said.

Not a bad Q. & A., Roland thought. He had enough to charge, enough to indict. When the lab stuff proved out, he'd have enough to convict. A nice package.

Delivering this package to Karp was a moment Roland had keenly anticipated, one that in his imaginings would be second only to the one when the jury returned a guilty verdict in *People* v. *Tomasian.* Roland and Karp went back a long way. They had entered Garrahy's old operation on the same day. In a system that put a premium on toughness, on hard work for little reward, on success in the arena of the court, both had flourished. Karp had perhaps flourished a little more, but that was because, Roland had told himself in his secret heart, Karp had sucked up to old Garrahy in politics and gotten hold of a bureau chief's job in the Criminal Courts Bureau.

Still, Roland considered himself Karp's equal in the courtroom, and more than his equal in the battle of life. Roland had done well in the market; Karp lived on his ungenerous salary. He had a parade of young lovelies in his bed; Karp was married to a one-eyed woman who, by all Roland's experience of her, was a massive pain in the ass. He lived in a five-room apartment in the Village; Karp lived in a converted SoHo factory. He had a perfect body: Karp was a semi-cripple.

On the other hand . . . what was it on the other hand? Roland had trouble pinning it down. Something about Karp irked him mightily. Perhaps it was his refusal to be patronized by Roland, his refusal to recognize that there was a contest going on. Karp was playing, and playing well, but he wasn't watching the score.

When Hrcany entered the office, Karp had his leg up on his desk and was engaged in wrapping an Ace bandage tightly around his left knee. Roland grinned and said, "You got another call from the pros? They can't live without your two-inch jumper?"

Karp returned a bleak look. "Screw the pros. I'm hoping I can make it to the can and back." With a movement of his head he indicated the case file Roland was carrying. "That the U.N. thing?"

Roland slapped the folder on Karp's desk and sat down. "Yeah, it's wrapped up. How do you like that?"

Karp's eyebrows rose a notch. "No kidding? The warrant paid off, huh?"

"Jackpot. The guy had an armory in his safe. We got threatening letters to the Turks. We got the parka he wore. It's all over but the details." He quickly filled Karp in on what the police had found.

Roland spoke confidently—in truth, with more confidence than he felt, for he was a careful and rigorous lawyer. Karp tended to bring out the boastful in him, and Karp understood this, if Roland himself did not.

Karp finished wrapping his knee and pulled his pants leg down. He smiled wanly across the desk. "Sounds great, Roland," he said. "It could be a record for tying up a major case. What's the guy like?"

"A little twerp. Got tired of making earrings, figured being a terrorist might be more fun. I mean, everybody else is doing it, right? Fucks it up, gets pinched the next day, now he wants out. He's hamburger."

"If you say so, Roland. It sure comes at a good time. Bloom's been on the horn three, four times, what's going down with the U.N. thing? You sure don't want to kill anybody with political clout on his watch. I presume you'll want to bring the good news personally to Mr. District Attorney."

Roland did indeed want to bring the news to Bloom, and stand next to him at the press conference that Bloom would instantly arrange, but he would die before admitting it to Karp. If Roland shared Karp's contempt for the D.A. as a legal mind, he was more attracted than Karp to power—not an unusual thing in bright and ambitious men, especially lawyers. Roland knew that, given a chance, he could manipulate the D.A.—in the interests of good, of course. The present case seemed an ideal opportunity to do so. Roland shrugged and said, "Hey, whatever."

Karp smiled again. "Go do it, Roland. Give him a kiss for me."

Roland laughed, a deep, loud rumble. "On the lips, Butch."

3

As soon as Roland left, Karp put the murder of the Turkish diplomat entirely out of his mind and turned to the contemplation of a kind of murder less distinguished but far more numerous. From the center drawer of his desk he extracted a large sheet of yellow paper. It was actually four sheets of the large-ruled stock that accountants call spreadsheets taped together. On it were written the names of his attorneys, the cases they were responsible for, and the schedule proposed for each case.

There was an elaborate computer system that was supposed to do the same thing, but Karp knew that system to be out of date and unreliable. He knew it to be unreliable because he had fed enough lies into it to make it so. Bloom and his administrative satrap, Conrad Wharton, placed a high priority first on pumping clearances through the courts and second, on putting forth special effort toward punishing culprits who had the temerity to harm important or interesting people.

Karp smoothed the sheet on his desk. There were nine hundred and fifty homicides listed, which gave each of his people an average of thirty-odd each. In practice, no one worked on thirty homicides; a single homicide trial was absolutely consuming for a single prosecutor, and some cases required more than one. The saving fact was that not all cases went to trial.

Karp ran his eye over the spreadsheets. Perhaps two-thirds of the killings were what the cops called grounders: perfectly obvious events in which someone had aced a loved one or acquaintance and there was absolutely no doubt about what had gone down. When the homicide was the result of the usual brew—poverty, frustration, the last unbearable insult at an unusually vulnerable moment, the convenience of a loaded handgun—the defendant would be allowed to cop to manslaughter one or two. They'd go up for anything up to twenty-five years, depending on the judge, but most would be out after the mandatory minimum—as little as five years for manslaughter two.

On the other hand, it was not a good idea to make a habit of it in New York County on Karp's watch. This guy Chester Hollis—Karp's pencil moved to touch *People* v. *Hollis* on the sheet—had just killed his third wife, two years after a six-year stretch upstate for killing a girlfriend. Before that he had killed his first wife and done sixty-two months for that. Mr. Hollis would not be allowed a plea, unless it was a plea to guilty on the top count of murder two. If Mr. Hollis chose to exercise his right to a trial (as he probably would) and if he was convicted (by no means a dead certainty) he would go up for twenty-five to life, and would serve at least twenty-five years, at which point he would presumably be too decrepit to attract a fourth sucker, or to use a hammer on her if he did.

Although there were legal limitations on what pleas could be accepted for what original indictments, A.D.A.'s had enormous discretion. Karp's job was to arrange and staff the flow of cases, within the number of trial slots he had available to him, so that a reasonable proportion of the truly wicked were removed from society for as long as possible. In general, the grounders took care of themselves. Except in cases of special circumstances, like Mr. Hollis, or where insanity pleadings or legal technicalities were involved, Karp allowed the system to crank along on autopilot. He had a competent staff he'd recruited himself, and he trusted them.

Besides the grounders, and making up about a third of all homicides, there were the mysteries: any case for which there was not an immediate suspect. The mysteries stood out on Karp's chart because he had outlined the little box labeled "defendant" in red. The little box was often blank.

Some were of fairly obvious provenance—a dead man on a mean street with a bullet through the chest and his pockets turned out—while others were exotic: two freshly severed female heads neatly placed on a table in a West Side motel room. All were problems.

They sometimes required elaborate investigations, and typically resulted in cases based on circumstantial evidence, which usually meant that the guy, when they found him, would deny it. Legally the A.D.A.'s were supposed to be in charge of these investigations, but in general the detectives tended to do pretty much as they pleased until they had a suspect. Most prosecutors thought it was wise to concede them that role, but not Karp. He insisted that his people visit the crime scene, handle the physical evidence, and attend the autopsies of the victims.

And among the mysteries, as a matter of course, were the cases that caused the greatest political heat, the ones where either the suspect or the victim was a taxpayer of note, or where members of one race had done in members of another, or where the vic was especially photogenic or endearing, or young, or had been done to death in a particularly elaborate way or in company with an unusually large number of others.

Roland's Turkish diplomat was one of these, naturally. Karp penciled the name Tomasian in the proper slot and moved on. He tried to hold to the belief that everyone's life was equally precious and entitled to the same protection of the law, even though he knew that many of New York's murder victims were not among those for whom the earth wept when they passed.

Like this one, for example. Karp frowned and made a tick mark against *People* v. *Morales,* and scrawled a note to Lennie Bergman, the A.D.A. in charge. Emilio Morales was a well-known murderous fiend up on East 112th Street. Karp believed he had stabbed any number of his mugging victims and probably killed a few, but he did not believe that Morales had cut the throat of his partner in crime, Snoopy Vega, and then kept the bloody knife and Snoopy's blood-soaked baseball hat sitting out on the dresser in the bedroom in the apartment he shared with his grandmother and sisters, which was where the cops had said that they found them.

Instead Karp suspected that the detectives who discovered Vega's body had decided to rid the city of the rest of the mugging team of Morales & Vega by pinning the hit on the partner. To many cops, one scumbag was like another scumbag. Morales had done killings for which they couldn't nail him, and now they had one they could plausibly nail him on, with the help of a little planted evidence. Sooner or later they'd get the guy who actually did Vega on some other crime, or maybe the street would save them the trouble. Or maybe Morales actually did do it, in which case it was nicely ironic that he was being framed for it.

Karp, although a big fan of irony, and although he had blinked at plenty of burglars being sent off for a ritual year in the slams on the basis of planted evidence, did not care to extend the technique to the prosecution of murder. He continued in the quaint belief that every scumbag was different, and that the guy who had done the murder was the one, and the only one, to convict for it. Quite apart from that, and of more practical importance, Karp believed they would lose the case on present evidence.

Because Morales, in the right for the first time in his miserable life, would hang tough for a trial, and at the trial, even if the case survived a motion to suppress, the defense would chew away at the tainted evidence like a bull terrier on a prowler's ankle, until something broke. Someone would remember seeing the hat on the street. The grandma, a saintly churchgoer, would testify that she cleaned his room every day and there had been no hat. Morales would have been playing hearts with five guys at the time of, and so the cops would have to go out and lean on the five guys to suppress the alibi, which would create more havoc at the trial, and Karp didn't have enough trial slots to waste on fuck-uppery like this.

Karp moved on to the next case and the next, building a tottering house of cards that he prayed would see the homicide bureau through another week without either embarrassment or miscarriage of justice beyond the ordinary run. Connie Trask stuck her head in, told him it was five-thirty and that she was leaving if he didn't want anything. He waved her away with a smile and worked on through the mysteries.

While Karp worked, Roland Hrcany was laboring in fields even less pleasant, chewing on a Tampa Nugget to keep the smell and his gorge down, and to show some class, while an assistant medical examiner scooped out Mehmet Ersoy's guts and placed them in a large basin. They were in the autopsy room at the Bellevue morgue, to which Roland had repaired after the press conference. The M.E. was a slight red-haired Irish immigrant named Denny Maher, who liked his work and enjoyed company while he performed it.

"A good liver," said Maher, probing the organ, "a rarity in a good liver, so to speak, as our friend here undoubtedly was. A well-nourished Caucasian male indeed. I take it from this that he followed the Prophet's admonition to abjure the water of life. No *poteen* for the Turk, and bad cess to 'em. Hah, here's another one."

Maher's forceps yanked something out of the mass of viscera and dropped it clinking into a kidney basin. There were three others, squat mushroom shapes, the remains of hollow-nose 9mm bullets. Maher spoke the details of his find into the microphone suspended before his face.

Roland watched impassively as Maher stripped the corpse's scalp down, cut the top of its head off, and removed the brain. The brain was uninjured, Maher reported, with no gross signs of pathology. He continued his spiel into the microphone, registering his opinion that death was due to exsanguination following the perforation of the anterior aorta and pulmonary arteries by bullets.

Maher switched the microphone off and quickly sewed up the now hollow places with coarse stitches. His assistant, a morose Puerto Rican, helped him move the body to a gurney, which he then wheeled away to the cold room.

"Ten hits, I counted," said Maher, "of which we have four. I presume the others are in the keeping of either the police or the Department of Sanitation. Funny thing, bullets: when I was in the E.R. during my residency, we had a lad who had thirteen bullet wounds in him, and not a one in a vital spot. He walked out in a week. Then we get them done in by a single .22. It's luck or artistry. This was not an artistic killing, Roland."

Hrcany grunted. He already knew the killers were amateurs; he was at the autopsy to see it established that the shots had killed the vic, which was perfectly obvious in the first place.

"Care for a drop, Roland?" asked Maher brightly. "It would help to underscore the gulf between good Christian men like ourselves and followers of the deplorable Mahound. Sad, that is: his immaculate liver didn't do him a hair of good, and he's dead as Murphy's cat in the prime of life."

"You still drinking lab alcohol, Denny?"

"Of course. It's nature's pure stuff, without all those confusing esters and adulterants."

Roland shook his head and, while Maher decanted a slug of ethanol into a small beaker, glanced over at another gurney. There was something odd about the shape under its cloth. "What's that? Another bag of parts?" he asked.

"No, not at all. But you might be interested in her, Roland, you being a connoisseur of the girls. That's what you might call an extremely flat-chested woman."

He drew the sheet off with a flourish.

Roland's teeth clamped down hard on the wooden bit of his Tampa Nugget. "Fascinating, Denny. What the fuck happened to her?"

"Took a swan dive off a six-story building and landed facedown. Interesting the way the internal organs have jetted out of the body orifices. It's going to be a messy one to do. The teeth are all over the place, assuming that they're not still back at the scene. It wouldn't surprise me one bit if I found some lodged in the brain. And of course we'll need them for an ID. The high school graduation picture won't do it for this girlie."

"A Jane Doe, huh? What, a suicide?"

"It appears so right now. No sign of foul play is obvious, but of course, the amazing Dr. Maher has not worked his forensic miracles yet."

Roland chuckled. "I guess this'll be one of the ones that doesn't get fucked by the staff."

"Well, as to that," Maher replied, "there are all sorts of tastes in the profession. I, of course, have never indulged; one imagines it's much like it is with an Irishwoman, but a bit warmer and without the crying and jabber afterward. Good day to you, Roland."

Hrcany left, laughing his booming laugh. Maher's assistant came in and asked hopefully, "You wanna knock it off for today, Doc?"

"No, Carlos," said Maher, "I want to work on our little pancake here. Hose down the table and help me get her on. You can take off at five."

At six, Roland Hrcany knocked on the door of Karp's office and walked in.

"Well," Karp said, looking up and rubbing his eyes, "were you on TV? Did they love your golden curls?"

"I was and they did. Bloom asked where you were."

"I bet. He likes to have me where he can see me. How'd it go?"

"Great, great," said Hrcany noncommittally. "The usual horseshit. Tomasian's been booked. We'll arraign him tonight. I'll probably want to go to the grand jury early next week."

"That fast?"

"Yeah, why not? We got plenty—or am I missing something?" Hrcany's bright little blue eyes narrowed.

Karp took a breath and threw down his pencil. "Roland, what do you say I buy you a drink? You deserve it."

Hrcany's tight expression turned instantly to amazement. "You want to buy me a *drink*? Butch, we've been working together for twelve years. You never bought me a drink before. Come to that, you don't even drink."

Karp rose to his feet and shoveled some folders into a large, ragged cardbord folder that served as his briefcase. "Well, maybe it's time I started," he said. He put on his suit jacket and a tan raincoat.

"She's giving you a hard time and you want to get your load on before going home, right?"

"It makes you happy to believe that," answered Karp mildly, "but really, I figured, you cracked a big case, we'll sit down, have a beer and talk about it, like regular people."

Hrcany had to be satisfied by that explanation. They did, in fact, go to a bar, one in a Chinese restaurant on Bayard Street, a favorite of bail bondsmen, cheap lawyers, and other Criminal Courts habituees. The place was full of these, enjoying after-work drinks, or pre-work drinks, if they were about to handle the late work of the courts, and practicing venality. Karp felt right at home.

The room was smoky and painted glossy red, with the usual character scrolls, misty paintings on silk, dying snake plants, and very old, thin Chinese men arranged in appropriate places. Karp and Roland settled themselves in a red leatherette booth. A blank-faced Chinese woman appeared instantly and took their order.

"Roland, I've always wanted to know: how come every Chinese restaurant in the world, no matter how crummy, has a fully stocked cocktail lounge?"

Roland shrugged. "They use them to launder money from Hong Kong and import illegals? I don't know. It's part of their plan for world domination."

"I thought that was the Jews."

"You guys missed your chance," said Roland. "Too much assimilation. The Chinese don't make that mistake." The waitress brought their drinks, a beer for Karp and a Dewars rocks for Hrcany. Karp put some bills out.

"You see that money?" Roland asked as the waitress swept it up. "Those bills will never touch white skin again. Once it's in the Chinese community, the money never leaves."

Karp grinned. "You're an engaging bigot, Roland. Okay, forget the yellow peril. What's your take on this Armenian and Turkish business?"

Hrcany drank half his scotch. Offhandedly he replied, "My take? A bunch of nuts, they got out of hand. They were writing letters about something that happened a million years ago, letters to the Turks, I mean. And somebody must have figured, the letters aren't doing much good, let's pop one of them, see what happens. They should've hired a pro. And for the cherry on top, look at this . . ."

Roland reached into his briefcase and pulled out a folder. He handed Karp two pages. "This one's the transcript of the tape of the call-in of the assassination. The other's a Xerox of a carbon we lifted from Tomasian's file cabinet. There's a typewriter there, and I guarantee you we'll show it was typed on that machine. Notice any similarities?"

Karp read the two texts. "I see what you mean. This part about 'thousands and thousands of the sons and daughters of the Armenian nation, cruelly butchered, cry out for recognition and recompense. If they do not receive their due, then the fighters of the Armenian Secret Army will extract vengeance instead.' It's word for word the same in both places. Pretty impressive, Roland. It'll play great in court." He handed the papers back and took another sip of beer. "I guess there's no question that we're going to have to try this one."

"For sure—there's no hint of a deal. He says he didn't do it and doesn't know who did, and I gotta say, he's a cool little fucker. Compared to the people I usually have up on murder, it's a pleasure doing business with him. His lawyer's also right by the book too. Another

Armenian, Hagopian his name is. Nice guy, looks like that guy used to do Perry Mason on TV."

"Raymond Burr," said Karp. "You're in trouble, Roland."

Hrcany laughed, "Yeah, right. No, we'll take him down. And I'll make another bet: in a little while we'll pick up the other guy too. Either Tomasian will rat him out, or he'll do something dumb. Yeah, I know I said he was being cool, but it hasn't sunk in yet. He hasn't thought about what it's going to be like for a nice middle-class boy looking at twenty-five to life with the smokes upstate. Plus, the momma and the daddy and the sisters and whatever haven't been to work on him yet. He'll deal. And if not, fuck him, we'll try and we'll convict. What's wrong, you don't think so?"

Roland had observed Karp rubbing his lower lip and staring raptly toward the upper left-hand corner of the universe, an infallible indication of dubiety.

"Well," said Karp after a pause. "You have a good case. I just don't think it's soup yet. The girlfriend, for example—"

Roland made a dismissive gesture. "Come on, Butch! Let's say she shows up . . ." In falsetto, " 'Yes, Officer, my honey was with me all night and until noon, and my squeeze is so sore I can hardly piss.' No problem on the girl. I'll take her apart on the stand. She fucked him, maybe she fucked someone else, she's a slut. I'll find people she told lies to. If she was a virgin, then she loves him, she'd do anything to save him from jail. If she's a dog, I put young guys on the jury. If she's a dish, I'll make sure it's full of bags and fags—the usual routine."

Karp nodded impatiently. "Right, Roland, I know how to impeach a witness. That wasn't what I meant. I meant, why isn't she here? Where is she? What's she doing? Are the Armenians holding on to her? Is Tomasian being set up for a sacrificial lamb by his own people? Okay, another thing, there's this business with the license plate and the guns—"

"Not the stupidity defense, please!"

"No, although in this case it might even work. I mean it doesn't jell, one with the other. If for some reason they didn't mind using their own license plate, then they'd want to be clean as whistles when the cops came around. The defense then attacks the eyesight or credibility of whoever spotted the plate. If for some reason they want the guns around, they have incriminating evidence on site, then they absolutely have to be anonymous when they do the hit. Then the defense can play them as innocent victims interested in self-protection. Which brings up the additional question of why a man who's got his hands on one of the most effective silent assassination weapons ever invented wants to pull a dumb stunt like shooting a guy in front of a dozen people while he's parked on a one-way street that's practically a dead end."

"I told you already, they're amateurs."

"Roland, amateurs, shmamateurs, it doesn't make *sense.* What's he got the silenced grease gun for? Fourth of July for the deaf? What I'm saying is, even if he's never done anything like this before in his life, if he wants this Turk dead, he hangs out at the guy's apartment late one night and hoses him down with the M3. There's another angle here that we're not seeing."

Hrcany finished his drink and signaled the waitress to bring another. He did not like the drift of the conversation, and it was not lost on him that the D.A. had asked none of these questions. In fact, Roland was a good enough investigator to have had similar reservations. But it was past time for these. It was now accepted gospel, broadcast to the millions not an hour since, that Tomasian was the guy. All of Roland's mental energy was now devoted to making sure that, weeks or months hence, twelve jurors would also believe it, beyond a reasonable doubt, to a moral certainty.

He said, "I know, there's flaky sides to the case, but I don't think they're that important, tactically. People watch a lot of TV killings; they think that's real life. They don't figure what's really going to happen if you do a crime in such and such a place and time. It'll be hard for the defense to get that point across—"

"No, Roland, look," Karp broke in, "I'm not talking tactically. I'm not saying it's not a good case. It's a good case. I'm asking, is it the guy? Did he really do it? It's not the same question as 'Is it a good case?' "

"Of course he did it!" snapped Hrcany. "What, you think it was a mugging that went sour? Who the fuck else could it be? He wrote the letter, he made the call, he has the car and the guns and the parka, he killed the guy. Case closed!"

Karp sighed and drank some more beer. His head was light, probably from the Empirin and codeine pill he had swallowed a few hours earlier, that and the unfamiliar alcohol, and he allowed that his incisive legal mind was probably not tuned to its highest pitch. So Roland was probably right; Karp, himself often a victim of second-guessing by incompetents, was sensitive to his own practice of that vice, and was, besides, disinclined to light his friend's notoriously short fuse.

Therefore he smiled pleasantly and changed the subject, which Roland was more than willing to do, and they spoke desultorily of sports for twenty minutes or so, and then Karp got up and said that he ought to go home.

Home was only six blocks away in a loft building on Crosby off Grand, and Karp walked there now, as he almost always did. His pace, however, was not his usual breakneck lope, but a careful and stately progress, like that of an ancient colonel on the esplanade of a resort. At his door, Karp still had to climb five steep flights of wooden stairs. This he did very slowly, flexing the bad knee as little as possible. It took him nearly ten minutes, and he was pale and faintly nauseated when at last he reached the red-painted steel door to the loft he shared with his family.

Entering, he staggered over to a tatty couch upholstered in red velvet and threw himself down on it, lifting his feet up on a low ta-ble made from a flush door set on concrete pipe. Beyond this table Marlene, his wife, sat cross-legged in a bentwood rocker, with a nest of papers on her lap. She regarded him over the rims of her large, round reading glasses and said, "Where have *you* been? It's past seven."

"I've been drinkin' away me pay down at the saloon, that's where," said Karp. He slipped his shoes off and shrugged out of his raincoat and suit jacket. "And now I want my dinner and a hug from my old woman."

She pushed her glasses back on her nose and resumed her study of a document. "Your dinner," she sniffed, "is congealing in a pan on the stove. There's bread and salad in the fridge. Pray help yourself. I'm answering motions."

She continued to work for a minute or two, but when Karp didn't stir, she looked up and examined him more closely.

"Butch? Are you okay? God, you look like death warmed over! Whatever got into you? You know you can't drink."

"Can too," said Karp.

"Nonsense! Jewish husbands don't drink or beat up their wives. I learned that at my mother's knee. If I wanted a lush I would've married somebody I could at least take to church. What's wrong with you, then?"

"Nothing," said Karp. "I'm just tired."

"Oh, horseshit! It's that goddamn knee again, isn't it? You said you were going to take care of it."

"I'll take care of it," said Karp. "Meanwhile, could you get me some ice?"

She dumped her papers on the floor and snapped her glasses off. Going to the refrigerator, she said, "I ought to make you crawl for it. Honestly, you're a complete infant."

She wrapped a dozen ice cubes in a baggie and a dish towel and brought the ice pack over to Karp, who had slipped out of his trousers in the meantime and unwrapped the Ace bandages that had held the errant joint together all day. His knee looked red, hard, and un-natural, like a pomegranate.

"Jesus!" she exclaimed. "You can walk on that? It looks like something in the window of a Chinese grocery that the Chinese don't even know what it is." She giggled, "God, you look nutty in your shirt and tie and no pants."

"Thank you for your support in my hour of need," Karp said stiffly.

"Oh, stop it! This is completely your fault, and I'm not going to feel all guilty and rush around being Florence Nightingale. I have an *actual* infant to take care of. Dammit, see a doctor! Get it fixed!"

"Okay, I'll do it," said Karp grumpily.

"Honest, swear to God?"

"Yeah, I'll see Hudson tomorrow. I'll tell him it's an emergency."

She looked at him closely to see if he was trying to fob her off with a facile evasion, and then, deciding that he was sincere, plopped down beside him on the sofa and put her arm around his neck.

He said, "That's better. Speaking of the actual infant, how is she?"

"*She's* perfect. *She's* an angel. But the child-care situation is deteriorating badly. Belinda has informed us that she is returning to her beautiful island home in two weeks."

"Why? I thought she liked it here."

"It's a family thing, which she told me in great detail and which I won't repeat. But that makes two exploited third-world women we've hired in the past three months to keep me liberated, and I'm sick of it. And don't give me that look! I'm not stopping work, even if I have to take Lucy into court with me, or better yet, drop her off in your office. You're a bureau chief. You can sit on your butt all day and give orders."

"Wait a second, I thought you were a bureau chief too."

"Yes, but my bureau, concerned as it is with trivialities like rape and child abuse, has only five attorneys in it, of whom I am one. I spend six times as much time running my ass off as you do."

"There's a child-care center—"

"No! I am not going to have our daughter stuck in a disease-ridden barn and shoved in front of a TV all day. Or worse."

"No, listen!" he said. "I heard Tina Linski talking to somebody today in the bureau office, a cop—no, she was a parole officer. Her sister had her kid in this group home and they were looking for another baby and she wanted to know if Tina wanted to move her kid in there. I just caught snatches of the conversation, but it sounded real nice. The woman's got degrees up the ying-yang in early education and child psych—"

"Who, the parole officer?"

"No, the woman who takes care of the kids. And the place is in Tribeca. You could drop her off on the way to work."

"What was her name, the parole officer?"

"I didn't catch it. A kind of chubby woman, short, dark hair. You could ask Tina."

"I'm on the case. But it sounds too good to be true. On the other hand, we should be due for some good luck. I got a letter from Lepkowitz today."

"What does he want, more rent?"

"No. It seems that nice old Mr. Lepkowitz in Miami Shores, driven to a final paroxysm of greed by Lepkowitz Junior, has decided to take this building co-op."

"Oh, shit!"

"Indeed. I talked to Larry and Stuart downstairs about it briefly before you got home. Stuart's been dickering with Lepkowitz Junior. Morton. He's talking as high as two hundred thou a floor, plus the maintenance is going to run at least four bills a month."

Karp felt his stomach turn over. "Christ, Marlene! That's almost twice what we're paying in rent. And how're we going to come up with two hundred large? Take bribes?"

"It may come to that," she said. "No, Stu and Larry have been running numbers like crazy. They tell me that if we put most of the forty-five grand we have in CDs into a down payment, and if we both keep working, we'd qualify for a thirty-year note. The monthly nut, principal, interest, taxes, insurance, and maintenance, will run about twenty-two hundred."

He gasped. "For this?" he blurted out quite spontaneously. Marlene scowled. It was a sore point between them. She had converted an old electroplating factory loft into a living space, years before the notion of SoHo had been concocted by real estate agents, or the loft area south of Houston Street had gone chichi. When Marlene moved in and did the grueling work of cleaning, painting, wiring, plumbing, and carpentry by herself, or with the help of her family, nobody but a few artists had lived in the area. It had been illegal to live in such buildings. In those days, she would sit on her fire escape and look out at square miles of blackness lit only by the windows of a dozen or so pioneers.

Now, in the late seventies, *companies* would convert a loft to the specifications of artistic millionaires. Loft buildings in this part of Manhattan had become gold mines for their owners. And Marlene's loft was a nice one. It was a single floor-through room over thirty feet wide and a hundred long, with windows on both ends and a big skylight in the middle. At one end, under the huge windows looking out on Crosby Street, was a sleeping platform. There was an enclosed nursery, and the rest of the space was divided by partitions, like a series of stage sets, into a bathroom (which held a rubber thousand-gallon tank that Marlene had rescued from the electroplaters and converted into a hot tub), a fully equipped kitchen, a living area, a dining room under the skylight, a sort of gym-cum-storeroom, and, at the end under the Grand Street windows, an office lushly crowded with house plants.

On the other hand, Karp thought it was no place to bring up a child. A child had to have, as in his Brooklyn boyhood, a street shaded by sycamore trees, and backyards, and other kids on the street to play potsy and ringelevio with, and there should be a mom who came out at around six, dressed in an apron, to call the kid in off the street. Karp valued his peace too much to actually express this fantasy to Marlene, but it was there in his mind, a constant irritant, now spurred to a fever by the prospect of having to actually buy this place.

Marlene, naturally, knew precisely what was going on in his mind and would have delivered a devastating riposte had she not been aware that Karp was in considerable physical torment. Instead, therefore, she said, lightly, "Well, we don't have to worry about it this minute. Lots of things could happen. Lepkowitz *père* could go out any minute—he's in his eighties—and with any luck the property could be in probate until Lucy's ready for Smith, and with a little more luck, Lepkowitz *fils* could go under a bus, and our problems would be over."

"Yeah, and the horse could learn to sing," said Karp glumly. He lifted the ice pack and inspected his knee. It was down some but not nearly normal; in this it was a model of his life.

Marlene said, "Yeah. By the way, who were you out drinking with? Some woman?"

The sudden change of topic threw Karp's mind out of the muddy rut in which it had been grinding, and left it spinning on the slick ice of Marlene's attitude.

"What! No, not a woman. Roland."

"That must have been fun. What prompted it? A sudden taste for bad lesbian jokes?"

"No, Roland cracked, or seems to have cracked, a big case. That shooting over by the U.N.—they found this pathetic amateur terrorist, an Armenian jeweler. So I thought I'd buy him a drink and discuss the case in congenial circumstances."

While he was talking, Marlene rose from the couch and went to the bathroom. She took an old blue plaid robe from a hook and carried it over to Karp. Then she busied herself with warming up some food. He watched her work. Her movements were precise, graceful, economical. She closed the refrigerator door just so, she picked up and used implements elegantly—there was never a mess where she had been. He watched her a lot; even after living together for four years, her movements still fascinated him.

Marlene Ciampi was a medium-sized woman just shy of thirty years old, with a thin, muscular body that her single pregnancy had touched hardly at all. She had a face out of the late Renaissance: cheekbones like knives, a long, straight nose, a wide, lush mouth, a strong jaw and chin. Her brows were heavy and unplucked, and underneath them were two large, dark eyes, only one of which was real.

"Discuss the case in a bar, huh?" Marlene turned from the stove and gestured with a spatula. "By which I gather you aren't in love with his Armenian," she said.

"How did you figure that out?" said Karp, amazed. He was barely aware of it himself.

"You forget I'm a trained investigator," she answered blithely. "Look, Roland's a friend of yours, but you don't go out of your way to socialize with him outside the office. He spends a lot of time hanging around saloons, and you never go into a saloon. So why should you all of a sudden decide to go into his turf? Because you wanted to break some bad news and, nice guy that you are, you thought it would go easier if he was comfortable and had a couple of scoops in him. Am I right? Yeah. So how did it go?"

Karp made a dismissive gesture. "I brought up a few points I thought he should look at."

"Such as?"

"You really want to hear this?"

"A little, but I get the feeling you really want to tell it. Here's your dinner."

She had made up a little tray, chicken stew and salad and a heel of Tuscan bread and butter, which she placed carefully across Karp's lap. He tore into the food ravenously. Marlene was a good cook, if you liked good bread, good coffee, and lumps of miscellaneous material generously sauced and served on rice or spaghetti, and you didn't mind eating the same thing several days in a row. Between mouthfuls he filled her in on what he had learned of the Tomasian case, and described his vague doubts.

"So you don't think this Armenian did it?" asked Marlene when he had concluded his story.

"I didn't say that. I said there's things about the case that would make me uneasy if it was my case, and I expressed that to Roland."

"How did he take it?"

"Not well. He was doing his massive jaw-clenching routine when I decided to drop the subject."

"I'm not surprised," said Marlene. "It sounds like it's a mega-case that could make him famous, and here's you throwing sand in the gears. He's jealous of you to begin with—"

"Roland? He's not jealous of me. I think he thinks I'm a little wimpy, if anything, because I don't drink and fuck everything above room temperature and talk tough with the cops."

"That's right," she replied, "and even though you don't, you're famous, and you have the best homicide conviction record in the city, and you got to play pro ball—"

"And I'm married to an incredibly beautiful woman—"

"In your dreams, and he can't stand not being the biggest swinging dick on the street."

"You know, you're really being unfair, Marlene," replied Karp. "Roland right now is probably the hardest-working and most successful A.D.A. in the office. He's got no reason to be jealous of anyone. Rivalry maybe—he's a competitive guy. So am I. It's natural. But I can't believe he'd let that influence the way he handled a case."

"Well you've always been totally naïve about that aspect of human behavior, especially where pals are concerned. Look, Roland's been at the D.A. as long as you, right? And, as you say, he's got a great track record, correct? But you don't see anyone hurrying to make him a bureau chief. And you know why? He's got a personality like a Doberman pinscher."

"So do I," said Karp defensively. "So do you, for that matter."

"In court, yes," replied Marlene. "Not otherwise. That's a big difference. And we're not talking about me. We're talking about you and Roland. I don't count for him because I'm just a wise-ass cunt, as Roland might put it."

"You never did like him."

"I like him fine, Butch. Roland and I have had many interesting and amusing conversations, especially after he finally got it through his blond head that I wasn't going to crawl into the rack with him. But he's got a thing going with you. And I'd want to watch him around Bloom and company."

"What? That's crazy, Marlene! He hates Bloom worse than I do."

"Yeah, but he thinks he can manipulate Bloom, which means he's playing on Bloom's court. You, on the other hand, decline the game entirely, which is what drives Bloom crazy. You just don't give a shit. Are you finished with that? I want to clean up."

"Yeah, thanks," said Karp, and then sat in silence, flexing his chilled knee and thinking about what Marlene had said. It didn't make sense to him, but he had learned over the years to appreciate Marlene's judgments about people, even when he didn't agree with them, and he treated her pronouncements like those of an expert witness in, say, blood chemistry—recondite but usable in court.

She finished her wash-up and sat down next to him on the couch. She lit her evening cigarette, one of the five she allowed herself each day.

"So what are you going to do about it?" she asked.

"Do? What can I do? It's his case and it's a strong case against his guy."

"But what if he didn't do it?"

Karp smiled. "Then because our system is just, he'll walk out a free man."

"I can see you don't want to discuss this seriously," she replied sharply, "but I am simply not going to believe you're going to let an innocent man get nailed for this, *and*—don't interrupt—*and* let the guilty party walk away laughing, just because you don't want to hurt Roland's feelings."

"Don't get started, Marlene," warned Karp. "I meant what I said about getting off, and you know why? Because in court we're not like the defense attorneys. It's not a symmetrical thing. They don't have to prove anything; they don't have to even believe their client is innocent. That's not their job. All they have to do is insert doubt. It's a simpler service, like dry cleaning."

"I know all this, Butch. What's your point?"

"My point is, if *we* don't believe the guy's guilty, it does matter. The doubt is there on the prosecutor's side and the jury can smell it."

"Oh, what horseshit! You mean to tell me that innocent people don't get convicted? Christ, there are even words for the process: framed, railroaded—"

"Okay, I'll modify that: not for homicide, not by conviction where there's competent counsel and not in New York City at the present time. Sure, in Coon Squat, Georgia, where they have one homicide in a decade, yeah, they grab the town asshole and nail him to a tree. But not here, not recently. Christ, Marlene, that's why these bozos Bloom put in have been copping stone killers to man deuce. That's what I'm trying to change. It's *hard* to convict someone who you're absolutely one hundred percent convinced is guilty. Trials are a bitch! And you could get wiped if you don't know what the hell you're doing. That's why they don't do them."

"Okay, right, but what if Roland is really convinced the guy did it?"

Karp thought about that for a moment, and then said, "Well, look: this case is two days old. Two days. They've made terrific progress, and Roland is hyped up about it. I would be too. Now if, after however many months, Roland brings this case to trial, then he'll really believe the guy did it, and moreover, if he does, then the guy really did it. Roland is good."

"You're going to leave it at that, huh?"

"What do you want me to do, babe? Second-guess him? Conduct a parallel investigation? You know I can't do that. Meanwhile, Roland'll do the right thing when the time comes."

"Well," said Marlene, "you have touching faith, but faith is as nothing without works. You might think about an ancillary investigation."

"How do you mean?"

"Where's the girl? The alibi? She's missing, a missing person. Her family will be concerned."

"What are you suggesting, Marlene? That I pump up the cops to find a girl who just happens to be a possible material witness in Roland's case? What do I tell Roland? Gee, Roland, there are fifty thousand missing persons every year in Manhattan, and I thought I'd pick one and put the max on it, just for laughs, and guess who it is—"

"Okay, okay, it's a lame idea. Why are we talking about this goddamn case anyway? It's not like I don't have my own problems. And speaking of which, since we're talking shop in the sanctity of our home, I think I can get Harry Bello to come over to the D.A. squad."

"You can? That's great," said Karp, genuinely impressed. Bello was a detective of uncanny skill, whose eccentricity, alcoholism, and general mulishness had caused him to be banished to a backwater in Queens, which had not prevented him from solving, in concert with the Karps, a case that the criminal justice hierarchy in Queens had not wanted solved. Bello had become, as a direct result of this, both dry and Lucy Karp's godfather, as well as persona non grata from one end of Queens to the other.

"Yes," Marlene continued, "the borough assistant chief was delighted to help. In fact, he gave out that if Harry never sets foot on his turf again, it'll be a day too soon. He'll start next Monday."

"I presume you'll monopolize him," said Karp.

"It's not a choice. I doubt he'll work for anybody else. You know Harry."

"Very clever, Marlene. Your own private investigator, and I bet it's a permanent steal. Harry's not going to show up on the D.A. squad's budget, is he? He'll be on the Queens detective chart until the day he hands in his tin."

She giggled. "How well you know me, my love. And I learned how to run that scam from you, if you recall."

"So you did," responded Karp, happy now that both the unpleasantness about Roland's case and the agony in his knee had abated. "And I believe it's time for us to stand clutching each other at our baby's doorway, watching her sleeping and making stupid noises, after which, if you'll help me climb that fucking ladder, I intend to take to my bed."

4

IT TOOK DENNY MAHER TWO AND A HALF HOURS TO FINISH THE FLAT-
tened Jane Doe. As he had feared, the teeth were all over the place,
from the windpipe to the base of the brain. He gathered them carefully and placed them in a plastic bag. There was evidence of careful
dental work; she had not been raised in poverty.

Death had been instantaneous, of course, from massive brain
damage, but the woman had at least been alive when she hit the
ground. The hyoid and trachea were intact, and there was no sign
that the woman had been strangled, stabbed, or shot. He examined
the hands, which had been placed in plastic bags. He took samples
from under the fingernails for later microscopic examination, and as
he handled the cold fingers he noticed that there was extensive bruising around the wrists. That was an odd note, although nearly any
mark could be explained by a falling-body death. Still, you got
marks like that when someone's wrists were tightly held.

He examined the woman's vagina, a difficult and tedious procedure, for the organ was badly torn by bone fragments from the disintegrated pelvis. He took samples and put them aside for later microscopic and chemical analysis. Ordinarily he would have taken samples also from the rectum and oral cavity, but these were so badly damaged and contaminated by the explosive eversion of the viscera and by direct impact that such samples would have had little forensic value. What did have value was something he discovered on the inside of the woman's thigh, high up near the crotch and protected by that location from the general ruin: the clear and unmistakable marks of human teeth. He rolled the body, first to one side, then to the other. More teeth. He got out the Polaroid rig and took photographs.

Maher secured and labeled his samples and covered and refrigerated what was left of the Jane Doe. Before going home, he stopped by his office and wrote a note to himself to call the police officers in charge of the case and, if what he now strongly suspected was borne out by the lab, the rape bureau of the D.A.'s office as well.

"Does that hurt?" asked the orthoped.

Karp, who had turned pale and nearly cracked a molar gritting his teeth, gasped, "Yeah, that hurts."

"How about this?" said Dr. Hudson, twisting. Karp let out a shrill yelp.

"I'll assume that's affirmative," said the doctor. Then he allowed Karp's knee to relax back on the examining table. Dr. Hudson rolled a little distance on his stool and examined a chart. He was a squat, muscular man with a gray crew cut and a squared-off face that seemed accustomed to issuing bad news.

"I saw you what? Four years ago?" the doctor asked, reading from his chart. "I told you to come back every six months and you didn't bother. So. What've you been doing with that thing?" He indicated the reddened lump that was Karp's left knee.

"What do you mean, what've I been doing? I use it when I walk," said Karp.

"No unusual strains? Falls?"

"Well, a little basketball."

The doctor's eyes widened. "Basketball? What, on asphalt? In the playground?"

"Yeah, that, and, um, I was on a pro team for a couple of months last winter as part of a murder investigation."

"You're joking! No, wait, you're that guy! D.A. Karp, they called you—played for the Hustlers, right?"

"Right," said Karp, an appeasing smile creasing his lips.

"Get the hell out of my office!" said Dr. Hudson.

"So did he really throw you out?" asked Marlene. It was lunchtime later the same day; they were seated in Karp's office, and she had brought him a sausage sandwich and a root beer from one of the cancer wagons that plied Foley Square. She herself sipped coffee. She had a lunch date later.

"No, worse," replied Karp, shoving bits of onion back into his mouth with his fingers. "He gave me a lecture. Apparently I've totaled the joint. He said he'll need to do an arthroscopy to be sure, but he thinks I'm going to need another operation, maybe a complete arthroplasty."

"That sounds pretty grim."

"It's grim, all right. I'll be on crutches for six weeks at least after the operation, not to mention the fact of how we're going to pay for it."

"But you've got medical—"

"No, I don't, not for this. It's a prior existing condition. I checked already; they won't pay."

Marlene's heart sank. "How much?"

"Um, we won't get much change from a ten thousand dollar bill."

Marlene finished her coffee and tossed the cup in the trash. She rose. "You mean, there goes our exclusive condo in the heart of one of New York's most desirable neighborhoods? Maybe, but I can't think about it today. I have to see this woman about our kid."

"The parole officer?"

"And her sister, the one with the kid. It's sounding better and better, and I know we're going to get in because we absolutely have to get a break right now." She blew him a kiss and whirled out the door.

Karp waited. Thirty seconds later she stuck her head in the door again, looking stunned. "Hey, if you're on crutches for six weeks, how are you going to get up to the loft?"

"The penny drops," said Karp. "As a matter of fact, I don't know how I'm going to get up the stairs. But I can't think about it today."

She grinned. "Smart move. See you around, cutie," she said, and closed the door.

Marlene took the elevator down from the sixth floor, where Karp had his office, to street level, and walked out of the special entrance reserved for the D.A.'s staff onto Leonard Street. She walked up Leonard to Church and a half block down Church to a branch New York State Parole office.

Inevitably, it was painted in the official bureaucratic colors, green to shoulder height and tan above, a scheme designed by famous scientists to increase suicidal tendencies, especially when lit by dim fluorescents. There were rows of plastic shell chairs in pleasing shades of avocado and pink, and a heavy-set clerk with streaked black and blond hair who sat behind a glassed-in counter munching corn chips and talking on the phone. Four of the chairs were occupied by the kind of people who have to visit their parole officers on a regular basis.

Marlene went up to the clerk's window and asked to see Geri Stone. The clerk continued talking and munching. Marlene asked again, louder. The clerk scowled and said, around a bolus of chip debris, "She's with someone. Take a seat!"

Marlene sat on her anger and decided not to flash her ID and make a scene. This was, after all, a private mission. She took a seat. The clerk talked on behind her window. Time stopped.

At least twenty minutes later, the door opened again, and a

pretty young woman entered, who belonged in such a place far less than even Marlene. She had her black hair cut in an artful shingle, she wore a mannish tweed suit that did not make her look mannish, and had that air of entitlement and confidence that even the City cannot strip from some bright and successful young women. Marlene checked the shoes and bag, found them expensive and tasteful, and thought, the girl's made a mistake—probably looking for a brokerage.

But no, the woman advanced on the clerk's station and, smiling, said, "Hi, Mavis, is Geri free?"

The clerk paused in her conservation and returned the smile. "Hi, Susan. I'll buzz her." Magic.

Marlene rose and went over to the woman. This had to be the sister, the one with the kid, thought the trained investigator, and so it was, Susan Weiner, mother of a three-year-old, an industrial designer, married to a rising TV producer, and a woman who obviously knew how to make New York sit up and beg. This information and this impression were conveyed to Marlene in a giddy rush as they walked together down a green, dimly lit hallway.

Weiner stopped by a frosted glass door, which opened, allowing the passage of a bullet-headed black man in his thirties, who glowered at them and brushed by so forcefully that they both had to jump back a step.

"A satisfied client," laughed Weiner, and went into the little office.

Geri Stone was the older sister, by perhaps five years, which made her early thirties. She was rounded, blurry, where Susan was crisply cut and lean, and had adopted a stern proletarian plainness in contrast to her sister's stylish flair. Her hair was a nondescript brown frizz, and she had on a lipstick that was too bright and a fuzzy sweater of an unfortunate blue shade that greened her sallow complexion.

She greeted her sister effusively.

"God, you look gorgeous. Get away from here, you're so thin."

"That's a gorgeous sweater," responded Susan. "Where'd you get it?"

And similar cooings. At length they noticed Marlene. Geri shook Marlene's hand in a formal, manly grip. They were all to go to lunch, Geri's suggestion when Marlene had called her to make contact with Susan. An odd arrangement, Marlene had thought at the time—why was Geri inviting herself along for a discussion about day-care? Now, of course, the reason was clear, a set of family dynamics you could explicate on the back of a business card. The dowdy social worker was in love with her glamorous sister.

They ate at a local bar. Geri turned out to be one of those people who justified their caloric intake by informing you about how little they had been eating for the past week. Marlene was not particularly hungry, but decided to order a cheeseburger with fries and a beer just for spite.

They chatted. Susan was witty and flippant, a game Marlene played back at her. Geri was more serious, in fact something of a bleeding heart. When Susan mentioned the guy who had almost knocked them down in the hall, Geri launched into his pathetic case history: mildly retarded, alcoholic, abused as a child, dragged through foster homes, a juvie sheet that went back to age twelve and a record of stupid petty crime that turned violent when he had a load on. She had struggled mightily to get him an early release from his last stretch and into a program that specialized in helping people with what she called "institutional malaise."

"Hmm, interesting," said Marlene, not really interested but making an effort to be polite in the face of a certain hostility she sensed coming from the parole officer. She was not sure whether this stemmed from her own job, as the kind of person whose delight it was to put poor, misunderstood victims of society in jail, or if it was a kind of jealousy for the attention of Susan Weiner.

Their food came. Geri fussed and harried the waitress over the crispness of her salad and the provenance of the salad dressing. Weiner caught Marlene's eye and rolled her own slightly, along with an indulgent smile. We the Thin.

It would have been easy to dislike them both, Geri for her fussy self-righteousness, Susan for her air of unthinking entitlement, but Marlene found herself warming to them, not as individuals precisely, but to the relationship.

These two sisters had something that Marlene had only read about in books, the kind of spiritual closeness that had entranced female writers in the nineteenth century. Marlene had two sisters of her own, whom she loved, of course, but conventionally. Annie was a housewife with a brood of kids out on the Island. Pat was a city planner in Philadelphia. She saw them at birthdays and holidays, and there was warmth then but no real intimacy.

Marlene did not envy them, precisely. If she had been Susan, she would have found Geri's combination of mother-hen advice and effusive praise unbearable. And as Geri, Susan's blithe princess act would have driven her to violence. But it was oddly pleasant to bask in the warmth of their relationship, which was as rare in the circles Marlene frequented as hot-chestnut vendors in Midtown.

The lunch ended, not without (as Marlene had expected) an unbearable niggling over who owed what on the check, presided over by Geri, wielding a pencil. At the point when she was calculating the tip, to the nearest cent, Marlene whipped a twenty out of her wallet, snatched the check from Geri's fingers, slapped the check and the bill on the table, and clunked a sugar dispenser down on both.

"My treat," she said. "Let's move, Susan."

"God, yes," said Weiner, glancing at her watch. "I already missed my Jazzercise."

"Your Jazzercise—" said Geri. "Honestly, it's like a religion with you."

"You should try it, Geri, seriously, I'm always trying to get her off her behind. Do something! Marlene, you work out, right? What, aerobics?"

"I box," said Marlene. A snuffle of unbelieving mirth. "No, I don't mean I get in the ring. I have a body bag and a speed bag, and I jump rope and curl dumbbells. My dad taught me, and I've kept it up."

"Really?" from both.

"Yeah, he was a welterweight contender at one time back in the forties, or thought he was before he spent six minutes in there with Kid Gavilan. He stuck to plumbing after that."

Polite smiles, but Marlene caught the little look that passed. The sisters Stone did not know people whose fathers were ex-pugs or current plumbers. One of the nearly invisible injuries of class that aren't supposed to happen in America, but which make up much of the grit in the national gears. Sacred Heart and Smith and Yale Law had taken much of the sting out of it for Marlene; still, she could re-call very much the same look on her own dear one's face when she had first told him about where she came from, under the fancy ve-neer. A brief thought, and a familiar one, brushed across her mind: that Karp might have been, not happier maybe, but more content with another perfect Jewish princess like Susan Weiner. She was glad now she had sprung for the lunch.

The day-care was on Lispenard off Church, a few blocks north. They walked up Church. Susan Weiner did most of the talking, much of it about herself and her nice life. Marlene let the talk wash over her, content to just swing along the street. It was a pleasant day in the City. That is, the sky was the color of a lizard's belly and the air stank of petroleum byproducts, but at least it wasn't raining ice.

And she had high expectations. A perfect being like this could not have found anything less than the perfect day-care.

And so it proved. The woman who took care of six children in her large, sunny loft was a matronly soul named Lillian Dillard, who affected an embroidered smock and a plait of gray-blond hair down to her butt. She made quilts and wrote poetry and would someday finish her dissertation on early childhood behavior. The children, ranging from eight months to three, obviously loved her. Susan's three-year-old boy barely acknowledged his mother's presence, which Marlene took as a good sign. There was no TV in the large front room, another good sign. Marlene turned on the charm, was ac-cepted, and wrote out a check for the first month in advance.

■   ■   ■

Back at her desk, feeling pleased with herself, she flipped through her messages, returning calls.

"Morgue, we doze but never close, Maher."

"Denny? Marlene."

"Ah, the pearl of Centre Street. How nice to hear your voice."

"Likewise. What's up?"

"Hmm. We've got a Jane Doe here. A splatter case. Went off a six-story building in Alphabet City. Some marks I don't like on the body, and the vaginal and esophageal smears are positive."

"You think rape and he killed her?"

"I wouldn't go that far yet," said Maher. "The girl was fairly torn up. On the other hand, I have some anomalous results on the secretion tests. We have more than one sperm donor here."

"What do the cops think?"

"They think a pross. They think suicide."

"They would. They made her for a pross? No, you said a Jane Doe."

"Right. Her face is jam. But the kicker is, I have clear human tooth marks, three bites, same guy, and deep enough to draw blood. That always makes me steer away from either a trip to the moon on gossamer wings or a straight commercial transaction. Of course, I don't date much anymore . . ."

"Drugs?"

"No tracks. Tissues are negative for barbs, amphetamines, and opiates. No booze either."

"Who caught the case?"

Marlene heard paper shuffle. "Camano. Ninth Precinct."

She wrote down the name and the phone number Maher gave her, thanked the medical examiner, and hung up.

The call from the M.E. was supposed to be automatic, but some of the medical examiners thought it too much trouble to call the D.A.'s office directly. They figured the cops were in charge and that it was their call. Besides, they had a lot to do.

Marlene looked at the name she had written down and wondered if it was even worth making the call. The cops had a lot to do as well, and so did she. About three thousand rapes were reported to the police in Manhattan every year, out of which Marlene would be glad if she secured fifty convictions. Of course, the woman had been murdered too, which meant the cops had to give it more attention. Lucky her.

The problem was that there were good and bad rapes. The good rapes were when the age, race, or social class of the perp and the victim were widely disparate, or when there had been notable violence. Rapes of prostitutes were, however, the worst rapes of all. The casual murders that were part of the occupational hazard in the City's sex trade were only slightly better. If the cops had decided that Jane was a whore who had taken early retirement, then convincing them that she was a whore who had been raped and killed would not get all that much more action out of them. Sighing, she made the call.

The homicide bureau occupied a small suite of offices on the sixth floor of 100 Centre Street. Only Karp and a few senior people like Hrcany had actual offices. These gave on to a large common area jammed with secretaries' desks, the domain of Connie Trask. The rest of the A.D.A.'s were stuck in glass cubicles in a large bay a short distance down the main sixth-floor corridor.

It was Karp's habit after lunch, and before court started again in the afternoon, to prowl his turf, poking into papers and confronting malefactors. This habit obviated any number of formal meetings, which he abhorred. In this way, emerging from his office, faintly redolent of Italian sausage, Karp made the discovery that brought him back into *People* v. *Tomasian.*

A clerk had just brought in a pile of Xeroxing, which she distributed among the wire baskets arranged for that purpose, one for each attorney, on a table in the corner of the secretaries' bullpen. Karp wandered over and thumbed through some of the still warm papers. One of the folders in Roland Hrcany's basket was labeled TOMASIAN. It contained copies of material produced by the arresting officers, mostly DD-5 forms, which cops used for describing in some detail what they had done to pursue the investigation and the results, if any. Karp skimmed the reports and the list of items seized under the search warrant. He dug deeper. The autopsy report. Deeper. A description of the items found on the victim. Here he stopped, puzzled, and leafed through the stack more carefully. Then he tossed the folder back into the basket and, frowning, strode off in search of Roland Hrcany.

Roland was not in his office when Karp looked for him there. He was in court, as it happened, for a bail hearing on the case in question. Karp sat in the back of the courtroom and watched Tomasian's defense counsel, a stocky, grave man who really did look a lot like Raymond Burr, move for the setting of bail. He pointed out Tomasian's clean record, the presence of a large and caring family, the defendant's gainful employment in a family business, his ownership of a condo. Roland rose to rebut and argued with equal vehemence that the defendant was accused of a particularly heinous crime; he had resources and contacts outside the country; he was part of an international terrorist network.

Karp sympathized with the judge. Justice was at least partially sighted in cases like this one, and able to read the papers and watch TV. Poor kids from the lower orders of the City who gunned down people on the streets were invariably remanded to jail without bail. On the other hand, the well-dressed and harmless-looking man sitting before him was supposedly innocent until proven guilty, and had a constitutional right to reasonable bail.

The judge was not used to jailing people in nice suits with, as the saying went, roots in the community. He pondered for a few seconds and, using his years of experience on the bench, pulled a number out of the air: "Bail is set in the amount of five million dollars."

Sighs from the small group of people sitting behind the defense table. Karp thought it a reasonable out for the judge. Bondsmen would not touch a bail like that, which meant that Tomasian and his near and dear would have to raise the face amount, which meant in all probability that the guy was going back inside.

Karp waited at the head of the aisle. When Roland reached him, he said, "Nice work, Roland. The City sleeps safer tonight."

Hrcany's face twisted. "It should have been a no-bailer. These are diamond people, for chrissake! Who knows what they've got squirreled away?"

"Maybe. Meanwhile, I'm glad I caught you, Roland. I was just curious: what did you find in the vic's safe-deposit box?"

"What're you talking about?"

"The box. The vic had a box key on him when he went down. What's in it?"

Roland's eyes narrowed slightly and his body tensed.

"What is this, Butch? You checking up on me?"

"No, it just happened to cross my eye. I have to go and sit down with Bloom this afternoon and tell him that the case is a wrap, which is the only thing he wants to hear. So I needed to know if it is."

A flush began to rise under Roland's jaw. "Wait a minute! Since when did you give a shit about Bloom?"

Karp ignored this and pitched his voice to its maximally calming tone. "That's not the point, Roland. The fact that a victim has a safe box suggests a repository of information that could bear on the case, and I need to know what was in it before I go talk to Bloom. So what was it?"

Roland, of course, had noted the box key first thing, but in the flush of success had neglected to follow up on it. He covered himself now by blustering. "How the fuck do I know? Cuff links? His birth certificate? What the hell does it matter?"

"You haven't checked it," said Karp.

"I don't believe this! You still don't get it. *This is the guy.* It doesn't fucking matter what's in the box. We don't have to trace the victim's movements or his fucking associates, or find out what he ate for his last meal. It ain't no mystery, Butch."

Karp shifted gears. "The alibi didn't check out, huh? You talked to the girlfriend?"

"The girlfriend is gone," replied Roland with an unpleasant

smile. "Her office says she's on leave. So I got a warrant to search her place, knowing, *knowing,* that you would bug me about her. They found a VISA counterfoil for a ticket to San Francisco. We checked with the airlines: she was on a flight that left late that Sunday. I wonder why."

"You think she's involved?"

"I know it. Her place was full of Armenian nationalist literature, some of it copies of the stuff we found in Tomasian's office. They were in it together. In fact, it wouldn't blow me away if we found out that she was the other gun."

"So we're looking for her."

"Yeah, she's out on the wire. But whether she turns up or not, it shoots the shit out of our boy's alibi."

Karp nodded agreement. "Yeah, it does, provided he needs one."

"What?"

"Roland, what happens to your open-and-shut case if there's five kilos of Turkish heroin in his box? Or a letter from a shark that says, 'Pay up or else!'?"

"This is horseshit, Butch!" cried Roland, going red again.

"Just open the box, Roland," said Karp, and walked away.

Detective Camano turned out to be one of those cops who had retired on the job. The Jane Doe from Avenue A was an easy clearance, one of hundreds of miscellaneous bodies and parts of bodies that turned up in the City every year.

"It ain't homicide to get a bite on the ass," he told Marlene confidently. "The M.E. says there was no sign of foul play."

"Biting isn't foul play?"

"I mean not a cause of death. Look, honey, there's no knife wound, there's no gunshot wound, she wasn't strangled, or tied up—"

"You haven't considered the possibility that she was raped and thrown out of a window?"

A long-suffering sigh on the line. "We checked the houses on both sides of the street. Nobody saw nothing, and there's no woman missing from any of the apartments."

"What about the street girls?"

A laugh. "They haven't missed a trick, is what I hear. Look, we got forty, forty-five homicides on the chart here that we know are homicides. We don't need to invent any, especially when the M.E. isn't ready to call it."

"What about the rape part?"

"We don't know that either. I got nobody on the block saying they saw this chick dragged into the bushes. Nobody's coming around saying where's my Mary. So what am I gonna go on? Fingerprints? Sperm samples? You know how I figure it? This chick gets off a bus, tries the sporting life, a customer gets a little rough, and she decides to take a jump."

It was a dead end with this guy. Marlene decided to waste no more time. She said, "I hope you're right, Detective Camano. On the other hand, if we get three more women's bodies turning up with bite marks in the same places, and one of them is the mayor's niece, I'll remember this conversation and bring it up whenever I can with whoever will listen."

She slammed her phone down and reached for the next call message in the stack.

After fuming in his office for a half hour and being rude to everyone within easy reach, Roland called Frangi at Midtown South and told him to get over to the bank where Mehmet Ersoy had maintained a safety-deposit box, with key to same. Roland stood impatiently over a secretary while a warrant was typed out, whipped into a judge's office, got it signed, and left immediately for the bank.

Frangi was already there. He had identified himself to the bank branch manager. Roland flashed his warrant, and they were allowed to follow a uniformed guard into the vault.

"What's going on?" asked Frangi.

"Nothing. My boss got a hair up his ass about this case."

It was one of the large kind, a smooth steel box nearly the size of a bus station locker. The guard used Ersoy's key and the bank's key to remove the box, and carried it with dignity to a little room, where he placed it on a table and departed.

Frangi flipped up the lid of the box. He let out a wordless exclamation. Hrcany looked inside and cursed and stamped his foot.

"How much you figure?" asked Frangi.

Both men had considerable experience in judging large volumes of cash. Roland rummaged in the box, flipping stacks of bills at random. They were hundreds, all of them, in fresh bank wrappers marked "$10,000."

"A million," said Roland, "at least. Maybe a little more."

"Thrifty guy," said Frangi glumly.

5

KARP SLOSHED HIS DRINK IDLY IN HIS GLASS AND LOOKED AROUND through the milling crowd for Marlene. As a rule, he disliked workplace parties. He had to pretend to like drinking, to find amusement in what drinking did to the brain and behavior (in order to avoid being thought a spoilsport, one of Karp's big fears, and somewhat justified), and to socialize with people he would not have shared three words with had they not had a function in his professional life, and, since his profession was criminal justice, that included socializing with an unusual number of unpleasant people.

He would have avoided this party, as he had many others, had not the guest of honor been Tom Pagano, the outgoing director of the Legal Aid Society offices for the Manhattan criminal courts and a man for whom Karp had immense respect and affection. Pagano had been copping pleas when Karp was still in grade school, and now, in his early sixties and tired, had been rewarded with a judgeship, which in comparison to running Legal Aid was a paid vacation.

There was Marlene, by the bar, of course, smoking and sucking wine coolers and talking animatedly to a short curly-haired man. Karp pushed his way through the crowd to her side.

She hailed him gaily. Marlene at least was enjoying herself. She liked parties, which was yet another reason for coming to this one, to forestall the "he never takes me anywhere."

She gestured possessively at Karp and said, "Paulie, this is my husband, Butch Karp. Butch, Paul Ashakian. He just started working for Legal Aid. He's from the old neighborhood; the Ashakians used to live across from us in Ozone Park. I used to run around with his sister Lara, and Paul and my brother Dom were on the gym team together at St. Joe. A giant family, bigger than ours. My kid brother Paulie used to think the Chuck Berry song was about them."

"Song?" said Karp.

"Honestly, Butch! Where *were* you? A Whole Lot *Ashakian* Goin' On? Get it?"

The two men shook hands. "Marlene thinks I'm culturally deprived, I missed rock and roll," said Karp, smiling. He gestured to the party at large. "You're losing a great boss."

Ashakian nodded vigorously. "Yeah, he recruited me, and now this."

"Any word on the replacement?"

Ashakian laughed. "Hey, I can barely find the men's room. I'll be the last to find out. You'll know before I do."

"No, they don't tell me anything either," said Karp. "I never hear the gossip."

"Nobody tells you gossip because you can keep a secret," said Marlene. "People come into your office and swear you to secrecy and tell you some juicy stuff, and then what do you do? You don't tell anybody! Of course they stop telling you—you never tell *them* anything. You're out of the grapevine, Butchie."

"Luckily, I have you to inform me," said Karp.

"Yes," said Marlene, "I blab. I'm so deep in the grapevine I'm covered with sticky purple juice."

"So who is it?" asked Ashakian.

Marlene threw down a healthy gulp of her drink. "I'm not gonna tell, since I've been sworn to secrecy. It's Milton Freeland."

Blank stares from both. "Freeland. From Sussex County Legal Services. Apparently a hotshot, hard-charger, good political connections."

"I wish I was impressed," said Karp. "I never heard of the guy. I was expecting a promotion—one of Tom's people."

"Go figure," said Marlene, "and speaking of blabbing, I was just telling Paul about your doubts on Tomasian."

Karp's face crinkled in disbelief. He glared at her and said in a strained voice, "It's not my case, Marlene."

She ignored the tone and said, "Paul doesn't care about the legal details. It's the Armenian connection."

"I don't understand," said Karp.

Ashakian was more than willing to dispel his ignorance. "That's the whole point. The Armenian community is really bent out of shape about this. I was at a meeting the other night at the Tomasians' house . . ." He put both hands to his plump cheeks and shook his head. "You would've thought the Turks were beating down the doors. Pandemonium. It was like, years of paranoia were sitting there, just waiting for something to spring it, and this was it."

"Paranoia?"

"Yeah, about the Turks," said Ashakian, and then seeing the incomprehension on Karp's face, sighed, as if he had explained something far too often, and continued, "Turks and Armenians? Cowboys and Indians? Nazis and Jews? The Turks killed a million and a half Armenians between 1915 and 1920, including one of my grandparents."

"And they're still doing it? Killing them, I mean." Karp considered himself something of a connoisseur of murder, both mass and individual, and he was vaguely aware of having heard something about the subject the young man had opened, but he was blank on the details. Nor could he understand what it had to do with the case at hand.

"No, they're not. They got them all, or they ran. Some were rescued by Europeans after the first war, some went to Soviet Armenia."

"I don't get it, then. What's the point of the terrorism? Or are you saying there aren't any Armenian terrorists?"

"Oh, there are Armenian terrorists, all right," said Ashakian grimly. "The point is that the Turks won't admit it ever happened. There wasn't any genocide, according to them. They won't acknowledge it, won't pay reparations to survivors, nothing, zip."

"That's impossible," said Karp. "It's like those nuts that claim Auschwitz never happened. Hell, the physical evidence—"

"No, it's not the same. Thousands of witnesses saw the Nazi camps. The camps were captured while they were still in operation. It was obvious what was going on, and the Germans kept good records. But the Turks didn't do it that way. They drafted the young Armenian men and massacred them in their barracks. They drove the rest of the population out into the countryside and marched them to nowhere until they all died of starvation and disease. Women and children! Babies tossed into ditches!

"No photographs, of course. Shit, there were probably about twelve cameras in Turkey in 1915. No records either. The only witnesses were German civilians, and the German government didn't do anything about it while it was going on because the Turks were their allies. After the war, all they had was oral testimony from survivors, Armenians. Suspect, obviously."

"I can see where it could be hard to believe," said Karp judiciously. Ashakian's face had flushed as he warmed to the subject, and a glint of fanaticism had appeared in his eye. Karp looked at Marlene for conversational support, but she was obviously enjoying the lecture and was not averse to seeing Karp discomfited. He had endured any number of lectures on the Holocaust from childhood onward, often with a we-Jews-have-to-stick-together-or-else subtext from people looking for emotional or substantive favors. He was holocausted out, in fact, as Ashakian clearly was not.

As if reading his mind, Ashakian turned to the familiar theme. "Look, imagine World War Two had lasted, say, another three years. It could've, easy. The Nazis would've been able to kill all the Jews they had. Then they tear down the death camps and pave them over, build parks or housing on top, get rid of all the shoes, the hair, and whatnot. They burn the records. Then, after the war, if anybody asks, they say, 'Jews? What Jews? They left. They're in Russia, China, who knows? Have another beer. Witnesses? It's hearsay, exaggeration. Besides, how can you trust Jewish testimony? It's self-interested. They were on top and we kicked them out, and now they're whining about a massacre.' That's exactly what happened in Turkey. You know what the Turks say? 'Trust a snake before a Jew, and a Jew before a Greek, but never trust an Armenian.' "

The three of them were silent for a long moment, thinking about this. Then Karp said, "Okay, back to the present. What's the tie-in with the Tomasian case?"

"The tie-in is somebody whacked Ersoy and they're framing Aram for it. Aram is an Armenian nationalist. Who has a hard-on for Armenian nationalists?" He laughed bitterly. "Who the hell even knows what an Armenian nationalist is?"

"You like the Turks for it? You think Ersoy's own guys did it and set up the frame?"

"Who else?"

"Another Armenian nationalist," suggested Karp mildly. "Or anybody who knew what you just told me."

"That's bullshit!" Ashakian cried, loud enough to draw stares from other drinkers. Then he remembered to whom he was speaking: one of the more powerful figures of the New York criminal bar and, not incidentally, a man twice his size. He flushed and mumbled something apologetic and added, "It couldn't happen. I mean, Armenians are a very close-knit community."

"So are the Italians," said Karp with a dirty look at Marlene. "They don't have much problem whacking each other."

She stuck out her tongue at him briefly and said, "Don't change the subject, dear. The question is, what are you going to do about it?"

"I told you, Marlene, it's not my case, and I don't want to talk about it." As he said this, he bore in his mind, as a griping burden, the knowledge about Mehmet Ersoy's safety-deposit box, grudgingly related by Hrcany the day before. The presence of the money meant that the odds against the murder being a simple terrorist act had gone way up. There were documents in the box as well, which were now up at Columbia being translated from Turkish. Karp was not inclined to reveal these discoveries as gossip at a party.

Ashakian looked disappointed. Karp could see the respect dying in his eyes. Why did these young lawyers expect you to pursue justice? After a few minutes more of bland conversation, Ashakian made an excuse and left Karp and Marlene together at the bar.

"That wasn't very smart, Marlene."

She finished her wine cooler and signaled the bartender for a refill. "No, it wasn't," she replied, "but I'm off duty. I don't have to be smart. He's a nice kid and he's worried. I thought it would perk him up to talk to you about it, since you also don't like the Armenian for it. I was wrong: sue me!"

Karp gave Marlene a long, appraising look. Her heavy, straight brows were lowering, and her exquisite jawline had assumed a cleaver-like sharpness. She'd obviously had a few and was moving inexorably toward righteous belligerence. It was not beyond her to go into a screaming scene in front of the entire New York County criminal justice establishment. Karp decided to forestall this possibility with a judicious retreat. He groaned and flexed his bad knee.

"Listen, I'm wiped out. I need to split."

"But the party's just getting going," protested Marlene.

"Me, not us. You stay, have a good time. You need a break anyway. I'm going to schmooze for two minutes with Pagano and then head for home. I'll relieve Belinda, be a daddy for a couple of hours."

Marlene didn't bother to protest; in fact, she beamed and laid a serious kiss on Karp, in front of judges and everybody, a kiss that was as good as Demerol for his aching body.

He rolled off unsteadily through the throng, and found Tom Pagano sitting at a drink-laden table, surrounded by well-wishers and cronies from Legal Aid. Pagano smiled broadly as Karp approached and waved him over. "Butch Karp! Here he is, guys, the Prince of Darkness. Sit down, have a drink!" The happy hubbub seemed to diminish slightly as Karp slid gratefully into a chair. Somebody put a full bottle of Schlitz into his hand.

Although the lawyers who faced one another every day in the criminal courts pretended to a genial collegiality out of court, it was an inescapable fact that the adversarial system was well named. Winning and losing was part of the game, but Karp won a little too often; in fact, in over ten years he had never lost in a homicide trial. Among the public defenders sitting around the table there was not one whom Karp had not trounced in court.

No, there was at least one. Karp felt eyes on him, and he turned to confront the intense gaze of a stranger. Who extended his hand across the table and said, "I'm Milt Freeland."

Karp took the proffered hand. "Tom's replacement, right? Glad to meet you."

"You have good sources of information: it's not even official yet. Of course, no one could replace Tom," said Freeland in a tone that implied that not only could Tom Pagano be replaced, but that it was about time. Freeland was in his late thirties, a thin, small man with a large nose, black horn-rims, and an aureole of reddish hair around a balding dome. He was wearing a too-tight baby-shit-colored three-piece suit and a dark red tie with little gold justice scales embroidered on it.

Karp said flatly, "No, no one could."

Pagano was looking down the table at the two men. He shouted out, "Hey, Freeland, that's the guy to beat."

"I intend to," said Freeland quietly. Karp nodded politely at this and stood up. He tapped on a glass with a swizzle stick and raised his beer.

"I'd like to propose a toast. To Tom Pagano, a great lawyer and a great guy—a man who could defend scumbags year in and year out without ever becoming a scumbag himself—well, hardly ever—the guy who, next to Francis Garrahy, taught me more about trial work than anyone else, and doesn't he regret it! Best of luck, Tom!"

Tom Pagano laughed, the table applauded, and after a few minutes spent in the usual raillery, Karp was able to slip away.

Marlene felt a touch on her upper arm and turned to look into a pair of familiar swimming-pool-colored eyes.

"Raney! What are you doing here?"

"A little security detail. Lots of important people wandering around drunk."

"Yeah, it would be a tragedy if anything happened," said Marlene. "Somebody tossed a bomb in here, it'd set criminal justice back four days. Well, it's been months! You're looking spiffy. That's quite a suit."

Jim Raney was a detective with the NYPD, with whom Marlene had a history going back several years. The suit—a double-breasted number in a very pale tan—did look good on his slim figure. He grinned and pirouetted. "You like it? I got a deal."

"From whom? Roscoe's Fashions for the Heavily Armed?"

"I wore it for you, Marlene," he said, rolling his eyes and batting his eyelashes, and placing a warm hand on her knee. He had them to bat, thought Marlene. Raney had never made a secret of his attraction to her, but hers to him was something she preferred not to think about. Those wild Irish boys! Their milky skin, their big blues, their golden hair, their crazy-making attitude toward women! Which was why, although ever on the cusp of falling for Peter Pan, Marlene had married Captain Hook.

She laughed and patted the erring hand. "Wanna dance, Raney?"

There was a three-piece combo playing tunes derived from the youth of Tom Pagano and his contemporaries. Later, when drunkenness was more general, they would play Italian kitsch—"Way, Marie!", "Hey, Comparé," "Come-onna-my-house"—and wizened judges would sway to the music and shout the words, whether they were Italian or not.

Raney and Marlene danced to "Dancing in the Dark." He was a good dancer, and she liked to dance more than she usually got to, married to Karp. He held her tightly, and his right hand slipped lower than its official position at her waist.

"So what's new, Raney? Any hot cases?"

"I passed the sergeants' exam."

"You did? Good for you. Does that mean a transfer?"

"Yeah, they got me slated to move into the Nine next month. They want me to finish up on this airport task force first."

"How's that going?"

"Umm, not all that great. The usual wise-guy horseshit. A couple of guys that've been boosting stuff from air freight for years got themselves whacked outside a bar on Ninth Avenue. We got the guy, or anyway, a guy who'll go down for it. Besides that, domestics and drug shit. The usual. How about yourself? They still raping them pretty good?"

The hand was now gently cupping her right buttock. She did not object, because she had just thought of something she wanted from Raney, whore that she was.

"Jim, there's something I'm interested in—in the Nine."

"Oh?" It was not an encouraging noise.

"Yeah, a Jane Doe, took a header off a building in Alphabet City. Camano's handling it as a suicide, a pross. I think it could be a murder, maybe a weirdo."

Raney's manner changed instantly from genial to chill. "What does the M.E. say?"

"Undetermined pending further investigation. But the woman was raped. She had teeth marks all over her."

Raney shrugged and relaxed slightly the intensity of his clutch. The music changed to "Cherry Pink and Apple Blossom White," but he didn't feel like a chacha. He said, "It takes all kinds, Marlene. Why don't we just wait for the further investigation?"

"Ah, shit, Raney! You know there won't be further investigation. Not if they got it pegged as a suicide. Not if there isn't a family making waves. All I'm asking is, just give it a shot. Just look into it." She smiled fetchingly and tweaked his tie. "Come on. For little me?"

Raney grinned at her. "Marlene, darling. You know I love you, but . . . let me say that if you were offering me a lot more than a cheap feel on the dance floor, a lot more, the absolute last thing I am gonna do is to stick my nose in another cop's investigation, especially in a precinct where I'm not even in there yet, and where I'm gonna have to move into a command slot. No way, baby."

"Oh, crap, you're just like my husband," she cried. "Okay, just forget it. I want another drink."

When Marlene arrived home two hours later, she was at that stage of drunkenness when the jolly effects of inebriation have begun to thin out, and the brain and body are about to take their revenge for having been flooded with a deadly poison. At this point one can drink more until oblivion arrives, staving off the reckoning until the morrow, or stop drinking and tough it out. Marlene had chosen the latter course, not wanting to render herself comatose in the midst of a pack of drunken lawyers, or in proximity to (the quite sober) Detective Raney.

Raney got her home in his beat-up Ghia. His behavior was beyond reproach, limited to a peck on the cheek at parting and a comradely pat on the thigh.

She could hear the wails from the first floor. Little Lucy was having one of her evenings. Entering the loft, she found Karp stumping to and fro like Captain Ahab, looking gray, holding the red-faced, squalling infant and patting her back despairingly.

Marlene threw down her coat and snatched her daughter. "I fed her," said Karp. "I changed her. I fed her again. She wouldn't calm down."

Marlene sat in the bentwood rocker. "Did you sing and rock?"

"Of course," said Karp indignantly. "It didn't work. She's been crying for hours. She's not sick, is she?"

"No. What did you sing?"

"I don't know—what does it matter? Rock-a-bye baby, nursery rhymes, the usual."

"That's the problem," said Marlene and began to rock and sing:

Chistu voli pani,
Chistu dici: 'Un cci nn'e,
Chistu dici: Va 'rrobba,
Chistu dici: 'Un sacciu la via,
Chistu dici: Vicchiazzu, vicchiazzu,
camina cu mia!

Ten minutes of this and the child was out cold. Marlene put her in her crib and returned to the kitchen, where she ate four aspirin and a glass of tomato juice. Then she collapsed on the red couch next to Karp.

"Thank God," he said. "I was going nuts. How did you do that?"

"Oh, sometimes a girl needs her momma. And sometimes her Sicilian genes need a special treatment."

"That song? What does it mean?"

"Um, something like: I'm hungry, I want bread. There isn't any. Then go and steal some. I don't know how. Come with me, old man, and I'll show you."

"Very nice, Marlene. When she starts muscling the other kindergarten kids for milk money, we'll know why. I'm writing to Mr. Rogers about this."

"Please, my head is coming apart. Speaking of crime future, I think I'm going to put Harry Bello on this Avenue A thing when he comes over."

"The jumper? I thought the M.E. didn't rule on that."

"Not on the homicide, no, but the rape part—I don't like it. It has all the marks of a particularly nasty sex crime—the bites, the sexual bruising. It looks like the kind of thing where if he's done it before, he'll do it again. And once, just once, I'd like to nail a serial weirdo before he gets going on the series. I'm telling you about it now because just in case we come up with evidence that it's a homicide, and we find a guy, I don't want it to get lost."

Karp didn't mind. He was happy to do Marlene a favor: anything to distract her from the Armenians.

On the following morning when Karp held his weekly trial meeting, the Armenians were much on his mind. At the trial meeting the assistant district attorneys who were planning trials laid the cases they had prepared before their peers, and Karp, who attempted to shoot them down: a sort of legal scrimmage. Such discussion was possible because trials were much rarer than murders. Of the thousand or so homicides brought to attention of the law in Manhattan, fewer than one in ten would get before a jury, the remainder being otherwise disposed of, usually by plea bargaining. Or the guy would walk because somebody forgot to do something important.

Karp looked around the table, the seats at which were reserved for presenters. There were four of them this morning. The rest of the staff sat along the walls in chairs they had wheeled into the room, or they were perched on Karp's desk or on windowsills. He nodded to the man seated to his right and said, "Okay, Guma, let's get started."

The man so addressed was short and squat and looked enough like Yogi Berra to turn heads on the street, the main differences being that he was not quite as handsome as Berra and could not hit a high inside curve ball, for which reason he had been denied a career in the majors. Besides that, he was a very good athlete, as were almost all the men (and the two women) crowding the room. Karp had found, or imagined he had found, that people who played high-level competitive sports made the best trial lawyers. They had thick skins and a certain casual brutality without which survival at Centre Street could be measured in weeks; they lived to win; they played hurt; they could work as part of a team. It was not a job for the legal intellectual: let them work on Wall Street or teach at Harvard, was Karp's thinking.

Ray Guma was a good example. It was not entirely clear that he could read. It was a fact that no one had ever seen him writing anything down. Yet he never forgot a face, or a name, or an incident from any case he had ever handled. Nobody in the D.A.'s office was more magisterial on the subject of the mob, its politics, its personalities, its plans. It had rubbed off; Guma was mildly corrupt in what he considered a good cause. He consorted with known criminals. He was an astonishing and indefatigable lecher. And though he shared no point of habit or moral standard with his boss, the Mad Dog of Centre Street, as he was known, was one of Karp's favorite people.

Guma began his presentation. "This is *People* v. *Cavetti*. Okay, Jimmy Cavetti was part of a gang that's been ripping things off from air freight out at Kennedy for years now. They did high-value stuff: wines, furs, art, antiques. Needless to say, the goombahs are in it heavy. It's under the Bollano family, a *capo regime* name of Guissepe Castelmaggiore.

"So, a cozy arrangement. They bought enough of the shipping clerks and expediters to get them the word on where the good stuff is. Joey Castles handles protection, plus fencing the stuff, plus divvying the cut for the families. The other two main guys in the gang were the Viacchenza brothers, Carl and Lou, solid Bollano guys. The vics in this case.

"To make a long story short, Joey finds out the Viacchenza boys are skimming the take, holding out. Joey has a short fuse. One night last November, the Viacchenzas are leaving the Domino Lounge on Ninth. They walk past an alley, and somebody takes them out with a twelve-gauge. There's snow in the alley, and we pick up a perfect heel print, which we match to Jimmy's shoe. That's the case. The shoe and the situation."

There was a brief silence. "How did we get the shoe?" asked Karp.

"Search warrant based on reliable informant. The usual horse-shit. This time the cops really got a reliable informant. One of the shipping clerks in on the theft deal. They nailed him on a dope thing and he gave them Jimmy C.—I mean that Jimmy fingered the Viacchenzas for the hit. He didn't name Joey Castles, needless to say—he wasn't that stupid. They'll move to suppress the shoe, but we shouldn't have any trouble."

Roland Hrcany, who was at the table, spoke up. "Did he do it?"

Guma snorted. "You mean, was he the trigger on the hit? Fuck, no! Jimmy's no killer. He's a thief. Nah, Joey Castles probably got a contract out. Jimmy was just there to finger, maybe drive. Oh, yeah, I forgot to mention. We got an eyeball says Jimmy was cruising around the Domino earlier on the night of, asking about the brothers, were they there yet, anybody seen them—like that."

"But he'll stand up on it?" asked Karp. "To murder deuce?"

"Yeah, maybe," said Guma, shrugging. "Jimmy was always a stand-up guy. On the other hand, he's never looked at twenty-five to life. But what you're asking is, will he rat out Joey Castles and whoever was the shotgun artist? I'd say no. Which is why we got the tap and the bugs on Joey."

"Let me get this straight," said Hrcany. "He didn't do the hit, but we're trying him for it?"

Guma turned himself and leaned forward so that he could look directly at Hrcany, who was sitting on the same side of the long table. "What kind of remark is that, Roland? The fuckin' guy was there. He was holding the shotgun's hand, for chrissake. He'll go down for it too, unless he deals."

Karp didn't like the way the conversation was drifting, and he knew very well why Roland had raised that silly point. Karp asked, "But *will* he deal when it comes down to it?"

Guma said, "No. He's saying, 'Convict my ass.' He figures we got a weak case, or that's what his lawyer's telling him. One heel print against his alibi. He got some bitch to say he was with her. (Sorry, ladies.) We shouldn't have much trouble impeaching her. They'll try to impeach our shipping clerk and our bar-flies. They'll get shoe experts. You know the routine."

Karp did indeed. He said, "Okay, good job, Goom. Tony?"

Tony Harris, a bright young left-handed pitcher from Syracuse whom Karp had raised from a pup into a competent and aggressive prosecutor, told his story: *People* v. *Devers*—a man, a woman, drugs, a gun. The D. had a record of atrocious violence, and had shot down the woman in front of three shrieking children. It was therefore one of the cases on which Karp had decided to hang tough. The defendant had done likewise, making the state work for it.

As usual, Karp questioned Harris closely about the details, and, following his example, so did the other lawyers. The M.E. evidence, the testimony of witnesses, the fact that all potential witnesses were sought out and interviewed, the defendant's alibi, the lab work, what the cops found.

After the questions were exhausted, Karp summed up the case. "The problem here is that the direct witnesses to the crime are minor children aged three to seven. Not convincing to most juries, easily confused on cross. So we build the case on indirect evidence, which is convincing. We have a neighbor who came out in the hall after hearing shots and made an ID. We have two young women outside the apartment, saw the defendant enter, heard the shots, saw the defendant exit. We have physical evidence in the form of nynhydrin tests that show the defendant had fired a gun recently. We have the murder weapon found in a sewer located on the direct route between the victim's apartment and the defendant's apartment three blocks away. It's a story. Anything wrong with it that we haven't brought up?" He looked around the room. Silence. "No? Okay, good job, Tony. Next."

Next was an A.D.A. named Lennie Bergman, and the case was *People* v. *Morales.* Bergman had just begun his account when Karp interrupted him. "Did you get my note on this?"

The attorney hesitated. "Yeah, I did."

"And you still want to go to trial on it?" Karp stared hard at the man, who met his gaze levelly. Bergman was a stocky, blunt-featured man, a defensive lineman out of Adelphi. Not an inspired mind, or particularly perceptive, but competent, tough, and certainly not a man to be moved by a disapproving stare from his boss. "Okay, make your pitch," said Karp.

Bergman presented his case, after which Karp tore into it, pointing out the absurdities in Morales's supposed behavior after the crime, the lack of direct witnesses to a crime that had supposedly taken place on the street, the fact that Morales's grandmother persisted in her story that the incriminating evidence had been planted. But nobody else seemed to smell a police scam, and Karp was left with the choice of either directly overruling a good attorney or letting him go to trial under a cloud based not on any direct knowledge but on Karp's experience and instinct.

Karp tapped on the table and looked at the faces sitting around it: Guma bored; Harris interested, inclined to be sympathetic, but confused; Bergman, pugnacious, defensive; and Hrcany. What was that expression in Hrcany's eyes? Challenging? Contemptuous, a little? What was he thinking? That Karp was afraid to try the tough ones anymore? That he had become too nice about the provenance of evidence?

They were waiting. Across Karp's mind passed the sudden wish that he had never gotten into the business of supervising other people's cases. Then he said, "Okay, fuck it, go for it. Roland, you're up."

6

THE SHOOT-OUT BETWEEN KARP AND HRCANY OVER *PEOPLE V. Tomasian* became the stuff of legend before the afternoon was well begun. In the outer office the secretaries were the first to know, as most of the discussion was carried on at such a volume that all work ceased and the women muttered nervously and fingered their telephones. After lunch the tale spread throughout the building, growing in drama and violence. They had come to blows. Hrcany had pulled a knife. The police had been called. Karp was in the hospital. Gunshots had been heard by reliable witnesses.

The news floated up to the eighth floor, where the district attorney heard it and was glad, though less so when it was explained to him that Karp had not really been stabbed by one of his own attorneys. Farther down the hall from the D.A.'s office, the story reached the ears of Conrad Wharton, the chief administrative officer, who understood what it meant, and considered how it might fit in with his perpetually evolving and lovingly maintained plan to ruin Karp.

Marlene heard the news late in the day, having been with the grand jury, and immediately sought out Ray Guma for the straight poop.

"Nah, the part about the knife is bullshit, and they didn't call the cops," said Guma confidently. "What it was, Connie stuck her head in when Roland kicked over his chair. She scoped the situation out and said, 'Should I call the cops?' After that they both calmed down. But Roland did throw the case file at Butch's head. That part's true."

"Did it hit him?"

"Nah, he was at the other end of the table. Lucky thing too. Roland gets up and kicks his chair across the room and he yells, 'You want the fuckin' case? Take it!' and he heaves the whole box. He would've gone for Butch too, but me and Tony stood up and stood in his way. Not that we could've stopped him. But it slowed him down and then Connie came in. It was like a schoolteacher breaking up a fight at recess in the schoolyard. Hell of a thing."

"How'd it start?" asked Marlene.

"It was when Roland had just finished doing his thing on the Tomasian case. It sounded okay to me, nothing special. But I see Karp is getting that look. You know what I mean? The Chinese warlord eyes? After Roland finishes, Butch stares at him like he just cut a fart. He says, 'What about the money, Roland. You didn't mention the money.'

"Roland gets all red and he says, 'The money's horseshit. It's not relevant to the case, it's extraneous, et cetera.'

"Butch says, 'You don't fuckin' know that, Roland. You haven't bothered to find out either. You haven't lifted a finger to investigate the victim's background. And what about the documents, they're irrelevant too?'

"Meanwhile everybody's looking at each other. Money? Documents? Nobody knows what the fuck's happening. Then Roland, he's yelling now, he says, 'Yeah, they're irrelevant. They're letters from his brother, in Turkey—just bullshit.'

"And Butch says, 'Oh, yeah? How come he keeps letters from his brother in a fucking safe-deposit box?' Then he turns around to all of us—I mean we're fucking . . . confused ain't the word, believe me—and he says, 'This is an example of a fucked investigation. This isn't even an investigation. It's a goddamn romance. He fell in love with this guy and that was it. It's not a case, it's not an indictment—it's a valentine.' Then some more shit about when the defense gets this stuff about the safe deposit on discovery, you can kiss this guy good-bye. They'll do a serious investigation, and then they'll know shit *we* don't know and so on. He was really wailing, dancing on Roland's head, and Roland's getting redder and redder, he's like a fuckin' Coke sign, and finally he breaks in, he yells, 'Well, fuck it, I'm not gonna give it to them! It's not part of the case, they got no right to see it. I checked it with Bloom and he agrees.'

"Good God!" exclaimed Marlene.

"Yeah, right. You coulda heard a pin drop. Okay, Butch goes dead white. He says, 'Bloom? You checked it with Bloom?' Then he points his finger at Roland, and he goes, 'If I find out that the defense doesn't have every single scrap of information you've assembled on this case, I will personally deliver it to defense counsel, *and* I will inform the judge of your conspiracy to suppress evidence.' That's when Roland threw the case file. Shit, it was like the movies!"

Marlene shook her head in amazement. "So what's the upshot?"

"Damned if I know," said Guma. "You oughta go talk to Butch. He might not bite *your* head off."

But late that day in his office, he seemed not biter but bitten, wan, and depressed.

"So, are you going to kiss and make up or what?"

Karp grimaced at this question, but left Marlene's head attached. "I don't know, kid," he replied. "I must be losing it. I still can't believe it happened. Me and Roland—for chrissake, we go back years. It was him going to Bloom that did it. Bloom! He hates

Bloom. And on a sneaky deal like this. And I blame myself for it. If I was a hundred percent, I would've played Roland different. The last thing you want to do with him is get into a pissing contest." He slammed the desk in frustration and looked at her with eyes that were dark-rimmed and full of pain.

"I hurt all the time. It makes me irritable. Running a staff isn't like playing ball, or even trying cases. Irritable is good in those. Now I got to be a fucking therapist."

"You do it, though."

"Yeah, but I don't love it. It's not my real thing. I'm trying to build a homicide bureau like we used to have, but I don't have the material and I don't have the support. Can you imagine what Garrahy would've said if Roland had delivered a case like *Tomasian*? I saw Garrahy make a guy cry once, and not a kid either, an old homicide prosecutor—reduced him to tears in front of a roomful of people because the guy had prepared an incompetent case. I'll never have that kind of authority, not over guys like Roland anyway."

"Maybe he should quit, then."

"But he's good," Karp protested. "I don't want him to quit. I wouldn't give two shits about him if he wasn't a terrific prosecutor. The pity of it is that he doesn't get the point, and I sense that a lot of the best guys were on his side. Bergman. Guma even. They didn't get the point, and if they didn't get the point, how the hell am I going to get the kids to get it?"

"The point being he picked the wrong guy?"

Karp sighed. "No, he may have the right guy. Christ, you don't get it either. Look, over on Mulberry Street around where we live, there used to be the old police headquarters, back in the eighteen-nineties. And in that building somebody got the bright idea of taking photographs of all the people they arrested and filing them according to crime. Very useful.

"And then it occurred to some other bright boy that when they had a mystery, they could reach into the drawer and pull out a photo of someone they were interested in getting off the street, and what they did was they put it in a frame on the wall, and then all the cops would lean on informants to come up with testimony that, yeah, this guy did the crime. That's how they built cases back then. That's where the word comes from, frame. It's still the easiest way to clear cases.

"But not to win cases. People talk about lenient judges and juries. That's bullshit. Scumbags get out on the street nine times out of ten because of prosecutorial incompetence. They're lazy: they buy the cops' story, like Bergman just did. Or they get entranced, like Roland. They forget that they have to learn everything about the case, not just the stuff that supports their indictment. Because if they have a halfway capable defense, it'll all come out in trial. The jury doesn't automatically believe the state and the cops anymore. Maybe the opposite."

"Gosh, this is just like being in law school," said Marlene, rolling her eyes. "But back to the matter at hand. What are you going to do?"

"I've been thinking about it. What I'd like to do is find out who did the murder. If it was Tomasian, fine. I'm an asshole, but at least we'll have a case that makes sense. If it wasn't Tomasian . . ." Karp grinned unpleasantly. "Then I'll have made my point. To Roland. To the homicide staff. And to Bloom."

"Are you going to make Roland cry?"

Karp laughed, a welcome release from tension. "Right now I kind of hope so.

"I hope so too. You could sell tickets," said Marlene. "And I can't fail to note that I told you so on this."

"Yes, dear," said Karp flatly.

"Ah, the Olympic passive-aggression team takes the field. Time for me to get small. You coming?"

"In a minute. I need to make a call."

She left, and he looked in his Rolodex to find a number that he called as infrequently as he could manage. It was late, but he figured the FBI's New York office would still be open, fighting crime.

The man who answered was about as unhappy to hear from Karp as he was to have to call. They wasted no time on pleasantries.

"I need some information, Pillman," said Karp.

Elmer Pillman was the FBI agent in charge of liaison with the criminal justice authorities of the greater metropolitan area. Once in the course of an investigation, he had made a very big mistake, a mistake that would certainly have ended his career and landed him in prison, a mistake that Karp had discovered. Karp had not ratted him out, however, for reasons of his own. It made for a peculiar and prickly relationship.

"About what?" asked Pillman after a meaningful pause.

"Armenian terrorism."

A pause. "You said Armenian? What, are you writing a term paper? You mean historical stuff?"

"No, current. Here, in the City."

"There ain't none. No, wait, this must be about that Turkish attaché who got popped the other week."

"That's right," said Karp. "You're interested in that?"

"Not particularly."

"Then you don't think it was a terrorist job?"

"I didn't say that," Pillman snapped. "Don't put words in my mouth. It's just that Armenian organizations have no record of assassinations in the U.S. We have no evidence that they're about to start. Europe, that's another story."

"They whack people in Europe?"

"They did at one time, a lot. Still do occasionally. Turks. Back in the twenties, they got all the people responsible for the so-called massacres. Gunned them down on the street, nearly every one of them. Recently? Not much. Couple of bombs, a shooting. Mostly young . . . I guess you can't call 'em young Turks, can you?" He chuckled. "Nothing like the Arabs. Or the Krauts for that matter."

Karp said, "But there is an Armenian nationalist movement locally, isn't there? You keep tabs on them, don't you?"

A longer pause. "I don't know about tabs. I wouldn't say tabs. Freedom of association and political activity is guaranteed by the

Constitution. We don't infringe on that unless we have reason to believe that such activity is a front for illegal activities."

"Thank you, Agent Pillman, and I hope you had a flag flapping in the background when you said that. Meanwhile, cut the crap: who runs the Armenian nationalists locally?"

"Hang on," said Pillman. The line echoed hollowly for four minutes. When he got back on the line he said only, "Sarkis Kerbussyan," and then an address in Riverdale.

Karp said, "Thanks, Pillman. As always it's been a—"

"We never talked," said Pillman, and hung up.

The next morning, a Saturday, Karp rose early and, after checking that his knee worked, grabbed a quick bowl of Wheaties and left the loft for an unpleasant but necessary mission. He took the BMT uptown to 8th Street in the Village, stopped at a bakery, walked a block and then up the handsome pale sandstone steps of a town house. He rang the buzzer energetically for a full minute until he was admitted. He climbed a flight and rang the bell.

Roland Hrcany stood in the open doorway, looking frowsty, with his long tresses in a blond halo, dressed only in a heavy black terry robe. He said, "I oughta punch you the fuck out."

"Yeah, and I oughta punch you out too, but you're not and I'm not. It's just another goddamn case, Roland. It's not worth it. So I came here to get this settled." He held up a redolent, warm paper bag. "I brought you a dozen onion bagels."

Roland tried to maintain his glare, but it collapsed seconds later into something between a scowl and grin.

"Bagels! Fuckin' guy! Okay, get in here, asshole!"

Roland stood out of the doorway, and Karp walked in. Hrcany had the whole floor, a two-bedroom with a large living room, a separate dining room, a real, as opposed to a Pullman, kitchen, and a nice view of 9th Street. It would have taken three-quarters or more of his salary to pay for it, except that he lived here for free, courtesy of his father, who was a substantial player in Manhattan real estate. Roland had the place furnished in Playboy modern: lots of black leather furniture, shaggy white rugs, chrome and glass tables and shelves, a Macintosh sound system with six-foot speakers, and big Warhol silk screens of Marilyn, one in yellow and one in red, chrome-framed on the walls. The place had an appropriate odor— sandlewood incense and some musky cologne. It stuck in Karp's throat and made him want to sneeze.

They went into the kitchen, where Roland set about making coffee, using instruments that looked like they belonged in a jet fighter. He ground beans, which Karp had never seen anyone do in a house before. Karp found a knife, sliced two bagels, and Roland put them on a plate with chunks of butter and cream cheese. Roland poured the coffee, telling Karp stuff he didn't much want to know about the origin of the beans. It tasted like regular coffee, thought Karp the peasant.

"So," said Roland, "this little visit, it means you're gonna get off my ass on Tomasian?"

"Well, yes and no, Roland. It's not that simple."

"Then let me hear the yes part first."

"Okay, Tomasian is your case. You do it how you want, and I won't make any more public comments about how you're handling it. I'm going to sit on my private opinion that the case is fucked."

Hrcany flushed and was about to say something, but Karp stopped him with a hand gesture and continued, "Hold on a second. Here's my problem. You're an experienced prosecutor. You got an instinct. You want to play it a little cute sometimes, a little closer to the horns than I do, than I'd like, that's fine. For you.

"But I got fifteen, twenty kids on the staff who don't know their ass from a hole in the ground. They weren't trained by Garrahy's old homicide bureau, like you and me. They see the stuff you pull, they think it's cool for them to do it too. And it's not. I can't have thirty or so cases I think are fucked up running all the time, and I can't nursemaid every case individually. You see the problem?"

"Assuming I do," said Roland carefully, "what're you going to do about it? This is the no part coming, right?"

"Yeah. Basically, I want to fill in around your investigation. You say the cash and the letters and the details of the vic's life are irrelevant. Fine. Go that way. But I need to find out for sure. And I'm going to."

"What, you're going to investigate my investigation?" asked Roland with some heat.

"No, that's not the point. I just want to check out the stuff you thought wasn't worth checking out. If it doesn't amount to anything, you're the hero and I'm the goat."

"And the opposite if it does, right?"

"No, as a matter of fact: I intend to feed you anything I find out. Like I said, it's your case. And if it turns out that Tomasian is innocent, you'll do the right thing. And it'll be a good lesson for the kids."

The glower was back in Roland's eyes. "Fuck the kids! I don't like this. It's like you're working D. against me."

"No, it's not," said Karp. "I'm just completing the investigation for the People." Roland snorted derisively, but Karp continued in the same calm tone. "The thing of it is, Roland, I'm going to do it either way. Now, we can duke it out in public and split the bureau and make Wharton and them real happy, or we can approach it like friends and colleagues who're trying to work out a difference of opinion. It's really up to you how it goes down."

Hrcany sipped his coffee and considered this at length. He thought Karp was chasing rainbows, but still, the notion that Karp would, in a sense, be working for him on the case was certainly attractive. And he knew he could depend on Karp's promise that any new stuff that came up would not be used in an embarrassing way. It was a covered bet, a two-way win, the kind that Roland liked best.

He looked Karp in the eye and rapped sharply, once, on the table. "Okay, deal." A smile spread across his face. "You wouldn't want to make it more interesting? A little side bet?"

"Okay, if I lose, I'll kiss your ass in Macy's window," said Karp.

"No, I mean for real. Money. Say a yard. Come on!"

"No bet, Roland. You know I don't bet."

Roland laughed. "Yeah, right. Okay, I'm mollified. How about a piece of ass as long as you're here?"

"What!"

"Yeah, in the bedroom. Seventeen. Got a cooze on her feels like she's only been fucked about a dozen times. Hah! That's not counting last night and this morning." He cupped his hand to his mouth.

"Hey, Mollie! You wanna fuck my friend here?"

From the direction of the bedroom came a querulous reply that Karp could not make out. Roland gestured in that direction. "Go ahead. In return for the bagels. I'm serious. She'll do you."

"Not today, Roland," said Karp, rising and suppressing a wince. "But I appreciate the offer. Catch you later."

Karp let himself out. The air was crisp and clean, springlike, not too laden with distillates, for which Karp was grateful. Although accustomed to wading ankle-deep in society's rotted pus, depravity on a more intimate level, as, for instance, practiced by friends, disturbed him. That it disturbed him also disturbed him. It cut him off in a way from the prevailing mood of his times, which, being at heart a companionable man, he would have liked to have shared.

But no, having dipped lightly into the fleshpots immediately after his first wife had run out on him, he had found that he didn't much care for casual sex, or any of the ordinary weirdnesses of his era.

He had just resigned himself to young-fogeyhood when Marlene dropped into his life. She had, in contrast, stinted herself nothing in the sexual phantasmagoria that was 1970s New York, and Karp was content to thus sample the fleshpots at, as it were, second hand. Feeling virtuous, warmed by recalling his most recent encounter just that morning with his very own sensual calliope, Karp walked back toward the downtown subway.

Marlene, at this moment, had completed the ever-wrenching transition from scented houri to cart horse. She was about to take her infant daughter to the park, an enterprise which, if one lives in a five-floor walk-up in the City and the nearest park is ten blocks away, requires nearly the equipment and preparation of an assault on the Eiger.

With the baby on one hip and a huge canvas bag on the other, and while balancing a collapsible stroller on her shoulder, Marlene clumped down the narrow stairs. Out on the sun-dappled, filthy street she set up the contraption and placed the child in it, and leaned over to strap her in.

It was a scene still oddly out of place on that industrial street. All around her, cursing workmen were off-loading huge spools of heavy wire from a truck and manhandling them to the cable hoist in Marlene's building, where they would be hauled up to the drawing mill that occupied the two middle loft floors. This was one reason why Marlene had decided to get out of her loft for the day. The ancient motor that ran the hoist was located in her home, and all morning it would be producing a deafening racket.

She set off down Crosby to Grand and then headed east. Soon she left the industrial loft zone and entered the heart of Little Italy. At Grand and Mulberry she passed the tenement where her grandmother had lived for most of her long life. From before Marlene could remember until she had left for college, she had spent every Sunday in that apartment, and afterward, on fine evenings, she had played on these streets, potsy and jump rope and the various lost street games of the City that amused children in the era before TV took over the hours between dinner and bedtime: ringalevio, red light green light, giant steps, Chinese handball.

The neighborhood was still the same on the surface. The shops were still nearly all Italian, as were the restaurants, although the Chinese were pressing in, especially around the junction with Mott Street. Yet Little Italy was shrinking and growing older. Marlene's parents' generation had largely abandoned it for the near suburbs, and most of her contemporaries were not interested in walk-up tenements.

The remaining old folks were out in force today, however, it being one of the first warm weekends of the year. Marlene stopped and spoke with several black-clad grand dames, friends of her grandmother's, who were sitting out in front of their doors on folding chairs. Lucy was made much of.

The old men were out too, and the doors of the social clubs, storefronts with their large windows painted brown or dark green, were open to catch the spring breezes. Marlene spent a few minutes chatting with a retired capo of the Lucchese family, who tried to give Lucy a cube of nougat exactly the right size to jam in a six-month-old's trachea. Marlene intervened in time to avert what might have been the old gentleman's first unintentional murder and moved on.

She had by this time quite recovered from her earlier irritation. She belonged here, in the old heart of the City; roots were worth a good deal of schlepping.

Marlene now entered an area that constituted one of the many open-air after-care clinics provided by the City for its mentally distressed. Sprawlers, sleepers, fighters, talkers to spirits, hearers of voices, disported themselves as if in a day room at one of the bad old upstate loony bins, although here they had the benefit of exposure to the healthful elements and were responsible for obtaining their own medication. Marlene could not help but observe this being provided by thoughtful citizens at many points along the street.

Crossing Chrystie Street, she entered Sara Roosevelt Park. There are still parks in the City where, on such a pleasant Saturday in spring, the quality disport themselves, and have elegant picnics, and tourists ride in overpriced carriages, and nurses wheel expensive perambulators, but Sara Roosevelt Park is not one of them. It is a narrow strip of asphalt decorated with tired lawns and dispirited trees, populated heavily not only by the distressed but by gangs from Alphabet City, which begins a few streets to the north.

On the other hand, even so pitiful a green space was rare enough in that part of the City to promote some accommodation. There was at least one section of the park, a lawn around a small playground and basketball court, where respectable people—mainly Puerto Rican families from the Lower East Side—could congregate and watch their children play.

The baby was asleep. Marlene sank gratefully onto a bench, lit a cigarette, and watched the action. Platoons of kids were shrieking in the playground, largely unsupervised, and on a patch of scabrous grass a Latina matron was setting out the ingredients for a picnic, while her husband lay on his back and drank a beer. Another Latino family group was starting a portable grill, laughing as the flames from their lighter fluid shot with a whoosh and a fragrant stink up into the sky.

A small Puerto Rican girl, perhaps seven, skinny and dirty, was weaving through the crowd, wrapped in some internal fantasy. She was dressed in a grubby pink satin dress several sizes too small for her, to which she had affixed a red crinoline which hung limply to her ankles. On her head she had placed a tiara made of crumpled tinfoil, and she had pinned chiffon scarves to her shoulders so that as she leaped and whirled, they fluttered behind her like wings.

Marlene's attention was distracted by angry shouts and the sound of breaking glass. She looked down the row of benches. Perhaps some drunks were fighting, but she couldn't see. The baby, awakened by the racket, began to fret, and Marlene reached into her bag for a bottle. When she looked up again, the little girl was standing in front of her.

"Are you a pirate?" she said without preamble. Marlene was wearing her black eye patch, covering the space where her eye had been blown out by a letter bomb some years back.

"Yes," said Marlene. "You're a fairy princess, right?" The child nodded. She was holding a long dowel that must have once been a balloon stick, the end of which was covered with a ball of the gold foil used by one of the fast-food chains to wrap sandwiches. She wore cracked patent leather Mary Janes and grungy white socks. Her knees were scabbed. A pinched little thing but pretty, despite the visible neglect.

"Is that your baby?"

"Yes."

"Can I play with him?"

"Her. No, she's too little to play."

The child smirked and whipped her wand back and forth. "I could, I could turn her into a frog," she said confidently.

"Yes, but please don't. I have zillions of frogs, but only one baby."

The girl pirouetted on a toe, to make her scarves flutter. She was holding her body very stiff in an effort to maintain the appropriate hauteur, and looking down her nose at Marlene in a way that would have been funny were it not so serious. Marlene said, "What's your name?"

"Princess, no, Special *Fairy* Princess Latameeshiana. The first. What's yours?"

Marlene introduced herself and the baby and then asked, "You live around here?"

"I live on the moon," said the girl, staring at an ordinary-looking man in a dark coat walking down the path. As he passed, the girl leaned close to Marlene and said in a stage whisper, "You see that man? He's a werewolf."

"I don't think so."

"You don't believe in *werewolves?*"

"Not that much."

"How about . . . witches? Do you believe in witches?"

Marlene thought seriously about it. "Yeah, I guess I do."

The child laughed out loud. "Ha-hah! There's no such thing as witches."

"No? Then what do you believe in?"

The girl intoned her credo portentously, ticking it off on her fingers. "I believe in werewolves, monsters . . . God, dinosaurs, vampires, fairies, and . . . angels. You can see angels. It's true."

Marlene let her face show an interest that was less than half patronizing. The sun was warm, the baby was sucking happily at her bottle, and Marlene was content to learn all about the characteristics of angels from an urchin. It was more interesting than condo-buying details, and more pleasant than listening to women talk about being raped.

More glass broke, the sound coming from around the bend in the path. The force of the argument rose a degree. The little girl stopped talking, and Marlene realized that she had asked a question.

The girl asked it again, "Did you ever see one?"

"An angel? No, I don't think so. Did you?"

"All the time. Do you know what happens if an angel is bad? God takes off their wings, and they fall down and smoosh. They have real blood and goosh in them. Really! Or they could become vampires. It depends."

"It's an interesting theory," Marlene agreed.

The child pirouetted again, admiring her wings.

"Fairies have special wings, so they could never get smooshed. I can really fly."

Marlene smiled uncertainly and gave the child a close look. Imagination was all very well, but the Princess, who, by the ragged look of her was not one of reality's darlings, might be taking it too far. Oddly, Marlene thought of the Jane Doe on the slab at the morgue. Maybe she had thought she could fly too.

"You know, Princess," Marlene began, "pretend wings are very pretty, but they're different from real wings, aren't they? I mean, birds have real wings and they can really fly—"

Marlene's introduction to ontology was interrupted, as such discussions so often are in the City, by a major felony. There was a hoarse scream, and a ragged man came racing down the asphalt path, staggering, his face a perfect mask of blood. Before Marlene knew it, she was on her feet, positioned between the gory apparition and little Lucy. The wounded man did not, however, spare them a look, but crashed through a low bush and across the picnic field, to a chorus of curses and more screams. His pursuers, two tattered louts, one with a knife in hand and the other clutching a broken wine bottle, came racing after. By that time Marlene was wheeling her stroller rapidly in the opposite direction. After thirty yards or so, she thought to look for her recent companion, but the little girl had entirely vanished. In this respect, at least, a fairy indeed.

7

"HAVE A GOOD TIME?" ASKED KARP WHEN MARLENE ARRIVED, BREATH-less, at the loft.

She put on a smile and declined to tell her husband that she had been chased from the park by armed thugs bent on murder. Instead she conveyed delight in the recreational opportunities of the neighborhood and then asked, "How did your thing with Roland go? Did he attack you with his triceps?"

Karp also put on a smile and declined to tell Marlene about Roland offering him a piece of ass. He did mention the idea of a bet on the Tomasian thing.

"You should have taken him up on it. We could use the money," said Marlene, placing the baby, with a full bottle stuck in her gob, on a large mat in the center of the living zone. She then went into the kitchen and set the kettle to boil. Karp followed her in and sat on a stool at the butcher block counter.

"Unless you don't think it's a lock?" she added, looking at him questioningly.

He took a while before replying. "I honestly don't know. I'd hate to think Roland was right, but like I said before, and like I said to him, that's not the damn point. Why doesn't anybody get this? The point is the investigation's fucked. And I've been trying to think how I can straighten it out." He paused, looked at her, and then glanced away. Then he asked, "Harry Bello's coming to work starting Monday, isn't he?"

"Yeah, why?" She caught the expression on his face, and her eyes narrowed and she snarled. "Oh, no! No fucking way! You're not going to take my *only* investigator away from me. You've got a hundred cops you could use."

"Yeah, but this is an off-the-books job. I can't set up a regular cop and go, 'A couple of your brother officers screwed up an investigation, why don't you go straighten it out?' Besides, where am I going to get them? Midtown South? Forget it! The D.A. squad? Those guys are all Roland's asshole buddies. They love him. No way are they gonna put anything real into a job like this."

"Harry's a cop," Marlene protested.

"In a manner of speaking. What he is is your personal ninja. There's no way I can make him do anything. Which is why this has to be a favor, you to me." He saw her jaw stiffen. "Honest, it'll be a short-term thing. And it's not gonna be anywhere near full-time. . . . Look," he continued as he saw that these words were having little effect, "why don't you do the whole thing?"

Startled, Marlene replied, "What! Butch, I'm up to my ears with my regular stuff. I can't take on a homicide investigation."

"It's not a homicide investigation, Marlene. It's just some checking up. Harry and you can do it in three or four days. See some people is all. Come on, you know you love this kind of stuff, cruising around with old Harry, the heavily armed semi-psychotic. Hell, you might even get shot. Make your week for you."

Marlene's mouth wriggled as she fought to suppress a grin. "I'm being manipulated," she said.

"Yeah, and it's working too. Hey, what's that noise?"

There was indeed a faint rattling sound coming from the living room. They both ran around the divider. The baby's mat was empty.

Hearts in throats, they followed the clattering noise to a corner of the living room where, under a rickety end table, their baby was yanking and sucking on an electric lamp plug she had just pulled from a wall socket, and seemed to be trying to pull the heavy ceramic lamp down on her delicate little head.

"My God! She can crawl!" cried Marlene, delighted and terrified at once. She snatched the infant out from under the table and held it to her breast, kissing it soundly. "Butch, get the baby whip! This child needs some harsh punishment. What were you thinking of, you birdbrain? (Kiss.) Plunging into danger? (Kiss.)"

"I wonder where she gets it from," said Karp. Marlene raised an eyebrow at that, but he understood that it was a done deal. In the quite recent past he would have fought hard against Marlene taking up a task that involved her wandering the streets with someone like Harry Bello. Now he had arranged it. It was the baby, he concluded. His considerable endowment of protective instinct had become transferred from his wife to his daughter. It was not so much that he cared less about Marlene than he had in the past. It was more that he had come to realize that she was going to put herself at risk from time to time, for her own reasons, and that if he attempted to thwart her at this, she would simply lie to him and the relationship would eventually collapse. Looking around at the loft, which now seemed to hide a baby's hideous death in its every cranny, he understood that this was the way it was supposed to work.

That Monday was, besides Harry Bello's first day, the baby's debut at Lillian Dillard's group day-care. Marlene arrived well before time in order to deal with any first-day terrors, but Dillard pounced on Lucy and charmed her out of her rompers. The faithless wretch didn't even glance up as Marlene sidled out of the room, feeling ridiculously annoyed. After all I've done for her.

Pausing at the entranceway, she watched Susan Weiner deliver little Nicholas with the aplomb of a Fed-Ex courier. Little Nicholas knew what was good for him too; he trudged into the center like a trouper, his shiny Sesame Street lunch box doubtless filled with food of matchless nourishment and perfectly free of harmful substances.

Marlene waved to Susan, who smiled and approached her.

"First day, huh? Any problems?"

"Not a one. It breaks my heart."

"Yes," said Susan, "it's a long day. That's why we try to schedule at least an hour of quality time in the evening."

Marlene gave her a look to see if she was serious and then smiled politely. Marlene didn't believe in quality time. Kids didn't have Filofaxes; their needs were unscheduled. Marlene wanted to be a full-time mother and a full-time prosecutor. That she could not was yet another indication that life sucked, and blathering about quality time to assuage guilt was not going to change the fact that both her child and her career were suffering a net loss because of each other.

Susan was talking about how she had to go because there was this big rush on at work, where they were designing a custom façade for a gallery, and the architect wanted to pin the marble on with bronze roses and they couldn't find exactly the right ones, and they ought to get together for lunch sometime.

Marlene wanted to kick her teeth in. She was wearing two grand on her back, and both her eyes were real and she had a perfect life and Marlene couldn't help liking her and wanting to bask a little in that sublime confidence and grace.

Susan said good-bye and skittered off down the street and of course found a cab instantly going in the right direction. Marlene clumped off disconsolately to Centre Street, where she found her secretary and her staff acting peculiar and Harry Bello waiting in her office.

"Scaring the help, Harry?"

"How's the kid?" asked Bello. Marlene knew that he did not mean Marlene herself, but her daughter, his goddaughter. Marlene told him about the new day-care and, seeing the look that he gave her, explained that it was a good place that she had thoroughly checked out and then added the name of the woman who ran it and the address. She knew that before long Harry would determine for himself whether or not Lillian Dillard had lived a blameless life back through grade school, and would also have checked out the other children and their parents and whether the facility was up to code in every respect. I ought to give it up and let him be the mom, she thought.

She looked at his face, which was the color of an old grocery bag left out in the rain for a long time, and just as empty of any human expression. He was unnaturally still too. He didn't twitch his hands or rub his nose or do any of the small motions we inherit from the great apes, but sat, barely blinking, like a zombie waiting for a command from the *hougan*.

Harry didn't talk much either; he never had, even when he was still tearing up the bad guys in Bed-Stuy with his partner. The partner had done all the talking. And Harry's wife had done all the talking when he wasn't at work. Then they had both died in the same week, and the partner's death at least had been Harry's fault, and that was, more or less, why Harry was what he was: a soul waiting for reincarnation but still visible to the rest of us. Old women crossed themselves when they saw him coming.

On the other hand, you didn't have to tell him anything twice. Or once either. Without a word Marlene handed him the folder on the Alphabet City Jane Doe. He read it silently. Marlene turned to other work. After fifteen minutes, he put it back on the desk and said, "You think he might do it again." Marlene felt a rush of gratitude and smiled at him. With no prompting at all, Harry had seen in the photographs and the autopsy report and the bare-bones investigation exactly what she had seen, and understood that of course this was why an anonymous death with some oddly sexual bits might be important.

She said, "Yeah. What do you think? Too stale?"

"I could try to find him."

Marlene's brows knotted. "What, the killer?"

He gave her a look, the one he gave her when she missed the subtext of one of his telegraphic messages.

"No, the guy who called it in. For starters," said Bello, rising and picking up the fat file. "Can I keep this?"

Marlene nodded and Harry Bello disappeared, and she wasn't entirely certain that the door had opened. Five minutes later, she cursed and banged her desk. She had forgotten about the agreement with Karp, about Harry and the Armenian thing.

Karp had sort of forgotten about the Harry part too, in that he was still personally on the case. At the moment he was emerging from an unmarked police car onto the gravel drive of a large Riverdale house. It was a lovely house, a two-story Italianate villa in rusticated brown sandstone with a red tile roof. The grounds were bright with flowering trees, and there was a flash of silver through the boughs from the Hudson. Karp rang the bell, and a maid in a white uniform showed him in.

He had called Sarkis Kerbussyan first thing that morning, and the man had agreed to meet with him immediately. Indeed, he seemed anxious to do so. The servant, a dour, elderly woman, led Karp silently through paneled halls that were floored with marble or dark wood where they were not covered with oriental carpeting. Karp was notably insensitive to works of art, but these carpets struck even him with their obvious quality, the depth and intricacy of their patterns, the brilliance of their colors. It was like walking on soft jewels.

The woman brought him at last to a large semicircular room, white paneled, its walls made of bookcases except on the curved side, where high French windows gave onto a formal garden, just turning bright green. The floor was covered with a ruby carpet bordered in vivid blue. On the carpet, in the approximate center of the room, was a light writing table of some pale wood, and behind the desk was an old man.

The woman left the room, closing the door silently behind her. This is like a movie, thought Karp, being of a class and generation that did not often enter houses of this style, and that instinctively used the fictions of Hollywood as a reference when encountering the remarkable in real life.

The old man rose stiffly to his feet as Karp approached, and smiled and offered his hand, introducing himself as Sarkis Kerbussyan. Karp said who he was and took the proffered chair.

"Nice place," offered Karp, and immediately regretted it, feeling the hick. Kerbussyan nodded politely. "Yes, I like it very much. I bought it because it reminded me of my grandfather's house at Smyrna, also on a hill above a river, also with a red tile roof and a garden in the back. I have been successful in growing figs here too, despite the climate. Perhaps, if you are interested, later I will show you the house and the garden." He paused and smiled. "But first our business, yes?"

"Aram Tomasian," said Karp.

"Yes. An unfortunate mistake. A tragedy for the boy and his family."

"I take it you don't think he did it."

Kerbussyan made a dismissive gesture. "An impossibility! I have known the boy since he was born, and also his father and his mother from a very young age. In Beirut, in fact. They were brought there as orphans, and my uncle arranged for them to come to this country. So I know them all very well. They are all businessmen, peaceful people, like me. There is no possible chance that Aram was involved in such a thing."

At that moment the servant reappeared with a tray containing a coffee service and a small plate of baklava. In the necessary pause while this refreshment was served out, Karp took the opportunity to study his host. Old, at least eighty, thought Karp, but not frail. Rather the opposite, with a full head of thick white hair swept back from a freckled, ivory forehead. He had a strong, fleshy nose over a thick, stiff-looking mustache, also white. He was dressed neatly, as for business, in a well-tailored gray suit, a white silk shirt, and a blue tie. He became conscious of Karp's examination as he poured the coffee and met Karp's gaze out of deep-set brown eyes.

The eyes held an expression Karp had seen before: veiled, layered, amused, ruthless, an expression common to powerful men of a certain stripe. Some of the dons had such a glance, and some lawyers around town, and Karp had also seen something like it in both an Israeli intelligence agent and a Nazi fugitive. Sarkis Kerbussyan was not a simple businessman, or a simple anything.

They drank, they nibbled. Small talk flowed. Kerbussyan, it turned out, had started as a rug merchant—a deprecating smile, denoting his concession that such a trade was almost a parody for an Armenian—and while expanding his businesses into real estate and investments, he had retained his love for carpets and antiquities. Karp learned that the rug beneath their feet was worth a good deal more than the house in which it sat.

"That's a lot of money for a rug," said Karp, willing to be impressed. "That's pretty nearly enough to bail Tomasian out."

An incomprehensible look, that could have been anger or pain, flashed across Kerbussyan's eyes for an instant. He put a stiff smile on his mouth and said, "That is being attended to. Five million is a great deal of money to assemble at short notice. As for the rug and other antiquities of value, I am afraid that the courts are reluctant to accept them as bailable items. Not like cash and real estate, you understand." He glanced away, seeming to take in the carpet and the room's other furnishings for the first time, or as if he were looking at them for the last time.

"Yes, a great deal of money. It is an Ushak medallion carpet made in the region around Smyrna in the seventeenth century. There was one like it in my grandfather's house. But there are only a few of this quality and size left in private hands in the world, and that is where value resides—quality, craftsmanship, beauty, yes, but uniqueness above all.

"Something else too. Objects, certain objects, have a kind of soul. Rugs, for example. In the old days, they say, the rug makers would buy little girls from poor peasant families and wall them up in rooms with a loom and wools of many colors, and the little girls would spend their entire lives working on a single rug. When you bought such a rug, you would, in effect, be buying a whole life, a soul.

"That people would do such a thing is an indication of our fallen state. After all, what is more unique than a human being? Yet we treat one another so badly; we murder for objects. There are objects in this very house that are dripping blood. If we were truly god-like, we would become connoisseurs of souls and not objets d'art, don't you think?"

"We have a way to go," said Karp. "Meanwhile, people kill for lots of reasons that have nothing to do with objects. Passions. Causes."

"Yes, but it takes a particular sort of man to kill for a cause, don't you think? To return to the reason for your visit, not a man like Aram Tomasian."

"No? He sure had enough equipment for it. And he's a member of an organization called the Armenian Secret Army, and he'd written threatening letters to the Turkish mission."

Kerbussyan put down his coffee cup, pressed his palms together beneath his chin, and looked at Karp. "Mr. Karp, I do not see many people anymore, outside my community, that is. I was curious about why the chief of the Homicide Bureau wished to see me, and so after you called I made some telephone calls of my own. It appears that there was recently a difference of opinion between you and the gentleman who is handling Aram's case."

"I'm not at liberty to discuss the internal operations of the district attorney's office," said Karp, irritated both by the other man's knowledge of his argument with Roland and by his own pompous response.

"Of course," agreed Kerbussyan, "it is a delicate position. But let us say only that you are not convinced that Aram is guilty. You have no wish to discommode your colleague, who is convinced. So what must you do? Obviously, you must find the person who actually did the shooting of this Turk." He shrugged and smiled. "But of such things I can tell you nothing. If I may say so, a visit to an el-

derly Armenian seems an unprofitable way to advance your investigation."

Karp's irritation increased. He was being played with in an
insultingly obvious way. He said, "Not if he's the local head of the
Armenian Secret Army."

To his surprise, Kerbussyan laughed, a dry sound like a bron-
chial attack. "Ah, yes, that. Tell me, Mr. Karp, what do you imagine
the Armenian Secret Army to be?"

"I have no idea. I'll bet you could tell me, though."

Another chuckle. "Yes, but then it wouldn't be a secret, would
it? All right, enough fencing. May I assume you have some knowledge of the Armenian genocide? Yes? Very good. One of history's
great crimes, but now almost forgotten. 'Who remembers the Armenians?' You know who said that? Adolf Hitler. The reasoning is clear.
The Armenians were ignored and forgotten and so would the Jews be
when they were all dead.

"You are yourself Jewish, are you not, Mr. Karp? A good deal
in common, the Jews and the Armenians, and not just the disasters
of the present century. Do you know that of all the ancient peoples
of the Near East mentioned by Herodotus twenty-five hundred years
ago, the Cappadocians, the Lydians, the Phoenicians, the Phrygians,
and the rest, the only ones to survive into modern times with their
cultural identity intact are the Armenians and the Jews? One won-
ders why.

"It is easier to see why a people obsessed by national survival
and the imagined wrongs of history, like the Germans and Turks,
should conceive a hatred for the champions of survival and wish to
destroy them. Perhaps it is similar to what I have heard of cannibals
who seek to obtain the virtues of their enemies by eating their flesh.

"The great difference, of course, is that the genocide of the Jews
was exposed by the victorious powers in the second war, and that,
overcome with guilt, those powers provided the Jews with an inde-
pendent nation. The Germans admitted their crimes and paid compensation to the victims. Little enough, but the world attempted

some justice. You should not be surprised that Armenians want the same."

The old man paused and looked at Karp with his deep and level gaze. This speech was a distraction, but from what? Or perhaps the old man thought it was the point. They had in any case drifted far from Tomasian's predicament. The silence continued. Karp said, "You mean they want a homeland?"

"I think there are some that do. The liberation of western Armenia. But it is complex. There are no Armenians left in that country to liberate, and of course, politically it is impossible; Armenia is a Soviet republic. The Turks are allied to the West. And besides, the Armenians are not like the Jews, or like the Jews imagine themselves to be. There is no serious Armenian Zionism, the tie to a particular piece of land. In the eleventh century, when the Seljuk Turks conquered Armenia, much of the nation moved five hundred miles south and founded another Armenia in the Taurus Mountains. The people, that is what counts, the people and the language and the Church."

"So what do you want?"

The old man's eyes flashed briefly. "A confession. From the Turks. That it happened. That they owe compensation. So, in our cause, Turks are killed. The Turkish ambassadors in Vienna, in Paris, in the Vatican. The consul in Beirut. The director of Turkish espionage in the Middle East."

"And Ersoy?"

Kerbussyan smiled and shook his head slowly. "Not Ersoy. As you know very well. And also, if an Armenian group wished to kill a Turkish official in New York, which would be a stupidity uncharacteristic of such a group, let me assure you that it would not have been done as this was done, and Aram would not have been the assassin. Not someone who is on record as writing letters of protest."

"And the weapons . . . ?"

"Mr. Karp, Aram travels to Europe and the Near East several times a year. He carries bags full of gems. He is well known to customs officials, and his paperwork is always impeccable. . . ."

Kerbussyan made a graceful gesture with his hand, indicating a cae-
sura into which a thought might be inserted.

"You're saying he runs guns?"

"You are saying it, Mr. Karp. But supposing an Armenian nationalist organization possessed an asset like Aram Tomasian.
Wouldn't he be the very last person to risk in a venture such as the
crime in question?"

Karp didn't know. He thought not, but then he wasn't a terrorist leader. Maybe that was exactly what a terrorist would do. On the
other hand, it was an additional confirmation of his feeling that
Tomasian had been purposely framed. He decided to voice this to his
host, since they were pretending to be frank.

"Okay, say I buy that. It means that someone went out of their
way to frame your boy. Who would do that? I mean, who among the
people who wanted Ersoy dead?"

Kerbussyan appeared to consider this for a moment, nodding,
his face all amused concentration. "Those are two separate questions.
First, we are not sure that Ersoy was a target. Perhaps Aram is the
target, or the Armenian community generally. Any Turk would have
done just as well for that. And Ersoy was obvious, accessible, and
regular in his movements. As for motive, whether the Turks would
like to discredit the Armenians, the question is hardly worth asking."

"You think they killed their own guy to smear the Armenians?"

Kerbussyan made a dismissive gesture. "I don't say that. But
they are a violent and inexplicable people. They have a military government with many quarrelsome factions. Perhaps someone wished to
kill two birds with one stone."

As Karp thought about that possibility, an ornate clock on a
side table chimed a clear note. Kerbussyan shifted in his chair and
said, "That is really all the advice I can give at this time, sir. If you
will excuse me, I have one of my infrequent appointments."

Karp rose, as did Kerbussyan, and they shook hands formally
across the desk. Karp felt as if he had just completed an unsuccessful
loan interview, which was not a way he liked to feel. As a result, instead of leaving amid polite pleasantries, he looked the old man in

the eye and asked, "What about the money? The million dollars in Ersoy's safe-deposit box. You wouldn't know anything about that, would you?"

Kerbussyan's face assumed a look of polite confusion. "I have no idea what you're talking about," he said.

Karp nodded curtly and left the room. The old guy was good, you had to give him that. He had played Karp nicely, giving away as little as possible, and only those things that would steer Karp in the direction he wanted him steered. Admitting Tomasian was a gun runner was good, and probably true. It cast a cloak of sincerity over the conversation, and over the suggestion that the killing might be a Turkish operation.

The servant entered and stood by the door. Karp followed her out, passing as he did so two stocky, scowling men wearing field jackets and handlebar mustaches. Terrorists in training.

Karp got back into the car, awakened the driver, and was conducted back to the City. Mulling over what Kerbussyan had said about the motive for Ersoy's death, Karp decided that it might be worth at least poking around in that direction. On the other hand, he had an instinct for the culpable lie, arguably the most valuable, to a criminal prosecutor, of all the subtle talents. The old man had indeed been frank about a number of things, but when he had said that he did not know about the slain Turk's hoard of money, he had been lying through his teeth.

When Karp returned to his office, he found a distraught Tony Harris waiting for him. The young man looked as if he had just lost his family in a freak accident: he was pale and sweating and his eyes were hollow. A bearing less like that of the ordinarily chipper Harris could hardly be imagined.

"I got wiped in *Devers*," Harris blurted out when Karp came in. So he had not lost a loved one, but a murder case, and one that should have been a lock. Karp gestured Harris into his private office and sat down behind his desk. His knee was throbbing again.

"What do you mean 'wiped,' Tony?"

"Wiped! Case dismissed. The fuck-head walked out smiling and shot me the finger. God! Those witnesses! I sweated bullets getting them to testify. I swore to them; I swore it was a lock, that Devers was sure to go away for twenty. Now they're gonna see him every day on the street. Or worse. Probably worse."

Harris looked like he was about to burst into tears. Karp understood the man's agony, if he had never shared it. He said, "How did it go down? This was at pretrial?"

"Yeah, the Legal Aid, Conyers, goes up for motions. I figured it was gonna be the old horseshit about the gun, its association with the defendant and all. But no, he moves to dismiss the eyewitness testimony. I was standing there like a frog on a rock. I didn't know whether to shit or go blind."

"What grounds?"

"*People* v. *Hackett.* I never heard of it. On lineups. Basically it holds that in lineups, where witnesses have specifically identified an item of clothing worn by the alleged perpetrator, such an item can't be worn at the lineup, so the witness supposedly ID's the perp, not the clothes. When I did the lineups down at the station house, Devers was wearing a leather hip-length coat. The two girls, it turns out, mentioned the coat to the cops, but the cops never mentioned it to me. I mean we *had* the guy. The girls knew him, for chrissake, and so did the lady in the hallway. So he went into the lineup in the coat. That was it. The whole fucking case trashed. Oh, yeah, Freeland was there too, enjoying the hell out of it, it looked like."

"Freeland? He was there?"

"Yeah, he waltzed in and talked to Conyers."

"The son of a bitch. He must have been in on it."

"In on what?" asked Harris.

"The scam. You were royally fucked, kid. Swindled."

"How? I saw the case. I read it. The judge read it. It was real. I mean, you could argue with the application, but—"

"*Hackett*'s an Appellate Division case," Karp interrupted.

"Yeah, I realize that, Butch; that's the fucking problem, they threw out the conviction on *Hackett,*" replied Harris impatiently.

"It was reversed by the Court of Appeals."

Harris opened his mouth, but no words came out. It was an old trick. New York calls its lowest felony courts "Supreme Court," and the first level of appeal is called the Appellate Division. The actual supreme judicial authority in the state is called the Court of Appeals. A Supreme Court decision can thus be reversed by the Appellate Division and confirmed by the Court of Appeals, and although every lawyer licensed to practice in the state has explained this odd nomenclature on the bar exam, people still get confused, even judges.

Harris still looked stunned. He was pale and shaking his head. Karp, controlling his genuine rage, made his tone gentle.

"Okay, there's no use crying over it. You got robbed. I'll have some words with Mr. Freeland tomorrow. You should take off. Go home. Get drunk."

"I can't. I'm on call this afternoon until eight."

"Don't worry about it. You're in no shape to do intakes. Scram. No, really—out. I'll cover the shift."

Amid protestations, not very sincere ones, Harris was packed off.

Karp had now traded an afternoon of sedentary desk minding for a long evening that might require considerable mobility. He had done this as much for himself as for Harris. That morning he had made an appointment for an arthroscopy, an investigative procedure that was sure to be followed by a major operation, one that was not certain to succeed. A week hence he would be disabled. In a couple of months he might find himself a cripple.

These thoughts bred in him an almost desperate desire to move, to act, to get away from papers and negotiation, to walk on the bloody margins of crime scenes, to talk with cops and skells, to breathe smoke and kick ass, while he still could.

All in all, therefore, given Karp's record, and this extra rocket up his pants, it was probably not the best afternoon in the year to murder somebody on the isle of Manhattan.

■   ■   ■

Murder was little on the mind of the man in the blue shirt as he walked carefully down the sunny aisle of Hudson Street, looking for a victim. He had most of a fifth of white port sliding through his body, cranking him up, giving him confidence. Two months out of Elmira, he was back at his chosen profession, purse snatching. He'd just quit his straight job, humping stuff at a warehouse. Actually, they'd canned him for being late too much. His daughter had booted him out on the street, and he had missed a meet with his parole officer. He had to score something today so he could get a place, and maybe find another job humping so the bitch of a parole officer wouldn't be on his case.

The West Village was a good place for it. Plenty of rich women by themselves. He needed a handbag off a rich white lady. Or a skinny faggot. Grab him, shove him in a doorway, take the purse, the wallet, the watch. Take all of two minutes.

He crossed 10th Street, moving north. At the corner a couple of obvious out-of-towners, a youngish couple, stood talking and studying a map. The woman had a shoulder bag.

The man in the blue shirt looked them over. The man was big and athletic-looking. It would've been a possibility with a gun, but all he had was a cheap kitchen knife with a five-inch blade. Besides, he didn't much like guns.

The man with the tourist map looked up and stared at him. He had nasty blue eyes and close-cut reddish hair. He looked southern, looked like he could handle himself. The man in the blue shirt passed on.

There she was. His heart accelerated and his gut roiled, as might happen to a man upon catching sight of a lover. A young woman, pretty, in a light coat, maxiskirt, and polished boots. A large, expensive-looking leather bag hung from a strap at her shoulder. She was moving right toward him on the sidewalk.

Now she turned and approached the entrance to an apartment building. This was perfect. All he had to do was follow her into the doorway and, when she stopped to open the outer door, lift the bag and take off.

She stood in front of the glass door and opened the bag to extract her keys. He made his move. She must have seen his reflection in the glass of the door, for she whirled to face him, her mouth opening.

He grabbed for the bag, caught its strap, and yanked hard, hoping to pull the woman off her feet. But she had wedged herself into a corner of the doorway and set her heels. And she had started screaming.

Echoing off the buildings, the screams seemed as loud as sirens. They hurt his ears. He heard footsteps behind him, and someone shouted. He let go of the strap and grabbed the woman's coat with his left hand and pulled his knife out of the waistband of his jeans and flashed it in her face. She screamed louder. He had to stop that noise. He stabbed her in her chest. She gave a last cry when he did this, different in tone from her screams for aid, a shriek like a baby's mindless call. Slowly she turned away from him and sank to her knees, still clutching the bag.

He cursed and stabbed her again, in the back, the force of the blow knocking her flat. She turned on her side and drew up her knees. Now she was quiet. The man in the blue shirt picked up his prize from the woman's limp hands and turned. A black man in a leather apron stood on the sidewalk in front of the shop adjacent to the woman's apartment building. There was shock and rage on his face. The man in the blue shirt spun away from him and ran south on Hudson Street. He heard shouts, and more screams, and the sound of running feet behind him.

On the sidewalk in front of her apartment house, Susan Weiner's perfect little life drained away in a widening red pool.

8

___

IT IS AN OLD-FASHIONED HUE AND CRY, THE KIND OF THING THAT ISN'T supposed to happen in New York anymore because people don't care. The man in the blue shirt runs south on Hudson and turns east on Christopher, heading for the twisty little streets and alleys of the West Village. A half-dozen people run after him, shouting. The amazed faces of the tourist couple flash by his eyes as he runs, clutching the handbag under his arm like a football.

The block of Christopher east of Hudson is a short one. The man cuts sharply across the street, runs down Bedford, and turns east on Barrow. If he can get under cover before his pursuers reach the corner of Barrow and Bedford, he might be safe. A sunken courtyard at 58 Barrow catches his eye, and he dashes down its steps. There is a restaurant built partially out over the courtyard, casting it into deep shade. Two doors lead from the courtyard. He chooses the one on the right and pounds on it.

A young man opens the door. He is an actor expecting a delivery of moo goo gai pan from a nearby Chinese take-out. He smiles and says, "Hi. What do I owe you?" The killer pushes by him and runs through the small apartment. He is no longer thinking very clearly, or even as clearly as he normally does, which is not with any particular depth or lucidity. The idea of escape fills his entire mind. Here fortune favors him. There is a door opening into the interior of the building, and he goes through it and up two flights to where the stairs end in a small landing, under a skylight.

By now he is exhausted. He rests for a moment, panting, and rummages through the handbag. He tears a thin sheaf of currency from the wallet he finds there, seven dollars in all, and thrusts it into his pocket. He tosses the knife and the bag into a corner of the stairwell. He listens; the building remains silent. He begins to walk quietly down the stairs and stops, because he has just had a thought. He strips off his blue shirt and throws it into a corner with the other stuff. He is wearing a bright red T-shirt underneath it.

The killer walks down the stairs, past the door to the young man's apartment, and down a dimly lit corridor. He sees a door, opens it, and finds himself again in the courtyard. The young actor is standing there. He has gathered around him a crowd of people, the remains of the crowd who had chased the man in the blue shirt from Hudson Street. They are exchanging experiences. The young man looks up, sees the killer, and shouts. The killer darts back through the door.

Continuing along the corridor, he finds the building's boiler room, stifling hot and black as midnight. He lights a match. There are some large pieces of cardboard lying about. He uses these to make a nest for himself in the space under the boiler, and lies down in it, carefully pulling the cardboard around him.

The first officer to reach the crime scene was patrolman Ray Thornby, a sturdy black man in his fifth year on the force. He summoned a patrol car on his portable radio, and in a few minutes the dying young woman had been whisked away. Members of the crowd that had gathered vied to describe the assailant and the direction he had gone.

A thin young man on a bicycle came to a screeching halt at the edge of the crowd and shouted, "They got him!"

"Where?" asked Thornby.

"Building at 58 Barrow. He's in the basement."

Thornby follows the bike rider to 58 Barrow. He sees that there is a crowd, an angry one, in the center of which is the young actor. The actor approaches the cop, introduces himself as Jerry Shelton, and explains what has occurred. A patrol car rushes up to a halt at the curb, and a sergeant and a patrolman get out. The three police-men learn that the actor was the only one who had actually seen the fugitive.

"This man actually came through your place?" asks Thornby.

"Yes! He pushed right by me like a madman, ran through my apartment, and out the front door."

"What, this door?"

"No, the back door. It leads to a hallway and the stairs. There's no way out of the building from it except back through the court-yard. Then I saw him again, over there." He points at the basement door, across the courtyard. The crowd murmurs assent.

"What did he look like?" Thornby asks.

"Around thirty, I'd say—not a kid. Shortish hair. About five-ten, maybe one-seventy."

"What was he wearing?" asks Thornby.

"Oh, let me see—blue, I have a blue picture. It all went so fast. A dark blue shirt and jeans, or some kind of work pants. Sneakers. No hat or anything. He was carrying something too. I thought it was my lunch."

"Race?" asks Thornby mildly. In the West Village you had to pry it out of them, especially if you were a black cop.

"Oh! He was black," says the actor, reddening.

"Dark complexion? Light? Darker than me or not as dark?"

"About like you."

"You're sure he's in the basement?"

"Yes, I told you, I just saw him," says Shelton. The crowd murmurs assent again, although most of them have seen nothing.

The sergeant goes back to the patrol car to call for backup, and Thornby and the other patrolman enter the basement.

Karp got the call eighteen minutes after Susan Weiner had been pronounced D.O.A. at St. Vincent's. Fifteen minutes thereafter, he was at the crime scene on Hudson, talking with the detective in charge, a short, saturnine man out of Zone One named Charlie Cimella.

Karp stared for a moment at the stain on the pavement.

"Who was she?"

Cimella said, "Woman named Susan Weiner. This is where she lived. The super ID'd her. She had a date with her hubby for lunch. Nice. Guy showed up just after it went down."

"Witnesses?"

"Yeah, a couple of out-of-towners saw the whole thing. And a bunch of folks chased the guy around the corner. I got the word out to the portables to round them up."

"Okay, when you get them, take them over to the Six. I'll interview them there. Any chance we'll pick up the perp?"

Cimella shrugged. "We could get lucky." He looked at the bloodstain too. "Hell of a thing. Nice neighborhood, nice building. Pretty kid, young. The papers, TV'll go batshit."

Karp nodded and went back to his car. Susan Weiner. The name stirred a memory, but he couldn't place it. A not uncommon name in the City. Maybe he had gone to school with a Susan Weiner. He told the driver to make for the Sixth.

In the lightless, sweltering boiler room of number 58 Barrow Street, Ray Thornby gets lucky. He checks the room with his flashlight beam and is about to leave when he spots the cardboard sticking out from under the boiler. He draws his pistol, kneels down, and tugs at the sneakered foot he finds resting on the cardboard. Slowly a man rolls out from under the boiler, blinking in the flashlight's glare. Thornby backs away and points his gun.

"Get up and put your hands against the wall!" he orders.

A high, whining voice comes from the man: "Hey, wha'? Hey, man, 'm just sackin' out, y'know? My daughter, she kicked me out—"

"Up!" says Thornby. The man staggers out and braces his hands against the wall, spreading his legs as he does so. An experienced mutt, thinks the policeman as he pats the man down and goes through the pockets of his grubby jeans.

No ID. Nothing but a crumpled wad of paper money, two singles and a five. And something else: a VISA counterfoil from Bloomingdale's with today's date made out to S. WEINER, crumpled up between the bills. Thornby puts the receipt in his own pocket and gives the money back to the man. At this time he does not know the name of the vic, but he knows it was a woman, and that Bloomingdale's is a high-end women's clothing store, and that the odds are long indeed that this man he has found under a boiler has just come from a spree in Better Dresses.

"What's your name?"

"Hosie Russell. Hey, what is this? I was just sleepin' off a drunk, man. C'mon, gi' me a break, man. I jus' got out of the joint. My daughter kicked my sorry ass out of the house."

Thornby can smell the truth of at least part of that statement. He looks Russell over carefully. Close up, he is a lot older than the initial description, closer to fifty than thirty. And his shirt is red, bright red, not blue. Not a blue picture. He hesitates. Russell catches this and smiles, says ingratiatingly, "C'mon, blood, gi' me a break. I'll jus' move along uptown . . ."

Thornby frowns. The guy could be just a wino, but Thornby doesn't like that receipt; he hates the receipt. More than that, he doesn't like being called "blood" by a skell. He whips Russell around and snaps the cuffs on him.

The crowd rumbled as they emerged. Some people clapped. There were two more blue-and-whites parked in the street, their lights flashing. Thornby brought his prisoner across the courtyard to the young actor, waiting with the sergeant.

"Is this him?" Thornby asked.

"Yes, definitely. Only he was wearing a different shirt."

Russell rolled his eyes and said, "Bull-*shit,* man! He don' know what the fuck he talkin' about. I never was in his fuckin' place. What he mean, all niggers look alike."

As if to confirm this statement, an elderly white man in a rumpled tan suit, who was standing on the curb, shouted out, "That's not the guy. I saw the whole thing. The guy who stabbed the girl was a different man."

Russell nodded his head vigorously. "See? He saw it! It wasn't me. Hey! What you doin', man? Hey! It wasn't me!"

As he continued to shout these and other protestations, he was muscled into a blue-and-white and driven off to the Sixth Precinct.

At a commandeered desk in the detective squad room of that precinct, Karp finished his preliminary interview with the Digbys. The couple were sensible, straightforward people, and they had seen the fleeing defendant at close range. They would have made superb witnesses had it not been for their Dukes of Hazzard accents, which for most New York juries indicated either slowness of wit or racial prejudice or both. Nevertheless, they had assured Karp that they could identify the man.

A detective walked over and said that Cimella was on the phone.

"We got him," said Cimella. "He was in a basement on Barrow Street. One of the uniforms found him, and we got a positive ID from a tenant in the building—guy ran through his apartment a few minutes after the stabbing. Name's Hosie Russell. They're bringing him in now."

"Great," said Karp. "Okay, run him by a lineup with the Digbys and the other people who chased him. Then stick him in an interview room and make sure nobody talks to him before I do."

Karp hung up and called his own office and asked Connie Trask to get someone to run a check on whether a black male named Hosie Russell had ever come to the attention of the law. Then he went over his interview notes until, ten minutes later, Cimella walked in with Hosie Russell and a black patrolman. They put Russell through a lineup, and the couple from Kentucky had no trouble picking him out. Neither did the young actor, Shelton.

Karp was introduced to Thornby, who filled him in on the details of the arrest.

"The funny thing was, the guy Shelton, he said Russell had a blue shirt on and was carrying something when he ran through the apartment, but he was wearing red when I found him. No shirt. No handbag. I thought for a minute he was just a piss bum on the coop. You think it really is the guy?"

"I don't know," said Karp. "We don't have any physical evidence, and it's hard to build a homicide case on just eyewitnesses, especially white eyewitnesses on a black perp."

Thornby looked startled. "Homicide? Holy shit, she's dead? I didn't know that. I thought it was an armed robbery and assault. But I do have some physical evidence." He handed Karp the receipt. "Does that help?"

Karp looked at the little slip of paper and then, sharply, back at the patrolman. "Where did you get this?"

Thornby told him.

"You didn't find the handbag?"

"No, it wasn't in the boiler room. The sarge got people out checking trash barrels and sewers. We didn't find his blue shirt either. Or the knife."

The phone rang, and it was Mel Channing, one of Karp's junior attorneys, with a copy of Hosie Russell's criminal record. Karp asked him to read it over the phone while he made notes. It took five minutes.

"What was that?" asked Cimella when Karp hung up.

"Our boy's yellow sheet. From here to Mars. Fifteen felony convictions—robbery, assault, larceny, burglary. Guy's fifty, can you believe it? He's spent a total of—let's see . . ." Karp made a rapid cal-culation on the pad he had used to take notes. "Twenty-two years in the slams, total."

Cimella said, "Gosh, maybe our system of rehabilitation isn't working. In any case, it looks good he's the guy."

"Oh, it's him, all right," said Karp. "He grabbed the cash out of her purse and didn't notice that the receipt was crumpled up in it. But it's nice to know he's not a pillar of the church. Okay, let's take a look at this sweetheart."

Karp and Cimella went into the interview room. Russell stared at them blankly. His eyes were red-rimmed, and the room was full of his sour odor. Karp introduced himself and explained the rights of the accused.

"Do you know why you're here, Mr. Russell?"

"Yeah, the cops fucked up. They got the wrong guy."

"Uh-huh. Tell me, what were you running from when you ran through Mr. Shelton's apartment this afternoon?"

"Who?"

"You ran through an apartment at 58 Barrow Street. The tenant saw you clearly and identified you to the police. What were you run-ning from?"

"I din' run nowhere. I was drunk all mornin'. My head feel like shit. Could I get some aspirin?"

"In a minute. Let me tell you what we know for sure. At about twelve-fifteen you stabbed and killed a young woman named Susan Weiner in the doorway of 484 Hudson Street and took her purse. Re-liable witnesses have identified you. Do you have any statement to make at this time?"

"Yeah, I want some aspirin. And a lawyer."

Karp shrugged and walked out of the room. A cop took Russell to the holding cells. Karp and Cimella went back to the squad room.

Karp said, "125.25; 160.15; 265.04, okay?"

Cimella said, "Sounds good," and so they booked Russell for murder in the second degree (two counts, one for murder in association with a felony and one for intentional murder), first-degree robbery, and first-degree criminal possession of a weapon.

"What's wrong?" asked Cimella, observing the tight expression on Karp's face. "You expected him to confess?"

"Hell, no. I'd just like to have the shirt and the bag and the knife."

"Why? We got the slip Thornby found on him."

"Yeah, but that'll be challenged on probable cause. Why did the cops pick on a poor innocent derelict? We'll probably win that, but we could lose it too . . . what's all that?"

There was a commotion, sounds of shouting and crashing furniture from the lower floor of the precinct house.

Cimella trotted down the stairs, and Karp limped after him. There they found police officers holding back a large, conservatively dressed black man who had apparently been trying to attack a prisoner. Approaching, they saw that the prisoner was Hosie Russell.

"What the hell's going on here, Maury?" Cimella demanded of the uniformed sergeant.

"Damned if I know, Charlie. This guy"—indicating the large black man—"came in and asked the desk who was on that Hudson Street thing, so I gave him your name and he headed upstairs. Then Ryan and Hardy came through with this mutt on the way to the cells, and the guy sees the mutt and yells, 'You swine!' and goes for his throat."

The man now seemed calmer and, in fact, embarrassed at his outburst. The officers restraining him released him, and Russell was removed to the cells without further incident. Karp introduced himself to the man, who turned out to be James Turnbull, the proprietor of the leather shop on the ground floor of Susan Weiner's building.

"Mr. Turnbull," asked Karp after steering the man to a quiet corner of the station-house corridor, "what was that all about?"

Turnbull shook his head, as if amazed, and spoke in a soft West Indian accent. "I just lost it, I guess. You see a woman, a neighbor, slaughtered before your eyes. When I saw him, I just wanted to smash his damned face in."

"Him? You mean the man in custody?"

"Yeah. He killed Susan."

"You're sure? You'd make a statement to that effect?"

"Of course. That's what I came down here for. I was too shaken up earlier."

They walked off to find a stenographer, found one, and Turnbull dictated a statement and signed it. As Karp was about to find the officers who had witnessed the altercation and obtain statements from them, Cimella hailed him.

"Look what I got," the detective said. He held up three sealed evidence bags, two large, one smaller. The two large bags held a dark blue shirt and a woman's leather purse. The small one held a short kitchen knife.

"Where did you get those?" asked Karp.

"Our friend Shelton. It turns out he was visiting a friend on the second floor of his building and found these under the stairwell. He called the house, they sent a car out, and they found the stuff. Cop just gave them to me."

"That's Susan's bag," said Turnbull. "I made it." He looked close to tears. Cimella said to Karp, "So, we got it all. Are you always this lucky?"

"It's clean living, Charlie," said Karp, grinning. "Luck has nothing to do with it."

"Yeah, well, in that case, you can go talk to the jackals. There's fifty of them outside the house. I told you they'd eat this one up."

Karp's shift on call lasted until eight. There were no more murders in Manhattan during its span, for which he was profoundly grateful. He had the police driver take him home and limped up the stairs.

The sound of heavy thumps and energetic grunting issued from the far end of the loft. Karp shouted a greeting, which was returned with a breathy "Hi." He then sat down on the couch, removed his clothes, put on a bathrobe, and applied a chemical cold pack to his knee.

He had just bought a carton of these, and kept them near the old red couch, which he had taken over as a dressing room and bed. He could no longer bear to climb the ladder to the sleeping loft. After a half hour, with the knee partially anesthetized by the cold pack, he clumped down to the gym, an ill-defined area beyond the wall of the dining room. It held, among other things, Karp's rowing machine and Marlene's speed bag and body bag.

She was pounding away at the latter, dressed in baggy red shorts, a cut down T-shirt, and sneakers. Karp watched her in silent admiration as her muscles bunched and played and shining sweat bounced off her face. The baby was in her recently purchased playpen, bouncing, cooing, and rattling her bars. Karp took a towel and played peek-a-boo with his daughter until Marlene finished her workout and began to strip off her speed gloves. When she turned at last to face him, he saw that her eyes were red-rimmed and swollen.

"What's wrong?"

"You were on the news."

"What? Oh, yeah, the West Village thing. That made you cry? My performance?"

"No, dummy, the vic. Susan Weiner."

Karp now recalled where he had heard the name. "Oh, shit, the woman from the day-care!" He went over and hugged her. "I'm sorry, babe—but at least we got the guy."

Marlene leaned against him and sighed deeply. "Yeah, I'm sure that'll make her family feel better. Her husband can sleep with a copy of the indictment."

She shook herself and wiped some sweat from her face. "I didn't mean that. Sure, it's great you caught the guy. I don't know why it's affecting me like this. I wasn't particularly close to the woman. It's just that her life . . . she seemed so on top of it all, like the grime didn't stick to her. You know how everybody in the City seems sour and cynical and paranoid? She had a shine on her that made you think, yeah, she's making it, she's happy, with a job and a kid and a nice place to live, and she doesn't look like a survivor of the Long

March. So it's, hey, she can do it, maybe I can do it too. Now she's a piece of meat on a slab."

"Speaking of meat, what's for dinner?"

She pushed him away and slapped at him with her towel. "Oooh, how could you say that? I can't believe you said that."

"What? What?" sputtered Karp, taking a step back. "Hey, what do you want? I'm sorry your friend got killed, but—"

"She wasn't my friend."

"Okay, I'm sorry your acquaintance got killed. What should I do, go into mourning eleven hundred times a year? Beat my breast? I'd be paralyzed in a week if I did that, and so would you. People get killed and sometimes, not very often, they're people like us. The only thing we can do is find the bastard who did it and make sure he won't do it again. Does this make a difference? No, there's ten more where he came from. Are things getting better? No, every year they get a little worse. It's useless and stupid, but we keep doing it because that's what we do. We're pros."

"What's your point, Spinoza?" snapped Marlene.

"I don't have a point," Karp admitted. "I just hate it when you get like this. You get pissed off about how shitty everything is, and you bring it home and take it out on me."

"Who else is there? But yes, you're right! I was wrong. I wavered for an instant from the absolute control you have every right to expect." She slapped her own cheek, twice. "There! I needed that. Now I can make your dinner in an orderly manner—"

"Come on, Marlene," he sighed, "don't do a number—"

"—while you provide your daughter with forty-six minutes of fatherly attention as per contract." She stomped away in a stiff robot-like walk. Clattering of pots. Karp picked up the baby, who needed changing, badly. A perfect day.

They ate dinner in an atmosphere of chill correctness. They were just clearing the dishes away, and Karp was struggling to think of some magic language that would get them out of marriage hell, when the phone rang.

He picked it up. A woman's voice: "What're you going to do to him?" She sounded drunk or drugged.

"I'm sorry, who is this, please?" said Karp.

"I killed her. I killed her. I let him out, the fucking nigger scumbag bastard fuckhead. I let him out and he killed her . . ."

The woman's voice dissolved into sobbing. Then there was a loud crash over the line as if the phone had been tossed against something solid, followed by a hollow cacophany of wailings and things being smashed, picked up by the unattended receiver. Karp hung up.

"Who was that?" Marlene asked, seeing the odd expression on her husband's face.

"I don't know. I think it was about the Weiner case. A woman, claims she had something to do with letting Russell loose."

Marlene went white and sat down on a kitchen stool. "Oh, shit, it must be her sister. The parole officer I told you about—the one I had lunch with when I met Susan. Russell must be one of her parolees. In fact, Christ, I think it was the guy she was talking about when we had lunch—the prize pupil. He had a weird first name, didn't he? Foley? Mosie?"

"Hosie Russell."

"Yeah, Hosie. Oh, God, what a nightmare! The poor woman!"

Karp embraced his wife and didn't say a word, and this time she clung to him fiercely.

"Who is this guy Kerbussyan?" asked Roland Hrcany, "and why did Karp go to see him this morning?"

Barney Wayne and Joe Frangi did not know, nor did they particularly care, after a long day. The Ersoy murder was a clearance as far as they were concerned. They had the guy. Hrcany's thing with Karp was his own business, and while they were willing to go some extra for Roland, seeing as how he was an okay guy, they had other stuff on their plate. Wayne pointedly looked at his watch. Frangi got out of his chair and looked out the window of Roland's office at the gathering dusk.

"Why don't you ask Karp?" Frangi replied.

Roland said, "I did ask him. I just this minute got off the phone with him." Roland could not keep a satisfied grin off his face as he said this. He had, of course, learned of Karp's morning expedition indirectly from his driver, a detective, via the Centre Street police grapevine, into which he was well plugged. That he had thereafter felt free to call his nominal boss at home after hours to pump him for information had given him considerable pleasure.

Roland continued, "That's why I want him checked out. According to Karp, he's some kind of Armenian political. He claims that Tomasian had the guns because he was a gun runner."

"You believe that shit?" snapped Frangi.

"It doesn't matter what I believe. It's a plausible story for a jury. We need to find out if it's true, and also whether Kerbussyan's ever been mixed up in any funny business. Speaking of which, Karp thinks that Kerbussyan knows something about the victim's little treasure chest."

"For instance . . . ?" asked Wayne.

"Karp doesn't know. But we should check it out. Why don't you guys go up to Riverdale and find out what you can about this guy?"

Unenthusiastic grunts of assent issued from the two detectives.

"The other thing," continued Roland, unfazed, "what's the latest on the girlfriend?"

Frangi brought out his notebook. "On that, we got a woman answering her description getting off a plane at San Francisco and renting a Hertz car on a credit card made out to Gabrielle Avanian. We got credit card charges in San Luis Obispo, stores and a motel, the following day. Then we got charges in Disneyland, Huntington Beach, Monterey, and San Francisco. Looks like she's on a vacation."

Wayne said, "I don't know. Disneyland: she could be targeting Mickey."

"Yeah, or a terrorist assault on the Turkish taffy stand," said Frangi. "I think we should all go out there, Roland. We might save countless lives."

"Very funny. Okay, we assume the girl is either too incredibly cool or else not involved. Also, assuming she reads the papers, she doesn't seem in any hurry to get back and spring her sweetie, which could mean the alibi is a piece of shit. In any case, will you do me one favor? Let's pick her up when she gets back. Just to dot the I's."

Frangi made a notation in his pad. "Dot the I's. Pick up girlfriend. It'll be soon. Master Card says she's running close to her credit limit."

The next day Karp went for his arthroscopy in Dr. Hudson's office. His knee was shot full of dope, but he could still feel the conducted vibration of the instruments rattling up his skeleton, informing him that someone was working inside his living flesh. He sweated bullets.

After the procedure, Dr. Hudson was characteristically blunt: massive destruction of cartilage, bone abrasion, chronic inflammation of the bursa. The whole thing would have to be replaced, and soon. Karp told Hudson to set up the operation.

In a somber mood Karp was driven to his next appointment, which was with Milton Freeland at the Legal Aid Society offices on Leonard Street. The offices were suitably shabby, to go with the clientele, but Karp observed that Freeland had replaced Dora, Tom Pagano's old secretary, with a shiny new model. Karp was ushered into the presence. It was wearing a yellow tie and yellow suspenders and a good false smile. Karp sat in an uncomfortable wooden visitors' chair without being asked.

"We have a problem, Milton," he said without preamble.

"Oh? What problem is that? Butch."

"Well, specifically, that stunt you pulled the other day on Tony Harris in the Devers homicide, but—"

"It's not my fault if your people don't know the law," Freeland interrupted.

"But," Karp continued, "but, I just wanted to get together with you at the beginning so as to make sure that the good working relationship that my office had with Tom's office continues."

"And what was that, pray tell?" Freeman was smirking. He could tell Karp was embarrassed and was enjoying it.

"A certain respect. A certain understanding of the position of the formal adversary. We don't break our word. We don't pull funny stuff in court. I don't railroad people or accept phonied evidence. You don't yell racism and police brutality when none exists—"

Freeman laughed out loud, unpleasantly. "Oh, be serious. The next thing you're going to tell me is that all the people you bring to trial really did it."

"No. But I'd say if I bring them, *I* believe they did it."

"What about Morales?" Freeland sneered. "Do you believe in that piece of shit case?"

Karp's stomach lurched and he suppressed a sigh. "Between us? No, and I didn't mean to imply we didn't ever screw up. But there's a good example. If Tom were still here, when he saw *Morales* he would've called me up and chewed my ass for a while and we would've worked it out some way."

"What way?"

Karp stared hard at the smug little face and looked for something that he was more and more sure was not there. "Are you asking hypothetically," he inquired calmly, "or are you interested in working something out?"

Freeland seemed to consider this for a while, leaning back in his swivel chair, with his feet on the desk, staring at the corner of the ceiling, tapping with a pencil.

At last he faced Karp and said, "Actually, no. I'm not interested in working something out. We intend to fry your Mr. Bergman's shorts publically, in open court, and do the same in every case in which an innocent defendant is framed. Especially homicide. And especially when your cops have picked some poor black or Hispanic at random. And from what I can see, in even the short time I've been here, there are plenty. And this West Village murder—the body wasn't even cold, before they dragged some pathetic piss bum out of a cellar and pinned it on him. It sucks, Karp! And it's not going to go on. I don't care what cozy little deal you had with my esteemed predecessor."

"Good speech, Milton," said Karp, "but allow me to point out one difference between *Morales* and the Weiner killing. In all probability Morales didn't do it. Russell definitely did it. That strikes me as significant."

"Oh, please! It's another FAN job. A white woman gets stabbed and it's grab the first available nigger."

"Well, since we're on the subject already, I presume that you won't be pleading guilty to the top count in Russell."

"The plea is not guilty."

Karp rose slowly to his feet and looked down at Freeland as at something adhering to his shoe. He said, "In that case, Counselor, I'll see you in court."

He started to leave, but Freeland said quickly, "Wait a minute! You mean *you're* trying Russell?" There was something flickering across his pale face: anticipation, excitement? Karp couldn't be sure. He said, "Yes, the luck of the draw. Why?"

"Nothing. It's a bullshit case. You're gonna get creamed. Well. Maybe I really will see you in court."

Karp walked across the small office, but paused at the door. "Tell me," he said, "I'm curious. This is about winning to you, isn't it? I mean, that's basically all it is to you, a game to win?"

Freeland snorted. "You mean it's not to you? What the hell are we doing here, then?" He gestured at his dingy office. "Making lots of dough?"

Karp ignored this. "You didn't play any ball in school, did you?" he asked mildly. "I mean letter ball. Varsity."

"No. Why?" Freeland seemed genuinely puzzled at the question.

"Just curious," said Karp, and left.

He went back to his office, spent the rest of the morning on routine paperwork, and was about to break for lunch when he got a call from the Tombs. It was Tony Chelham, the captain of the day shift. Karp listened to what the man had to say with growing disbelief.

"Hold on a minute, Tony, Russell wants what?"

"He wants his blue shirt. We had him signing for his stuff, you know? And he says, 'Where's my blue shirt? I ain't signing without my blue shirt.' "

"Holy shit! Um, did he want the knife he killed her with too?"

A booming laugh. "No, but I thought it could be something, the shirt. He said the cops had it down by the Six. So I called."

"You did great, Tony. Okay, here's what I want you to do. Get with Charlie Cimella at the Six. Have him bring the shirt. Get Russell in a cell by himself. Show him the shirt and say, 'Is this the blue shirt you asked for, Russell?' Let him handle it, sniff it, whatever. If he says, yeah, it's mine, just say something like, okay, but we have to hold it for a while—you'll get it back, we'll put a note saying that in the effects bag. Then leave. Don't say anything else at all, no questions, nothing. Make sure Charlie understands that too. Then both of you get over here and we'll make out a statement."

"Okay, check. I'll get right on it."

An hour later, Karp watched as the two officers signed statements to the effect that Hosie Russell had positively identified the shirt as his, amid much rolling of eyes all around.

"You know, guys," Karp said, "this is what makes this job such a challenge—matching wits with Professor Moriarty."

9

HARRY BELLO WALKED THE NIGHT STREETS OF ALPHABET CITY, THAT part of the upper lower East Side of Manhattan where the avenues are named not for great men or events but for letters of the alphabet, as if it might have been inappropriate to name them after anything admirable. There are many slums in New York that have fallen from better times—Harlem and Bedford-Stuyvesant were once proud middle-class districts—but Alphabet City was built as a slum and had not risen in the world. It contains block after block of New Law tenements, five-story walk-ups with fire escapes and air shafts. Down the bleak avenues parade the storefronts of bodegas, liquor stores, cheap furniture and clothing marts, record and hairdressing rooms, pentecostal churches, and the rest of the economy of poverty, all heavily grilled and shuttered at night.

In the sixties, tens of thousands of young people seeking bohemia flooded into New York, and naturally gravitated to the famous art enclave of Greenwich Village. They were thirty years too late; the rents there were designed for art patrons rather than actual artists and their friends. So they moved east, displacing elderly Ukranians, and the East Village was born. There, middle-class kids on the bum could live in agreeable squalor, take drugs, catch sexual diseases, and (a few of them) make music and art.

Where the East Village ends and Alphabet City begins is a question only real estate brokers care much about. To a homicide cop like Bello the presence of a borderland like this one, between the faux poor and the hard cases, meant mainly that it was a place where taxpayers' children in search of excitement were particularly likely to get themselves killed.

Every night for the past week Bello had walked the streets around midnight. This was after a full day's work acting as Marlene Ciampi's private detective on a variety of other cases. Bello didn't need much sleep, and he had no hobbies except Lucy Karp, who was not available in the wee hours.

He was looking for a middle-aged black man, the man who had called 911 at 1:58 one evening a month or so ago and said, "There's a dead woman on Fifth Street off Avenue A." When the operator had asked for his name and number, he had shouted, "You heard me. Fifth and A," and hung up. Bello had listened to the tape many times. The pronunciation was diagnostic: "there's" was "deh's"; "Fifth" was "Fi't"; "dead" was "daid"; and, most interesting, "heard" was "hoid." You didn't get that much among the recent generations. The guy would be over fifty.

Bello had canvassed all the houses on both sides of 5th between avenues A and B and come up blank. A lot of "*no comprende*" on 5th Street. Bello understood enough Spanish to understand that something was being hidden, but not enough to squeeze for it. So he continued to walk the night streets. He bought cigarettes and coffee in the bodegas. He stared down the *guapos* swaggering on the streets. He was polite, almost courtly, to the women.

After a while the people got used to him, and when they found he was not interested in their minor grifts, they almost forgot about him, except that, to the majority of the people, it was nice having their own private *lajara* on the street at night. He became invisible. He was good at it; he felt invisible.

On this night Harry Bello crosses Avenue A to a little *comidas y criollas,* where he buys a cup of excellent coffee and a greasy sugar bun. He reads the *News,* the other three men in the place, Puerto Ricans and a Dominican, chat, smoke, read *El Diario.* Two whores come in for beer, indulge in light raillery, leave with a scream of tires. An elderly black man in dark green work clothes comes in, buys a pack of Camels and a newspaper. When the man gives his order, Bello puts down his paper. There is a brief, inexplicable hiatus in the Spanish conversation.

The black man leaves. Bello, without a word, rises and drifts out behind him. The black man is mid-sixties; he walks stiffly, but his shoulders are square and his back is erect. He enters a building on A off 7th Street. Bello follows him into the building. The man hears a step sounding behind him, whirls in fear. Bello holds up his gold shield. He says, "Tell me about the girl. How she died."

Marlene said, "He said they were laughing?"

"Yeah," said Bello. "Laughing their heads off. Shouting stuff. Have a nice trip. Like that. Two of them, that he saw over the parapet."

They were in her office, and Bello was telling her what he had learned from William Braintree, sixty-four, a Con Ed maintenance worker who, walking home from his swing-shift job at a local substation, had nearly been struck by the falling body of a young woman.

"No, he couldn't ID them," Bello continued, anticipating as usual. "Just saw silhouettes." Pause. "The problem is proof."

Marlene struggled to keep up with the detective. "Um, Harry, you know who did it?"

"Oh, yeah. There'll be somebody saw it. Let you know." He got up and left.

■   ■   ■

Weeks now pass. The season moves into full summer, the City heats ups, and geographically literate New Yorkers recall that they live at the steamy latitudes of Madrid and Naples. Having no *corrida* to distract them, the poor cannot pass the unbearable summer like the dignified Madrileños and so take up the habits of the Neapolitans, shooting and stabbing one another in increasing numbers.

Lennie Bergman's case against the despicable Emilio Morales collapses amid scandal. Bergman receives a scathing lecture from the judge. Karp is subjected to a public tongue-lashing by the district attorney, who is able to use some tough-guy lines that he has been saving up for years. ("What kind of whorehouse are you running down there, Karp? You can't keep your people in line, maybe I better find someone who can!") Karp takes it calmly, as he does most things these days. He is convinced that he will never recover from his impending operation. Nevertheless, he prepares the case against Hosie Russell for the grand jury and gets his indictment.

Lucy Karp grows two tiny fangs. She is not amused. Sleep is banished. In desperation, and secretly, Marlene dips a rag in marsala wine and sugar and sticks it in Lucy's little gob. It works like a charm. Marlene decides not to think about her daughter's brain cells perishing in squadrons, or what Karp will have to say if he finds out.

Emilio Morales returns to his neighborhood, to no great enthusiasm among the home boys. The People's Republic of East 112th Street having not, like the state of New York, suspended the death penalty, Morales is found one sunny morning among the trash cans with two through the ear. Another listless murder investigation begins.

Frangi and Wayne do as little as possible on the Tomasian case. It is the height of the murder season, and they have much to occupy them. They visit the mistress of Mehmet Ersoy, from whom they learn that the late Turk was a big spender, unsurprising information. They also learn that Sarkis Kerbussyan is precisely what he appears to be, a wealthy Armenian art collector with no obvious criminal ties. Aram Tomasian languishes in jail. Gabrielle Avanian is still among the missing. She had never returned from California after the credit card ran out. The police have ceased to look for her with any ardor.

Geri Stone, the sister, collapses the day after Susan Weiner's murder. She is briefly hospitalized and then released, laden with tranquilizing drugs she forgets to take. Her grooming slips, her work deteriorates. She revokes the paroles of an unacceptably high proportion of her case load, and her supervisor asks her to take extended sick leave. She haunts the Criminal Courts building, mumbling, occasionally shouting at nothing. She fits right in.

On 5th Street, in August, around midnight, a woman was being tortured. Her screams and the heavy, meaty sounds of blows shot out into the blackness and melded with the other sounds of the moist summer night—the Spanish music playing on the big radios propped up on the stoops, the punk and heavy metal and salsa from stolen stereos, the roar of cars, the shrieks of children out too late, loud conversation from small knots of men dealing drugs, the buzz of a thousand televisions. It was not an unusual addition to the summer symphony in Alphabet City. Nobody called the cops.

Later that night, two men emerged from 525 East 5th Street, carrying a long bundle wrapped in a dirty green blanket. They walked a half block west to a housing project on Avenue A, cursing the unwieldy weight, and tossed their burden unceremoniously next to a blue Dumpster. They walked away. The bundle moved slightly and a mewling sound arose from it, but no one noticed.

■　　■　　■

"This is a bad one," said Mimi Kellerman, passing Marlene an eight-by-ten photograph. "They took this at Beekman when they brought her in." Kellerman was one of Marlene's four attorneys in Sex Crimes, a birdlike woman with a crisp head of curls and a hard eye. If she said it was bad . . .

Marlene looked. It was a photo of a woman naked from the waist up. It was bad, and Marlene thought for an instant of her Jane Doe. The woman's face was one huge bruise, but worse that that, it had been crumpled like a beer can: the optical orbits and the cheek-bones crushed, the nose flattened, the teeth bashed in, the jaw broken. Bruises also covered her upper body, and there was a gaping hole full of clotted blood on the surface of one breast. Above the hole, obscenely grinning, was a small tattoo of a skull with a red rose in its teeth.

Marlene tossed the photo down. "Sexual activity too, no doubt?"

Kellerman read from a page in a folder. "Raped repeatedly and sodomized, substantial tearing of the vaginal and anal mucosa, internal bleeding, foreign objects forced into both anus and vagina—"

"What objects?"

"Let's see . . . in the anus, a rubber grip from a motorcycle. In the vagina, a folded-over plastic card, some sort of credit card. Nice, huh?"

"I'm enthralled. I assume an autopsy has been scheduled. Who's handling it for Homicide?"

Kellerman gave her an odd look. "What homicide? She's alive."

A bubble of nausea rose in Marlene's belly, and she felt the dampness of sweat on her forehead. That the tortured flesh in the photograph was still vulnerable to pain seemed a grosser violation than mere murder.

"How is she? Can she talk?"

"No, she's still unconscious. Not that she would be able to actually say anything—he did a good job on her mouth."

Marlene picked up the photograph again. "Christ! It's hard to believe anyone survived this. She's got a hole in her chest the size of my fist."

Kellerman looked at her folder again. "Oh, that—that's the least of her problems. It looks like hell, but it's superficial compared to the head and facial damage. Apparently he took an actual bite out of her."

"A bite? And this was where, Alphabet City?"

"Yeah, as a matter of fact. Why?"

"Because he did it before. A Jane Doe, except then he tossed her off a roof after he chewed on her. Not 'he,' I should say 'they.' Harry found the guy who called in the Jane Doe, and he saw two people throw the Jane Doe off the roof. Speaking of which, do we have an ID on this woman?"

"Not exactly," said Kellerman. "She was nude under the blanket they found her in. But, um, that credit card? It had a name on it." She read it off. "Gabrielle P. Avanian." Then she said, "Marlene, why is your mouth hanging open?"

"Yes, Marlene," said Karp, "I do think it's crazy, but luckily it doesn't matter what I think. I'm going into the hospital tomorrow. I'll be lying on my bed of pain, clinging tenuously to life. Somebody else can think about the Armenians."

"I hate it when you play for sympathy," said Marlene, getting up and walking to the window of his office, "especially for a minor operation. What about me? You think it's going to be fun being a single parent for however long? I don't see why you can't just stay at home until your cast is off."

"I explained this already, babe," he said, controlling his irritation. "I'm starting the Russell trial. I can stay in my office while it's on. After, I can get somebody to carry me up the stairs and take some time off."

Marlene stiffened her jaw and turned to look at him, ready to spew invective, but something in his eyes made her check. Was it fear? Karp wasn't afraid of anything. He was the solid, steady, unchanging one. She was the nut prone to weird fantasies. A tide of empathy burst through the elaborate structure she had built, as a quasi-modern woman, to keep the "relationship" on track and prevent herself from being trodden on. She walked over to him and touched his hand. He gripped her fingers, tight enough to sting. They remained that way silent, for minutes, while the sounds of the working day flowed in through the glass of the door.

Karp cleared his throat, and spoke again about what she had discovered, as if nothing important had happened.

"I think it's a good break, this woman, but tying it to the Tomasian case is speculation beyond the facts. It's loopy to tie a sexual predator to a political assassination—"

"But we agree that it looks less and less like a real political assassination," Marlene objected. "Tomasian's being framed. Look, what's the big anomaly in this case? The money. Where did the money come from? Blackmail? Maybe Ersoy knew somebody with money who was into snuff sex. The victim decides a hit is cheaper than paying off forever. The killer decides to frame Tomasian. He knows Tomasian has an alibi, so he has to wax the girlfriend too. But she runs. When she has to come back, maybe because she's broke, they grab her and do her like they did the Jane Doe."

Karp held up an admonishing hand. "Marlene, stop! You don't know any of this. Even if the same guy did Avanian and the other girl, it could still be a nutcase selecting at random, like you thought before. There's nothing else solid to tie these Alphabet City cases to Ersoy."

"Then why did she split?" Marlene asked with some heat. "Why did she leave town the day after the murder? With her boyfriend accused of the crime? It wasn't like she just decided to take a vacation and didn't know about it. This case made the network news, for chrissake. She went on the lam for a reason, Butch."

"Okay, Marlene, you're right," said Karp crankily. "It's a great story. So what are you gonna do with it? Where does it take you? Nowhere. Roland'll laugh in your face if you bring him that connection." Then, observing the growing tightness of her jaw, he temporized.

"Look, let's review the plot here. What do we know as facts?" He ticked them off on his long fingers. "One, Ersoy is killed. Two, he has a big pile of money in a box. Three, Tomasian's alibi disappears after the crime. Four, a woman who may be Gabrielle Avanian is badly beaten. Five, another unidentified woman is thrown off a roof, the only association with Avanian being they both were bitten. What else? Okay, not quite a fact, but I'm almost positive that Kerbussyan was lying to me when he said he didn't know anything about Ersoy's cash."

"I still don't see why it couldn't be a sex thing."

"You have sex things on the brain, Marlene," said Karp, snappish, "and don't tell me all about how you were right about sex rings that once. You want to know what I'd do? I'd find out where that money came from. And I'd find out who killed those women."

Marlene did not like being lectured to by Karp in this way, which was one reason why she had maneuvered in the past to get out from under his direct supervision. On the other hand, she had laden him with enough lectures of her own, and regarded that aspect of their marriage as an inevitable result of two lawyers literally, rather than figuratively, screwing one another on a regular basis. Also, to her credit, she was able to see, through the fog of conjugality, the reason in what he was saying. Her preferred view was still little more than a fairy tale.

"Okay, how would you approach the money angle?" she challenged. "Kerbussyan?"

"No, he's extremely slick and hard to get at. I'd go through Ersoy's connections. The Turks at the U.N. His hang-outs."

"Wasn't there a girlfriend?" Marlene asked.

"Uh-uh, the girlfriend's a semi-pro. She knows from nothing, according to the report Wayne and Frangi filed—he was just one of her regular dates. But come to think of it, I don't recall that anybody checked out the U.N. yet. I mean, why should they, since they had the guy already?"

"Look," she said after a moment of thought, "don't get mad, but this is starting to look like a big complicated thing. On the assumption that my cases are connected somehow to Tomasian—no, don't look like that, I said assumption—why don't me and Harry do some poking around on the Tomasian case while you're loafing in the hospital? Maybe drop by the U.N., see what we can shake out."

"No, but you'll do it anyway. But do you really think a diplomat hung out in the East Village and threw a girl off a roof and beat another one to a pulp?"

"Well, as to that," said Marlene blithely, "I was thinking more of a diplomat paying to have it done. Harry already knows who did the jobs on the women."

"*What?* Who was it?"

"Harry won't say yet," she replied.

"He won't say? What the hell does that mean? Why did we just go through this whole song and dance if he's already found the killer?"

Marlene shrugged. "What Harry knows and what you can bring to court are two different things."

"What kind of statement is that, Marlene? If he has evidence sufficient to identify the killer, he should bring it to us to see if there's a case. He's not supposed to make those judgments. Or are we talking about his mystic intuition?"

"Come on, Butch. It's Harry. You know he has his little ways."

"Okay, fine," Karp said grumpily. "Do your thing. Just keep Roland informed, okay?"

"You're upset," she said inanely.

"No, I'm not. Yeah, I am. I think that's why I'm hot to do this Russell case. It's clean. The guy did it. We caught him. We have a case. We'll convict. It's like a cold shower after all this horseshit Armenian business."

After Marlene left, Karp took two little white pills. Since he had scheduled the operation, he had become more generous to himself with respect to codeine. He figured he wasn't going to become a junkie because of a few days' excess, and he was willing to trade a slight fuzziness for increased mobility—that and surcease from continual pain and the irritability it caused.

Over the next half hour a pleasant numbness crept through his body. He signed some routine papers and then, growing restless, he walked down to Ray Guma's office to talk about some things he wanted done while he was in the hospital.

"Well, you look happy," observed Guma as Karp came into the steel and glass cage that served him for an office. Raney, the cop, was there too. They had been listening to a tape recording. Guma flicked the machine off, and Karp sat down clumsily in a spare chair.

"Raney, I think you oughta make him pee in a bottle. I think he's been tapping the evidence lockers."

"I have a prescription," said Karp with dignity.

"That's how it starts," said Raney. "Then it's boosting car stereos and gold chains. Do you have a street name yet?"

"Yeah, Butch the Crip. What was that tape?"

"The thoughts of Chairman Joey; it's from the tap we got on Castelmaggiore's phone—on the Viacchenza shootings. Wanna hear? It's pretty interesting if you like stupid dirty talk."

Karp made a go-ahead gesture. Guma pushed the rewind. As the taped whined backward, he said, "Okay, on this part you're going to hear, he's talking to Little Sally Bollano, who's sort of the smoother-over for the family at this point. They got another guy who handles it when they don't need to smooth it over. The problem is Lou Viacchenza, the older brother, was a made guy. He'd done a lot of good business for the Bollanos over the years, and Joey had him whacked without clearing it with the family. So Joey's got to show it's for business, not, like, he just got pissed and had them taken out."

"I understand," said Karp. "It's the principle of the thing."

"You got it," said Guma, "not to mention he has to discuss this problem without actually coming out and saying anything indictable. He hopes."

"You figure they know there's a tap in?"

"They'd be assholes if they didn't," replied Guma, and pushed the play button.

The first voice on the tape was Little Sally Bollano's, a nasal snarl.

"What the fuck, Joey, you don't know how we do business? How the fuck long you been doing fuckin' business, Joey? Answer me that!"

"A long time, Sally." This voice was low and grumbling: Joey Castles.

"So you shoulda fuckin' known better, right?" the voice of Sally Bollano continued. "Lemme tell you something, Joey: the Don don't know shit about this, I been making sure of that; he finds out, old as he is, he'd fuckin' have your *culliones* on a plate. So, what I'm saying, this thing, it gotta be put right. Okay, the women, the kids, they gotta be taken care of. You understand what I'm saying, Joey? Out of your fuckin' pocket. Not my fuckin' pocket. Not the Don's fuckin' pocket. *Capisc'*?"

A significant pause on the line. Then Joey said, "It was business, Sally. It wasn't, like, they parked in my fuckin' parking place, like personal. They were taking us off, Sally. They had their own fuckin' little like warehouse over by Ozone Park—"

"Hey! I din' say they shouldn'ta been. Did I fuckin' say that? Been up to me, hey, go do it! It was the way it went down, Joey. No talk, no . . . no fuckin' courtesy. Guys are fuckin' pissed."

"Okay, they're pissed, the cocksuckers—what, I gotta open my fuckin' veins? I'll do the right thing with the family—what the fuck's it to me? But, you fuckin' believe it, man, next time some cocksucker rips all a you off, I din' see nothin', I din hear nothin', I ain't gonna do nothin'. The fuck I care, right?"

"Hey, that kinda talk, Joey—"

"Hey, cut the shit, Sally, I'm fuckin' shakin' already. So, is that it? Everybody's fuckin' happy now?"

"No, that ain't all. They're fuckin' unhappy about the Turk, they wanna know he's gonna hang in there."

"Hey, let me worry about the fuckin' Turk. The Turk ain't gonna do nothin'."

"And what you said, before, this thing goin' down, it's still on with them all?"

"Yeah, yeah, it's okay—hey, here's a fuckin' tip, Sally, you worry about your business and let me fuckin' worry about mine—"

Karp cleared his throat and said, "Hold it there, Goom. Roll it back about a minute." Guma did so; the machine squawked and played the last few sentences of dialogue again.

"What is this Turk business?" asked Karp.

"Street name. We think it could be Turk Minzone."

"Who is . . . ?"

"A Bollano soldier—Red Hook boy, nobody special."

"You like him for the shotgun on the Viacchenzas?"

Guma waggled a hand, palm down. "It's not his usual line of work. He does sports action and a little sharking. Joey could've called in a favor, though, had him do the hit. I mean, it's not like he got scruples about it."

Raney asked, "Why do they call him Turk?"

Guma said, "Turk? It's an expression. They say, '*Il fuma' com' un turco.*' The guy chain-smokes De Nobilis; he's always got one in his face. The story is he ground one out in Jilly Manfredo's eye when Jilly wouldn't come up with his vig."

Karp said, "Yeah, but he said 'the Turk,' not just 'Turk.' Why would he do that?"

"No big thing, Butch. It's like saying 'the Babe' instead of Babe Ruth, no? Or, what, you got another idea?"

"Um, I don't know. We got a murder involving an actual Turkish person."

"What, the hit on that dip? Roland's thing? You think there's a connection? But that's the vic. Why would Sally be worried about a Turk being under control if the Turk's already dead."

"Another Turk?" suggested Raney.

Guma wrinkled his nose and curled his lip back. "Guys, come on! This is your basic gangland slaying, like they say in the papers.

Don't fuck me over with Turks, Assyrians, Armenians, or whatever."

"Maybe I'll check out where Minzone spent the night of," said Raney.

"Now, *that* makes sense," said Guma.

Marlene and Harry Bello rode up the elevator in One U.N. Plaza, the undistinguished building across the street from the great glass Secretariat of the United Nations, where the missions had their offices. Like most people educated in the City, Marlene had made the ritual visit to the place in the fifth grade, and never again thereafter. Harry made no sign that he was impressed with the world body. They rode up with three men chatting in an incomprehensible guttural tongue. For all they knew, it might have been Turkish.

The second secretary of the mission, a Mr. Abdelaziz Kilic, welcomed them gravely into his small office, sat down behind his cluttered desk, and indicated chairs for them to sit in. He was a smallish man with slicked-back graying black hair and a nervous hatchet face. He was wearing a double-breasted suit that seemed to date from the first time that such suits had been popular. Marlene recalled having read that it was always 1937 in Istanbul, and she now understood what that meant. Kilic's desk was covered with brown folders tied carefully with literal red tape.

Mr. Kilic was in no hurry to get to the meat of the appointment. Coffee was ordered and delivered by a large, swarthy woman in a severely tailored black suit. They drank the heavy, sweet brew and talked about the heat of the day, whether it was hotter than in Turkey, which Mr. Kilic pronounced Turk-*iy-eh,* and about the many and varied differences between the two nations. That done, the talk switched to crime in general, to crime in the City, and at last, with many a parenthesis, to the crime in question.

"A truly dreadful happening," observed Kilic. "We at the mission were most shocked." He shook his head rapidly back and forth to indicate the severity of the shock. "But please, you must tell me what I can do for you. As I understand it, the investigation is concluded. You have hands on the criminal, isn't it so?"

Marlene was about to speak when Harry, to her surprise, answered the question. "Yes, we do have a suspect in custody, sir," he said, "but in order to complete our case, it's necessary to find out all we can about the victim of the crime, especially to discover any reasons the victim might have been killed other than the reason we tell the jury he was killed. That way the defense won't be able to place a doubt in the jury's mind."

This was the longest sentence Marlene had ever heard Harry utter, and she had to struggle to keep herself from gaping at him.

Kilic registered profound puzzlement. "What doubt can there be?" he asked. "Mr. Ersoy was assassinated by Armenian terrorists."

"And why would they want to kill Mr. Ersoy?" asked Bello. "Was he a particular enemy of Armenians?"

Kilic smiled at this naïveté. "They are terrorists, Mr. Bello. Mehmet was a Turk; one is as good as another. This man you have arrested is well known to us. He has written abusive letters to us, full of the usual provocative lies."

Somewhat to her surprise, Marlene found herself asking, "What lies are those, Mr. Kilic?"

An elegant dismissive gesture of the hand. "They accuse us of massacre during the first war."

"And that's not true? The Turks didn't kill any Armenians?"

He gave her a sharp look, then smiled appeasingly at Bello. Who is this silly woman? "It was wartime. The Armenians were allied with the enemies of the Turkish people. Some were therefore removed to places where they could not practice their mischief. Of course, there were some deaths in the traveling, but massacre? There was none. We have rejected these lies authoritatively many times, and—"

Harry broke in. "Be that as it may, sir, we're really more interested in Mr. Ersoy's personal affairs. For example, sir, to your knowledge, did Mr. Ersoy have any business interests in the United States?"

"Business? No, he was a professional diplomat. He was not in business."

Bello inscribed this information into a small notebook. "How about relatives? Did Mr. Ersoy have any relatives in the States?"

This required some thought. "I do not believe so. He was unmarried."

"But he had a family—in Turkey, I mean."

"He had a brother, I know. A quite prominent curator of one of the national museums, and an archaeologist as well. Other than that, I would have to look up. Is it essential?"

"Not for now," said Bello. "Did Mr. Ersoy have any close personal relations with any of the mission staff?"

"Personal . . . ?"

"Yes, close friends, people he was always with."

Kilic shrugged slowly and elegantly. "Mehmet was a friendly man. He was friendly with everyone."

"Did he keep a desk diary, or did his secretary keep one, and may we be allowed to look at it?"

A significant pause. "To answer your question, I suppose he did keep a diary, for appointments, but I believe the chief of mission would have to authorize such an inspection."

At this remark Harry scribbled again in his notebook, but this time he looked over at Marlene and fixed her with his eyes, which made at that instant a tiny motion toward the door. Then he continued with his interview. "Might we see a list of all the employees of the mission with their responsibilities?"

A list was produced. Harry read it and began to discuss individuals with Mr. Kilic. Marlene excused herself and slipped out.

She did not know quite how she knew, but she understood precisely what Harry Bello had asked her to do with his millimetric twitch of the eyes. Outside the office, at a secretary's desk, she spotted the grave woman who had served the coffee and asked her where

Mehmet Ersoy's office had been. Following these directions, she found herself in a similar secretarial anteroom. Here the person at the desk was, fortunately, a young man. Marlene smiled and introduced herself, and perched on his desk in such a way that the slit of her maxiskirt dangled open, revealing to his gaze a rich slice of nyloned thigh.

It was thereafter not hard for Marlene to get this young man to inform her that the office diary of Mehmet Ersoy was in the hands of Mr. Ahmet Djelal. Mr. Djelal was with the economic section, the young man told Marlene, but when he said the name, he averted his eyes in a manner that suggested to Marlene that whoever Djelal was, he was not the man to see about the General Agreement on Trade and Tariffs.

Undismayed by this setback, Marlene asked if the mission kept a telephone log, adding that Mr. Kilic was particularly anxious that Marlene have a look at it. The young man seemed delighted to provide her with this document, which Marlene rapidly scanned, taking notes in shorthand.

When she returned to Kilic's office, she found the diplomat and Harry Bello deeply involved in a discussion of the table of organization of the Turkish mission. Kilic was smiling and seemed willing to carry on all day about who reported to whom on what issues. Harry brought the conversation to an abrupt halt as soon as he saw Marlene come in.

"I think that's enough for now, sir; you've been very helpful," he said, closing his notebook and standing. The diplomat rose too, smiling and bobbing his head, uttering polite phrases. Harry paused and seemed to think of some detail. "Oh, one other thing. Mr. Kilic, can you think of any reason why Mr. Ersoy should have had nearly a million dollars in U.S. currency in a personal safe-deposit box?"

An indeterminate look passed over the diplomat's bland face. They waited several beats in uncomfortable silence before he spoke.

"Ah, that. An embarrassment. I had not thought that this

would have a bearing on the prosecution of the criminals. Surely, it is not necessary to have this exposed to the public view?"

"That depends on what the money represented," said Bello. "But you say you knew about it?"

"Ah, yes. One of Mr. Ersoy's tasks was cultural . . . shall we say, retrieval. Türkiye is the repository of much ancient treasure, as I'm sure you know. Unfortunately, now and in the past, some of our patrimony is diverted by smugglers and thieves. Much of this comes to New York, for the art market here. My government finds it convenient to repatriate these treasures quietly and without the notice of the law. A payment is made in cash, the object is returned under diplomatic seal." He paused and tapped his mustache. "I tell you this to avoid any shadow of impropriety falling on poor Mehmet, and so that the way will be clear to punish the terrorists responsible. My government, and perhaps your government as well, would appreciate it if these dealings would remain confidential."

Marlene said, "If, as you say, this money has no connection with the shooting, there's no reason for it to come out."

After that, in a flurry of pleasantries and bows, they left. In the lobby of the Secretariat, Marlene clutched Harry's arm and said, "Harry, Harry—you can talk! It's a miracle! I brought out the big guns for you, Harry—my rosary with the transparent plastic beads filled with water from Lourdes. And it worked."

The corners of Bello's mouth lifted a fraction of an inch— paralytic hilarity. He said, "So?"

Back to the gnomic. Marlene realized that Bello could slip into the persona of a skilled and articulate interviewer the way he could melt into a doorway during a tail job. It was part of the equipment.

"I got a look at the phone logs. He spent a lot of time on the horn with this Ahmet Djelal, the one who has his diary."

"Security chief. It figures. The art."

"Yeah. Another thing, the last couple weeks of his life he made about a dozen real long outside calls to the same number."

Bello took out his notebook and wrote down the number

Marlene gave him. He went to a phone booth in the lobby and dialed the reverse directory service the phone company makes available for the police.

"Who was it?" asked Marlene when Bello returned.

Bello read from his notebook. "Somebody named Sarkis Kerbussyan."

10

KARP CAME FLOATING UP OUT OF THE PENTATHOL FOG, OUT OF THE dream he always had when he was anesthetized, the one with the little room full of dead people in it, people he knew, his mother, his grandparents, and victims of murder. They were whispering the secrets of the dead, and however hard he strained his dream ears, he could never quite make them out.

He opened his eyes. A white shape swam into view, and resolved itself into Marlene's face. Karp tried to speak, croaked, and touched his lips. Marlene passed him a plastic cup with a bent straw attached. He drank and said, "I survived."

"Of course you survived, you big silly. How does your knee feel?"

Karp looked down at the massive plaster log lying on the bed where his leg used to be. "I don't know—it feels different." A thought struck him. "My God, I have an artificial organ."

"This disturbs you?"

"It's better than being crippled, assuming I'm actually not crippled. Did you see Hudson, the bastard?"

"Yeah, we conversed. He said it went fine, and provided you don't abuse it and come to physical therapy like you're supposed to—which he doubts you'll do, by the way—you shouldn't have any trouble."

"Thank you, Dr. Hudson." He relaxed back on the pillows, and they chatted about Lucy and about inconsequentials for a while. Karp's head slowly cleared. He said briskly, "So, what's up in the big world? Did you see Roland?"

"Yeah, I made his month with that information about Ersoy's loot. He was practically cackling."

"Let him cackle. It's still a frame job. Anything on the connection with Kerbussyan?"

"No. Hey, it's been one day, okay? I plan on getting with V.T. to see if there's a money trail connecting the two of them. Maybe Kerbussyan got hold of ripped-off Turkish art treasures and the Turk was buying it back."

The Turk. The conversation with Guma still plucked at Karp's mind. Turks and Armenians. Funny money. A gang of wise guys that specialized in taking things from airports. And the Alphabet City women. The pattern wouldn't emerge, and maybe there wasn't one at all. Maybe he and Marlene had been doing this too long, so that the need of the mind to make sense of the random and unpredictable violence of the City was producing hallucinations of meaning.

"What about the sex maniac?" he asked.

"Harry's going to take me around there tonight, show me the guys."

"They have cops for that, Marlene," he rumbled. "Heavily armed and trained cops."

"I don't want to hear this, Butch."

He said a curse under his breath, reached for the water cup, found he couldn't twist his body far enough around to reach it, and fell back, frustrated and angry.

"I hate this," he said as she passed him the cup. He held her hand, running his thumb across the warm meat of her palm. "And I'm horny."

"That's good news," said Marlene. "A complete recovery can be expected. Does the door lock?"

"You're not serious."

She got up from the bed and discovered that while the door didn't lock, the hallway outside was deserted. She went back to the bed and pulled the curtains around it.

"Actually," she said, wriggling out of her panties, "I should be wearing a white nurse's uniform for the absolute height of lubricity. Do you mind? You know how I am about weird places to do it. And having you helpless there is more than I can stand. I'm gushing."

"Be gentle with me," said Karp.

"The big one, long hair and the sideburns," said Harry Bello. "Vincent Boguluso. Calls himself Vinnie the Guinea. The skinny one with the pizza face is Eric Ritter. Monkey Ritter. The one with the headband and the red beard is Duane Womrath."

"What, no cute nickname?" asked Marlene. They were sitting in Harry's Plymouth on 5th Street, where they had a good view of the three men sitting on the stoop of 525, drinking malt liquor out of quart bottles. A steamy night on 5th Street off A, people out on all the stoops, young men and girls doing the *paseo,* the street full of cars, their stereos blasting Latin, little boys racing up and down with toy guns, screaming, other boys, a little older, with real guns, moving envelopes of dope.

"No, just plain Duane," said Harry. "There's half a dozen others live in there. Men. Plus girls. Everybody else has been chased out. They use a couple of the apartments as a garage for their bikes." He pointed at four gleaming, chopped Harleys lined up against the curb.

"And these guys did it for sure?"

"When the girl was beaten, the yells were coming from that house. Also the bites. Forensics says the wound are consistent with the same set of teeth. But."

"Yeah, we can't tie them positively to the roof job. Get me a witness, Harry."

Bello didn't answer, but stared out the driver's side window at the three men on the stoop. After a few minutes they appeared to become aware of his inspection. The big one, Vinnie, stood up. Marlene measured his size against the doorway and gasped. "Harry, he's a monster! What is he, six-eight?"

"Six-nine, three hundred ten pounds the last time he was in jail. I think he put on a little weight since then. Got a sheet on him: assault, disorderly, car theft, burglary—"

A green quart bottle glinted in the streetlight as it arced toward them and shattered on the pavement inches short of their car. Harry Bello had the door handle jacked and was halfway out the door before Marlene put a restraining hand on his arm.

"Harry, no!"

He resisted her pull for a moment and then relaxed and closed the door. "Do it right, Harry," she said.

He nodded, started the car, gunned the motor, and sent the vehicle roaring off in a sweeping half circle that knocked over the four Harleys in a racket of bonging chrome and tinkling glass.

"That must have felt good," said Marlene as they drove at a sedate pace up Avenue B. And then she snapped her head back, looking over her shoulder. "There's that little girl again."

"Hm?"

"A little girl I met in the park, the fairy princess. She was just there." Marlene had caught just a glimpse, but the thin child was unmistakable. She was wearing a long bridal veil of white tulle as she skipped between the cars.

Bello checked the rearview mirror but saw nothing.

"What about her?"

"Oh, nothing, just a funny little kid. I was worried about her—she thought she could really fly."

Morning, a week has passed. Marlene in her lonely bed was awakened by a call from Lillian Dillard at the day-care center.

Dillard was down with a bad cold and neuritis, and the care group was canceled for the day.

Marlene cursed vividly, her cries joining the chorus of the thousands of working women to whom this very thing was happening at this very moment all across the City.

Lucy wailed from her crib, and Marlene struggled to suppress the sour juices of resentment, so as not to present a harridan's face to her child, who in fact she dearly loved. She threw on her tattered blue robe, cleaned, diapered, and ate with the baby, watching *Sesame Street,* and placed Lucy in her playpen. Then she cleaned and dressed herself and called her office.

Luisa Beckett, Marlene's deputy, responded competently to the procedural disaster that Marlene's absence represented. The other attorneys would have to be shuffled to fill the places where the People had to be represented, motions would have to be filed or opposed, meetings would have to be canceled and rescheduled. Competent but not all that sympathetic, Luisa had no children, nor did the other female attorneys on the rape bureau staff. Marlene hung up the phone, depressed and irritated, and with no human being in range to unload on but a tiny child.

Not to be tolerated. She swept up the baby and clumped one flight down the stairs to Stuart Franciosa's loft. There she found the proprietor, a small, elegant bearded sculptor, and his mate, still smaller and more elegant, a Creole from Louisiana named Larry Boudreau, at ease in their dressing gowns, sipping coffee and watching *All My Children* on a small color television.

Marlene breezed in, deposited Lucy on Larry Boudreau's lap, and went to the kitchen, where she poured herself a cup of coffee. Stuart's loft, unlike her own, consisted of a formal two-bedroom apartment, constructed of dry wall, and a large studio equipped with workbenches and a disreputable orangish sofa, on which the roomates now reclined.

"No work today?" asked Stuart.

"Day-care conked out on me. And I had a million things to do. I'm heading into a ferocious depression."

"And so you dropped down here, where fun ever reigns supreme, in hopes of a cheerful word?"

"Not for nothing are we called gay, Stuart," said Boudreau, holding Lucy's hands and goggling at her as she tried to walk up his belly. He was a nurse. He had delivered Lucy Karp in an adjoining bedroom, Marlene having been caught short by an emergency involving a pair of Mafia gunmen. Larry doted on Lucy; this was not surprising, given his current position as chief nurse in the children's ward at Columbia-Presby: she was cute, affectionate, and not dying from fulminating meningococcemia.

"What about you, Larry?" Marlene asked. "Vacation?"

"Not at all, mah dear child. Ahm night-shiftin' it this week. Stuart heah will be rambling through wicked SoHo, breakin' hearts while Ah attend the sick."

Franciosa rolled his eyes. "We're having a spat. It's too tawdry and boring. He's being the martyr, and I'm the heel."

Boudreau sniffed and leveled a hooded and disdainful look at his lover over Lucy's bouncing dark head.

"Meanwhile," said Stuart brightly, "I have two passes to a tony reception, uptown. Shrimp and champagne. Are we interested?"

Larry said, "Ah'd love to, deah, but Ah have to wash mah hay-uh," in a tone that could have etched bronze.

"God, I haven't been uptown in months," sighed Marlene.

"Why don't you take Marlene, Stuart?" said Boudreau silkily. "She'd love it. Ah'll watch ouah little darlin' heah. Mind, y'all have to be back by two-thirty . . ."

Franciosa hesitated, neatly trapped. Marlene would insure that he behaved himself, while Larry would get to sulk nobly at home. "Want to?" he asked, after a moment's pause.

"Since you ask . . ." she said. "Just twist my arm a little harder."

Forty-five minutes later, Marlene sat in a cab with Stuart Franciosa, wearing a yellow 1950s sundress bought at a thrift shop, thong sandals, and a Panama hat with the brim turned up. She was working hard, fighting guilt, trying to bring her mood up to match her sprightly appearance. Around 14th Street, guilt retreated snarling into its cave, and Marlene turned her attention to the prospect of a delightful afternoon consuming elegant viands in the company of lovely people, none of whom spent much time examining mutilated women.

"So, what's with this gallery? Are you in it?"

Franciosa, who had been doing some sulking of his own, shone a weak smile at her. "No, Sokoloff handles nothing but the old: antiquities, plus Byzantine and other Eastern stuff. They're one of the main houses in the City for that."

"So why did you get an invite?"

"They've used me to make copies. Lost-wax jobs, in precious metals. Scythian bracelets, Egyptian rings, that sort of stuff. Little statuettes. It's a nice little business for them, and I get some good contacts out of it."

"Wow, treasures of the mysterious East. It sounds deliciously romantic and decadent."

"You got it, sister," said Stuart, brightening.

They arrived. Sokoloff's occupied a corner at Madison in the fifties. Inside were three spacious rooms, painted white, with track lights on the ceiling and oriental carpets on the floor. The treasures were arranged in glass cases on the walls and on pillars. Glomming the artifacts and loading up on canapés, shrimp, and Moët were perhaps fifty people, the men prosperous-looking, the women dressed in the sort of clothes one needs an appointment to buy. Marlene was introduced to the proprietor, Stephan Sokoloff, a portly old rake who lingered a tad too long over the continental kiss he placed on Marlene's hand. Stuart ushered her away before she could object.

"Stuart!" she said in a stage whisper, "I'm dressed like a hick. I thought it was going to be arty, people with blue spikes and vicious leather."

Franciosa laughed. He was himself wearing all black under an Italian silk double-breasted jacket in the palest possible tangerine, worn open. "It doesn't matter what you wear when you're the most beautiful woman in the room, dear. As you are. You saw how Sokoloff drooled over you."

He started and placed his hand on his breast. "Speaking of which—be still my heart! Who is that dish?"

Marlene followed his gaze. It had been a rhetorical question, and she was astounded that she was actually able to answer it. "It's V.T. Newbury. What the hell is he doing here?" The man in question was a smallish ash blonde with the perfect Anglo-Saxon features of a portrait by Copley.

"You know him?"

"Yes, and you can stop that panting, you slut."

"He's *not* straight."

"Like a T-square. Want to meet him anyway?"

"Maybe later," said the artist morosely, at which point he was shanghaied by a person in a feathered hat.

Marlene ambled over to Newbury, who was in rapt conversation with a squat, swarthy man dressed in a cheap and ill-fitting three-piece polyester suit. V.T. was his usual exquisite Paul Stuart self. They made an odd pair.

V.T's eyes widened in surprise when he saw Marlene, but she forestalled whatever remark he was about to make.

"Not a word, V.T. I'm not here, you never saw me. Gosh, that's a lovely thing. What's he smiling about?"

They were standing in front of a glass case containing a small statue of a boy done in some hard, bright stone. The tag said "Kouros, 14.5 cm, alabaster, Miletus, ca. 600 B.C."

The swarthy man said, "It's what they call the archaic smile. It's a symbol of personality." This delivered in a thick New York accent. *Poisonality.*

Marlene gave him another look. A blunt, square face, pock-marked, and a black crew cut. Intelligent eyes, but they had a hard, cynical light in them that Marlene recognized all too well.

"Not something most cops would pick up," she said. The man laughed, and V.T. made the introductions. The swarthy man was in fact Detective Lieutenant Ramon Rodriguez, and he was in charge of the small unit of the New York Police Department that investigates art frauds and thefts.

"So, V.T., you're working?" she asked. V.T. was a light of the D.A.'s fraud bureau.

"Yes, I suppose I am. And isn't it pleasant? That's why I love fraud. You get to mix with an altogether tonier class of people than in Homicide."

"Yeah, and the food's better too," said Rodriguez, snagging a caviar-heaped cracker from a passing tray.

"So what's the scam?" said Marlene, doing the same. "Is it a fake?"

Rodriguez looked at the little kouros again. "Well, it's kinda hard to say. With stone like this, you don't have the chemical tests you have for your organics, like wood and cloth, or pigment tests and X rays for old paintings. All you have is, you can do crystallographic analysis to see where the original stone came from and if it has weathered the way it ought to if it's ancient. Other than that, it's all stylistic. And provenance, of course."

"Which means?" asked Marlene, all at once fascinated, and not because the subject was inherently gripping. Something tugged at her mind.

"Well, stylistic is Sokoloff got some guy from Yale and some guy from the Met to say it's a realie," said Rodriguez. "Provenance means you got documentary proof of a chain of ownership; that, or the thing's been under observation in some church since the year one. But you can forge or fake provenance. Or explain not having any—hey, you just dug the sucker out of some tel in Iraq. Example: in 1960 a Brit named Mellaert discovered a trove of stuff at Haçilar in Turkey—pottery mostly, very old. Turns out the 'peasant' who led Mellaert to the find was a forger named Cetimkya, who ran the pots off himself. Of course, once you have a 'find' it's open season; who's to know the stuff's not something ripped off out of the dig before it was catalogued? Pre-Columbian stuff is the worst for that. Robbing graves is a major industry down there, and collectors don't ask questions. And they get ripped like crazy.

"The hard part is making them complain; nobody likes to be a mark, especially rich connoisseurs." *Connowsewers.*

"So why are you here at this particular gallery? Routine?"

Rodriguez smiled, showing large, yellowish teeth. "I like the food. No, actually, I'm following up on an Interpol bulletin. Somebody popped a warehouse in Istanbul that was being used to keep stuff from the Topkapi collection. Nobody knows what the hell was in there, but a bunch of collectors in Milan, Paris, and London have been stung by phony antiquities and Byzantine stuff, supposedly the loot from Istanbul. It would be natural for whoever's doing it to move their operation to New York too. So, watch and wait.

"I'll say one thing for whoever's doing this. They know what they're doing—the craftsmanship's outasight. C'mere, I'll show you something."

The three of them trooped over to a case by the wall. On black velvet a small painting glowed golden.

"*Christ Judged by Pilate,*" said Rodriguez. "Byzantine, ninth century. Okay, the wood's right, it's an old panel. The paint's egg tempera, the blues are crushed lapis, the red's cochineal—not modern pigments. The gold in the frame is really beaten, not milled. Milling wasn't used until the tenth. But . . ."

He paused significantly. "Stylistic analysis. The soldier holding Christ. His helmet, his armor, even his stance and the expression on his face is right off a cross reliquary and icon of the Passion now in the treasure of the Primatial Basilica of Hungary—early thirteenth."

"But why couldn't the Hungarian piece be copied off this one?" Marlene asked.

"It don't work that way. Stylistically, that figure's too late to have been done by a Byzantine in the ninth. Here's something else, even more interesting."

They moved to the next case.

"Five-pointed Armenian tiara decorated with star and two eagles, gold and gems, circa 90 B.C. Same thing: the workmanship is terrific. Lost wax casting, no drawn wire. There's one just like it in the Armenian state museum at Erevan. I mean, just like it. I'm not saying it's a fake; it could be an ancient duplicate or a slightly later copy. But ..." He waggled his hand. "In any case, it convinced Kerbussyan enough to buy it."

"Kerbussyan!"

"Yeah. Why, do you know him?"

"I heard the name. How do you know he bought it?"

"Little red dot there on the card. Has to be old Kerbussyan. Nothing that good from Armenia comes through the New York market without him scarfing it up. He's probably the major collector of Armenian art in the world. Look, here's something else he bought."

The next case held a small panel painting. The card gave *Burial of St. Gregory* as its title, and there was a tiny red stick-on dot there too.

"It looks a little like Giotto," said Marlene.

Rodriguez raised an eyebrow. "Very good. It's a contemporary of his, Tóros Roslin. 'School of,' more likely. Worked in southeastern Turkey—what they called Cilicia or Lesser Armenia. Funny, it's not quite an antiquity—out of Sokoloff's usual line."

They studied the painting in silence for a few moments. A haloed saint was being placed in a tomb, with the usual attending mourners and angels waiting to conduct his soul to glory.

"Why is his face like that?"

"Oh, that's the famous mask," said Rodriguez. "St. Gregory the Illuminator was the founder of Armenian Christianity back in the fourth century or thereabouts. It's, um, a complicated story, but the upshot was the king and queen were real broken up when he died, so they had a death mask made of his face, and after a while they used it as a cast for a solid gold mask adorned with jewels. According to one version of the legend, Gregory's actual eyes were incorporated into the mask, miraculously preserved from corruption. It had the usual holy powers. Heal the sick, make the blind see. Gregory's right hand, by the way, is wrapped in a silver gauntlet reliquary in the treasury of the Catholicos of Cilicia in Beirut."

"What happened to it? The mask, I mean."

"No one knows ... if it ever existed, which I doubt. Art history's full of legendary treasures like that. I'll tell you one thing, though. If it ever comes through New York, Kerbussyan'll buy it." He looked at his watch. "Shit, I'm due downtown in court in half an hour. Nice to meet you, Marlene. Coming, V.T.?"

"Just a sec, Lieutenant, one question," Marlene said. "Did you ever hear of a guy named Mehmet Ersoy?"

Rodriguez frowned and chewed his lip. "Name sort of rings a bell. Turkish name. What about him?"

"Well, I just thought that since his business was buying back stolen Turkish antiquities, you might have run across him."

"Stolen Turkish antiquities? Who told you that?"

"I heard it from their guy at the U.N., in confidence, that the Turks have a program to locate and return to Turkey ancient stuff that is taken out of the country illegally and is being sold abroad. Had some serious money behind it too."

Rodriguez shrugged. "Well, hey, it's possible, but I never heard anything about it. I mean, from the Turks' perspective, it don't make a hell of a lot of sense."

"Why not?"

"Because when the Brits and the French and the Greeks and the Italians try to get their antiquities back, they're dealing with their own heritage. The stuff was made by their ancestors, or people they'd like to believe were their ancestors. But the Turks didn't get to Anatolia until the Middle Ages. That statue, the tiara, and those paintings—it ain't their stuff. It belonged to people they beat the crap out of back then. That's why it'd be a little weird if they were buying back antiquities. I always thought they'd kinda like to forget anyone lived there before they hit town."

V.T. and Rodriguez left. Marlene mooched listlessly around the exhibit, drinking more wine than was good for her, until the existence of a class of people who spent their time buying expensive trinkets and clinking glasses of champagne, instead of wading neck deep through the dregs of society, produced in her in an unbearable state of disgust mixed with guilty longing. She dragged a protesting Franciosa away from a coven of glittering art hags and fled the gallery, returning with a churning mind and a heavy heart to the steaming streets and motherhood.

Karp had a wheelchair in his office, but he refused to use it in public. Instead he clumped on crutches from courtroom to meetings, grasping a ratty brown folder in two fingers as he slogged away down the bustling halls.

Now he was sitting in the conference room of the district attorney with the other senior bureau chiefs—Fraud, Rackets, Supreme Court, Criminal Courts, Appeals—and the D.A.'s administrative deputy and hatchet, Conrad Wharton. Karp did not have much in common with any of these men. They were Bloom's creatures all, adept at public relations, smooth administration, coordination, the judicious use of prosecutorial power. Karp was the only one of them who was a serious trial lawyer.

There was some good-natured joshing about Karp's leg, to which he responded in the same tone. Wharton did not join in this. He never talked to Karp if he could help it, or noticed his existence in any way, except under the absolute press of business. He wrote Karp a lot of memos though, mostly to point out deficiencies in his management of his bureau.

It was curious. Karp had sent any number of vicious, depraved monsters to prison, where they certainly did not wish to go, but he doubted that any of these hated him as much as the baby-faced little man at the end of the conference table, to whom Karp had never, to his own recollection, done a personal injury. It was a mystery, one that annoyed him, although it cannot be said that he tossed nightly in his bed because of it.

Still, he recognized that Wharton's hatred caused him trouble. Whenever administration could trip up a bureau, there was Wharton's ankle in Karp's way. Karp reflected, in fact, that there had been an unusual number of D.A.'s meetings called during the week he had been on crutches: perhaps Wharton was taking some sadistic pleasure in seeing him hobble around.

The D.A. entered, in shirtsleeves and red suspenders; to his credit, these did not have tiny golden justice scales upon them. The D.A. was in his early fifties and looked like a suburban anchorman: razor-cut, blow-dried tannish hair going attractively gray; even, pleasant, if undistinguished 'features; terrific teeth. He was charming.

He began the meeting by charming his minions. Karp was charmed by solicitous concern about his knee, plus a remark about not having to worry anymore about hiring the handicapped, which raised a gust of dutiful, unpleasant laughter. The bureau chiefs gave their reports. Wharton handed the D.A. a sheet of paper on which was written a set of probing questions about various cases that might get the D.A. into trouble or show the office in a bad light.

Karp's questions were about the Hosie Russell case and the Tomasian case, as he had expected.

"What about this Russell? You're sure he's the right guy?"

"Yes. It's a circumstantial case, but it'll go the right way."

"That's not what I hear. The word is the cops picked up the first black lush they came across in the neighborhood and cooked up a bunch of incriminating evidence. The black community is pissed off."

"If that's what you hear, you're talking to the wrong people. We have two positive witnesses, one of them a black man, tying Russell to the crime. The evidence is good, and it'll hold up under challenge."

"That's what you said about Morales. And Devers. Those were embarrassments, but they were nothing to what we'll have if this case gets fucked up. A young woman stabbed in broad daylight in front of a good building . . ."

Karp felt his face heat and felt the eyes of the other chiefs on him. He had gotten angry before. He had tried arguing from the perspective of a trial lawyer. None of it had done any good. This had nothing to do with the job he was doing and everything to do with Karp himself. He paused for a number of seconds before answering.

"You're the D.A. You sign the indictments. Would you like me to let Russell go?"

The D.A. looked startled, as he did any time someone (usually it was Karp) reminded him of his legal responsibility.

"No, of course not! But I'm holding you responsible for seeing that this comes out right. Now, on this Tomasian thing. The U.N. liaison office is still extremely upset. I was on the phone with a man for a half hour this morning, assuring him that terrorism was not about to take over the City. I hope to hell I wasn't wrong and you've got your act together on this one."

Karp said, straight-faced, "I think it's absolutely certain that terrorism isn't taking over the City."

"You know what I mean," snapped Bloom. "I don't like what I hear from your operation on this thing. Dissension. Duplicate investigations. I don't think you realize what'll happen if the press gets hold of these stories."

"There's nothing for the press to get hold of," said Karp calmly. "There's one investigation. Roland Hrcany is in charge of it. We have an indictment and a defendant in custody."

"And he'll go for it? You can promise that?"

"No, as a matter of fact, I can't."

"Why not? Is there something wrong with the case?"

"No," said Karp after a brief pause. "It's a good case." He was about to add that the only problem with the case was that the defendant hadn't done the crime, but decided against it. The D.A. wouldn't be interested in stuff like that. What he said was: "It could be better. We're working on it."

"Do that!" the D.A. said, and moved on briskly to other business.

Karp went back to his office and worked on the Russell case. He wanted to move it swiftly through the courts and, for a wonder, it was moving swiftly. They had opened up a new Supreme Court part a few weeks ago, and its calendar was not loaded yet. Theoretically, it was possible to dispose of a murder case in two months from arrest to sentencing, if you had the right court and it was not to the defense's advantage to slow things down.

Unfortunately, it usually was. Witnesses forgot or died. Pleas were more acceptable after a decent interval in jail. But this time Freeland seemed almost eager to rush things along, as if he could not wait for the personal confrontation with Karp. That suited Karp just fine. Pretrial was set for the morrow, and he was busy researching arguments for the motions the defense was likely to bring when his wife walked in.

"It's conventional to knock," he said.

"In an office, yeah," said Marlene, "but this is your bedroom and I'm your wife. I have conjugal rights."

"Which you intend to exercise now?"

"Dream on." She looked around the office. Karp had set up a steel folding bed he had snitched from the jail infirmary. A steel clothes rack on casters from one of the courtrooms was hung with his suits. There was a suitcase standing nearby with shirts and other necessaries.

"I still can't believe you're doing this," she added. "Nobody lives in their office."

"It's only for six weeks, Marlene, maybe less. We've been through all this. I have to be here for Russell, and I can't get up and down from the loft, and we can't afford a hotel right now."

Marlene slumped down in a visitors' chair and lit a cigarette she didn't really want. She smoked in silence for a while. Karp went back to his reading. She stood up abruptly. "Well, so much for domestic felicity. I'm going to pick up Lucy. What do you want for dinner?"

"Chinese?"

"Good choice. MSG helps build strong bones. See you."

She left. Karp worked until his eyes burned and then lay down on his bed of pain. He drifted off and was awakened by his daughter's tiny fingers probing his facial orifices.

"She misses you," said Marlene, setting out white cardboard containers on the conference table. "She's been whiny all week. Her little schedule is all disturbed."

"I'm sorry," said Karp lamely, kissing the child.

They ate, Lucy sitting on his lap, grabbing for indigestible morsels and making a mess.

"What's going on in the big world?" he asked to break the silence.

"Um, the usual. I saw Geri Stone again today down in the lobby. She's stalking the halls, dressed in black and buttonholing strangers and trying to convince them it wasn't her fault the guy she sprang whacked her sister. She's become one of the Centre Street characters, like the Walking Booger and Dirty Warren. Everybody calls her The Sister. I think she's deteriorating.

"What other news? I'm following up on what we learned from the Turks and at that art gallery. V.T. is working the banks, trying to get a line on whether Ersoy had moved any serious money out of the U.S. before he got shot.

"Harry located Gabrielle Avanian's parents today. The father says he hasn't got a daughter and hung up on him. He spoke to an older brother later. Apparently the father disowned her when she moved out and started shacking with Tomasian. The brother is supposed to come down to the hospital tomorrow and give us an ID on her. She's still out of it.

"Harry also did a repeat canvass of the buildings across from the murder scene on Fifth Street. No luck, so we're still looking for a witness that'll tie those mutts in the motorcycle gang to the Jane Doe killing."

"Something is jelling in my brain about all this," said Karp, "but I can't quite get it to come clear."

"Yeah, I know what you mean, me too. Here's a thought. The U.N. guy, Kilic, said that Ersoy's money was for buying art. I don't think so. But maybe he was selling art."

"Huh? Why do we connect him with art at all? Why not dope or sex?"

"Because Kilic is covering up something, and he was the one who suggested that Ersoy was in the art business. He must have known that we'd look into it and wanted to be covered in case Ersoy's name came up in connection with the art trade. And, of course, there's the one man whose name shows up in both ends of this business—the Armenian nationalist and art collector, Sarkis the K. I'd like to have a chat with him."

"I miss you," said Karp.

She looked at him for a while, her face unreadable. "Yeah, well, me too. If I'd wanted to be a single mother I would've started at age sixteen and my kid would've been going to proms by now. This can't go on."

"What can we do?"

"I don't know," answered Marlene wearily. "I'll think of something."

11

NOTHING IMPROVED KARP'S SPIRITS LIKE BEING IN COURT. IT WAS HIS gambling, his girls, his heroin. He glanced around at the courtroom. Milton Freeland was at the defense table, along with a young Legal Aid acolyte and the defendant, Hosie Russell. Russell had clipped his hair and was wearing glasses. He looked like a deacon.

The judge, a large, olive-skinned, beetle-browed man, was already seated at his presidium, peering over his half glasses and discussing some business with his clerk. His name was Martino, and Karp was very glad indeed to see him. He could not have asked for a better judge. Martino knew the law; he knew the difference between rights and legal trumpery; and he was ferociously impatient with lawyers who didn't know what they were doing, into which class Karp thought that Milton Freeland very likely fell.

A pretrial hearing is like a dress rehearsal for a trial, a clearing of decks, a showing of cards, so that the trial proper may proceed expeditiously, if it proceeds at all.

No jury is present, of course. Karp was expected to expose his critical evidence and his official and police witnesses to demonstrate to the judge the veracity of the evidence and the probity of the identification of the defendant, all of which had been challenged by Freeland.

Motion to suppress the Bloomingdale's VISA slip taken from Russell at the scene: the basis—no probable cause for a search. The judge heard Freeland out and decided that a police officer finding a man answering the description of a fugitive hiding under a boiler in a building where a dozen people had seen him go was probable enough cause. Motion denied.

Motion to suppress the blue shirt and the handbag and the knife. But the knife had human blood on it. The bag was the victim's bag, the blue shirt had, according to several witnesses, been worn by the perpetrator; the defendant had, in fact, identified it as his own. Motion denied.

Here Freeland raised an objection. "Your Honor," he said, "I must protest. The testimony that the blue shirt was the defendant's was elicited after arraignment and in the absence of counsel. It was the product of an illegal interrogation."

The judge said, "How was it an interrogation, Mr. Freeland? Both Captain Chelham and Detective Cimella have testified that the statement was voluntary on the part of the defendant. He asked about his shirt and they brought it to him and he identified it."

"It's still incriminatory," Freeland shot back.

That was interesting, thought Karp. He's not reading the judge. He's bugging him, but he doesn't care; he's getting objections on record, trying for a reversible error. Fat chance.

"How is it incriminatory?" asked Martino, his brows twitching. "He says, 'It's my blue shirt.' I have a blue shirt too. You have a blue shirt. Admission that we have them is not incriminatory. Statement of the defendant was not in response to any interrogation connecting defendant with the crime or with any other statement of the defendant. Motion denied."

Freeland did not seem flustered by this rebuke. Karp had to admit that he had a good courtroom demeanor. A strong voice, a snappy appearance.

Next motion. Move to suppress defendant's priors under the *Sandoval* rule, which says that a defendant cannot be cross-examined on his criminal record unless those convictions speak to the credibility of the defendant as a witness. Karp struggled to his feet, and they went through Russell's fifteen convictions, one by one. The judge allowed the burglaries, the larcenies. The jury can know that the guy steals things. On the assaults, Freeland began to argue from a parole report—the defendant was subject to uncontrollable rages—when Martino stopped him abruptly. "Is Counsel arguing mental incompetence here?"

"Ah . . . no, Your Honor, it speaks to circumstances mitigating the effect of the convictions on the credibility of the witness."

The judge lowered his head for a moment as if to clear his throat, and the court clerk thought she heard him say, "What total horseshit," which was impossible, and then the judge said, out loud, "Either argue it or don't! I will strike four of these convictions: two narcotics possessions, the carrying a deadly weapon, and this receiving stolen property. The rest stand."

It suddenly struck Karp, and the thought inspired a vague queasiness, that the parole reports that Freeland had just used had been written by the dead woman's sister.

Next, Freeland turned to the witnesses, arguing from *Ward* that the lineup was so unnecessarily suggestive as to be unfair. The point of this was to throw out the identifications made by the Digbys and Jerry Shelton. The judge studied the photographs. All the people in the lineup were black men of about the same height and build. Motion denied. The same thing happened to Freeland's motion to suppress the spontaneous identification made by the leather-shop owner, James Turnbull.

Freeland objected. "Judge, if you're going to allow this eyewitness testimony, defense should have the opportunity to examine the People's witnesses at this time. Also, I move that the prosecution should be required to supply us with the names and addresses of all witnesses they intend to call."

Karp rose. "Your Honor, the People have no obligation to provide names and addresses of civilian witnesses. Statements of potential witnesses are not discoverable under New York law, Section 240.20, Criminal Procedure Law."

"Thank you, Mr. Karp," said the judge. "I am familiar with the statute, but it is also true that New York precedent gives the trial judge broad discretion to compel disclosure, although People's witnesses should be compelled only on a showing of most unusual and exceptional circumstances. Are you prepared to make such a showing, Mr. Freeland?"

"Your Honor, since the physical evidence in this case has no direct or obvious connection with the defendant, the testimony of the identifying witnesses is of extreme importance. Also the nature of this case—the murder of a white girl, this incredible rush to select a black indigent as the murderer. I would construe that as unusual and exceptional, certainly."

"Would you?" asked Martino. "Well, I would not, within the guidelines suggested by *People* v. *Hvizd*. Denied as to the discovery."

Karp saw an odd look come across Freeland's face, a nervous look but touched with something mischievous, as when a boy is deciding whether to heave a snowball at a cop. Freeland spoke again, confidently, "Your Honor, citing *People* v. *Blue,* Appellate Division, 1973. The court found that the pretrial hearing was inadequately and improperly conducted in that the identification witnesses were not called by the prosecution to testify at it and that the hearing court would not permit the defense counsel to examine the witnesses as to their original testimony to the police."

Blue? thought Karp, suddenly asweat. What in hell was *Blue?* He should know all about any cases that bore on prosecution witnesses. Protection of witnesses was essential to winning trials—if Freeland could get all Karp's civilian witnesses up on the stand now, he could probe for weaknesses, confuse them, establish a record of contradictory testimony, alienate them—it would be much worse than simply getting their names and addresses.

But *Blue* was a mystery. Unless . . . He looked again at Freeland, and all at once he was sure.

"Shit! He's trying it again!" The words appeared in his mouth before he could stop them.

"Excuse me, Mr. Karp, I didn't get that," said the judge inquiringly.

"Oh, sorry, Judge. I meant to say, I believe the Appellate Division ruling in *Blue* was reversed by the Court of Appeals."

"Mr. Freeland, were you reading from an Appellate memorandum?" asked Martino, frowning. "Yes? Okay, five-minute recess. Get the law."

The look on Milton Freeland's face was worth a month's salary.

In front of 525 East 5th, the street and sidewalk were full of tattooed men in sleeveless T-shirts and leather pants, sitting on big, shiny, customized Harleys, drinking beer and wine from bottles, looking corpselike under the glare of the sodium lights. They were shouting and scuffling, grabbing and kissing similarly attired tattooed women and each other, and doing all the other things that outlaw motorcycle clubs do to make themselves loved and admired by the general population, all this to the sound of music that seemed to be largely composed of guitar feedback played at the max.

They were also dealing drugs fairly openly, despite the fact that Harry Bello was standing across the street, leaning against the stoop of number 528 and watching them. Or maybe they were doing it because Bello was there.

He didn't mind. He had no intention of making a drug bust, but he wanted them to know he was there and watching.

Something swift and bright appeared in the corner of his vision. It was a thin girl of about ten, dressed outlandishly in a tattered bridal veil and a lacy pink party dress. She had come darting past the stoop to talk with a Puerto Rican woman. The woman had dyed blond-streaked hair and was wearing pink shorts, a sequined halter, and sandal spikes. She was leaning against a parked car, drinking with several similarly attired Puerto Rican women.

The little girl was arguing with the woman. Their voices grew shrill. Bello's Spanish wasn't that great, but he gathered that the two were mother and daughter and that the mother wanted the girl in the house, and the girl wanted some money to go down to Avenue A and get ice cream.

A smack sounded, a hard one. The girl shrieked like a vole in a trap. A flurry of blows. The bridal veil was torn loose. Sobbing, the child gathered it up and ran into the house. The woman in the sequins laughed and resumed her chat with her sister whores.

Bello stared at the woman. He recalled her; her apartment had a good view of 525, he had interviewed her twice. She was one of the tribe of din-see-nothins. Bello tried to think about how to make her some trouble.

He watched the gang across the street some more. A young woman in light green coverall and a head scarf, a woman going to a night shift somewhere, walked out of an adjoining building and started west on 5th. When she saw what was going on, she checked and crossed the street.

One of the bikers saw her cross and made a run at her, laughing. He threw a clumsy arm around her shoulder and tried to kiss her, but she shrugged off the arm and ran across the street. Harry tensed and put his hand on the butt of his revolver.

The man saw the gesture and snarled and shouted something and went back to his pals. His friends egged him on, attributing homosexual qualities to him in colorful language.

Bello walked behind the young woman down to Avenue A. In an all-night, he called Marlene.

She was used to getting calls from Harry at odd hours. The baby had been so cranky these last days she wasn't getting much sleep anyway.

"It's not Avanian," he said without preamble when she picked up the phone.

She nevertheless felt cranky. "Is that a new greeting, Harry? I like it. Let's not say, 'Hello, Marlene, sorry to disturb you.' Let's all start saying, 'It's not Avanian,' when the other person answers."

"The brother was by Beekman," said Harry, ignoring this.

"I don't get it, Harry. That's the woman went to the coast and came back. I thought you checked with United."

"It's the woman who went, but the woman who went wasn't Avanian."

"Harry, what about the credit card? Where did Avanian's plastic come from?"

"It was the tattoos. We should have figured. I'm slowing down."

"What tattoos, Harry?"

"On the Beekman girl—woman. Avanian didn't have any that her brother knew of. But the woman in Beekman had tattoos. Quite a few. So do the women who hang out with Vinnie and his friends."

Marlene hated playing the straight man. She tried to kick her brain into gear. "Okay, so if she wasn't Avanian, she was somebody who had at least one of Avanian's possessions, or knew someone who had, and if she was also connected with the gang, that means . . ." What did it mean? Then it hit her, with a cold chill.

Before she could speak, Harry said, "The Jane Doe is Gabrielle Avanian. She lived in the neighborhood. She was walking down the street that night and they grabbed her. I almost saw it happen to a woman tonight."

"Just at random?"

"Sure. The fuck do they care? Our Beekman woman must have boosted her stuff, her credit card, and her ticket, went off and had a little vacation. Disneyland, L.A. Vinnie and them were probably not too pleased about that. She must have blown five, six grand. Then she came back, like an asshole, and they found her and did her. We could confirm it was Avanian through dental records. I'll get on that first thing." He paused. "Still no witness. We could roust their place."

Marlene considered it briefly. Could she get a warrant on the basis of a witness seeing two silhouettes on a roof and a crazy theory? Maybe. Then what if they found evidence connected to the victim in apartments occupied by the gang? The mutts could play nobody-knows-nothin' or he-did-it forever. There was probably a substantial transient population going through there anyway; without eyewitness testimony or a confession, they didn't have a case that would stand up.

She was about to share these considerations with Bello when he said, "I saw your little friend tonight. The princess."

"Oh, yeah? Where?"

"Building across the street from the mutts. She lives on three. Her mom's a pross. She was giving the kid a hard time."

It popped into Marlene's mind all at once. Angels falling from the sky and getting smooshed. It had to be that.

"She lives across the street from where the murder took place? With a street view?"

He caught the tone in her voice. "Yeah. What's up?"

"She saw it, Harry. She's our witness."

"Witness? A flaky kid?"

"And if she saw it, the odds are her mother saw it too."

"I asked her already. Zip."

"Yeah, but we didn't know. Now we know! Get her, Harry. Squeeze her."

The following day, Concepción (Chica) Perez proved to be squeezable. Most prostitutes are. After obtaining a guarantee that the police would find her another place to live, she admitted that she and her daughter had watched as Vinnie Boguluso grabbed Gabrielle Avanian off the street, picked her up like a doll, and carried her into his building, amid the laughter of Eric Ritter and Duane Womrath and several others she could not identify. An hour later, she saw the woman being thrown over the roof parapet. She also observed the three men standing on the sixth-floor fire escape attempting to urinate on the body in the street below.

Marlene read over the formal Q. & A. she had taken from Perez after Harry had finished with her.

"I'm going to warrant all three of them. Let's pick them up right now. Who're you going to take?"

"I'll do it."

She looked at him to see if he was joking. It would have surprised her. Harry didn't go in much for joking. He wasn't joking.

"Harry, these guys are dangerous."

"To girls," he said.

He did go by the Fifth Precinct and collect a RMP and a driver, and they drove to 525 East 5th Street. It was nine-thirty in the morning. Harry told the driver to wait in the car and went into the building alone. The gang occupied the first two floors. The apartments on the upper floors were either abandoned, their fixtures and wiring ripped out, or home to a transient population of junkies and runaways.

He knocked on the scarred door of Apartment 1-C, and knocked steadily for something like three minutes. These were not early risers. A surly voice shouted, "Who the fuck is that?"

Harry shouted, "It's Harry Bello. Open up!"

Monkey Ritter threw open the door, dressed only in grayish Jockeys and a sagging T-shirt. He saw Harry and his eyes widened. As he drew breath to shout a warning, Harry's fist caught him solidly in the solar plexus and he crumpled; only a strangled whine escaped his throat. Harry cuffed him and frog-marched him unresistingly down the hall, out into the street, and into the back of the RMP.

"Keep him quiet, would you?" said Harry to the amazed young cop. "And can I borrow your cuffs? I only brought one pair."

The driver gave him a set. "You sure you don't need any backup?" he asked.

Harry shook his head and went back into the building.

He found Vinnie in the back bedroom of 1-C, lying on a mattress with a girl. Also in the room were piles of dirty clothes, a new nineteen-inch television set, a red steel toolbox, a disassembled 1956 Harley-Davidson Electra-Glide, and, lying near the mattress, a sawed-off shotgun.

When Bello entered the room, Vinnie said, "What the fuck do you want, pig?"

Harry said, "Get up, Vinnie. Let's go."

"I'm not goin' no fuckin' where with you," said Vinnie, his eyes moving to the shotgun.

"Look at me, Vinnie, not at the gun. You're not going to go for the gun." His voice was calm, as if instructing a dull child.

Vinnie looked at Bello's face, at his eyes. It was a revelation. Vinnie had never looked at a face that held no fear, even when he looked in a mirror, and he was an expert; people were afraid of Vinnie Boguluso. This man didn't care whether he lived or died, and certainly didn't care whether Vinnie lived or died. Vinnie saw his own death written on this face.

He licked dry lips. "Hey, what's this about?"

Harry said, "Get up, Vinnie. Don't fuck me around anymore."

"I wanna get dressed."

"Make it quick."

Vinnie hesitated, then rose clumsily to his feet, using the blanket to cover his crotch, and uncovering the girl, who shrieked and cursed him. Vinnie kicked out at her and told her to shut the fuck up, exposing himself in the process.

Vinnie went into the corner and put on jeans, a T-shirt, and boots, and Harry then cuffed him and led him out.

Bello put them in cells in the Fifth Precinct and read them their rights. Neither asked for a lawyer. He talked to Vinnie a while, but Vinnie had regained some of his bravado and was uncooperative. That didn't matter. It was Eric Ritter who was going to crack. Ritter's toughness went about as deep as his many tattoos. Harry explained to him that he was going to do time, but the kind of time—where and how long—depended on whether he cooperated or not. He pointed out the various things that might happen to a skinny white boy in Attica after hours, especially one who had a big iron cross and swastika tattooed on his chest. He asked Eric to think about fifteen years of that.

In the afternoon, Marlene came down to the precinct. "How's it going? I see you're still in one piece."

Harry said, "The Monkey's about ready to go."

"Get a stenographer." Marlene had decided that she wasn't going to prosecute the homicide. She hadn't the time; one of Karp's people could do it. But she wanted to take the initial Q. & A. to round out her investigation. And she wanted to get a crack at Vinnie.

They went with a police stenographer to the interrogation room, where Eric Ritter was sitting. He seemed startled when Marlene walked in and sat down across from him. She introduced herself, explained what was happening, identified everyone for the steno, and offered to provide Ritter an attorney.

He said, "I don't need no lawyer. I didn't do nothin'."

"Okay, Eric, let's start with what happened on the night of March 13, this year. You were sitting with some of your friends on the stoop at 525 Fifth Street."

"Yeah. We like saw this chick walking down the street, toward us. And Vinnie, he goes—"

"Excuse me, this is Vincent Boguluso?"

"Yeah, Vinnie the Guinea. So Vinnie, he goes, 'I'm gonna fuck that.' So we all, we go, 'The fuck you are,' and like saying he doesn't have the balls and all. So when she comes by, he grabs her and drags her into the place."

"What happened then?"

"Well, he gets her in the apartment; he's got her in this choke hold, and she musta passed out or something. We all go in there to see what he's gonna do.

"We're all crowded in the door of Vinnie's room. I was, like, in the back. Vinnie was pissed everybody wanted to watch. Even the bitches. Evelyn, she was yelling at Vinnie, and he raps her a couple and slams the door."

"Who's Evelyn?"

"Evelyn. Vinnie's main squeeze. Or was. That's why she took the stuff and split. She was fuckin' pissed. Drunk too, or stoned, or she never woulda done it."

"This is the woman who was beaten up last week?"

Ritter giggled. "Yeah. She took the chick's bag offa the street. Fuckin' bitch sent Vinnie a postcard from Disneyland. He went fuckin' crazy, man. About the credit card. And the ticket. Then the crazy bitch comes back, if you can believe that."

"Okay, let's go back to the night of the thirteenth. Vinnie's in the room with the woman he abducted. What happened then?"

"Well, after a while he comes out and asks if anybody wants sloppy seconds. He had her tied down by then. He stuffed his shorts in her mouth. So, like, everybody did her."

"Including you?"

A pause. "Yeah, well, everybody was in on it."

"Then what?"

"Um, Vinnie was getting into the wine pretty good by then. This was a couple hours later. So he goes, 'Hey, let's fuckin' throw the cunt off the roof.' So he did."

"All alone?"

"Yeah, well, I think Duane helped him out. I don't remember that part too good. I was wasted myself."

"That's Duane Womrath you're referring to, right? Do you know where we could find him?"

Shrug. "He's around. I heard he was shackin' up with some chick over on C."

"Right. Up on the roof. Vinnie and Duane take the woman up there. Was there anyone else around?"

A sideways look. "Yeah, we was all up there."

"You all watched him do it?"

"Yeah, I guess."

"And she was alive at the time?"

"I guess. She was pretty beat up. But she was movin' when he dropped her over that little wall they got up there. Then Vinnie and

Duane and some guys went out on the fire escape and pissed down on the street, seeing could they hit her or not."

A few more questions about the beating of the biker woman, which Ritter had also observed at close range, and the interview was over. He was taken back to the cells, and Vinnie Boguluso was brought in. Marlene did the usual formalities in a hurried monotone. She was not that interested in Boguluso anymore. She had him.

Vinnie looked at Harry Bello and then looked quickly away. He looked at Marlene and grinned. He had large, widely spaced greenish-yellow teeth. Marlene couldn't help thinking about the bite marks on the two victims and what an easy job it would be to present a convincing match-up as evidence. She thought about this in preference to thinking about what the last hours of Gabrielle Avanian had been like.

"What the fuck you lookin' at, cunt?"

Marlene saw Harry start to move and held up her hand, shouting, "No, Harry!"

The stenographer looked up from her machine, startled. "Do you want that in?"

"No," said Marlene, "and I think you can go now. Tell them we're done with him. Unless Vinnie wants to make a statement. Do you want to make a statement, Vinnie? Like about how you kidnapped, raped, tortured, and killed Gabrielle Avanian on the night of March 13 at 525 East Fifth Street?"

"I ain't done nothin' and I ain't gonna say nothin'."

The stenographer left. Marlene said, "That's too bad, because your buddy Eric gave us an earful. According to him, it was your show from start to finish."

"He's a lyin' fuck, then."

Marlene gathered up her files and rose. Two big cops appeared at the door. "Okay, Harry, back to the pens with this one. Charges are murder two, rape one, assault one, kidnapping, on the Avanian. We'll charge him later on the girlfriend."

She looked Vinnie in the eye and took a deep breath. He was smirking at her. "You're gonna die in prison, Vinnie," she said matter-of-factly. "You will never, ever walk on the street again, ride a motorcycle, touch a woman, have a beer. What're you, thirty? You could live another forty years. That's almost sixteen thousand days. And that's because I'm gonna make sure you never get out. Every parole hearing you get, until you're dead or I'm dead, I'm gonna be up there telling them exactly how Gabrielle Avanian died."

Vinnie stood up quickly, his face pale. Bello and the two cops tensed. "Fuck you, cunt!" he screamed. Then he gripped his crotch and thrust his hips back and forth. "I'll get you, bitch. I'll fuck you in half, you dried-up cunt!"

The cops moved forward and grabbed him. Foamy spittle flecked his lips as he continued to roar vengeful obscenities.

In the uproar it was remarkable that Harry's voice could be heard clearly. He said, "Marlene, the reason he talks that way is that he has a very, very tiny little dick."

Marlene snorted, then giggled, then burst out in a belly laugh, helplessly. "No kidding, Harry? How little?" she snorted. The cops were laughing too, even as they cuffed the struggling and roaring Vinnie.

Bello held up his thumb and index finger, separated by an inch and a half. Everyone laughed some more, except Vinnie.

They dragged him away. He didn't seem to be fighting that hard, considering how big he was. He seemed to have lost considerable steam. Marlene watched him go and said to Harry, "It's funny. He's probably going to do just fine in Attica. He'll have a little gang, and respect, and plenty of terrified skinny kids to rape and torture. Three hots and a cot. Drugs. It doesn't seem fair. What seems fair is if we just took him out right now, this minute, to an air shaft full of rotting garbage and rats and just shot him in the head and left him there for the dogs and the rats." She shuddered. "Christ, what am I saying?"

"It could be arranged," said Harry.

She gave him a sharp look and then slapped his sleeve playfully. "You old thing! You're so bad for me, Harry. You trigger all my worst Sicilian instincts."

"Go for coffee?"

"No, thanks, I need to get back to Centre Street and wind this up and then pick up Lucy—and then!—I want a long, slow, hot bath. Not that I'll probably get one until fucking midnight."

Karp limped on his crutches down a dank hallway in the Tombs. The Manhattan House of Detention, to give it its official name, is attached to the Criminal Courts; it is essentially the same building, joined by many corridors and passageways, so that the accused can be expeditiously transferred from cell to court and back again.

Karp was going to take a shower in the guards' locker room. He did so every evening after work, after first wrapping his cast carefully in a dry-cleaning bag. Then he hung his suit and shirt and tie on a hanger and put his shoes in a sports bag and dressed in sweatshirt and sweatpants and one sneaker and clumped back to his office, gripping the hook of the hanger in his teeth and the strap of the bag by a thumb.

He looked and felt ridiculous. It was a stupid idea, living in his office, but having decided on it, he felt bound to continue. It was only another couple of weeks until the trial.

He took his shower, alone in the steamy room. The shower was used only when shifts changed, and Karp was careful not to use it at those times. He was just pulling on his sweatpants, sitting on a locker room bench, when he heard a clanking sound behind him.

It was one of the trustees on the clean-up crew. Karp pulled up his pants and knotted the cord. He slipped into his sneaker and got his crutches under his arms. When he tried to stand, one of his crutches slipped on a wet spot and skittered away across the floor. Karp sat back down on the bench heavily, cursing.

The trustee left his bucket and got the crutch and brought it over to Karp. He looked up, and his smile froze on his face. It was Hosie Russell.

Karp cleared his throat and said, "Thanks."

Russell nodded. It was silent for a while there in the locker

ROBERT K. TANENBAUM

room, except from the gurgle of water in pipes and, far off, the continuous murmur of thousands of confined men.

Russell wasn't wearing his glasses. He was dressed in an orange jail uniform with TRUSTEE stenciled across the chest and back. Karp wondered for a moment why they had let Russell be a trustee, and then it struck him that no one was better suited than this man, who had spent two-thirds of his adult life behind bars, who understood the routines of jail and prison perfectly, who had never given his various warders a lick of trouble.

Russell broke the silence. "You got a cigarette?"

"No, I don't smoke." Then, to his own surprise, he added, "I could bring you some. I'm here every night about this time."

12

"ROLAND," SAID KARP THE NEXT MORNING, "EVEN YOU HAVE TO AD-
mit that this U.N. thing is looking less and less like a terrorist
crime." They were in Karp's office, trying to have a professional
conversation about late developments connected to *Tomasian*. They
were doing fairly well at it, considering. Karp was snappish and
Hrcany was sulky, but they were avoiding actual violence.

"Why? I don't see how all this shit that you and Nancy Drew
have dredged up affects the basic case against Tomasian in the slight-
est."

"Roland, it's the context. It's reasonable doubt," explained Karp
wearily. "Look, let's review the bidding here. First, we find out that
Gabrielle Avanian was killed the night of the murder day in a random act. That shuts down the theory that she was involved in some
kind of Armenian plot."

"She was. Tomasian admits it."

"What?"

"When we went in there and told him his girlfriend was dead, he said she'd been going out to northern California to raise money for the cause. A lot of Armenians around there."

"What 'cause'?"

"How do I know?" Hrcany replied in a tone of annoyance. "Some business connected with his secret army. He didn't expand on it, and I didn't press him." -

"How did he take his girl getting killed?" Karp asked.

"Pretty broken up. Of course, it could've been because there went his alibi."

"In any case," Karp continued, "you're still looking for the other guy on the hit, who seems to have vanished into thin air. That's another weakness. You assumed Tomasian would crack in jail and give up his partner, but he hasn't. That makes me think he didn't have one, because he wasn't there. And a jury will too. No, wait, let me finish.

"There's still the money. The Turk from the U.N. says it was a slush fund to buy back antiquities. But Rodriguez, the art cop, says the Turks aren't likely to do that, and he never heard of Ersoy buying art on the shady market.

"Finally, we know there's a connection between Ersoy and Kerbussyan. Ersoy called him from his office in the U.N. mission a whole bunch during the month before he was killed. That's a connection we haven't explained, and it's one that Kerbussyan is anxious to keep quiet. He was lying about not knowing about Ersoy's money."

"How do you know that?" Hrcany challenged.

"I just know. Also, I'd like to know why two wise guys are talking about Turks in relation to an airport theft operation."

Hrcany shook his head in mock rue. "I don't know, Butch. I think hanging around with Marlene is starting to soften your brain. None of this has anything to do with the case. Focus on the case! Tomasian's car, Tomasian's jacket, Tomasian's threats against the Turks, Tomasian's gun collection. That's the case. Who the fuck cares the vic called another Armenian? He could've called the Pope too.

"Same with the money. There's no evidence the money had any goddamn thing to do with the crime. Remember evidence? You used to think it was pretty important. Hey, here's an explanation. The Turk's into art, Kerbussyan's into art. They discuss, they trade. Could be, right? It don't matter if it is or isn't. It doesn't affect the case."

"The case sucks, Roland. The D.'ll blow you away."

"Wanna bet?"

There was a beat when everything stopped except the whirling in Karp's brain, and then he said, "Yeah, I do; five grand says Aram Tomasian never goes down for killing Mehmet Ersoy."

Hrcany snorted in amazement. "You're kidding."

"The fuck I am." Karp scribbled on a piece of yellow bond and whipped the page across the table to Hrcany. He had written, "I owe Roland Hrcany $5,000 if and when Aram Tomasian is convicted of the murder of Mehmet Ersoy," and signed and dated it below.

Hrcany read the thing and looked narrowly at Karp, his eyes pinpricks of gas-flame-colored light in their deep sockets. "You fucker," he said, "you know something."

Karp raised his hand in oath-taking position. "I swear, Roland. You know absolutely everything I do, just like we agreed, the whole truth, so help me God."

"Then how the hell can you bet five grand?" said Hrcany, his voice strained. "You don't have that kind of money."

"No, but you do, which is why I won't mind taking it off you. You jumped for this guy because you have the killer instinct, which is good, but you also have a hard time arguing against yourself, asking the questions the defense is going to ask, trying to wreck your own case. When the great Roland has decided you're gonna take the fall, you better take the fall.

"But Tomasian's not gonna take the fall, Roland. Because he didn't do it. As for how I know: I know cause I *know.* I can smell when a case is right and when it's not. Because I'm the best, Roland, and you're the second best. Now put up or shut up."

Roland's face went brick red, and the muscles of his jaw popped up like immies. He scratched an opposite-bet IOU on the bottom

half of the sheet, tore it across, shoved it over to Karp, and walked
out of the office without another word.

"You did what?" shrieked Marlene.

"It's okay, Marlene. It'll be fine." Karp calmly took another bite
of the sausage and pepper sandwich she had brought him from the
cancer wagons.

Marlene shoved the plastic spoon into her yogurt cup and
slammed the cup down on the desk. Bits of Dannon spattered an af-
fidavit.

"What do you mean, it'll be all right?" she said, her voice
shrill. "How could you have done something so moronic? And without telling me? How could you take a risk like that while we're trying to buy the loft and pay for your operation? Besides, it's unethical!
Two prosecutors betting on the outcome of a homicide case! If it got
out, you could be disbarred, the both of you. You have a piece of
pepper on your chin."

Karp dabbed himself with the flimsy paper napkin. "It won't
get out. Roland'll pay up and contract instant amnesia. You think he
wants anyone knowing I skunked him? And we won't tell. So there's
no problem."

"There is one problem, Einstein. Tomasian could go down for
it, despite everything."

"No way. Because we are going to find and convict the actual
killers."

"You're that confident?"

"Of course." He grinned at her. "I have you, don't I? You're always accusing me of not having confidence in you or your ideas. You
were the one who first sniffed out it wasn't Tomasian, you got that
stuff from the U.N. guy, and you're going to find who did do it. I'm
a cripple. You have to grab the banner from my failing hands."

She stared at him, her face flashing a series of emotions. "You're
such a rat. Only you would've turned us working together into a ma-
cho game with Roland."

Karp laughed and looked skyward. "Dear God, what do they want?"

Eventually she laughed, too. "Okay, wiseass, what's our next move?"

"Follow the art. What deal went down between Kerbussyan and Ersoy? And find out about the art frauds. It's got to be that. Somebody killed him because he was about to blow a scam. That, or because of some pricey trinket that got misplaced or ripped off."

Marlene followed the art. She gathered up the notes she had made at the U.N. and the other materials from the case and went to visit V.T. Newbury. His cubicle was on the eighth floor in Fraud, another typical assistant district attorney's tiny veal-fattening pen, although V.T. had made some improvements. He had his own furniture: a Sheraton-style desk, a Tiffany desk lamp in mauve and cream glass, a worn but genuine oriental on the floor, a signed (real) Matisse print, and a fake (but pretty) Utrillo street scene on the wall.

"V.T.," she said, sliding into the cane rocker he kept in his office for visitors, "let's talk about art. Tell me things."

V.T. looked up from a catalogue raisonné he was studying.

"Post-modernism is dead, assuming there ever was such a thing."

"Not like that. About what you and Rodriguez are doing. The fakes."

"Oh, that. That's going nowhere. As I recall Ramon telling you at Sokoloff's, art fraud is a hard thing to demonstrate. The victims are embarrassed, so they take their lumps without complaining. If they do complain, the dealer smiles and buys the stuff back, and the next day it's crated and on a plane to Taiwan or Brazil. They just sell it again. You can't touch the dealer; he just does a Bogart."

"Pardon?"

"Like Bogart in *Casablanca*. When Claude Rains asks him why he came to Casablanca, he says, 'I came for the waters. For my health.' And then Rains says, 'But there are no waters in Casablanca. Casablanca is in the desert.' And Bogart says, 'I was misinformed.'

The dealer has his provenance and his opinion from some art school guru he keeps on retainer. So he's cool. The only way to nail them is if you have solid evidence that they knew the art was fake, like if they actually commissioned some SoHo hack to whip out a Cezanne. Then it is prima facie scheme to defraud, a Class E. Or if we have evidence that the art was actually stolen, and the dealer knew about it. Even then it's dicey. This is not a guy with fifty hot TVs in the back room. Except if they actually arranged the theft, which is incredibly rare, they'd usually plead down to Criminal Possession Five, misdemeanor level."

"So what's the point? Of what Rodriguez and you are doing?" Marlene asked.

"The point is the rings. Art fraud nowadays isn't a solo operation. You don't have many guys like Van Meegheren faking Vermeers on his own anymore. It's an international operation involving groups of dozens of people for each major scam. It's Big Con. So Rodriguez works very tight with Interpol and the people who do the same kind of work he does in the major art centers. The idea is to understand the con and roll up the whole ring at once—craftsmen, dealers, middlemen, and all, close down the workshops and grab the money. That's the most important thing."

"This is where you come in," Marlene observed.

V.T. was an expert, perhaps the reigning expert in New York at that time, on how people disposed of ill-gotten gains. He smiled and made a deprecating gesture. "That, and my magisterial knowledge of the quattrocento. But I'm drawing a blank on this one. Ramon is much vexed."

"How come?"

"We don't know the seller, for one thing. Sokoloff regards it as a trade secret, and we can't demonstrate knowing fraud on his part, so we can't pressure him to give it up. The only thing he'll say is that the stuff comes from Turkey. That's the other problem. The Turkish authorities are being less than fully cooperative."

"Because they don't care about antiquities? Like Rodriguez said?"

V.T. pursed his lips and cocked his head: an expression of polite disagreement. "Hmm. As to that. I think there are various factions involved. I think that probably some Turks don't care, or would like to forget the previous inhabitants of Anatolia, just as Ramon says. I think others, when they bother to think about it at all, resent the looting of their country. After all, the stuff is there; it belongs to them now, whoever made it. I'm not a Sioux, but if a bunch of Turks arrived and started to loot Indian artifacts, I might get upset. And then there are the people who just see a buck to be made. Tourism et cetera."

"But you do think it's at least plausible that this guy Ersoy was buying stolen artifacts back for Turkey."

"Plausible. Yes, at least plausible."

Marlene did not particularly want to hear this. She wanted Ersoy to be scamming in some way, but she knew she wanted it, and so she was careful not to let jell in her mind a dependence on that view of things.

"V.T., I think you should check on some stuff for me and Butch. It's a long story. Have you got a minute?"

"Yes, it's a life of leisure here at Fraud. Shoot."

Marlene gave him a brief history of the investigation into the killing of Mehmet Ersoy, including what she and Harry Bello had learned at the Turkish mission. Shortly after she began, V.T. got out a pad and started to take notes.

"This is really fascinating, Marlene," he said when she had finished. "Especially this business about the brother in Turkey. The archaeologist. A family business maybe. You said there were some letters from the brother. Could I take a look at those in translation?"

"Sure, I'll get them for you. You think it's something?"

"Yeah, it has the right odor. What you need in these scams, for authenticity, is a credible story that you have access to good stuff, either a theft from a museum or a discovery. Alfredo Kappa, for example."

"Who was . . . ?"

"This was three, four years back. Kappa let it be known on the

Rome market that he had discovered an Etruscan grave site and was keeping it hidden from the art authorities. He moved a hundred and eighty works in a single week, all fakes, of course. Knowing that they might get something that nobody else has is irresistible to a certain class of collectors. The illegality just adds some spice. In this case, though, we have a quasi-legit dealer moving the stuff openly—some of it, anyway."

"There could be more?"

"I'd count on it. The open market just heats up the bidding. You go to the guy who lost out on the Lydian brooch and hint that there's another available off the books."

"Which is a fake."

"Doubtless."

"So Rodriguez was right? Sokoloff's stuff is phony?"

V.T. made his lip-pursing gesture again. "I'm not so sure. The Roslin painting is real enough. What I smell is something really large. A coup. You move some genuine stuff, museum quality. You make a big deal about how important the pieces are, scholars write articles, the *Times* does a spread. You focus attention, get the serious money interested, spread the story, line up the customers, sell your fakes, and you're gone."

Marlene thought about this for a moment, chewing her lip. "Okay, let's go ahead on Butch's supposition. Ersoy was dealing with Kerbussyan. Kerbussyan buys art . . . uh-oh."

V.T. grinned. "Ah, yes. It just struck me too."

Marlene rocked forward and rapped her knuckles on the desk. "Crap! Ersoy sells Kerbussyan fakes, and he finds out and aces him. Christ, it wouldn't take much to get him to shoot a Turk. Damn! It could be we've gone around in a big circle for nothing."

"You mean it might actually be Tomasian. Kerbussyan tries to recover Armenian national treasures, gets cheated by the hated Turk, and sends the Secret Army out for revenge. Yes, there's that, but in that case you'd also want to bring in the old man too. Okay, put that aside for a minute, and look at the other alternative. Let's say thieves fell out. Who would Ersoy be connected with on this scam?"

Marlene paged through her notes. "Ahmet Djelal. Ersoy spent a lot of time with him. And he was in charge of security at the mission. And he's got Ersoy's desk calendar."

"It's worth checking."

"Yeah. Okay, I'll send Harry around. What else?"

"Well, from my end, I'll start pulling the wires on the brother, and you get me those letters. We'll see if his bank account is consistent with the salary of a humble archaeologist."

Marlene sighed. She was oppressed by the idea that the Armenians were in fact involved with the murder. "I guess I should go tackle Kerbussyan. I don't see how it's going to do any good. I mean, why the hell should he talk to me? Butch's been at him already, so have the police, and we haven't got anything new to wave in his face."

"Oh, I wouldn't see Kerbussyan yet," said V.T., a sly tone creeping in.

"Oh?"

"No. I think you should talk to Sokoloff first."

"Why? We have nothing on him either."

"Yes, but he doesn't know that. Cast some broad hints. The last thing he wants is to be involved in a murder investigation, the old smoothie. If he's not actually the middle man between Ersoy and Kerbussyan on any art dealings they may have had, I guarantee you he knows who sold what to whom. And if it was real."

She saw Sokoloff the next day in the office above his gallery. She went alone. Harry was off on bureau business, talking to people who might know whether some guy in Washington Heights had been raping his nine-year-old stepdaughter. She had told him about Djelal, and he had said he would look into it. She was at least mildly guilty about using Harry to investigate something outside her official (and his official) purview, essentially as a favor to her husband. The other women in the office were getting miffed about it too, although they were careful not to show it.

Harry wouldn't work directly for them in any case; they had to go through Marlene to get him to do anything. Since they were all ambitious women with substantial egos and a certain quickness to take offense at the slights that came daily from what was still virtually an all-boy environment, this did not add to the joy of working in the Rape Bureau. They called Harry, behind his back, "the Dobe"—Marlene's Doberman pinscher.

So she sat uneasily on Sokoloff's nearly real Louis Quinze settee, making small talk with its charming owner, in his charming, exquisitely decorated office, feeling vaguely blue. She had not yet told him why she had come, but he had assumed that she was working the fraud thing with Rodriguez and she had not contradicted this.

"You sell a lot to Sarkis Kerbussyan, don't you?" she asked.

"Yes, I've placed a number of very fine pieces with Sarkis over the years."

Placed. Like abandoned children in foster homes, but with infinitely more concern.

"Armenian artworks, right?"

"By and large. Sarkis has one of the largest private collections of Armenian art, both ancient and medieval. Why do you ask?"

Marlene ignored this question. "Would you say he's a connoisseur? That he knows what he's doing?"

Sokoloff nodded and smiled. "Oh, yes. He has a good eye. There is still a little of the rug merchant in him."

"Is it likely that he would be taken in by fakes, if they were offered?"

The temperature of Sokoloff's smile dropped a few degrees. "Fakes. Well, dear lady, we can all be taken in by clever fakes. Not everything can be analyzed in the laboratory. If we took the time to do so for every item, the art business would collapse. We all have to rely on taste and provenance and the integrity of a reputable dealer. So I can't really tell you if any fakes have been unloaded on Mr. Kerbussyan. Certainly he never got one from me. Knowingly, that is."

Marlene looked at him, waiting. After a brief silence he took a deep breath through his fleshy nose and continued.

"On the other hand, the specialist collector is perhaps more susceptible to that sort of thing than the general collector, odd as it may seem."

"Why is that?"

"Because the specialist is interested in the specialty, not necessarily in the aesthetic or technical qualities of the art itself. Despite his greater familiarity with his narrow field, his desire for possession may overcome his prudence. For example, back in the mid-sixties there was an enormous surge in the market for Judaica. Perhaps it was the Six-Day War, who knows—a stimulus for Jewish patriotism. In any case, many wealthy American and European Jews were willing to pay anything for old synagogue silver, the *rimanim,* the little bells and decorations hung from the Torahs, North African Hanukkah lamps, silver menorahs, and such things. Enamel betrothal rings with Hebrew inscriptions.

"And, of course, the market responded. There was a cottage industry digging out old tea caddies and carving them with Hebrew to make *ethrog,* the little boxes to place matzoh in, and converting Victorian silver chalices into medieval kiddush cups. Probably half the forgers in Italy were studying Hebrew.

"What's interesting is that there were very few complaints about all this. Only the historians were affronted. The customers were delighted, mostly. And you have to wonder who got hurt. Some fakes are fine art in themselves. Vlaminck painted a fake Cezanne, which Cezanne thought was a very nice painting. Picasso owned a fake Miro. Funny, heh?" He laughed, to show what funny was.

"So, the point is," he concluded, "Sarkis and some others like him want Armenian, they'll get Armenian. Real or fake."

"I see. Do you think that a Turkish diplomat named Mehmet Ersoy might have sold things to Kerbussyan? Real or fake."

The art dealer raised an eyebrow. His smile was now purely formal, a faint upward tug of his thickish lips. He said, "Miss, ah, Ciampi, is it? Perhaps it would save time for both of us if you simply told me what you are here for."

"You recognize the name?"

He nodded. "The man who was shot. At the United Nations?"

"The way you say that, Mr. Sokoloff, suggests to me that you knew Ersoy's name even before he was shot," Marlene said, and then, to forestall the response she saw building in the man's face, "No, you asked why I was here. Okay, I'm going to tell you, frankly. I'm not interested in art fraud per se. What I'm interested in is who killed Mehmet Ersoy and why."

"But I thought—"

"Yes, we have a suspect, but we have reason to believe that whether or not he actually did it, the reason had nothing to do with political terrorism. The reason Mehmet Ersoy was killed involved the sale, or theft, or forgery, of objects of art. Which is why I want you to tell me everything you know about Ersoy, about his dealings in the art world, and about his relationship with Sarkis Kerbussyan."

She was looking directly at Sokoloff as she spoke, and she imagined that she could see the calculations going on behind his dark eyes. She added, "I should also tell you that I have no reason to believe that you have been personally involved in any of this, and you are not at this point the subject of any investigation. However, you *are* obliged to give me any information that you have; failure to do so is called hindering prosecution, and is itself a felony."

The words sounded absurdly formal in Marlene's own ears, but she could see that Sokoloff took them seriously. V.T. had been right; the art dealer did not want to be mixed up in anything to do with a murder. He chewed on his lower lip, and dropped his eyes, and sighed—a picture of surrender that Marlene hoped was not a complete dramatization.

"Well. You're a forceful young woman, Miss Ciampi. Of course, I will help you in any way that I can. You will forgive my not being forthcoming at first. There is, ah . . . a certain confidentiality associated with my business, which I would not have liked to breach without good cause. In any case . . . I did know Mehmet Ersoy, from, say, two years ago. Naturally we met. He was cultural attaché at the mission, I am an antiquities dealer, much of my business is with goods originating in Asia Minor, so of course we had much to discuss.

"Then—I forgot how it came up—he asked if I would be interested in handling some items, some antiquities, on the New York market. His brother is an archaeologist and a museum director in Turkey. I had no problem with that. His paper was in good order. He said these pieces were being de-accessioned from Turkish museums, and he was credentialed as agent.

"The pieces arrived, beginning last November. I remember a small figurine of Tiamat from Pergamum, in ivory, some Ionian red-figure work, some jewelry. A beautiful tetradrachm of Tigranes the Great. Small but very high quality. I had no trouble selling them. Kerbussyan, of course, snatched up the tetradrachm." Marlene looked blank. "An ancient Armenian coin," he explained.

"We do some more business. The pieces get better and better. This is all private sales, by the way. He doesn't want an auction or a gallery show, even though I tell him he can do much better than he can selling privately. About six months ago, he stops selling to me. I think I half expected it."

"Why is that?"

Sokoloff shrugged and, with a watery smile, replied. "I've seen it before. A seller comes to town. Puts a few pieces with you. You do okay by him. Everyone's happy. Then, bang, you find he's all of a sudden the competition. He knows who your best customers are. They've bought his things. He approaches them—let's do a deal, minus Sokoloff's commission—who needs him?"

"What do you do when that happens?" Marlene asked. "Or, did you do anything in this case?"

"What can I do? They're both free agents. But, of course, dealing with someone on the side like that exposes the customer to certain risks, which he doesn't have when he buys from me."

"Like fraud?"

"Like fraud. Even so, I was surprised when Kerbussyan started dealing directly with Ersoy. Sarkis, I told you already, is a maniac for Armenian pieces. I hear things, on the street, in the Armenian community. You didn't know? Yeah, I'm an Armenian, too; half—my mother, God rest her. She got out of Zeitun just before the big attack

in 1915. Her parents sent her east. She kept moving, one step ahead
of the Kemalists, and ended up in what became Soviet Armenia during the civil war. She met my father there, and they got to Odessa,
where I was born, and then out in 1925. What a life! So, yes, I've
known Sarkis for years. And I'm hurt; it's not like him to take bread
out of my mouth for no reason. So I invite him. We meet. At the
Russian Tea Room, in fact. I ask him what's going on, he's buying
direct from the Turks. It's like a joke. I know how he feels about the
Turks, right? He apologizes. Then he tells me a story." Sokoloff
paused and shook his head sadly. "A crazy story. He says, 'Stephan,
Ersoy has got the mask. The *Suurp Timag.*"

"I'm sorry, the what. . . ?"

"The Holy Mask of St. Gregory the Illuminator," said Sokoloff,
a tone of awe creeping into his normally dry voice. Marlene remembered the conversation she'd had with Rodriguez and Roslin's painting of the internment of the saint.

"Which is what, exactly?" she asked.

"It's a myth," said Sokoloff. "A dream."

"But Kerbussyan believed it?"

"Yes, I'm afraid he did. He was obsessed with it, as both a
collector and an Armenian nationalist. When it was offered to him,
he suspended all disbelief. It's strange. Otherwise he's such a clever
man. I suppose we all have a weak spot . . ."

"But he must have seen some evidence."

"He said a photo. In color. I tried to tell him it was a plot, a
forgery racket. But he went right ahead."

"He actually bought it?"

Sokoloff's forehead wrinkled, as if under the press of an unpleasant memory. "I don't know what he did. When he saw I was scoff-
ing, he closed up. He can do that. A very proud man sometimes. We
haven't discussed the matter since then."

Marlene nodded and asked, "Mr. Sokoloff, in your opinion, if
Kerbussyan thought that Ersoy had defrauded him over something as
important as this mask, could he have arranged to have Ersoy murdered?"

A tight smile. "I suppose everyone is capable of murder under the right circumstances."

"Is that a yes?"

An inclination of the head, with tightly pressed lips.

"And would he have used Aram Tomasian to do it?"

Sokoloff's face broke into a smile. "My dear young lady, if you had a perfectly good hammer and you had to bang a nail in, would you bang it in with a Meissen vase instead? Believe me, if Sarkis wanted to kill someone, he has people to do it who could eat little Aram for breakfast. And you wouldn't have caught them either."

When Marlene returned to her office, there was a note on her desk saying that the district attorney wanted to see her immediately. Marlene said, "Shit!" in a high-pitched voice that provoked a burst of laughter in her office, grabbed a yellow pad, and headed for the elevator. As she rode up, she tried to think of any high-profile, newsworthy rape cases that might have engaged the interest of the D.A. She drew a blank. No politician's or big shot's daughters, no nice white girl raped by black beasts, no nice black girl raped by gangs of Nazis, no day-care scandals. Not this week.

Thus, she was curious and mildly apprehensive when she walked into the D.A.'s outer office and announced herself to the receptionist. This glittering person informed her that Mr. Bloom had been called away and that she should speak to Mr. Wharton instead.

Marlene's heart sank. Whatever it was would have nothing to do with her or with her bureau—not really. She felt a brief surge of resentment against her husband, which she quickly stifled. It wasn't fair, but it was a fact that anyone closely associated with Karp in the office came in for a share of harassment from Wharton, and it was now her turn.

Wharton was sitting behind his desk when she entered. Late afternoon sunlight from his two big windows glinted off his round glasses. He looked at her with his kewpie-doll's face drawn into its characteristic expression of mild distaste. He didn't ask her to sit, but she sat anyway, and steeled her jaw.

There was no point in small talk. Wharton said, "Henry Pinnett tells me you've been harassing the United Nations."

"Who's he?"

"The mayor's liaison with the U.N. He called Mr. Bloom this morning, and Mr. Bloom hit the roof."

"I haven't been harassing anyone."

"According to my information, you made a visit to the Turkish delegation to the U.N. last week, during which you misrepresented yourself and rifled through confidential files."

"I was conducting a legitimate interview as part of a murder investigation. There was no misrepresentation. The information I collected was freely given."

"A murder investigation?" said Wharton. "What the hell were you doing investigating a murder?"

His tone said he didn't really want an answer, so Marlene remained silent and worked on controlling her wise mouth, a technique she had brought to perfection during the eight years she had spent under the absolute domination of Sister Marie Augustine, compared to whom Conrad Wharton was the merest twit.

After an appropriate wait to inspire terror, Wharton said, "It has to stop. You are not to contact any U.N. official for any purpose without clearance from the D.A.'s office. Is that perfectly clear?"

Marlene said, "Yes, it's perfectly clear."

Wharton gave her a final dirty look and turned to pick up his phone. Marlene rose and walked out, much relieved. She had thought that she was going to be warned off Sarkis Kerbussyan too.

13

"SO I THINK WE SHOULD GO SEE KERBUSSYAN AGAIN," MARLENE SAID. "As soon as possible. Now, maybe."

Karp considered this. His wife had burst into his office and spilled out the whole exotic and confusing tale of her interview with Sokoloff.

"You like him for Ersoy, right?" Karp asked. "Kerbussyan."

"I think he's connected, sure. Whether I like him? I don't know."

"Umm . . ." Karp rolled his eyes.

"Yeah, I thought of that too, God forbid," she said quickly. "But Sokoloff said Tomasian was the last person Sarkis would've used, and that's supported by what Mr. K told you when you went to see him. Tomasian's a courier, not a shooter."

"So he must've used somebody else. What makes you think he'll be more forthcoming now than he was with me?"

"We know he lied. He said he didn't know anything about Ersoy's money, and I guarantee you it came right out of his own bank account. He dealt with the vic, for chrissake! So we got him anyway for obstructing. It's a lever."

Karp nodded. "Okay, I'll call." He called. And it turned out Mr. Kerbussyan would find some time around five.

Marlene went back to her office. Harry had left no messages, which worried her. She had sent him out again after Djelal, *before* she had been warned off the U.N., but she didn't think that detail would matter to Wharton if Djelal or the ambassador made a stink. It could be very bad indeed. She could lose the bureau.

In this mood she scrambled through paperwork and made herself generally unpleasant to her minions. Being the kind of minions they were, they were unpleasant back. Thus, she was in no mood for playtime when Jim Raney stuck his head in her door and flashed his patented charming Irish grin.

"Go away, Raney, I'm busy."

He slipped past the door and closed it behind him. "Go ahead, I'll just watch." He pulled a visitors' chair around so that it was touching Marlene's chair, and sat down in it, still grinning.

"Raney! Go away!"

He placed an arm across the back of her chair. "You seem tense," he said. "I hear the marriage is breaking up. You're probably not getting much lately. You ready for an indecent proposal from a deserving Irish lad?"

"The marriage is not breaking up," she said snippily, suppressing a giggle. Raney had that effect on her, the same effect as the strutting neighborhood swains of her teen years—infuriating but crudely seductive at the same time.

"Oh, yeah? How come I hear he moved out?"

"He had an operation on his knee; he can't climb our stairs."

"A good story. Stick to it. On the other hand, I'd figure out how to climb those stairs with two busted legs, if you were at the top of them." This last was whispered a half inch from her ear. His hand slipped down off the back of the chair to her neck.

Harry Bello walked in the door without knocking, as was his habit. There was a moment of frozen embarrassment. Marlene shot to her feet, knocking back her chair with a clatter.

Bello said, "You're busy."

"No, Harry, come in," she answered in a voice that cracked. "Um, Harry, you know Jim Raney. Raney, Harry Bello."

Raney stood up too. He seemed amused. "Yeah, Harry Bello. I heard you brought in Vinnie the Guinea by yourself. Very impressive."

Harry said in a flat voice, "Jim Raney. I hear you shot four guys in the head in four seconds. Very impressive."

Raney flushed, and his jaws stiffened. Another moment of strained silence, which Marlene broke by saying breezily, "Jim was just leaving."

"Yeah," said Raney, his grin returning. "I just came by to invite you to the big touch football game this weekend. Bring the family. Two at the Sheep Meadow, rain or shine. Be there or be square. I could pick you up."

"Do that. I wouldn't miss it," said Marlene. Raney left.

"Don't you dare look at me like that," said Marlene. "It's just the way he is. He saved my life once."

Harry shrugged and sat down like a cat. He said, "He's got a Mercedes 300SL."

"Who, Raney? No, he doesn't . . . oh, you mean Djelal. Did you talk to him?"

"No, just checked him out. Nice condo in the fifties too. They must pay pretty good, the U.N."

"I love it! This is looking a lot better. I also love it you didn't roust him." She explained Wharton's orders about bothering the U.N., and told him what she had learned at Sokoloff's.

"Butch and I are going to see Kerbussyan this afternoon—oh, crap! Look, Harry, could you do me a terrific favor and pick up Lucy at day-care and take her home? I'll give you my key."

"No problem," said Harry, a little pale light starting up in the dead of his eyes.

After Harry left, Marlene called Ray Guma, who, as it turned out, had caught the homicide prosecution of Vinnie Boguluso.

"What do you think, Goom? Of the case, I mean."

"Hey, it's locked. Any time you want to do all the work up front, let me know. I could use a break."

"He'll go for the top count?"

"Rest assured. The little scumbag's testimony and the toothmarks, and the Perez woman—it's a lock. Grand jury this week, no problems. We go to pretrial probably the week after, but I can't see the defense coming up with anything. The warrants're good. So's the evidence."

"Have you talked to him?"

Guma chuckled. "Yeah. He's a fuckin' piece of work, Vinnie. You know, he's really got a thing for you, Champ. I think you pissed him off. I think you insulted his manhood."

"I'll try to live with it. Any word on the third guy, Duane?"

"No, we got the usual APB out on him, but I'm not holding my breath. He got any sense, he's in fuckin' Texas, or someplace where there's more Duanes to blend in with."

"Yeah, really. Okay, let me know how it goes . . ."

"Hey, one other thing, you gonna see Butch the next coupla hours?"

"Yeah, I'm going out with him right now on something. Why?"

"Just tell him to get with me. I got some more stuff about Turks on my wire into Joey Castles. He was interested the other day."

"Turks?" she asked. "What's a mob guy doing with Turks?"

"Hey, the fuck I know. Joey called Ready Eddie Scoli, you know, the fence? Handles heavy theft? He says the Turk got the product and they're getting ready to process it. I thought, fuck, it sounds like scag—you know? Process? But Eddie doesn't do scag—he's into gems, metals, furs. So tell Butch it looks more like my theory that the Turk is this Brooklyn guy, Minzone. Minzone I could see getting hold of a shipment of dope. Maybe he's cutting it or something and Eddie's supposed to cover the financing, or maybe—"

"Hold it, Goom," she interrupted. "This is getting too complicated, and I got to meet a car like five minutes ago. I'll tell him to call you."

One of the D.A. squad cops drove Karp and Marlene up to the house in Riverdale, and they told him to wait. The door was opened not by the housemaid but by a burly, bushy-mustached man in an olive drab T-shirt and chinos who looked as if he had just put down his assault rifle. He gave them a severe look and led them through the paneled and carpeted hallways, stopping impatiently from time to time to let Karp, clumping along on his crutches, catch up.

He took them not to the study where Karp had originally interviewed Kerbussyan, but through a solarium full of huge houseplants and then through French doors to a small brick terrace overlooking the garden. There he left them. Karp collapsed gratefully into a white wicker armchair. Marlene walked out into the garden.

It was a lovely place, smelling of wet earth, crushed foliage, roses, and lavender. It sloped to the west, and from the terrace end one could see the river and the cliffs of the Palisades. She strolled down an aisle of roses, turned around the heavy green arch of a grape arbor, and came upon Sarkis Kerbussyan clipping grapes.

The old man was dressed in a white silk shirt and pale linen trousers, slightly stained with green but crisply pressed, and a black-banded straw hat.

He nodded formally. "Miss Ciampi, I believe," he said.

"Yes. How did you know?"

"One is informed. The Ashakians speak highly of you. And, of course, you made an impression on Stephan Sokoloff: a formidable woman, he said. Formidable and beautiful."

He finished his pruning, and placed his clippers and the cuttings in a small basket. "These are raisin grapes. Or sultanas, as they should be called. Raisins to me are still dried currants. These, you know, don't dry well in this climate, but I grow them anyway. My uncle had a whole vineyard full of them in Smyrna. Shall we return to the terrace?"

Civilized, thought Marlene. Not like interrogating Vinnie the Guinea, although she suspected that Sarkis Kerbussyan could eat any number of Vinnies like raisins. They sat in the wicker armchairs around a wicker and glass table. Coffee and little cakes appeared, brought by the silent housemaid. Kerbussyan talked to Marlene about the garden, and they watched the lush late-summer twilight gather over the dark trees.

Marlene could see Karp getting more irritable. He liked interrogations to take place in smelly, green-painted rooms. Finally he said, "Mr. Kerbussyan, this is all very nice, but you know we're not here to talk about your roses. We're investigating a homicide, one in which you're more involved than you led me to believe at our previous meeting."

"I? How involved, Mr. Karp?"

"You lied to me last time I was here. You said you didn't know anything about Mehmet Ersoy's box of cash. In fact, that was your cash he had, some of it, at least. You'd been buying art objects from him for months before he died."

"Buying art is not a crime," said Kerbussyan after a brief silence.

"No, but concealing evidence in a homicide investigation is. You remember last time I was here, we waltzed through some likely scenarios about why Ersoy was killed? Let me add one. A patriotic Armenian art collector starts buying Armenian art objects from a Turk whose brother is smuggling them out of Turkey. At first he buys them through an art dealer, but after a while the source is so good that he decides to do private deals. The Turk starts slipping him fakes. The Armenian gets pissed off and has the Turk shot. You like that one?"

"Mr. Karp, do you believe that I would employ Aram Tomasian, a child I have known all his life, as an assassin in an act of revenge?"

"It doesn't matter what I believe," said Karp sharply. "It's what a jury will believe. It explains Ersoy's money. Tomasian is linked to you. When it's presented, it'll be devastating."

Kerbussyan seemed not to hear this. He repeated, "But do *you* believe it?"

Marlene said, "I don't believe it."

The two men stared at her in astonishment. Karp opened his mouth to say something, but she pressed on. "This is what happened. Ersoy offered you items. Some of them were fakes. You bought them anyway. You knew they were fakes, but you didn't care, because you knew that Ersoy had something that you had to have and you thought that if you kept him on the line he'd eventually offer it to you. This whole thing is about the St. Gregory mask, isn't it, Mr. Kerbussyan? And that's why you're going to help us, to work with us, to find the killers. Because whoever killed Ersoy has the mask. That's why they killed him."

Karp could see from the stony look that passed briefly across the old man's face that Marlene's words had struck home. He recalled her mentioning something about a mask to him when she told him about her interview with Sokoloff, but he hadn't registered it as more than an oddity. Now it seemed to be central to the whole case. Karp had no idea how Marlene had just put all of it together, but he knew a fat opening when he saw one. He said, "Maybe you better tell us about this mask, Mr. Kerbussyan."

"It's not a myth, is it?" asked Marlene.

Kerbussyan studied both their faces before answering. "No, it is not. It exists."

"What is it?" asked Marlene. "Sokoloff mentioned that you had a line on it, but he didn't say much about it. Why is it so important?"

Kerbussyan took a deep breath and looked back at his garden, at the declining sun lighting the Palisades. Then he faced them again and said, "It is a long story. Everything to do with Armenia is a long story, but this is longer than most. You may not credit that the hand of the past can reach forward to kill a man in the streets of a modern city."

Marlene said, "A couple of years ago, a friend of mine, a cop, was blown to pieces because of something that happened in the fifteenth century in Serbia. So try me."

"Well, then," said Kerbussyan. "Ancient Armenia. A pagan kingdom caught between the declining power of Rome and the Persian Empire. In 224 A.D. a revolution in Persia overthrew the Artaxid dynasty and brought Artashir and the Sassanids to power. Khosrov, the king of Armenia, was related to the Artaxids, and he went to war against Persia. During this war a noble named Anak, who was loyal to the Sassanids, killed Khosrov, and the Persians took over the country. Anak himself was killed later.

"Two boys, the sons of Khosrov and Anak, were left fatherless by these events. They are close friends, nobles, raised at court. But they are separated. One, Trdat, son of King Khosrov, was taken to Roman territory as a ward of the imperial court. The emperor Diocletian was always interested in a royal pawn to use against the Persians. Anak's son, Krikor, was sent to Caesaria, in Palestine, where he came under the influence of the bishop and was raised as a Christian. He becomes a priest.

"Time passes. Trdat is now a famous warrior. He does great service for the emperor, saving his life, and as a reward Diocletian gives him military support. Trdat raises the Armenian barons, and the Persians are thrown out. The young man is crowned in Vagharshapat as Trdat III. Tiridates the Great, as he is known to the West.

"At about the same time, Krikor returns to Armenia to preach the word of God to his old friend. But Trdat now learns about the conspiracy of Anak. Krikor is the son of the man who killed his father. He has Krikor tortured and thrown into a deep pit to starve."

"Get to the mask," said Karp.

Kerbussyan smiled wanly. "Patience is essential to an understanding of Armenian affairs, Mr. Karp. Where was I? Yes, there was at this time in Nicomedia, where Diocletian reigned, a beautiful Armenian nun named Hrip'sime. The emperor desired her; she resisted and fled to Vagharshapat and the protection of Trdat. But Trdat was as lustful as his sponsor. He too attempted to rape Hrip'sime and when she fled from him, had her tracked down, tortured, and killed.

"After that, God cursed Trdat and sent him mad. The legend was that he turned into a wild boar. He was an animal for ten years. The king's sister, who was a secret Christian, had a dream in which Krikor rose from the grave and saved her brother. She had the pit investigated, and there was Krikor alive and well, a miracle.

"So, of course, Krikor cures King Trdat, who in his gratitude and repentance converts to Christianity. Krikor preaches to the Armenian nobility, a sermon that lasts for sixty days. The whole nation becomes Christian, the first nation to do so. Krikor becomes known to history as Krikor Lousavorchi, Gregory the Illuminator. This is a little after 300 A.D.

"St. Gregory, as I should call him now, now goes through the Armenian nation stamping out paganism. He dies old, mourned by the king and the people. On his deathbed a plaster mask of his face is made, and a casting is made from this, in gold. Gregory's bones are taken by monks to a secret place in the mountains. The mask becomes part of the treasure of the Catholicos in Ejmiatzin.

"Nearly two centuries pass. Rome falls; Byzantium rises as the second Rome. Byzantium is now Christian too, of course, but a different sort of Christian from the Armenians. I won't bother you with the theological details. Zeno becomes emperor of Byzantium. He is interested in reuniting the churches.

"At this time the body of Gregory is discovered by some shepherds, in a cave. Preserved, you see. Another miracle. The word spreads to Byzantium. The emperor naturally wishes to do something grand for the Armenian church. So he sends craftsmen, gold, and jewels to holy Ejmiatzin. They take the original mask, and they make it into the centerpiece of a great reliquary triptych. Solid gold, chased with silver, decorated with a thousand pearls and a thousand jewels, including the famous sapphires known as the Eyes of Cappadocia, offered from the Byzantine crown jewels by the devout empress Ariadne. These were placed in the eye sockets of the mask, over the actual eyes taken from the body of the saint. Thus was made what we call the *Suurp Timag*. The Holy Mask."

"What happened to it?" asked Marlene.

"For centuries it rested in the Holy City, in the great cathedral. It was brought out on the saint's day only, at which time, of course, it performed miracles. The Bagratid king Gagik brought it to his capital at Ani around the year 1000, and built a church to contain it, the church of St. Gregory.

"Ani fell to the Seljuk Turks in 1064. By that time many Armenian nobles had exchanged their lands for estates in southeastern Anatolia. There they founded the kingdom of Lesser Armenia, with its capital at Sis. The ecclesiastical treasures, including the Holy Mask, were removed to the see of the Cicilian Catholicos at Hromkla.

"In 1292, Hromkla fell to the Mamluks, and the church treasures were looted. The Holy Mask disappears from history. All assume it was taken with the other treasures by the Mamluks. But there is a curious note in the manuscript of Sir John Maundeville's *Travels into Great Armenia,* written in the middle of the fourteenth century. He describes a miraculous relic to be found in a castle near the port of Lajazzo on the Gulf of Alexandretta, what he called 'a head of St. Gregory, of gold and jewels, that weepeth real tears from its eyes.' The Mamluks took Lajazzo in 1345, but no such object was found."

He fell silent. The sun dipped behind the cliffs across the Hudson. Marlene said, "So?"

"So, let us discuss my dealings with Mehmet Ersoy. He had a brother, Altemur Ersoy, who is an archaeologist. I see you know this. I began to buy pieces from Ersoy through Sokoloff. I am quite pleased. I am certain the pieces are stolen from Turkey, but who cares? They stole from us.

"Then Ersoy calls me, I believe just before Christmas of last year. He says his brother has made a great discovery in the excavation of a medieval castle in the neighborhood of Payas. On the Gulf of Alexandretta. Payas is Lajazzo. When Ersoy told me that the mask still existed, I did not, of course, believe him. He provides a photograph. I pretend indifference, of course, but my heart is in my throat. I say I would consider buying it if it is genuine, but, of course, I know it must be genuine. No one could forge such a thing."

"Why not?" Marlene asked.

"The investment! That is, if one could even lay hands on large cabachon and square-cut stones of such quality and in such quantity, not to mention the gold itself. Twenty-five pounds of gold, more or less? If the raw materials of the thing he showed me in the photograph were genuine, their intrinsic value alone would be in the neighborhood of eight to ten million. And they would have to be genuine because, of course, it is the easiest thing in the world to expose fake jewels or precious metals. No, it was real. We agreed on a price—"

"How much?" Karp asked.

"Thirty million dollars. A million on account and the rest on delivery. Of course, raising that much cash is not a trivial task even for Armenians. I had to send representatives to Armenian communities across the country, to Chicago, to California—"

Marlene asked, "That was where Gabrielle Avanian was going, wasn't it? She was working on this."

Kerbussyan placed his hand on his cheek and shook his head. "*Ayt kheglj poriguh!*" he said.

"Pardon?" said Marlene.

"I'm sorry. I slip into the old tongue from sorrow. That poor child, I said. Yes, she was to go to San Francisco and Fresno. Torn to pieces by beasts . . ." He was quiet for a moment, swallowing, his face working. Then, his composure regained, he continued, "Of course, by that time Ersoy had been assassinated. We assembled the money and waited, but no one has contacted us."

Karp said, "You're sure the mask is in New York?"

"Fairly certain. Ersoy hinted as much."

"What about the other stuff? Did any of Ersoy's things turn out to be fake?"

Kerbussyan smiled faintly. "Of course. He and his brother were in it together. They were running an international ring selling fake antiquities. We knew that. I paid for fakes gladly, once I was sure that he had the Holy Mask."

"But why did you think he was going to be such a sweetheart about the mask? Didn't you suspect a trick there too?"

"Naturally. Thirty million in cash is a tempting prize. But I had taken precautions."

"Including murder?"

Kerbussyan rocked his head slowly from side to side. "No, Mr. Karp. I confess that I might easily have killed Ersoy if I thought his death would bring me the Holy Mask. But I would never have killed the only man who knew where it was."

"How do we know you haven't got it now?"

For the first time a flush of angry color touched Kerbussyan's cheek, and his voice grew loud. "How? How? Do you think I sought the *Suurt Timag* to stick it in a hole as it has been hidden for six hundred years? If I had it, Armenia would know. The whole world would know. I would shout it from the rooftops. Hide the glory of Armenia to cover up the murder of a Turk? Me?"

Marlene spoke up in a mollifying tone. "No, I don't think you would, Mr. Kerbussyan. The thing is, we're still back to the old question. Who killed Ersoy and why?"

Kerbussyan looked genuinely puzzled, and this time Karp knew he was telling the truth when he answered, "I honestly can't help you there. I believe you are correct when you say that whoever killed him probably has the Holy Mask. It may be that Ersoy had accomplices and that these betrayed him, or he tried to betray them and they found out. Thirty million, as I say. . . . Or someone found out about the negotiations and decided to intervene. My hope is that we will be contacted again by whoever has it now."

"In which case," Karp said sternly, "you'll contact us."

A slight pause, and an affirmative nod of the head.

"Like hell he'll call us," said Karp when they were again in their car, driving south down the Henry Hudson. "He's not going to do shit unless he's got his hands on that statue. By the way, how did you figure all that out?"

"I don't know. I just took a chance. When we knew it was all about art treasures, there was a good chance that the killing was about a particularly big one."

Karp laughed, and then gave voice to his sole artistic talent, a remarkable gift for mimicry. "It's the shtuff that dreams are made of," he said as Bogart in *The Maltese Falcon*. And then, an explosive laugh, Sidney Greenstreet, "The black bird, Mr. Spade, ha-ha!"

"You're not taking this very seriously," said Marlene.

"Ha! It's looney toons, that's why. We're in a goddamn movie. I expect guys in dirty white suits and fezzes. *Reeck! They are after me, Reeck!*"

"That's from a different movie. Rick is in *Casablanca*. Good Peter Lorre, though." This triggered a memory. "Oh, speaking of guys in fezzes, I talked to Guma before we left. He wants you to call him. Some weird complicated thing about some sleazeballs he's got on a wiretap. I couldn't make it out."

The driver let Karp off at the Leonard Street side of the Criminal Courts, where there was a direct elevator to the D.A.'s office and he didn't have to negotiate any steps.

She got out of the car and hugged him tight.

"What's this about?"

"I miss you, you bum. We *have* to figure out some way of getting you home."

"How about moving to an elevator building?"

"I mean besides that. I don't think a respectable married lady should have to whip off a quickie in her husband's office after hours, and then have to go pick up her baby, absolutely oozing, and of course, everybody knows. I might as well be having an affair."

"You only did that once. The quickie."

"Yeah, once was enough. I mean seriously. This sucks!"

"*We'll always have Paris. Shweetheart.*"

"Idiot!" She reentered the car with a slam, and it pulled away.

Back in his office, Karp took off his jacket and tie and spent a pleasant ten minutes chasing down itches under his cast with a long bamboo back scratcher. Then he spotted a folded sheet of paper stuck in the dial of his phone. A message from Roland—call him at home, important. He called.

"What's happening, Roland?"

"Lots. Where were you?"

"We were out seeing Kerbussyan. Interesting stuff."

"Oh, yeah? Like what?"

"The vic was selling him art objects. That's where the money in the safe-deposit box came from. He'd just made a payment of a million on a fancy statue, a holy object of some kind—worth thirty mil apparently."

"Ersoy double-crossed him and he had him aced," said Hrcany confidently.

"Not according to Mr. K. He claims the deal never went down."

"I bet," said Roland, a sneer in his tone. "And speaking of bets, kiss yours good-bye, sucker. Tomasian admitted the whole thing."

Karp's stomach roiled, and bile filled his throat.

"What?!"

"Yeah, today. His roomie in the Tombs gave him up. A check kiter named Dave Medford. Came forward like a good citizen, contacted Frangi, and made a statement."

"And you bought it?" Karp said, incredulous.

"Yeah. Why shouldn't I buy it?"

"Oh, for crying out loud, Roland! The guy denies everything for months, in jail, and then all of a sudden unburdens to a cell mate? What do you think this Tomasian guy is, a mugger with a sheet? Have you got any corroboration for this guy? Anybody else who heard Tomasian spill his guts? Or any information that wasn't in the papers?"

Roland laughed. "I'm hearing a sore loser."

Karp struggled for a moment with his growing temper.

"Roland, tell me I shouldn't be thinking what I'm thinking right now. Just tell me!"

"What, you think it's a plant?" Roland yelled over the phone. "I planted Medford? I set up phony testimony?"

Karp thought, and it made a sick sweat break out on his forehead and run down his sides beneath his arms. What he thought was that he could not really believe that Roland Hrcany had conspired to suborn perjury, to concoct a fake jailhouse witness. Both he and Roland had trained in Francis P. Garrahy's hard school, a school that had turned out tough but straight prosecutors for nearly thirty years. Roland's straightness was perhaps a little wavy on the edges, but if he was truly bent, then the whole business, everything Karp believed in, was meaningless.

Karp swallowed and said, "No, Roland, I wasn't accusing you of anything, or even implying. It just seemed, um, overly convenient. This Medford, there's no deal with him, is there?"

"*I* didn't make any deal. Shit, of course when he goes up, his counsel's gonna tell the court the mutt did a good deed, maybe get him some slack on sentencing, but what else is new? That's how it works in snitch land."

Which was true. Karp's head felt full of grout; he was void of any sensible ideas, but he didn't think that this lapse required him to listen to Roland's crowing. He cut short the conversation, hung up, and called a local place for a pizza and a Pepsi and a pack of Camel filters. The guard at the main desk called when it arrived, and he hobbled down to get it.

Fed, he crutched himself slowly through the passageway to the Tombs, to wash the day's grit off his body. In the steaming shower, he heard the clanking sounds of a man with a mop and steel bucket in the locker room, and when he emerged he saw, as he had expected, that it was Hosie Russell.

Russell looked at the pack of Camels when Karp proferred them, then at Karp, suspicion in his eyes. But he took the pack and opened it and lit one up, drawing gratefully at the smoke.

"What you want with me?" Russell said after a few deep puffs.

It was a good question, but one that Karp could not easily answer. At least he could not give the real answer, which was that he had come to feel, over the past weeks of confinement and isolation, that he and Russell were fellow prisoners.

He shrugged and said, "I appreciate you being around. If I fell or lost my crutch like last time, I'd have to lie on wet tile until the shift changed. It wouldn't be much fun."

Russell nodded and walked back to his bucket. He swished the mop with practiced ease while Karp clumsily pulled on his clothes. Then Russell stopped and looked carefully at Karp. "I know you," he said.

Karp, surprised, smiled and said, "Yeah, sure you do. I'm prosecuting your case."

"Naw, not that. I mean from somewheres else." He thought for a few seconds, his eyes narrowed, his mouth slack. Then he smiled, "Yeah! You that ball player! You played for the Hustlers, in the NBA. Last year. I saw that game you shot that sixty-footer, the Celtics."

"Yeah, that. It was a fluke shot."

"Yeah, but it went the fuck in. That how you bust your leg, playin' ball?"

"In a way. I fucked it up in college ball. Then when I played pro for that little while, it went bad on me."

"I played me some ball," said Russell, smiling. "I played with the Helicopter, that Knowings. Sixty-two, back then, sixty-three. You ever see that man play?"

"Yeah, as a matter of fact. I guarded him in Rucker ball once. Summer of sixty-three, I think. Just before I hurt my knee."

"You guarded the Helicopter? How'd you do?"

Karp laughed. "Not too good. I think he scored about forty off me. Guy got a three-second whistle once, he was in the air all the time."

Russell laughed too and sat down on the bench across from Karp. "Shit, so you played Rucker League, huh? I pro'lly played you a time or two."

"It's possible, if you were any good."

"I could jump over your head, man! I could cut you up." He stood up abruptly and did a little basketball dance, miming the ball—fake, shift, pump fake, jump, release.

"You convinced me," said Karp. "Anyway, those days are gone forever. I don't know if I'm ever going to be able to walk right on this piece of junk, much less play ball."

"Yeah, but at least you got a shot in the pros. How the fuck you do that, old as you are?"

"It's a long story," said Karp. "How'd you get into the mugging business?"

Russell shot him a dark look, then relaxed. "How? Well, first I didn't get into fuckin' Harvard, then my daddy lost his millions in the stock market. How the fuck you think, man? Just scufflin', tryin' to get by. Like everybody else up in the ghet-to."

"Not everybody. It was everybody, this place'd be the size of the Chrysler Building."

"Hey, you don't know what you talkin' about, white man," snapped Russell, his voice rising.

"You're probably right," said Karp equably. "So tell me. What's it like? The mugging business."

"Why the fuck you care? You tryin' somethin'?"

"No. There's nothing I have to try. I got my case against you, and I think it's a good one, and next week I'm going to prosecute it and try to send you away for twenty-five. I can't talk to you about the case. Nothing that passes between us can come out in court. In fact, if your counsel knew I was sitting here talking to you, he'd have a shit fit."

"So why're you doin' it, then?"

Karp shifted his shoulders and settled his bad leg more comfortably. "I don't know—I'm stuck here. You're sure as hell stuck here. I could go watch TV at the guard station, but I'd have to watch what they were watching, which I've done already. You could finish mopping and go back to your cell, but you probably don't find that much of a thrill anymore. Or we could just sit here and shoot the shit for a while. No big thing."

"They come for me, I don't get back there in a little."

"No problem. I know the captain. I'll cover it. No, the thing is, I'm curious. I must've put ten thousand guys like you in jail, and I never spent any time talking with them—just enough to make the case. And they sure as shit didn't want to talk to me."

Russell's face stiffened, and he threw the butt of his cigarette hissing into a damp corner of the locker room. "Well, fuck your 'curious'! I ain't no fuckin' museum."

Karp nodded and extended his lower lip in the have-it-your-way expression, finished tying his sneaker, got his crutches under his armpits, and stood up. "In that case, see you in court, Hosie," he said amiably, and carried himself, careful of the wet patches, out the door.

The same evening, Marlene, entering her shadowy loft, was greeted by a scene of touching, if unconventional, domesticity. Harry Bello was lying asleep on the red sofa, and his goddaughter was sleeping facedown on his chest, her face resting on his neck and her little butt stuck up in the air.

Actually, she observed, coming nearer, Harry was not sleeping at all, or perhaps he had awakened, instantly and without motion, just as she entered. She could see tiny glints of the pale evening glow from the skylight reflected from his eyes.

Without a word Marlene scooped up her daughter and put her in her crib. When she returned, Harry was up, standing and rolling his shoulders to release the kinks. There was a damp patch of baby drool around his collar. He walked over to the rack above the stove that held Marlene's pans and utensils and retrieved his revolver, which he had hung there to keep it away from Lucy's tiny trigger fingers.

"World's safest baby-sitter," said Marlene. "Thanks, Harry. A buck fifty an hour all right?"

Harry made a hmmp and said, "Do any good?"

Marlene told him the good they'd done at Kerbussyan's.

Harry didn't comment on this information but said, "I saw our guy, that Duane, today."

"Yeah? Where?"

"Right here, when I brought the kid home. He was sitting on his bike, corner of Crosby and Broome. I called it in, but he took off before the blue-and-white got here. I wasn't gonna chase him with Lucy."

"She would've been thrilled, probably. The youngest assist on a collar in NYPD history. She could've whined at him until he gave it up."

Harry was not amused. "It's you. He's checking you out for the other one."

Marlene did not want to hear this. In general, prosecutors are, oddly enough, the safest of the participants in criminal justice. Witnesses get killed, cops get killed, mutts shoot their own lawyers, occasionally somebody goes after a judge, but the D.A.'s don't seem to attract much violence. It is as if the nature of the job—that D.A.'s are by profession prosecutors—prevents, by a sort of vaccination, the violently inclined from seeing them as maliciously inspired, and fit subjects for vengeance.

On the other hand, Marlene had been blown up (if mistakenly) and kidnapped, and Karp had been shot, although if the truth be told, they had been asking for it by straying from the safety of jurisprudence and into direct contact with the criminals in question on the street.

She said, "You don't know that, Harry. He could live in the neighborhood. Tribeca, SoHo—good places to get lost."

"I'm staying," said Harry.

Marlene was about to object, reflexively, but stopped herself. It was actually a terrific idea—good for Harry, good for her and the baby. And he had a car.

She made up a bed for him in the gym, on a stack of exercise pads, good for the lower spine. As she was about to leave him, he said, offhand, "I forgot to tell you. Our Turk's got a cousin."

"Which Turk, the vic?"

"No, the one with the high life. Djelal."

"So? He has a cousin, what about him?"

"Guy runs a restaurant on East Forty-six. Vic ate there all the time. Ate there the day he died. The Izmir."

"And?"

"Guy used to manage it, but he bought the place three months ago. Paid cash. Nobody I talked to could figure out where he got the money."

Marlene grinned nastily. "Yeah, and he doesn't work for the U.N."

14

"A TERRIBLE CRIME HAS BEEN COMMITTED," SAID MILTON FREELAND, looking at the jury, stoking the sincerity. "We all feel for Susan Weiner and her family. How can such things happen in broad daylight? we ask ourselves. We all want justice for Susan Weiner."

Do we? thought Karp. He looked sideways at Hosie Russell, sitting at the adjoining table. He looked a lot better than he had in the harsh light of the locker room. He was neatly dressed in a suit and tie and wearing the glasses. Karp wondered whether their lenses were really ground to a prescription or if Freeland kept a stack of odd peepers in his desk for show.

Karp had thought that Freeland would go the emotional route. Karp had not done so in his own opening. He never did. The opening for the prosecution should be dry, like a table of contents: first I say what I'm gonna say; then I say it; then I say what I just said. You wanted the impression of a carefully woven, mutually supporting net of facts; leave the emotion to the defense. Good advice, given ten years ago by an old homicide D.A. who had helped train Karp.

Freeland was pacing slowly before the jury, drawing out the words, as if each one had popped that instant from the oven of his warm heart. ". . . yes, a young woman was brutally murdered— there's no doubt about that. And the state will try to show that my client, Mr. Russell, is that murderer.

"Indeed, they must show it, beyond a reasonable doubt; that is Mr. Karp's job. It is his show. I could sit here sleeping during the trial, and so could Mr. Russell, and it would not matter. My client is innocent until proven guilty, beyond a reasonable doubt. That is what the prosecution must do. But, ladies and gentlemen of the jury, that proof will be impossible if you are the reasonable and decent people I know you to be. Because Mr. Russell is innocent of this dreadful crime.

"He stands accused today for one reason and one reason only—he was in the wrong place at the wrong time. He fell victim to the fervid desire of the police to find a culprit, any culprit for this spectacular and highly publicized murder in the shortest possible time.

"Mr. Russell was ideal for this purpose. He is poor. He is homeless. He has severe emotional problems. And he is black."

As Freeland said this, Karp knew, he would be looking directly and intently into the eyes of the three black members of the jury. Karp thought back to the voir dire. The jury selection had taken five days, probably longer than the trial itself would take. Karp thought the whole thing was a waste of time nine times out of ten, but the voir dire was dear to lawyers, especially defense lawyers, who almost always believed that they had a mystical ability to pick an acquitting jury. Also, it was to the defense's advantage to drag the thing out as long as possible, especially in a case that depended as much as this one did on the testimony of witnesses.

Reasonable doubt—Freeland had to cultivate it like a gardener. All he needed to win was one tender green shoot, and time was the best fertilizer. What? You mean to tell us that you can remember a face you saw once, five weeks or ten weeks, or eight months ago? So Freeland had used all his peremptory challenges to fill the jury with people who might be swayed by the idea that the cops had dragged in the first available brother off the street, and Karp, of course, had tried for a group of solid taxpayers.

Neither had succeeded, of course; the jury was what might have been pulled out of a hat. Freeland had got his college student with collar-length hair and his matronly black woman. Karp thought that his black security guard captain and his black retired schoolteacher would provide a balance, and do the right thing. Freeland was going to play the race thing up, and so hadn't objected to the two black men. That might have been a mistake, Karp thought. But he only had to hit once.

Freeland was well into his peroration. ". . . and I think, I know, you will conclude that Hosie Russell's only crime was being one of society's forgotten men. He is as much a victim as Susan Weiner, a victim of the desire of the police and the prosecution to find a scapegoat that would get the press off their backs. But the real killer of Susan Weiner still walks free. If you convict the wrong man, you will be denying that young woman justice. If you listen to the prosecution's illogical tale of concocted evidence and mistaken, so-called, witnesses, if you give it a moment's credence, then you will be compounding injustice and denying justice forever to the victim of this horrible crime. Thank you very much."

Karp stood up. The crutches cramped his style. He liked to move forcefully from evidence table to witness stand to jury box during a trial, confident that his size and athletic movements would rivet attention and keep the duller jurors awake.

He called the first witness, a civil engineer. This was a departure from the usual practice. Since it was a legal necessity to show that a murder had in fact taken place in New York County, the early witnesses were generally those who could establish that fact—the medical examiner and other forensic experts. But Karp wanted first to establish the scene of Russell's capture firmly in the jury's mind from the outset, because the only reasonable defense was that the man found in the basement under the boiler was not the man whom the crowd had chased from the murder scene and who had briefly invaded the apartment of Jerry Shelton.

He led the engineer, a thin, scholarly man with wire glasses, through the layout of the apartment complex at 58 Barrow and introduced as an exhibit a large chart showing the building's floor plans. Freeland peppered him with meaningless objections, all of which were overruled. Freeland still hadn't caught on that Judge Martino liked dispatch and a thorough understanding of how trials got done in the big city.

Freeland's questions on cross were, of course, directed at establishing reasonable routes of escape for the putative other man. He chose the one Karp had expected: the skylight at the top of the stairs.

Freeland asked, "Now, sir, there is a skylight at the top of the stairs there, leading to the roof, is there not?"

The engineer confirmed this and pointed it out on the exhibit when asked. He agreed that once on the roof there were a half-dozen routes down to the street or across other rooftops to other streets.

Then he asked whether a man could get up out of the skylight, and Karp snapped an objection, rising briefly on his good foot. Calls for a conclusion based upon speculation. Sustained.

The next witness was the police photographer—routine. The photographs of the murder site and the Barrow Street complex, then the knife were duly admitted into evidence. The next witness was Ray Thornby, the arresting officer. But it was by then four-fifteen, and Judge Martino adjourned for the day.

Not a bad start, Karp thought as he packed up his papers. He walked up the aisle and out of the courtroom, and suddenly there was The Sister, in voluminous black, staring at him. He tried a false smile and started to say something, but she turned away and left the courtroom. He felt unaccountably chilled. For some odd reason, he felt that The Sister was not on his side.

■   ■   ■

Harry Bello walked into the Izmir Restaurant from the kitchen, in the slack hour right after lunch, flashing his badge at the astounded and undoubtedly illegal scullions. He found Aziz Nassif, the cousin, punching away at an adding machine in a small storeroom-cum-office behind the main dining area.

Bello showed his shield. Nassif frowned. He was a stocky, strong-looking man of thirty-odd with a thick head of hair and a brush mustache. He said, "I got the door clear and the sprinkler fixed. What you bothering me again?" He had a guttural accent, quite unlike that of the elegant Mr. Kilic at the United Nations.

"I'm not from the building department, Mr. Nassif. I'm investigating a murder." A little bombshell, but there was no dramatic reaction. Nassif paused and asked, "What murder?"

"Mehmet Ersoy. Sunday, March 13, this year."

Nassif looked sorrowful and wagged his head. "I talked already with police. Then."

"You knew the victim?"

"A customer. Very good, come here all the time. Very sad thing."

"Yeah. He was here on the morning he was shot, wasn't he?"

"Yes. Almost every day have breakfast here." Nassif nodded vigorously to affirm this information. A young waiter came into the office on an errand. Nassif turned on him, his face contorting briefly, and snapped, *"Çek arabaru!"* The boy gaped and scuttled out.

"And where were you when the shooting took place, Mr. Nassif?" Harry continued as if nothing had happened.

"Where I was? Here. In restaurant."

"All morning?"

"Yes, all. All day." Harry stared into the man's face, which remained blank and unrevealing.

"While you were here with Ersoy in the restaurant, did he say anything to you? Anything that would have suggested he was in danger?"

"No. Just hello, how are you. Like this. Is just customer."

"Uh-huh." Harry gestured broadly and said, "This is a nice restaurant. You own it?"

"Yes."

"Expensive. East Side, nice neighborhood. Do you mind if I ask what you paid?"

Nassif opened his mouth, closed it, opened it again, and said, "Two hundred thousand."

Harry registered surprise. "Whew! That's a pile. Where'd you get the money? A loan?"

"I save."

"You save. Good. Well, thanks for your help, Mr. Nassif." He produced a card. "You think of anything else the victim said or did, give me a call."

Nassif took the card mutely and looked at it without apparent interest. Harry paused at the door and said, "By the way, did Mr. Ersoy ever mention to you that he was running an art-forging operation?"

Blankness remained. A mute shrug, a shake of the head.

"No? Okay, thanks again for your help."

Harry went out into the street. It was muggy late August weather. In Bed-Stuy, where he used to work, and around the less desirable addresses in Manhattan, blood would be flowing. Harry didn't miss it much. He walked across the street and lounged in a shady doorway.

He wore a shabby gray seersucker suit, a white shirt and black and tan tie, and heavy, rubber-soled black cop shoes. He stayed still for twenty minutes. Harry was good at staying still. Sometimes, off-duty, he would just zone out, perfectly aware of everything but feeling no need to stir, a man literally with nothing to do. In his doorway he was as invisible as a leopard in an acacia tree.

Here he waited for an hour or so, to see what Nassif would do with the little zinger that he had just received. Nassif did nothing. No panicked race out the door, looking over his shoulder, no hurried arrival of the cousin to consult. Nassif was either innocent or cool, Harry didn't know which.

■   ■   ■

Karp hobbled back to his office from the courtroom, looking forward to a nice cool Coke and a lie-down. As soon as he entered the secretarial bay, however, Connie Trask informed him that he was not about to get it.

"He wants you," she said with that upward tilt of the eyes and head that identified the He Who Wanted.

Karp sagged, let out a breath, dropped his fat folder on Trask's desk, pivoted on his crutches, and went back out the door.

After the customary maddening wait in an antechamber, Karp was ushered into the D.A.'s throne room. Bloom was sitting in his special raised chair at the end of the conference table. Next to him sat Conrad Wharton. Karp's heart sank; this was going to be a crappy administrative matter, something that could have been handled with a phone call. It served to confirm his suspicion that Wharton liked to see him dashing around the building crippled.

Therefore he was surprised when Bloom, after the usual false pleasantries, asked, "How's the Weiner trial going?"

"It just started. Openings and a couple of official witnesses."

"But he'll go down for it, for murder two, this guy, uh . . ."

"Russell. Yeah, he'll go for it."

"Yes. It's an important case. Lots of press on this one. The 'seven-dollar killer' they're calling it. It'd be a disaster if he walked out of there. You're sure?"

Karp wondered what this was all about. The D.A. seemed nervous. Wharton had on his usual unreadable plastic-doll smile and a fixed stare. Karp answered, "Well, no jury trial is ever a lock. But we have a good case. And the guy did it."

"And you always win murder cases," said Bloom. "Well, good. I'm happy to hear it. Good work."

This statement amazed Karp more than if the district attorney had leaped up on the table and done the dance of the seven veils. He tried to recall the last time Bloom had complimented him, and came up blank. He nodded and murmured an acknowledgment.

"Well, is that it? Anything else?" said the D.A. breezily.

Wharton still hadn't said anything. Karp wrinkled his brow, confused. It was *their* meeting.

Bloom rose to his feet and so did Wharton. Karp heaved himself out of his own chair. Bloom walked him cordially to the door of the conference room, another first.

"Lucky break on that Tomasian thing, huh?" Bloom said casually. "That'll nail it down."

He meant the jailhouse snitch. Karp was noncommittal. "If it's legit," he said. "I haven't really followed the details since I've started this trial. I could get Roland to give you a ring and fill you in."

"No, that's okay," said the D.A. quickly. "I'm sure it's in good hands."

Karp left, puzzled, as if he had just finished a conversation in a foreign tongue in which he was not quite fluent. I missed something, he thought. What was Wharton doing there? What was Bloom afraid of?

It was by now past five, and Centre Street was moving into its evening routine. Karp had a list of things to do, prepared by Trask, which, of course, he had not done, having been stuck in court all day. At the top of the list: call Ray G.

He called, figuring only an even chance of finding Guma in. Guma kept odd hours. Long divorced, he maintained a Queens highrise apartment that he rarely visited, preferring to crash in the Manhattan apartments of one or another of his many girlfriends. If he didn't have a court appearance, he was likely to take off early and go to the track or a ball game, or hang out in a bar. On the other hand, when a case struck his interest, he might be found working at midnight.

He was in. Karp asked what was up, and Guma said, "I'll come by."

"It's this Joey Castles thing," said Guma when he had settled himself in one of Karp's chairs, "I can't figure it anymore." Karp was stretched out on his cot with his casted leg elevated. Guma did appear more than usually disheveled. His enormous tie knot was pulled down to the third button, and his thinning, greasy curls were awry and flying, witness to many runnings of fingers through them. He had a heavy five o'clock shadow.

"What's the problem?"

"What it is, is they, Joey and Little Sally, they keep talking Turk this, Turk that. So, like I told Marlene the other day—she told you, right?—uh-huh, I figured Minzone was in deep on it. That was the theory. So I think to myself, let's see what old Turk is up to. Raney checked it out for me.

"Turns out, for the last three weeks Minzone's been in Madison Park hospital, getting carved. The Big C. I was fuckin' amazed—the guy was an ox, you know?"

"Maybe there's justice after all."

Guma looked pained. "Hey, Minzone whacked some people in his time, but cancer . . . besides, he's about my age. I mean, have a heart."

"All those guinea stinkers caught up with him. So, if it's not Minzone, who's the Turk?"

"Damned if I know. An out-of-town thing? The point is, they're getting anxious. Little Sally is. Joey is telling him not to worry, that the whole thing'll be wrapped up by Thursday next week, Friday the latest. Eddie Scoli is gonna move the stuff, he says—"

"Scoli the fence? Where'd he come from?"

"Yeah, see? It's like that. Look, go back to the beginning. Joey ran the operation lifting stuff from the airports. The Viacchenzas went into business for themselves. Joey didn't like that, so, we figure, he had the Viacchenzas whacked. We got Jimmy Cavetti for it.

"Little Sally is real pissed at Joey, but Joey sets up a deal on the side that'll take some of the pressure off him. Sweeten the pot for the Bollanos. That's what all this Turk talk is about. Only we don't know what the deal is. Drugs? A big diamond deal? We don't know."

"If Eddie Scoli's involved, it could be diamonds," Karp mused.

"Yeah, right, but, again, who's the Turk? I hit the records. I talked to Safe and Loft. In town, outa town, I can't find any big-time heavy theft guy with that street name."

Karp said, "You know, this may sound crazy, but there's a possibility that they're talking about an actual citizen of Turkey. That's why I was curious in the first place when I heard that tape in your office. I got Turks out the ears on this other thing, the U.N. hit."

He was silent for a moment, reflecting, running isolated events and discoveries from the past four months through his mind. A pattern, unlikely at first and then increasingly plausible, came into focus, like a photographic image rising out of blankness in a tray of developer. He snapped his fingers and pointed one of them at Guma. "Look, here's what we need to do. You, me, Roland, Harry Bello, Raney, Marlene, and, um, V.T. need to sit down and talk. I think we're stepping on each other's jocks here. Let's set it up for tomorrow, right after court. And meanwhile, why don't you have a chat with Jimmy Cavetti?"

"Jimmy? Why? He won't say shit."

"I don't mean about the murder," Karp replied. "Just ask him exactly what it was that the Viacchenzas ripped off."

Guma left, and ten minutes later Marlene came in, bearing a large, flat box.

She said, "You awda a pizza?"

"Yes," said Karp. "If that's the one with pepperoni and mushrooms and a hot girl to squirm on my lap and bite my neck and give me the kinda kisses that I'd die for."

Marlene glanced at the ticket taped to the box. "Yeah, check: pepperoni, mushrooms, squirm, bite, kiss. What you want, the pizza foist or afta?"

"Afta," said Karp. She sat on his lap and delivered. "Watch your hands, I don't want to get all runny and gasping," she said, gasping.

"Why the hell not?" Karp breathed into the hollow of her neck.

"Because," she said, straightening, "I'm a mom. I have to function. I have to tear myself from your embrace, gulp down a cooling pizza, race home, have an Alka-Seltzer, and get the baby fed and ready for bed, not to mention talking to her so she remembers that I'm her mom and not somebody who tears her away from the nice day-care lady."

Karp looked at his watch. "Speaking of the kid, where is she? I thought day-care closed up at six."

"Harry's got her. He's been picking her up the last couple days."

"Good for Harry," said Karp. "He doesn't mind?"

"He adores it. It makes him feel temporarily human. And Lucy loves him. It's the most perfect deal in the City."

"Well, she's for sure the world's safest baby," said Karp, opening the pizza box. Marlene brought two cans of soda out of her bag, and they ate.

"Anything new on the loft?" Karp asked as Marlene lit up one of her rationed cigarettes.

"Oh, just that we are going to be thrown out on our asses for sure now. Stuart says Lepkowitz has raised the ante. Now it's a quarter mil. And considering the hit from the surgery and the five grand you blew with Roland—well, hi ho! I could sell my white body on the mean streets . . ."

"Who gave you the nickel?"

"What?"

"You know, Morris's business is on the rocks, so he sends his wife out to trick, and she comes back in the morning with fifty dollars and five cents, and he says, 'Who gave you—?' "

"Oh, yeah, 'Everybody!' Honestly, it's not a joking matter, Butchie. We could be under the bridges this time next year."

"Well, first of all, I haven't blown my five large yet. The case isn't over."

"No? I thought Roland had a snitch who dropped one on little Tomasian."

"Yeah, I thought it was kind of peculiar they got a snitch this late in the game and off a guy like Tomasian."

"You thinks it's a ringer?"

"Got to be. And no, it wasn't Roland who set it up. It could've been the skell himself, heard some shit on the jailhouse telegraph, figured to cut a deal. I don't know."

"So what do we do?"

"Same same. Find the real guy." He told her about what he had learned from Guma and about the brainstormer he had organized for the next day.

"I'll be there," said Marlene, "and another thing—tomorrow's Friday, and I am not going to spend another weekend by myself."

Karp mimed desolation and clunked his cast against the desk.

She said, "And fuck your cast too! I will find a way; count on it!"

After Marlene left, Karp saw that she had "forgotten" an almost full pack of Marlboros on his desk. That was part of the reduced-smoking campaign. She left packs of cigarettes behind her wherever she stopped, like the spoor of a deer. Without thinking, he scooped the pack up.

To his mild surprise, Hosie Russell was waiting for him when he arrived at the staff locker room for his shower. Karp had thought that after their last interview, Russell would avoid him, but there he was, glowering, hesitant, yet exhibiting an expectant attitude. What did he expect? Karp wondered.

"You bring any cigarettes?" he asked.

Karp handed him the Marlboros. Russell broke off the filter on one, lit it, and sucked greedily. Karp stripped, took his one-legged stance under the shower, and emerged hopping from the steam, wrapped in a towel. He always tried to keep his cast dry in the shower, but since this was virtually impossible, it had started to become spongy on the outside and to unravel around the toes. The bright messages written on it by his co-workers had run, becoming indecipherable, if decorative, swirls of color.

"So," he said when he was seated on the bench, "what's happening, Hosie? They treating you okay? How'd you like your day in court?"

Russell said, "That lawyer's fucked up big-time, man."

"Freeland? Why? I thought he did pretty good."

"I don't mean how he did. I mean how he is. Treat me like a dog. A dog fool."

"Well, you know, you have the right to ask for another attorney. I mean, it's your case, not his."

"Wouldn't do no fuckin' good. Jew lawyers all the same. Fuck 'em all!"

"Suit yourself," said Karp, beginning the difficult process of working the leg of his sweatpants over the lumpy cast.

Russell said, "You want some help with that?"

"Sure, if you don't mind."

Russell helped Karp dress. Karp thanked him. Russell sat across the locker room aisle on a bench and smoked. The mumble of the imprisoned and the burble of water pipes blended distantly, a background to their silence.

Then, out of nowhere, Russell began to talk, disjointedly, in spasms, interrupted by long pauses and the snap of matches as he chain-smoked.

It was a complaint. He had never had a break. He was the second youngest of seven children, and the only survivor. The others had died, in wars, in jails, of suicide and murder. He had been brought to New York by his parents at the age of four with his younger siblings and raised in Harlem, the glittering Harlem of the thirties and forties.

Hosie had not participated in the glitter. Someone had dropped a load of bricks on his father. The family had sunk to the lowest echelon of poverty. They were "nigger poor." He had "scuffled." He had dropped out of school in the fifth grade and run numbers. He had tried to become a pimp and failed. His first theft was recalled, a purse-snatching. He had been grabbed and pounded by the cops and done juvie time.

He hung out on the street, doing casual labor, getting fired a lot, sometimes for petty theft, sometimes for drinking. He drank heavily. He got hooked on heroin. He became a small-time burglar. No rough stuff, he added; he had never carried a gun.

He had fathered children with several women, all of whom had betrayed him, abandoned him. A daughter had turned whore. A son had been shot to death in a dope deal. Another daughter had cast him out.

He was as incompetent at crime as at everything else. He had spent twenty-two years of his forty-odd years behind bars. He had missed the Korean War in prison on a six-year robbery stretch.

Karp listened quietly, noting that the criminal justice system had had at least one effect on Hosie Russell. It had given him an alternate language to describe his life. His speech was peppered with sociologist's jargon. He said, "I'm a recurrent alcoholic." He said, "I got low self-esteem." The tale had a rehearsed quality, as if he had told it any number of times before, to parole boards, to social workers. He had probably told it to the sister of the woman he had murdered.

He went on and on. He was sorry for all his crimes. He regretted them. But what else had life offered him? He said, "I never got a chance to reach my potential."

When this last came tumbling out of his mouth, Karp asked, "What do you think your potential was?"

"Say what?"

"Your potential. If you hadn't had to scuffle, if you'd had the money, what would you have done?"

Russell thought for a moment. Then he said, "A artist. I always liked to draw and paint and shit like that. I did a lot of that in the can, like when I was in Lex for the dope thing, I had this therapy—they let you alone. You could paint. They said, the lady there, said I had a talent for it."

"Do you still do it? Draw?"

Russell snorted. "Yeah, on the fuckin' floor with a mop. What you think?"

Karp shrugged. "You could take it up again. You'll have plenty of time."

Russell bristled at that, the confidential mood broken. "What good's that gonna do? All y'all care about, put the nigger away. What damn good is it?"

"No damn good at all," agreed Karp affably.

"But you do it anyway? What the fuck, man. I go in, there's fifty little jitterbugs out there pick up the slack. You pathetic."

"Uh-huh. But it's my job. It's what I do. And you're right—it is pathetic. People shouldn't grow up like you did. I shouldn't have crippled my knee. Susan Weiner shouldn't have died on the street with a knife through her heart. Life stinks. On the other hand, we're supposed to at least try to make it better, or leave it so that our kids have a shot at making it better, God help them."

"That's what's gonna make the world better? I go upstate fuckin' forever?"

"Well, yes," said Karp, as if making a discovery, "it will. You won't kill any more young women. It's not much, but that's all we got."

"I never killed nobody," said Russell, almost to himself, almost as if he didn't expect anyone to believe him.

"Uh-huh, and if the jury buys that, you walk out." He stood up in his crutches. "Big day tomorrow. Got to go."

Russell said, "You ain't gonna give me no break or nothin', are you?"

Karp paused and looked carefully at the other man, and shook his head. "Here's the thing, Hosie. This is nothing personal. I mean, if you weren't a criminal, I'd probably enjoy going down to the courts with you, shoot some hoops, crack jokes, and so on. I mean, I don't think you're a devil or anything. I understand why you turned out how you did, the story of your sad life and all.

"Okay, I understand, but what good does that do? Doesn't do me any good. Somebody once said, 'To understand all is to forgive all.' Fine. I understand you, and I forgive you. Maybe her family can forgive you too someday.

"But then what? Acts have consequences. You drop a brick, it falls to the ground. You couldn't live in a world that didn't have some physical order in it. There's a moral order too; it's dim but it's there. Or maybe we just have to pretend that it's there so we can get out of bed every day. I don't know. You following me here, Hosie?"

Nothing.

"And here's another thing: understanding never helped *you* out. It probably hurt you, come to that. You figured it as part of a hustle, get you out of a jam. I mean, you been hustling me, in a way. We all figure that, you understand somebody, you go easier on them. But why? Maybe when we understand, we should be harder, not softer. Maybe that would fucking work."

15

THE NEXT DAY, THE FRIDAY, IN PART THIRTY, VINNIE BOGULUSO WAS
scheduled for arraignment on the grand jury indictment for the
murder and lesser crimes committed on the body of Gabrielle
Avanian. Part Thirty, a felony arraignment court, had the atmosphere
of a bus station in an underdeveloped nation. The floor was brown
linoleum, much scuffed. The yellowish window shades were tattered. The mural behind the judge's presidium was peeling; the
allegorical figure of a woman with a sword and scales had no
face.

In the well of the court gathered a dozen or so A.D.A.'s, clutching capacious folders. Around them, like bees about blossoms, moved
a smaller number of defense attorneys, harassed and shabby if they
were with Legal Aid, sleeker and better-dressed if private. Behind
them in the rows of wooden benches sat relatives or friends of defendants. On the bench, Judge Rosemary Slade, a black woman of

vast experience and legendary arraignment velocity, called them up and shut them down.

The room rumbled with talk, like a marketplace. Formally, the arraignment was the place at which a secret grand jury indictment was made public, where the People let the accused know the nature of his crime against them. In practice, for nearly all cases, it was where one copped out, confessed to a lesser crime, in exchange for a reduced sentence or no sentence at all.

Part Thirty was a marketplace, in fact. The marketing was done between the A.D.A.'s and the defense attorneys, who circulated through the little mob of the People's representatives, seeking deals for their clients. The A.D.A.'s were often little more than children a few years, or a few months, past their bar exams. While in principle they had wide discretion, in reality they were bound tightly by the tinkerings of politicians in Albany, about what deals they could actually make, and even tighter by the blizzard of policies and memos that issued from the office of the district attorney.

Ray Guma stood placidly amid the familiar bustle and awaited the arrival of his opposite number in *People* v. *Boguluso.* This was a Legal Aid named Jack Cooney, an old war horse of approximately Guma's own vintage. They had worked opposite each other for nearly twenty years, and Guma grinned when he saw Cooney's familiar, beat-up face appear in the courtroom doorway.

"Counselor," said Cooney when he got next to Guma, "well, well. A fine piece of shit this morning. I've just come from my client, speaking of fine pieces. He wants to know what's on offer."

"Offer?" Guma rolled his eyes. "In his dreams, offer. Guilty to the top count is the offer. Twenty-five to life."

"He'll never plead to that, my friend."

"Fuck him, then, Jackie. Trying this scumbag will be a day at the beach. I look forward to it."

Cooney shrugged. Although he did not want Vinnie out on the street any more than Guma did, he was also a pro. "Not such a day at the beach. Your witnesses are a whore and her wacky kid, and an accomplice to the crime, this Ritter, who by the way was brutalized by the arresting officer."

"I got the teeth marks, Jack," replied Guma airily. "He had the vic's stuff in his apartment. His girlfriend—" Guma stopped, his eyes widening. "Hello," he said, "I'm in love. Will you look at that?"

She had just walked through the courtroom door, a young bottle blonde with a sharp little face, chewing a wad of gum the size of a golfball. She was an obvious paralegal of some sort, one of the many who darted like guppies in and out of courtrooms.

A new one, perhaps: she seemed lost and was outfitted inappropriately for her job. She wore stiletto-heeled sandals, a deeply vee-necked, very snug baby blue sweater, and a shiny black skirt so tight and short that she was nearly hobbled, swaying precariously as she walked. She was carrying four fat legal files, two under each arm. The burden pulled her shoulders back and thrust her high, conical breasts into sharp relief.

She paused at the little gate that led to the well of the court. Two court officers practically collided as they leaped to open the gate and let her through. She smiled at them, giggled, walked around the end of the defense table, and approached the court clerk, followed by every male eye in the house. She spoke briefly to the clerk. He shook his head and gave her directions. Poor thing! She was in the wrong courtroom.

An arraignment was just finishing, having lasted six minutes, about average for Judge Slade. The defendant looked longingly at the blond woman as he was led away to the Land of No Girls. He said something naughty to her, and she giggled. Judge Slade frowned. The clerk tore his attention away and called the next case: "Calendar 2606. Boguluso."

The young woman headed back out again, but as she passed the corner of the defense table, she seemed to wobble on her spike heels, to stumble. The four folders went flying and crashed to the linoleum, scattering a deep drift of paper around and under the defense table. She let out a little shriek and knelt down to retrieve her documents.

In this she was not alone. A half-dozen men, court officers, A.D.A.'s (with Guma in the fore), a defense counsel rushed to her aid, eager to help a fellow servant of criminal justice, to peer down her gaping neckline, and to look up her nearly exposed thighs.

Thus the task was quickly done, and the young woman soon rose, burdened again, flushed and apologetic. In a moment her small, shiny butt had wiggled its way out of the courtroom. Nobody noticed that when she left she was no longer chewing gum.

A few flights up from this scene, in the nobler precincts of Supreme Court Part 52, *People* v. *Russell* continued. Milton Freeland had begun the day by moving for a mistrial. The *Post* had done a story on the start of the trial in which Russell's criminal record was featured in some detail, and Freeland was arguing that the material was prejudicial. Judge Martino growled, but he had to drag all the jurors out one by one and ask them if they had seen the offending article. They hadn't. The morning vanished.

The delay meant that Karp's witness, the arresting officer, Patrolman Thornby, would have his testimony broken by the lunch recess, reducing its probable impact on the jury. A cheap but often effective trick.

Thornby was a good witness. He had good presence and a clear voice, and the color of his skin didn't hurt either. The story of the chase and of hunting through the baking, dark basement was told, and the Bloomingdale's charge slip with the deceased's name on it was placed in evidence.

On cross, Freeland seemed obsessed with the time the sales slip had been recovered, and the reason for the delay between the time Thornby said he had taken it off Russell and the time he had delivered it to Detective Cimella at the Sixth Precinct house. Karp knew why too.

Freeland was saying, "And when you took the sales slip off the defendant, what, if anything, did you do?"

"I wrote my initials down on it," said Thornby.

"Did you write down the time?"

"No."

Freeland asked, "Wouldn't it in fact be very good police procedure to put on a piece of evidence the time that it's recovered?"

Karp objected and was sustained. Freeland asked that the sales slip be circulated among the jury. While this was happening, he walked back to the defense table. The court clerk looked at his watch and said, "This is a long one, Judge. We don't get out of here soon, I'm gonna miss my train to Hempstead."

Thornby remarked, "You think you got problems? We just had our first baby, and my wife's waiting on me to get her home from the hospital."

There was a ripple of mild laughter, and Judge Martino spoke briefly to the cop about women and children. He himself had six kids.

At last the jury was done with feeling the sales slip, and Freeland continued questioning Thornby.

"There's nothing that requires you to put on the time?"

"No."

"But there's nothing that says you can't do it either, is there?"

Objection. Sustained.

Freeland looked ruffled. "I'd like to know the basis for the objection."

Martino replied, "There's nothing in law or police regulations that requires it, Mr. Freeland. The officer didn't do it, and he's already testified to that effect."

"I'll show you common sense requires it!" snapped Freeland. Martino gave him a long stare. Freeland said, "No further questions," and walked back to the defense table.

Martino dismissed the jury for the weekend. Two guards took Russell back to the cells. The press and all the spectators left. When the room was nearly empty, Freeland approached the bench.

"Your Honor, with due respect to the court, and as much as it pains me to make this application, I have to ask that the record show that while the jury was examining the sales slip, there was a . . . some sort of colloquy between Your Honor and Officer Thornby, such that it might have an effect on the jury of making Officer Thornby's testimony more credible. Therefore I must move for a mistrial at this time."

Karp heard snatches of this and definitely caught the last line. He cursed under his breath, got to his feet, and crutched over to the bench.

Martino gave Freeland another long stare, and his cheeks darkened. He snapped at a court officer, "Get Thornby back in here!"

Thornby was brought back in and, as the stenographer tapped away, Martino went through everything that had been said in the little colloquy for the record.

Karp could see the judge's jaw working. He had to give Freeland credit for balls, anyway. He was trying to infuriate the judge, not a usual tactic among lawyers, to say the least, but it occasionally paid off. The Chicago Seven gambit. If he could make Martino lose control, he might provoke a reversible error and get any conviction tossed out. That would establish the basis for a new trial, and perhaps months of delay.

That and the doubt about the time the sales slip had been found seemed to be all Freeland had, Karp thought. But maybe not.

Down in Part Thirty, they brought Vinnie Boguluso in, creating a momentary stir. The Tombs had sent the first team to accompany the huge defendant to court: a former professional wrestler named Walker, who was taller even than Vinnie and built with a lot less fat on him, and a weight lifter named Amico, who could, it was said, jerk and press anyone in the jail.

They took Vinnie's cuffs off and sat him down at the defense table, and then took up their posts behind and to either side of him.

Jack Cooney came over to his client and looked him over. Vinnie had not had any clothes suitable for court, and he was a hard fit. He was wearing a black leather jacket, a new one without gang regalia, black jeans, and a brown shirt with a collar. He had shaved, at least, and his hair was cut short. He seemed curiously detached and content, not at all like a man about to be arraigned on a murder charge.

"Okay, Vinnie, here's the deal," Cooney said. "There's no deal. So it's up to you. I have to tell you, you got nothing to lose right now by going to trial."

"Can I get bailed out?"

"Yeah, if you got about a million bucks. You own any property? Real estate?"

"Fuck, no. I look like I own any fuckin' real estate?"

"Right. So we plead not guilty."

"Yeah, sure, whatever."

The judge called the two counsel to the bench, determined that there was no offer and that the defendant was pleading not guilty. She nodded. The system was working for a change.

The reading of the indictment was waived, the judge asked for a plea, and Vinnie stood and said, "Not guilty." The judge looked at him and curled her lip and asked the court officer to spin the drum that contained the names of all the Supreme Court trial judges. The court officer picked out a cardboard square and read a part number and a judge's name.

Walker and Amico cuffed him behind his back and walked him out of the courtroom and down the passageway back to the holding pens.

Vinnie walked carefully. Stuck in his jockey shorts was the five inch switchblade knife that Duane's girlfriend had managed to stick into the near left corner of the defense table with her wad of bubble gum while she was pretending to pick up her papers. Vinnie had palmed it as soon as he was seated and slipped it into his fly.

Court ended at four, about average on Fridays. Judges must roll home before the traffic, though the heavens fall. By four-thirty, Karp's office was full of people he had invited.

Karp himself sat at the head of the long oak conference table, but sideways, with his bum leg propped up on an upended waste basket. To his right sat Ray Guma and then Marlene and Harry

Bello. Across the table from them were Jim Raney and V. T. New-bury. Roland Hrcany came in last, accompanied by Detective Frangi, and sat next to Raney.

"What's this about?" asked Hrcany in a peremptory tone. "It's Friday. I got a date."

Guma made a show of looking at his watch. "Jesus, Roland, what's your rush? School just got out. Give her time to get her milk and cookies."

Laughter, and Roland flushed and gave Guma the finger. Karp took this opportunity to start business.

"This won't take long. It looks like *People* v. *Tomasian* is expanding."

Roland's brow congealed. "What's that mean, expanding?" he said suspiciously.

"Just that there are more players," Karp answered. "Somebody may have launched Tomasian. Somebody may have set up the vic. *Tomasian* seems to be related to at least one other murder case, a double murder involving wise guys, and a big fraud operation. That's why I thought we should all sit down and see which end is up.

"Okay, let's start with Guma. Goom, what's the hookup with *Cavetti?*"

"Yeah, okay, here's the deal," Guma began. "I went to see Jimmy C. out at Riker's, like you said. I say to him, 'Jimmy, you're in a bad situation here, and I'd like to help you out, but I know you're a stand-up guy and I'm not gonna get shit out of you on this Viacchenza thing. But there's something else you can help us out on that's got nothing to do with any of that business.' I said it could do him some good. And totally off the record.

"So I could tell he's sort of listening. Jimmy's a thief. I don't figure he's ever seen himself up on a murder, for that kind of stretch upstate.

"I say, 'Jimmy, what I want to know is, like, it's been bothering me—why the fuck did the Viacchenzas do it? I mean, they had a pretty good deal going. It's years they've been ripping it off down by

Kennedy. What could it be worth, crossing Joey Castles. Diamonds? Gold? Bonds? What?'

"He says, 'Fuckin' caviar.'"

Here Roland snorted a laugh and said, "What is this shit? What does this have to do with Tomasian? Caviar?" He laughed again.

Karp noted that Frangi was not laughing, and seemed unduly nervous. Karp said, holding up his hand in a mollifying gesture, "Listen and learn, Roland. It's a long story. Go ahead, Goom."

Guma continued, "So I go, 'Caviar?' And he says, yeah, this guy's been around the Domino and Ciro's, where Carl and Lou used to hang, looking for somebody to take something off. It's common. Like you want to buy stocks, you go down to Wall Street, hang around Merrill Lynch, somebody'll come over, sell you some IBM.

"So this guy says he knows they're shipping some prime caviar in by air freight, knows the flight and the freight terminal, and he wants a piece of it. He says this'll be a continuing thing: the shit comes in every month, the boys'll lighten the shipment, and they'll get paid. He says he'll give them thirty large."

He paused, and Karp looked at V.T., as perhaps the only person at the table who could quote from his head prices for caviar in bulk. "Does that sound right?" Karp asked.

"How much was involved?" V.T. asked.

"He didn't say, but he did say this guy needed two guys to lift the crate, so figure, what, two hundred, two hundred-fifty pounds?"

V.T. looked doubtful and said, "If it was actually beluga caviar, the thief isn't making much. That'd be close to the wholesale price."

Guma said, "Yeah, well, Carl and Lou probably weren't that much into caviar. They figured it was a nice, safe sideline. It wasn't like this guy they were boosting it for was a wise guy or anything, somebody who could tell somebody and it would get back to Joey. And thirty large, regular. They figured it was worth the risk."

"Who was the guy if it wasn't a wise guy?" asked Marlene.

Guma smiled broadly, showing a remarkable collection of mismatched yellow teeth. "Ah, yeah. It was a Turk, as it happens. Said his name was Takmad. Ran a restaurant, he said, which was why he wanted caviar. He said."

"So they lift the crate," said Karp. "What happened then?"

"That's where Jimmy got a little vague. Lifting it—no problem. They're so wired out by Kennedy, the clerks, the guards, it's like going to a fuckin' K Mart for them. So they deliver it. So I say to Jimmy, 'So, you find out they went into business for themselves, you ratted them out to Joey.'

"He got a little testy there. He don't rat, he says. So who, then? I ask him. Jimmy don't know, but somebody dropped a dime the day after the boys delivered the box. Not only the caviar, but the snitch tells Joey they'd been doing it for months."

Karp said, "Great. Hold that thought for a minute. The next act is the art business, starring V.T. and Marlene."

Marlene summarized the interview with Sarkis Kerbussyan and the story of the search for the Gregory Mask. V.T. added what he had learned from his investigation into the financial life of the various Turks and Armenians involved in the case.

"Summing up," he concluded, "Kerbussyan has been pursuing liquidity to an unusual degree for the past nine months. He's sold some property he should have hung on to, and he hasn't bought anything else, not in real estate anyway. So, a lot of cash floating around. Some pretty big wire transfers to Switzerland. Also he's received very substantial inflows of cash from wealthy Armenians in the U.S. and overseas. In the neighborhood of thirty million. This is since mid-February.

"On the Turks, Ahmet Djelal has a modest bank account, but he spends like a pimp. Aziz Nassif, the cousin, bought himself a nice location for his restaurant, and nobody knows where he got the cash. Nobody buys real estate in New York for actual folding money. The seller recalled it clearly.

"Mehmet Ersoy had, as we know, a nice wad in a box when he died. What we didn't know until a day or so ago is that in the past year he has sent a total of"—here V.T. paused to check through some sheets of scribbled-on paper—"a total of, $1,835,000 to the account of his brother, Altemur Ersoy, at Esbank, Istanbul.

"Another interesting thing. NYPD art fraud has been working with Interpol on a series of fake scams run across Europe in the last two years, centered on Rome and London. The period of these scams fits almost exactly with the periods that Mehmet Ersoy was stationed in those two cities."

He paused. "Now to the letters Ersoy also had in his box. They're in a kind of crude code. Family bullshit, but not really. 'I'm sending you a nice present. I hope Fatima will like it.' 'Thanks for your recent gift.' Always uses the same locutions, either a 'special present' or a 'very fine present, just like the special present.' Genuine art and forgeries? It makes a nice story. In any case, the Ersoys are apparently generous people. There are presents and thank-yous mentioned in every letter.

"Okay, late February, early March, there's repeated mention of a 'special present' coming. Also, old Altemur seems pretty worried. Talks about 'our unpleasant relations' trying to look in his windows. I think the cops were starting to pinch at him. Probably why they didn't use the phone. 'This will be my last present for a time,' he says on February 22. 'I will send it air express on March 10.' "

"The Viacchenzas pulled their heist when, Ray?" Karp asked.

"March 11." Everyone was silent, thinking about that for a while.

"Did he say what the presents were going to be, or just 'presents'?" Marlene asked.

V.T. smiled. "Yes, interesting question. Not normally. It just indicates with a name—a present from so-and-so. Obviously they'd worked the code out beforehand. But for this last one he did. He said, 'I'm sending you a big case of your favorite caviar.' "

■   ■   ■

Vinnie was taken to change his clothes and was then returned to his cell, a ten-foot box designed to house two prisoners in reasonable discomfort, but which now held six. He lay down on the lower bunk. He heaped his blankets on the upper part of his body, including his head, and began to groan and writhe, shaking the three-tiered structure. While he did this, he used the knife to peel strips of thick crusted paint off the wall opposite his face, until he had a crumbly little mound about the size of an ice-cream scoop. He placed the paint chips in his mouth, deep in his cheek, like the tobacco cud of a ball player. Then he stuck the blade inside his mouth and made a long slit on the inside of his cheek. It didn't hurt much; the knife was extremely sharp.

His groans and cries increased in volume. He rolled out of the bunk and, after staggering a few steps, collapsed on his side in a fetal position. A trickle of blood oozed out of his mouth. His roomies began to raise an alarm, yelling for the guards, delighted with this opportunity of getting rid of a man who was possibly the least desirable cell mate in the Tombs.

A guard arrived, checked out the problem, went back to a wall phone, and called for Walker. That was the informal policy: when Vinnie moved, Walker moved him, and it was obvious that something was seriously wrong with the big son of a bitch. He was bleeding from the mouth, and his face was flushed and covered with sweat.

Walker arrived, entered the cell, and heaved Vinnie to his feet. Vinnie immediately began to cough spasmodically; then he vomited a crimson lumpy mass all over the front of his own jumpsuit, the floor, and the tips of Walker's shoes.

Walker jumped back, his face expressing both distaste and concern. Ulcers are as common among criminals as they are in the advertising business. Most experienced jail guards have seen the typical bloody, granular vomit of a perforated ulcer, and many have learned how fast a victim can bleed to death through one. Walker thought of the investigations, of the paperwork he would have to do if Vinnie punched out on his shift.

"Vinnie! Can you walk? Should I get a trolley?" he asked nervously.

"I can walk," said Vinnie in a thin, cracked voice.

So he could, barely. The other guard locked up the cell, and Walker half carried his charge down the barred corridors toward the jail infirmary.

A small man in a white smock looked up in alarm as Walker dragged the huge bloodstained prisoner through the swinging doors.

"Knife fight?"

"No," said Walker. "Popped his ulcer. He's puking blood."

As if to demonstrate, Vinnie heaved again, splashing a gout of blood across Walker's white uniform shirt. Cursing, Walker wrestled Vinnie into a plastic chair.

Vinnie groaned. "I gotta go . . . toilet. Got the shits."

Walker looked at the slight ward attendant and cursed again. "Should I take him, or . . . ?"

The attendant nodded. "Yeah, go ahead. And then get him up on a gurney. Cuff and strap. There's one in the hallway. I'll call Bellevue. We can't handle a perforated ulcer here. Wait! Sign him over first."

Walker signed a blank form. The medic picked up the phone, and Walker got Vinnie moving down the hall to the toilet. He installed the prisoner in a doorless booth and turned to one of the sinks. He started dabbing at the bloodstain on the front of his shirt. He had reduced it to a large pink smear when he heard a faint sound behind him and turned.

Vinnie had squat-walked up behind him so as to keep his reflection out of the mirror. As soon as Walker turned, Vinnie sprang forward, rising, and drove his knife deep into Walker's chest. Again. Walker collapsed without a sound.

The medic had finished his call and was busy typing out the transfer form. He saw a man in a guard uniform walk past him and called out, "He okay?"

"Yeah," the man mumbled, and was gone.

. . .

"Cut to the chase," said Roland irritably. "What's it all mean?"

Karp looked around the conference table. He had everyone's attention. "What does it all mean? Okay, here's my take, but anyone else, you got any ideas, jump in. Mehmet Ersoy, our victim, had a brother who had access to art treasures. The brothers had a racket going. They worked some European cities and then, late last year, started in New York. He brought the head of security for the Turkish mission, Djelal, in on it, and maybe Djelal brought in his cousin Nassif."

"How do we know that, Butch?" asked Hrcany. "Because they got money? Hell, I got money. Maybe their family's loaded in the old country. We don't even know these guys hang out together. I sure don't with my cousins."

"They hang out," said Bello. Everyone turned to look at the cop, amazed, as if a file cabinet had started talking. "I followed Nassif. He went to the mission offices, then the two of them headed out in an embassy car."

"Where did they go?" asked Marlene.

"They bought paint on Canal Street. I saw them heaving a big carton into the trunk of the Caddy. Big carton. They had to tie it down. Then they went back to Djelal's place on 56th. They left the carton in the car."

Roland laughed. "Very suspicious. We could get them for Attempted Felonious Decorating with a Bad Taste Color."

Karp resumed: "Okay, at least it's established that they're buddies. Anyway, Ersoy, and whoever, started selling artworks through the Sokoloff gallery, some genuine pieces but also a lot of fakes. It was the same scam he'd used in Europe. They sold a lot of material to Sarkis Kerbussyan.

"Late last year, Ersoy told Kerbussyan that they'd gotten hold of this super treasure, this Mask of Gregory. Kerbussyan agreed to buy it and began gathering serious money from the Armenian community. He puts something like a million bucks down on it, most of which we find in Ersoy's bank box after his death. At about the right time Ersoy's brother sends this box of caviar."

Karp paused and looked meaningfully around the table again. "Anybody want to bet that it was caviar in that box? No, me neither. Let's say this mask was in the box. It goes out from Turkey on March 10, arriving at JFK March 11.

"Okay, now it gets complicated. A little prior to this, a Turk had contacted the Viacchenza boys and set up a theft from air freight. A box of caviar. He pays heavy cash in advance, with a promise of more. The Viacchenzas do the heist on March 11, late. This is a Friday. Two days later, Sunday, Mehmet Ersoy is murdered. Two days later, somebody calls Joey Castles and tells him the Viacchenzas are ripping him off. On the 18th, the Viacchenzas are gunned down. Maybe the snitch was the mysterious Turk, maybe not.

"Meanwhile, after all this, Joey is still talking to Sally Bollano about Turks and making some big score off them, with the involvement of a major fence. So. That's it. How many animals can you find in the drawing?"

Roland spoke first. "Simple. Ersoy screws Kerbussyan on an art deal. Kerbussyan wants to get even. Tomasian wants to be a martyr to the cause, so he pops Ersoy."

"That doesn't explain the theft from the airport," Marlene objected. "It doesn't explain the Bollano deal."

Roland answered blandly, "That's a detail. Ersoy arranged for the theft. Or maybe the thing didn't ever exist. It really was caviar, or a box of bricks. Then he tells Kerbussyan the thing got ripped off, and by the way, the million is nonrefundable. Kerbussyan has him killed, like I said. Now we got these other two Turks, they got a load of high-value objects they want to move. They're scared to run it through the auction houses—there's too much heat now. So they contact the mob and set up a deal with a heavy fence."

"What about this guy Jimmy said hired the theft? What's-his-face, Takmad?" asked Guma.

V.T. tapped a squat green-covered book he'd been leafing through. "It means 'nickname' in Turkish. Cute. No, it's got to be either Djelal or Nassif. Roland's story is interesting, and it fits all the facts."

Karp could see Guma nodding, satisfied. Karp might have been satisfied too if he had never met Sarkis Kerbussyan face to face.

16

"WHAT'S GOING ON?" ASKED MARLENE. SHE WAS SITTING NEXT TO HARry Bello in his car at the junction of Leonard and Centre, and they could see, and hear, that something was not right a block north at the Tombs. There were a half-dozen blue-and-whites parked near the corner occupied by the jail, their lights flashing. Sirens heralded the arrival of others. Harry moved the car onto Centre and was stopped by a uniformed cop who was directing traffic around the confusion.

Harry flashed his shield and asked, "What's up?"

"Escape. Scumbag knifed a guard and walked out through the courthouse."

"Who was it? The escape?"

"Name of Boguluso. A big motherfucker, they say. Shouldn't be too hard to catch. Probably hiding in the neighborhood."

Harry doubted that, the part about being easy to catch. He headed around the blockade toward the day-care center.

He was silent, but Marlene picked up his mood. "You're worried," she said.

He nodded and grunted assent. "Don't be," she said. "He's a punk. They'll pick him up. It's not like he could vanish into Chinatown. If he had any brains, which I doubt, he'd be halfway to the moon by now."

Not to the moon, but only to Hempstead, Long Island, at a house belonging to Duane Womrath's girlfriend's grandmother. Granny was in a nursing home, and Rita was watching the house.

The three of them sat in the living room, drinking beer and smoking dope, while the TV blared game shows.

"We should go west," Duane said. "Fuckin' Arizona."

"Yeah," said Vinnie without enthusiasm. He was wondering how to get rid of Duane for a while so he could hit on Rita. She'd go for it. Or if not, he'd pop her anyway. He was glad to be out of jail, sure, and it was Duane and Rita who'd planned it all out and pulled it off as slick as it went, but that was then. Vinnie was a child of the now.

He drained his beer and said, "We should get some more brew," looking significantly at Duane.

Duane said, "Fuck the brew, Vinnie! We gotta make some plans. We got to get out of state. That screw checks out, it's murder one, and they'll never stop lookin' for you."

"Don't fucking tell me what I gotta do," Vinnie rumbled.

Duane got up and paced. "Okay, fine. Do what you want. You want to stay here till somebody spots you, fuck me! Go do it! This ain't Alphabet City, bro. It's fuckin' Hempstead, Long fuckin' Island."

"Yeah, fuck it," said Vinnie after a considerable, tense silence. "Okay, we'll head west and all. But I got to do something in the city first."

"The city! You're outa your fuckin' gourd, Vinnie!"

"Don't fuckin' worry about it," said Vinnie confidently. "I'm in and out, no sweat. But I need to borrow your bike."

■　　■　　■

Marlene and Harry picked up Lucy at the day-care. She squalled briefly at the changing of the guard and then fell asleep in Marlene's arms.

"Home?" asked Harry.

"Yeah—no, could we stop by Canal and Lafayette first? I said I would pick up a roll of butcher paper for Lillian."

No problem. Harry parked the car on Canal, took the baby, and Marlene got out. It was close to six, and the merchants were starting to take in their sidewalk displays. Between Hudson and Centre streets, Canal is a vast emporium, whose many small merchants supply goods both ordinary and exotic, from war surplus to plumbing supplies, to hardware, to art supplies, to specialized equipment for all of the City's trades. You can buy a slightly used meat freezer, a bolt for an 1898 Mauser, a Norden bomb sight, a box containing a thousand assorted brass zippers, a length of anchor chain, an anchor to go with it, or (as in the present case) a roll of brown butcher paper suitable for the scribbles of preschoolers. Marlene bought her paper and staggered out with the heavy roll on her hip.

As she crossed the broad sidewalk, her eye was caught by an object fluttering from the awning rail of a military-surplus business next door. It looked like a gigantic pair of training pants in international orange, suspended by four heavy cables from a pulley. Marlene studied it for a moment and then went into the store. After a brief conversation with the proprietor, she bought it.

"Harry," she said when she was seated again in the car, "I got another big favor. After you drop us off, could you go back to Centre Street and get Butch and bring him back to the loft? Tell him I figured a way to get him home for the weekend."

"You must be out of your mind," said Karp when he saw what Marlene had wrought.

"I don't see why," she said blithely. "It's a navy breeches buoy. They used to use them to transfer people between ships at sea. Just sit in it and hold your crutches, and I'll go upstairs and haul you up on the cargo hoist. It's perfectly safe."

Karp looked doubtfully at the orange canvas object rotating slowly in the dusty light of their building's lift shaft. He was familiar with how the building's industrial operations acquired their raw materials. He also knew how frequently the lift broke down, suspending a load of wire in mid-shaft. Marlene had secured the lift hook to the shackle conveniently placed above the pulley block of the contraption. Thereby it swung, glowing and ominous.

"Come on. It's just like the Parachute Jump," encouraged Marlene.

Indeed. It was a lot like the vanished ride at Steeplechase in Coney Island, that once lifted screaming fun lovers two hundred feet into the air and then released them to float down to earth on parachutes. Karp had been on the Parachute Jump at the age of eight. Once—and tossed a heavy meal of hot dog, fries, and root beer over the assembled throng below.

On the other hand, at age eight there were only his brothers to mock him and call him chicken. Now he had Marlene. Leaning on her, he fitted himself into the apparatus. Five minutes later, the lift roared and jerked him into the air.

"There, that wasn't so bad," said Marlene cheerfully when Karp was at last standing in their loft.

"It was hell on earth, and I'll never forgive you," he replied.

"Thanks a million, Harry," said Marlene. Bello had gathered his small belongings and was about to slip away without ceremony. Marlene hugged him and kissed him on the cheek.

"Watch yourself," he said. "You going anywhere this weekend?"

"Harry, honestly! I'll be fine."

Harry looked doubtful, glanced at Karp hovering in the background, and after promising to pick Marlene up on Monday morning, made his exit.

Harry didn't go home. He drove around Alphabet City for a while, and stopped in several bodegas, restaurants, and bars, hoping to pick up some information about the fugitive. Nobody heard nothin', nobody seen the big guy. He got back in his car, feeling uneasy in a way he had learned, during the past thirty years on the streets, to trust utterly. He drove back to Crosby and parked fifty feet down the street from the door to Marlene's loft.

Karp seated himself at the kitchen table. "What was that all about, 'Watch yourself'?"

"Oh, nothing. Harry's a mother hen. It's the escape. He's worried that Vinnie might try something."

"With you?"

"Yeah."

"And you're not?"

"He's a punk, Butch. A loud-mouth asshole. Besides, I have a big man to protect me. Can I sit on your lap?"

"I insist on it," he said.

After a while, Karp, breathing hard, asked, "Have you thought about how I'm going to climb up to the bed?"

"I already brought the mattress down under the sleeping loft," said Marlene. "I'm completely handicapped-accessible, as required by law."

"You thought of everything," said Karp.

At which point Lucy awakened, squalling.

"Except that, of course," said Marlene.

The next morning, the two of them lay sated in a sticky embrace, having, as Marlene remarked, stored up enough for the coming week.

"I've been thinking," said Karp. "What if we offered Tomasian a deal?"

Marlene groaned. "Who's Tomasian?" She slithered up onto his chest. "Is he the author of the best-selling *How to Make Love to an Armenian*?"

"Seriously . . ."

"Seriously, I expect your thoughts to be focused entirely on the romantic during the tiny fragment of your time you devote to connubial duties. Begin with how much you love me and why."

"Okay, great face, hot body, terrific comprehension of the nuances of the adversarial system, which is why I put it to you that if we offer Tomasian a real sweetheart deal, and he doesn't take it, it'd be another indication that he's the wrong guy. Ow! That hurt, Marlene! Those are delicate organs. Don't you want to have any more children?"

"Not if they're like you." She got to her knees and stretched her arms out wide and flexed her torso from side to side. They were lying on the mattress in the space under the sleeping loft, which Marlene had fixed up as a library. Three walls were lined with a miscellany of bookcases, from brick-and-board to a huge, battered mahogany glass-fronted cabinet that she had salvaged and repaired. She examined her image in the reflection provided by this.

"Am I still beautiful?"

"You're gorgeous," he said.

She placed her hands beneath her breasts and frowned. "Badly sagged."

"Luscious and still perky," he replied.

"Perky? Really?"

"I swear," said Karp fervently. "Turning now to the other matter—"

Marlene flopped back on the pillows. "Yes, well, I don't think we need any further demonstrations that Tomasian is a patsy. We can't pressure Kerbussyan. We can't get to Djelal. No evidence links Nassif to any crime. So the only live action is the link to the Bollanos and Guma's wiretap. That, and the one piece of information that still doesn't make sense."

"Which is . . . ?"

"Why the two Turks were buying paint. They should want to keep away from one another. They know the heat's on. If they're actually the guys that Joey was talking about, they must be keyed up, ready to run this big deal. So they're painting? Doesn't make sense."

"Maybe they're doctoring the mask," said Karp. "Painting it

black. Or making a fake. Like the Maltese Falcon." As Sidney Greenstreet: "Nheh-heh-heh! Nheh-heh! By gad, sir. The black bird!"

"That's a thought," Marlene agreed. "Paint stores sell plaster too. We could check it out—"

This speculation was interrupted by a car horn out on Crosby blaring "shave-and-a-haircut."

"Oh, my God!" cried Marlene. "It's Raney."

"Well, invite him up. It's a queen-sized bed. Or did you forget that I'd be home?"

Marlene jumped out of the bed and ran to the bath. A sound of splashing. Karp called out, "So much for the tiny fragment of my time. When Raney calls . . ."

Marlene rushed dripping from her whore's bath and up the ladder to the sleeping loft. Drawers slammed open and shut. Panties, denim cutoffs, black Susan B. Anthony T-shirt, sweat socks, Converse high-tops. Down the ladder.

"Don't be a goon. I forgot I said I'd go to the park for touch football. You know, the detectives' game—we always go." She stopped and put a hand to her face. "Oh, Butch, I forgot to tell you. I'm sorry!"

"No, no problem. You go ahead."

"No, really, get dressed, and I'll get Lucy. We can all go."

"Hey, relax," he said. "Look, really, you've been cooped up here with the kid full-time for weeks. Take an afternoon off. I'll be fine. In fact, I'll enjoy it."

"You're sure?"

"Positive."

She planted a hot one on his lips and scooted for the door.

"Just don't break anything," he called after her.

Harry Bello saw Marlene get into Raney's beat-up Ghia and zoom away. Shaking off sleep, he cranked his engine and followed them at a discreet distance.

■　　■　　■

Two hours later, Marlene was lying propped up against the base of a big maple, her third Schaeffer chilling her hand, staring dreamily up through the mosaic of toothy leaves and blue sky. She had a bruise on her hip and a skinned elbow, grass in her hair, and drying sweat all over her body, and she felt wonderful.

There were about a hundred people attending the game and picnic, all current and former Manhattan detectives, their wives, dates, and children. Marlene supposed she qualified as a date. Several touch football games of varying levels of formality were taking place simultaneously: the "official" North-South game restricted to male detectives, a "ladies" game, a kids game, an old-timers game. Marlene had participated in the ladies game without resentment. Cops played rough. So did the ladies, for that matter.

She shifted her weight to ease the pressure of a root against a sore place, and felt an unaccustomed pressure against one buttock. Raney's wallet. He had been red-dogged as quarterback, and the wallet had popped out. She had been spectating at the time, and he had given it to her to hold.

The afternoon wore on. The games became more uncoordinated and hilarious as players drifted off the field, got their load on, and drifted back into the game. At last no one but kids remained on the grass, and everyone else repaired to the grills to scarf up chicken, burgers, franks, potato salad, chips, and more beer.

"We should get back," said Marlene woozily. Raney slipped a hand around her waist and fingered her belly above her cutoffs.

"We should," he said. "But first, how about slipping into the bushes and fooling around?"

"Get married, Raney," she said, laughing.

"I'm waiting for you, babes," he said. "You really want to go? They're gonna let off fireworks later."

"Next year," she said. "No, really. There's no food in the house, and my husband's hopping around there on one leg. I could grab a cab if you really want to stay. . . ."

Raney drove her home, carefully. He was fairly loaded too. The

Chopin tape he always had going on the car stereo played the *Polonaise in A-flat major,* and Marlene nearly drifted off.

In front of the loft, she kissed him solidly on the mouth, thanked him for a terrific day, and ran upstairs. Harry Bello's car sneaked around the corner two minutes later, cruised by the front door of the loft, and parked across the street.

Karp was on the floor with the baby when Marlene came in, the baby banging a spoon on a pot and on Karp—an appealing domestic scene. She joined them, hugged the child, kissed Karp.

"Whew!" he said, fanning the air in front of his face. "A few beers, dear?"

"A few, if you must know. How have you two been amusing yourselves? Did I miss anything exciting?"

"Yeah, actually you did. Watch this! C'mere, Lucy."

Karp rose on his good knee, reached for the baby, and stood her on her feet. "Go ahead, walk to Mommy."

To Marlene's incredulous delight, Lucy took three tottering steps and fell giggling into her mother's arms.

"I'm squirming with guilt now. I missed her first steps."

"Unnatural mother!" said Karp. "But that's nothing. Okay, Lucy, let's show Mommy." He picked up a pink sponge ball and handed it to the baby. Then he made his arms into a wide horizontal loop. "Okay, there she goes. She's driving down court, she's in the lane, she fakes, she fakes again, there's the shot . . . shoot it, Lucy!"

Almost on cue, with a convulsive heave Lucy shot the ball straight up into the air so that Karp, by contorting his body and shuffling on one knee, was able to arrange for the ball to fall through his arms. "Two points, and the crowd goes wild!"

Much was made of this, and there ensued a period of the sort of wordless familial being that stands at the root of any human capacity for happiness.

After this, time to eat. Marlene decided to take the baby with her to the store so that Karp could relax, deep ethnic and gender conditioning causing her grossly to underestimate the amount of time a man can be alone with an infant without murdering it, abandoning it, or suing for divorce.

Passing 23rd Street, making for the Queens-Midtown Tunnel, Jim Raney was suddenly aware of an emptiness in a characteristic place below the base of his spine. He cursed. Marlene still had his wallet. He couldn't face the weekend without cash or plastic. He whipped his car into an illegal U-turn and headed south again.

Marlene changed the baby, filled its bottle, and carried the child downstairs. At the ground-floor landing she paused to unchain the stroller from its pipe. She put Lucy in the stroller, rolled it down the shallow steps to the sidewalk, and set its brake. It was quiet on Crosby Street this late on Saturday. No more deliveries and almost no through traffic. Crosby Street, narrow, cobbled and inconvenient, is only six blocks long and goes nowhere in particular. This is one of its virtues as a place to live.

Harry Bello saw Marlene emerge from her building with Lucy. He briefly considered getting out and saying hello to them, but thought that Marlene might be pissed at him for hanging around. Instead he drifted back to his consideration of the case of Mehmet Ersoy. He already knew who had done the killing. That was the easy part. The hard part was why, and if he didn't know that, it would be almost impossible to assemble a compelling case. There was a treasure, with a willing buyer, and then it hadn't been sold to the buyer at all but stolen from the seller, and it was now about to be sold to the mob for what must be a lower price. It didn't make sense. Harry cogitated, staring blankly at Marlene, Lucy, and the empty street.

Vinnie Boguluso came swiftly out of the alley where he had been hiding and ran across the street, barely twenty feet in front of Harry's windshield. Marlene had her back to him. She was double-locking the big front door of the loft.

Harry Bello, heart in mouth, flung open the car door and pulled his .38 in almost the same motion. "Vinnie! Freeze!" he shouted.

Marlene spun around and saw Vinnie coming toward her, toward the baby. Vinnie checked in surprise when he saw the cop with the gun, but then continued toward Marlene.

Harry's gun was pointing at Vinnie, but there was no way he was going to fire a pistol with Lucy anywhere near the line of fire.

Vinnie reached the stroller. He yanked the baby out by her arm and clutched her roughly to his chest. He had his switchblade knife out. He pressed its blade into the tender flesh of the baby's neck.

"Drop the gun!" he shouted.

Harry didn't move. Marlene stood frozen against the door. She couldn't breathe.

"Drop it! I'll cut its fuckin' head off!" screamed Vinnie.

The baby became frightened. Her face grew red and crinkled up, and she began to wail. Tears sprang from her eyes, and then from Marlene's eyes.

Slowly, carefully, Harry Bello bent his knees and placed the pistol on the cobblestones.

"Back away from it!" shouted Vinnie. Slowly Harry did so, never taking his eyes off Vinnie, part of his mind cool under the terror, considering options, looking for an opening. Vinnie would have to put the baby down or take the knife away from her in order to pick up the gun. That's when he'd make his move.

Harry was a lot faster than he looked. He figured he'd have to take at the most two bullets before he got to the guy.

Vinnie shuffled forward into the street, toward the pistol. Marlene followed behind him.

Then the roar of an engine gearing down filled the canyon of Crosby Street, and a green Karmann-Ghia whipped around the Howard Street corner and screeched to a halt twenty feet from where Vinnie stood. Jim Raney stared at the scene through his windshield. It was not hard to figure out what was going on.

Raney got out of his car and walked a few steps toward Vinnie. He took his Browning Hi-Power out of its holster, jacked a round into its chamber, and took up his stance, pointing the weapon at Vinnie's head. "It's over, Vinnie," he said. "Put the kid down."

Vinnie had no intention of putting the kid down, not until he had a gun. With the baby under his knife, he was in control of the situation. He had seen all the movies. The cops always dropped their guns when you had the kid. He shouted, "Fuck you, cocksucker! *You* drop it! I'll rip its throat out, I swear . . . !"

Raney looked at Marlene. She stood white-faced behind and to Vinnie's right. Their eyes met. In a conversational voice he said, "Marlene. Red dog. On three."

Vinnie heard this. He didn't understand it, but he didn't have to. He was in control. Again he shouted.

"Drop the fuckin' gun!"

Raney took two deep breaths and let the second one out very slowly. Holding the pistol in both hands, he brought the little Day-Glo dot on the front sight in line with Vinnie's sloping forehead. He said, "Hut, hut, hut."

On the third "hut" he pulled the trigger.

On the third "hut" Marlene started to move.

Vinnie saw the flash of the gun. He formulated a thought: he would stab the baby and grab the woman.

This thought was still turning itself into neural impulses when Raney's 115-grain 9mm parabellum silvertip hollow-point punched through the bone of Vinnie's forehead as if it were wet cardboard, expanding to the diameter of a champagne cork as it did so. The resulting shock set up a cone of destruction in Vinnie's brain tissue, turning that thought and all the other thoughts he had ever had, and all his memories, and his unpleasant personality, into a reddish slurry that was, within the next hundredth of a second, ejected out the back of his skull in a graceful arc.

The decorticated mammal exhibits limb extension. The body of Vincent Boguluso did so; the legs stiffened, the arms shot wide, a fleshy crucifix. Squalling, Lucy Karp dropped like a brick.

Marlene was airborne in a low dive. She twisted in the air, her back crashed along the stones, her cupped hands reaching under her falling baby to cushion its skull. She felt the warm weight in her hands and whipped the little body around, pressing it to her breast.

She looked up at the standing corpse. Desperately she started to roll away from it, but there was no need. The knees buckled, they hit the street, and it fell over slowly onto its side.

"Are you all right?" Harry Bello was kneeling by her side, his face the color of cheap toilet paper.

"Yeah," said Marlene. She checked the baby. She was still whimpering, and her sundress was torn, but the only marks on her were a thin red bruise on her neck and finger impressions on her arm. Marlene shuddered and tried to force deep breaths into her lungs.

There was a loud, disgusting noise. It went on for some time. Harry looked up.

Marlene said, "It's okay. He always does that."

"What, puke his guts?"

Marlene nodded. "When he kills people."

Harry said nothing. He was pretty sure that if Raney had missed, if he had hit Lucy, Harry would have taken his own gun and killed Vinnie, Raney, and himself, in that order. He put the thought out of his mind and helped Marlene to her feet. Then he went to his car and called the incident in on the police radio.

Karp had slept through the whole thing: the screaming, the shot, the sirens. Rancy and Bello said they would handle the clean-up and the various official acts New York considers necessary when one of its citizens has his brains blown over one of its streets. Marlene returned to the loft alone. She got the baby interested in some toys in her playpen and poured herself a tumbler full of red wine. Which she drank and poured another.

There was still dinner to get, she thought, horrific event or no, and, naturally, she had not gone to the store. She was not going to go either. Maybe she would never leave her loft again.

No food in the house. Of course, there is always food in the house. She found half a Spanish onion, some faded escarole, and a chunk of salt pork. There was a bulb of garlic and olive oil.

She gets down an iron pot, splashes in some oil, cuts up the onion, chops in half the garlic and the salt pork, and puts the pieces in the oil, with the gas on low. She doesn't know what she is going to cook yet, but she knows that it is going to involve garlic and onions.

There was a can of tomatoes and one of tomato paste. Impossible there there should not be, in Marlene's kitchen. She pulls out a handful of dry spaghetti, but sees it is not enough for two and puts it back. She had been going to shop for pasta today.

There is a bag of flour. She gets out her largest pottery bowl and pours a mound of flour into it. She adds water and an envelope of yeast and makes dough. The dough rises, and she scours the back of the refrigerator and comes up with a bag of dried mushrooms and the end of an ancient sausage. She cuts the moldy parts from the sausage. The knife shakes in her hand, and she works slowly.

She opens the can of tomatoes, drains it, and dumps the contents into a steel sieve. She pushes the tomatoes through the sieve into a bowl. The pulp is brighter in color and in texture not very much like Vinnie's brains blown out across Crosby Street. Nevertheless, vomit rises in her throat, and she has to stop for a moment and lean over the table on her knuckles, breathing, her eyes closed. Then she throws the tomatoes into the pot, adds oregano and bay, covers the pot, and turns the flame down to sharp blue dots.

Karp wakes up and rises, attracted by the sounds and the odors. He comes into the kitchen on one crutch.

"What'd you get?" he asks.

"I didn't get anything."

He sees her face. "What happened?" he says in alarm.

She takes a deep breath and tells him. He's horrified, guilt-stricken. He looks at the child, who is in her playpen, banging two blocks together and crooning to herself.

"She's fine," says Marlene. "She's forgotten it already."

He senses Marlene doesn't want to discuss it now. "What's for dinner, then?" he asks.

"Pizza," she says.

He is amazed. She amazes him further by pounding out the

risen dough and flinging it up in the air. She has done this before, but never for him. A certain ethnic embarrassment: during the summer of her fourteenth year she did it fifty times a day at the restaurant owned by her father's brother in Belmar, New Jersey. It is obviously something you don't forget how to do, because Marlene can still do it.

She flings the dough high in the air again and again. Karp and the baby watch this, rapt. The dough enters the realm of pure ballistics, suns and galaxies tug at it. It becomes round and thin. Not a fast food this pizza.

Marlene puts it in a greasy pan and pours her sauce on it, and the mushrooms, escarole, and sausage. She bakes it. They eat, baby Lucy chewing on a crust.

By the time they have finished, Marlene is calm again, but changed, in the way this life has been changing her for some years. Ever less Smith, ever more Sicily.

17

DROPPING FIVE STORIES ON A WIRE WAS NOT KARP'S IDEA OF HOW TO start a day when he was on a trial. It did not make him feel like Peter Pan, especially since the belt slipped during the descent and he had to dangle in mid-shaft for a half hour while two employees of the wire factory on the third floor labored, amid loud Spanish controversy, to repair the fault.

When he emerged from the shaft gate, his brow was dark, and his police driver decided not to express any of the several cute remarks he had thought of while observing these events.

Marlene remained in the loft. She had called in sick, although there was nothing physically wrong with her. But if she could not take a mental health day after a weekend during which her child had been assaulted by a gigantic felon, when could she? She spent the morning lounging comfortably in bed, drinking coffee and sharing TV cartoons and cookies with the baby.

Karp passed his morning less pleasantly, finishing up the official witnesses in *People* v. *Russell*: Thornby, the arresting officer; Marrano, the cop who had taken the famous blue shirt, the victim's handbag, and the knife to the station house; Cimella, the detective who had received all this, plus the sales slip found on Russell; and two men from the medical examiner's office, who established that Susan Weiner had died of stab wounds and that the wounds were consistent with the knife found on the stairway of 58 Barrow, and that the stains on the knife blade were human blood.

The cross went as Karp expected. Freeland pounded away at the time issue. The implication he was trying to plant in the jury's collective mind was that the cops had found the handbag where the real killer (not Russell) had dumped it, found the sales slip within, and lied that they had found it on the defendant four hours or so before the bag had been located.

At least the trial was moving. Freeland had at last exceeded Judge Martino's level of tolerance, and Martino had responded in a way that did the defense no good. After a particularly fruitless and time-wasting series of questions about an alternate blood-testing system addressed to the medical examiner's blood pathologist, a man of magisterial expertise, Martino had called counsel to the bench.

"Mr. Freeland, what is the purpose of this line of questioning?" asked the judge.

"Your Honor, my purpose here is to draw out for the jury the failure of the medical examiner to test for blood type from the stains on the knife purportedly found."

"The witness states that the amount of blood was too little for those tests."

"Yes, but I've located articles in the *Journal of Forensic Medicine*—"

"Mr. Freeland, the witness has stated that those tests are not accepted by his profession."

"Yes, Your Honor, but—"

"Mr. Freeland, do you know what an expert witness is?"

Freeland flushed, coughed, and said, "Of course, Judge."

"I don't think you do. An expert witness is assumed credible when speaking within the confines of his expertise. You have spent half an hour questioning him about the validity of tests that he says are garbage, despite repeated objections by the People, which I have sustained. If you wish to challenge the expertise of the People's witness, the appropriate measure is to call an expert of your own. Do you plan to do so?"

"Uh, no, Your Honor, not at this time. But, Your Honor—"

"Be quiet, sir! Let me ask you, have you ever tried a homicide case before?"

Freeland's face was brick now. "Uh, no, sir, this is my first."

"It'll be your last in my court if you don't stop wasting my time. Unreasonable delay and contentiousness for its own sake are not acceptable strategies in this court." Martino paused for a beat. "And I want to say that if you can't cut it, I will have you replaced as counsel by reason of incompetence."

Points for the judge, thought Karp, moving back to his seat. The threat of removal for incompetence would be particularly telling when counsel was the new head of the local Legal Aid Society office. He looked over at the defense table. Freeland was thumbing through notes and making marks. His color was back to normal, and he seemed relaxed for someone who had just had his shorts fried by a judge.

Marlene let the phone ring. It was lunchtime, and she was feeding the baby mashed bananas. But when the message machine clicked on and she heard the voice, she abandoned Lucy in her high chair and raced to the phone.

"Ms. Ciampi? I'm so sorry to disturb you at home, but I thought it was important."

"No problem," said Marlene. "What's up, Mr. Sokoloff?"

"A gentleman called on me today. He presented himself as an associate of Mr. Ersoy's, with similar contacts. He said his name was Nassif."

"What did he want?"

"He had some things to sell. A very nice figured reliquary in silver—Armenian, fourteenth century. And some Byzantine coins ranging from the ninth to the fourteenth century. The reliquary is real, I believe, but the coins are not."

"What did you do?"

"I, ah, said I had to consult with some potential customers. I invited him to call on me tomorrow."

"Very good, Mr. Sokoloff, that's very helpful. Look, I need to talk to some people and then I'll get back to you."

Clever man, thought Marlene after he had bid her good-bye. Just the right move to dispatch any lingering doubts about the complicity of Sokoloff Galleries in a set of art frauds that may or may not have led to a murder.

Marlene got on the phone then and spoke with V.T. and then with Rodriguez, the art fraud cop, setting up a sting. Then she called Sokoloff back and told him what he had to do.

Lucy during this period had managed to cover herself and every object within range of her flinging power with a thin slime of sticky banana. Marlene laughed, hugged the child to her, stripped both Lucy and herself, and plunged the two of them into the bathtub.

In the afternoon, Karp presented his last official witness, Tony Chelham, the jail officer for whom Russell had identified his blue shirt. This was critical because all the witnesses who had seen Hosie Russell fleeing the murder scene and entering 58 Barrow Street had seen a man in such a shirt: the Digbys from Lexington, the actor Jerry Shelton, and James Turnbull, the leather shop owner. Karp brought those forward during the remainder of the afternoon. They all did well, both on direct and on cross. Freeland's only option, since they had all obviously seen someone, was to suggest that whomever they had seen, it was not the defendant.

He implied that, to the Digbys, all black people looked alike. He implied that Shelton, a homosexual actor living in Greenwich Village, was probably besotted with drugs as a matter of course—he actually asked whether Shelton had been smoking marijuana on the

afternoon in question. He implied that Turnbull, who had spontaneously identified Russell in the police station and had attacked him as
the murderer, had been put up to it by the police, which implication
Turnbull, a man of immense dignity and presence, passionately rejected.

It was not a particularly good cross, thought Karp. Freeland appeared to be drifting; a lot of his questions didn't lead anywhere in
particular, as if he was just going through the motions. It didn't help
him that the witnesses were all solid citizens. Attacking such witnesses tended to piss off the jury, composed of the similarly solid.

After Turnbull stepped down, Karp said, "Your Honor, that is
the People's case."

Martino excused the jury, Freeland made the expected motion to
dismiss, which was rejected, and Karp was through for the day, at
least with trials. He went back to his office and caught up on
paperwork until seven, ordered take-out Chinese, ate it, and clumped
off to the jail to take a shower.

He tried not to think about the trial. There is a certain letdown
after the presentation of a major case, and it was entirely possible to
drive oneself into a frenzy of doubt about the various errors that
could have been made, and which might even now be bubbling in
the minds of the jurors, cooking away at an acquittal.

The case had weaknesses, of course: no witness had turned up
from the crowd who had actually followed Russell from the murder
scene to 58 Barrow, although the police had seen dozens of people
doing so. The guy on the bike—who had told Thornby that a man
was hiding in that building—was a particularly unfortunate no-
show, and the cops, urged on by Karp, had tried strenuously to locate
him.

And, of course, Freeland still had his turn at bat. Karp had no
idea what the defense was going to present; Freeland had flatly refused to tell Karp who his witnesses, if any, were going to be. There
was no point in speculating.

Karp turned off the water and reached for his towel. He found
himself, surprisingly, wanting the trial to be over. The whole thing

irritated him: the stupidity of the crime, the arrogance and fatuousness of Freeland, the enforced isolation, the goddamned cast; he even regretted getting to know Russell in these after-hours meetings.

Here he was, mopping, as Karp emerged. Karp nodded curtly and began to get dressed.

"You got any smokes?"

"Sorry, I forgot," said Karp. He sensed Russell staring at him, but he did not acknowledge it, or make any effort to start a conversation.

"Hey, man," said Russell after some moments, "I heard some things."

"Uh-huh, like what?"

"You know, stuff. Around the jail. Like you might wanna know about." Russell had his pathetic sly expression on.

"Uh-huh. So, you going to tell me?"

"I could. Depends on what I get."

Karp pulled his sweats on. Water had dripped down inside his cast and was itching. He said, "I got nothing to give you, Hosie."

"You sure about that? This, what I got, it's a big case."

Karp got his crutches under his arms and stood. He looked Russell in the eye. "Well, here's the thing, Hosie. First of all, like I said a while back, there's no way I'm going to discuss your case in any way whatever without your attorney present. If you have something you want to deal for, he's the guy to see.

"Second, right now I'd say that if you gave me the guy who did JFK, you'd still be looking at twenty-five to life. The time to deal is past. You decided to go for the trial, and you got the trial. They find you not guilty, you walk; you're guilty, it's the max. That's how it works.

"And there's no point you looking at me like that. It's nothing personal. You can't be on the street. You're a career criminal, you've already spent most of your life in the slam, and now you're going to spend the rest of it inside. That's your part in the play. It's my part to put you away, and it's Freeland's part to try to stop me. It's a puppet show. Or like a mechanical bank—you put the penny in the slot and the little clown spins around."

"It's like that, huh?"

"Yeah, I guess," said Karp after a sigh. "Sometimes I think it is."

"Whatever you do to me ain't gonna bring her back."

"There's that. You know, when I was in law school, I heard a guy lecture on the philosophy behind punishment. What he called 'the supposed justification.' He did a pretty good job of proving that there wasn't any—rehabilitation is a joke, deterrence is unethical, revenge is immoral."

"Didn't convince you much."

Karp smiled. "No, it didn't. Or to tell the truth, I saw the logic of what he was saying, but it didn't feel right to me. You hurt someone, you got to suffer. There has to be justice or the world doesn't make sense. I'm talking gut level, not all the legal horseshit.

"So let me give you some advice. You heard something in the cells. Maybe somebody admitted doing something that somebody else is going down for. Or somebody has some information about a crime that the cops don't know about. You figure you can use it to get a better deal, because you're a hustler. You're looking out for number one. That's what you've always done, your whole life. Well, look around. Here you are. Here you're gonna stay. That's what hustling got for you.

"What I'm saying is, think about it; maybe you should start doing the opposite. Do something for somebody else, a stranger maybe. You can't fuck up your life any worse than it's already been, and who knows? It could change your luck."

He stumped out leaving Hosie Russell looking at him blankly, as if he had been speaking Armenian.

Marlene, baby on hip, pounded on the iron door of Stuart Franciosa's loft, which, after a considerable wait, was opened by the proprietor, looking harassed. He wore a heavy reflective apron over his usual black sweatshirt and black canvas pants, and he had a pair of dark goggles pushed up on his forehead.

"Sorry, I'm in the midst," he said. "What's up?"

"I'm going shopping," said Marlene. "You want me to pick anything up?"

"How considerate! How about the severed head of the odious Lepkowitz?"

"Oh, God, don't remind me. The deadline's getting close, isn't it?"

"Less than a month. How're you doing on it?"

"Doomed. I'm starting to get my head adjusted to the possibility that the fucker could actually kick me out."

"Oh, you'll think of something. But, really, shopping? Thanks, but we want for nothing. We eat like birds, as you know. Say, I heard about what happened Saturday. You really have to stop being attacked by criminals, Marlene. It's bringing the neighborhood down."

"I'll think about it. What're you doing in there, by the way?"

"Casting. Want to see? It's quite *dramatique*."

The big workroom was hot and smelled of burning.

"It's just a little bronze, a test really," said Stuart. "I just got this neat little electric furnace. It was starting to be a pain in the ass to go up to the foundry for every little thing. Don't look directly in the door."

Stuart used a set of tongs to open the door of the squat cylinder. Harsh yellow light and a blast of heat shot out. He reached in with the tongs and drew out a glowing crucible and poured a stream of liquid bronze into a small mold, throwing a shower of sparks and a cloud of smoke.

Marlene and Lucy watched with interest. Lucy was fascinated by the fireworks. Marlene was looking more at the metalized label stuck to the side of the device.

"Where'd you get that thing, Stu?"

"Pearl Paint, the artist's venal friend. Why?"

"Nothing. I've just been a jerk. See you."

■   ■   ■

Later, her shopping done, the baby fed and napping, Marlene worked the phone, trying to locate Harry Bello. She finally had to leave her number with the police dispatcher, saying it was an emergency.

Harry called back within ten minutes, concern thick in his voice.

"What's wrong?'

"Nothing's wrong, Harry."

"They said it was an emergency. I thought, the kid—"

"The paint, Harry. It wasn't paint."

"This you give me a heart attack for? The paint isn't paint?"

"Where was it, the store you saw the Turks at?"

"On Canal, that Pearl's Paint."

"Harry, Pearl Paint is the biggest art-supply store in lower Manhattan. You saw them carrying a heavy box out, say about the size of a big TV?"

"Yeah. So?"

"My next paycheck says that wasn't a set of watercolors. It was an electric jeweler's furnace."

"They're gonna melt that thing, the mask," said Harry, no flies on him.

"Not if I can help it," said Marlene.

The defense's first witness in *People* v. *Russell* was, to Karp's surprise, a familiar face. Paul Ashakian took the stand and was sworn in. He looked young and blank-faced up there.

Freeland took him through the usual background material, schools, profession, the fact that he was not a bodybuilder or involved in any athletics at present, and then on to the meat. Freeland had set up an experiment. He had taken Ashakian up to the stairway in 58 Barrow, and there Ashakian had propped up the skylight, jumped up, grabbed the lip of the skylight base, and chinned himself up to the roof. He testified that once up on the roof, he had observed numerous ways to leave the building.

Freeland asked, "Now, Mr. Ashakian, is there any doubt in your mind that a person of approximately your height and build could enter the skylight as you did and escape from the roof in any of the ways you have described?"

Karp objected. "Speculative."

"Sustained."

Freeland asked, "Well, then, did you yourself have any difficulty whatever pulling yourself up through the skylight to the roof?"

Ashakian said it had been easy.

Karp rose for cross. He had been about to ask that the entire testimony be stricken as speculative and irrelevant, but a memory flashed into his mind and he approached the witness.

"Mr. Ashakian, you testified that you attended St. Joseph's High School. While there, did you participate in any sports?"

"Yes, I was on the gym team."

"You started for the St. Joseph's gymnastic team?"

"Yes."

"And during that time, were you ever required to perform on the high bar?"

"Yes, I was."

"Did that entail leaping up for a bar set nine feet above the ground, pulling yourself up so that your legs were on the bar, and rotating your whole body rapidly around the bar?"

"Yes, it did," said Ashakian. To his credit, he seemed embarrassed.

"No further questions," said Karp.

Freeland's second witness was a thin, elderly man named Walter Tyler. Tyler testified that he had been walking down Hudson Street and that he had seen Susan Weiner stagger, bleeding, out of her doorway and a man running away from that scene. The man had glanced over his shoulder as he ran, and Tyler had seen his "full face." The running man had not been Hosie Russell.

Tyler testified further that he had gone with the crowd to 58 Barrow, had shouted out that Russell was not the right man, and had been ignored. Later he had gone up to a cop and had given his story, which the cop had written down. When he saw that the police were continuing to charge Russell, he had gone to Freeland.

Karp looked over at the jury. They were listening with interest. Wrinkles of doubt appeared on their faces. They had all watched enough Perry Mason to believe that the defense could pull in a secret witness at the last moment to overturn the prosecution's carefully constructed case. Disaster loomed.

Marlene, dressed in her best black, perfumed heavily, attempting to radiate class, sat in an uncomfortable Louis XV chair in Stephan Sokoloff's cozy office and looked at Aziz Nassif, who was sitting in a similar chair. Sokoloff sat behind his desk smiling genially upon the supposed transaction taking place. On the desk, on a tray covered in black velvet, were four coins.

"Thirty thousand for the four," said Marlene. "It's my best offer."

Nassif licked his lips, hesitated, then nodded. Sokoloff's smile broadened. He said, "I've taken the liberty of preparing a bill of sale. I'll just write in the price, here, and Mr. Nassif, if you'd just sign it . . ."

Nassif read the document and scratched his name on the appropriate line. Marlene took it, folded it, and put it in her bag. The door to the office opened. Ramon Rodriguez and Harry Bello walked in and arrested Nassif for art fraud.

Rodriguez took the protesting Turk away. Marlene pulled a paper out of her bag and gave it to Bello.

"Okay, Harry, this is a search warrant for Nassif's restaurant and his apartment. It's for the art fraud charge. You're looking for phony art objects or other evidence of fraud. Just like it says on the warrant. Of course, if you should happen to find any evidence of other crimes not named in plain sight, then you can seize that too."

Harry raised an eyebrow. "Smart."

"I thought so," said Marlene.

■   ■   ■

Karp stood and addressed the bench. "Your Honor, since this witness was not known to us before now, I request that Mr. Freeland turn over to the People all notes and statements pertaining to Mr. Tyler."

Freeland rose instantly and said, "Your Honor, the only records I have from this witness are personal notes, personal working notes, which I don't believe I am under any obligation to turn over."

Martino beckoned them to the bench. He addressed Freeland. "You have no statement from this man?"

"No, sir."

"No statements? You interviewed this witness without taking notes about what he told you?"

Freeland said, "Well, yes, but they're just rough notes—"

"That's what I want," said Karp.

"I don't have to give them," said Freeland, petulance creeping into his tone.

The judge said, "You have all Mr. Karp's material, notes, police reports, statements from witnesses. . . ."

"That was Mr. Karp's option in that he thought those materials fell under *Rosario,* which he was obligated to give up. I am under no such obligation."

"I am directing you to turn them over."

"Your Honor, I'd like to know under what rule of discovery, or case you are directing me to."

Martino squinted his eyes in thought. "Rule of discovery, it's . . . what?" He glanced at Karp.

"*Dolan,* Your Honor," said Karp.

"Right, *Dolan.* That's *Dolan,* Mr. Freeland: D-O-L-A-N."

"I'm not familiar with that case, Judge."

"Not my problem, Mr. Freeland. I'm going to recess now for five minutes, during which you can peruse the law, and during which you will turn that material over to the People."

It was as Karp had expected. Eight sheets of yellow paper covered with scribbling that contained almost none of the testimony that Tyler had just given, except for his insistence that the man who had committed the crime had worn a blue shirt. The actuality was easy to reconstruct. An elderly man had seen something dramatic, a murder. He'd seen a figure race away. He'd followed the crowd to 58 Barrow. When the cops dragged out a man wearing a red T-shirt, he'd called out, "That's not the guy." Somehow Freeland had located him, or he had drifted in to Freeland, and the original story had been fertilized by suggestion and encouragement and the desire to be important, and Freeland's unprincipled ambition, until the current testimony had appeared, like a gross and noxious weed. Perjury.

"Mr. Tyler," said Karp, "could you stand up and come down here where I am?" As Tyler did so, Karp continued, "Your Honor, could we have Mr. Tyler demonstrate for the jury how the man was running and how he turned his head?"

The judge assented.

"Mr. Tyler," Karp continued, "now, this man you saw, was he running fast or slow?"

"He was running fast."

"All right, could you do that, could you just run away from the jury box and show the jury how the man was running and how he turned his head?"

Tyler broke into a clumsy trot across the well of the court and, after a few steps, threw his head back over his shoulder, then continued on for a few more steps. It was a good demonstration that if a man is running away from you and he looks over his shoulder, you can't see his full face.

Karp said, "Now could you tell us exactly how far this man was away from you when he turned his head?"

"Thirty feet. I said thirty feet."

On his crutches Karp backed slowly away from Tyler. He stopped at the rail dividing the well from the spectators. "About here?"

"No, farther than that."

Karp opened the little gate and moved up the aisle. "Here?"

"Yeah, that's good," said Tyler.

Karp turned his back on the witness. "Mr. Tyler, can you see my back?"

"Yes."

"Mr. Tyler, you see that I can't run very well now, but I'm going to look over my right shoulder at you. Was this how the man on Hudson Street looked over his shoulder?"

"Yeah, like that."

"Mr. Tyler, can you see my full face?"

A pause. "Well, it wasn't just like that . . . he sort of stopped a little."

"Answer the question," said Martino.

"No, I can't."

"And it follows that on Hudson Street that day, you couldn't really see the full face of the man you saw running away, isn't that true?"

"Yes."

"So what you actually saw that day was a portion of a man's face at a distance of perhaps thirty feet for about one second, isn't that true?"

Tyler agreed that it was.

Karp said, "Mr. Tyler, when Mr. Freeland first interviewed you, didn't you say that you were forty-five feet away from the man when he turned?"

"No, thirty feet."

"But Mr. Freeland's notes, which I have here and which I now submit in evidence, state clearly forty-five feet. Is this the incredible shrinking distance?"

"Objection!" from Freeland.

"Withdrawn. Did you say you were forty-five feet away from the over-the-shoulder glance when you first spoke to Mr. Freeland?"

"Objection! These are personal notes. What I wrote down there may or may not be what Mr. Tyler told me, and they shouldn't be used to cross-examine the witness."

There was a moment of stunned silence, and the judge gave Freeland one of his long looks. "Mr. Freeland, are you stating that

Mr. Tyler did not just testify to the same facts that he told you originally, or that you didn't write down what he said then correctly?"

"Uh, no, Your Honor, I was not saying that."

The judged turned to Tyler. "Answer the question."

"It was thirty feet."

Karp then questioned him about the cop who had purportedly interviewed him. Tyler couldn't remember the cop's name or give a convincing description of him, or explain why he hadn't gone to the police, or the D.A. or a judge with his testimony. Karp dismissed the witness, feeling confident that he had creamed him pretty well. Freeland declined to recross, which was a good sign.

"Defense calls Geri Stone."

It took Karp a moment to comprehend who Geri Stone was. When he did, he rose and said, "Offer of proof on this witness, Your Honor?"

Freeland said, "This witness was the defendant's parole officer. She knows the defendant quite well and was in fact instrumental in obtaining his release from prison. She will testify as to the defendant's propensity for committing this type of crime."

"Approach the bench, Your Honor?" said Karp.

Martino beckoned them forward.

"Your Honor, this witness is the dead woman's sister. It strikes me as . . . obscene, to trot her in here as a character witness for the defendant."

"She's an expert, not a character witness," Freeland retorted, "and her relation to the deceased has no legal bearing on her suitability as a witness."

Martino looked at the two counsel bleakly. He had seen it all, and it hadn't improved his view of human nature or the imperfections of the law. "I'll allow the witness."

Karp protested, "As an expert only?"

"Yes, as to her expertise." To the court officer: "Swear her in."

The Sister was no longer in black. She wore a blue linen suit over a white blouse with a complicated scarf at the neck. She was heavily made up, and her hair had been recently done over with reddish highlights. She looked like a waxwork in the bureaucrats' hall of fame.

Freeland took her through her professional qualifications and her relationship with the defendant. Then they began on what a swell guy Hosie Russell was. Freeland read copiously from the parole officer's notes Stone had written, how Hosie was the victim of society and his own weaknesses, how he had tried so hard and, more to the point, how she believed that he was basically nonviolent, a disorganized, dissociated alcoholic, a sneak thief, not an armed robber. Stone confirmed her agreement with these opinions, her voice a low monotone.

Karp waited for the payoff, and he was not disappointed.

"Ms. Stone," Freeland asked smoothly, "have you or a member of your family ever been a victim of a violent crime?"

"Yes, my sister is the victim in this case."

"Objection!" cried Karp. "Irrelevant to the expert testimony."

"Sustained. The jury will disregard."

The damage, of course, was done. If Karp now tore Ms. Stone apart on the stand, tore apart the victim's sister, the jury would never forgive him. They would walk Jack the Ripper.

Freeland said, "No further questions."

Karp stood and said, "No questions, Your Honor."

Martino said, "Members of the jury, that completes the testimony in this case. All that remains are the summations by the respective counsel, after which the court will charge. Have a pleasant evening and do not discuss the case among yourselves."

The courtroom emptied. Karp gathered his papers.

"Need a hand?" It was Marlene.

"A leg, you mean."

"How'd it go?"

"Were you here?"

"No, I just came in. What happened?"

"Oh, nothing, just fucking Freeland called Geri Stone."

"As a defense witness?"

"Yep. As the parole officer, to the effect that Hosie was God's gift to New York. And she did it. She sat up there and mouthed that crap about the guy who knifed her sister. I can't understand it. I mean, I could understand Freeland doing it—it's brilliant in a filthy way. Getting the vic's sister to stand up for the mutt charged, and of course he slipped it in that she was the sister. But I can't see why she would agree to it."

"Oh, I can," said Marlene. "I mean, what else does she have anymore? She loved her sister and, God help us all, she loved her work. She thought she was doing good. She got Russell out on the street and he did her sister, what's she going to do—admit she made a mistake, that her whole approach to life is fucked? That this mutt she made a pet of and patronized and manipulated was really manipulating her? No way."

Karp sighed. "You think so? Maybe. It's hard to believe, though. I mean, *we're* not that crazy—about all this, I mean." He gestured wildly at the courtroom, taking in the legal profession and the law's grim majesty.

"Speak for yourself, dear," said Marlene unhelpfully.

18

"THIS IS GETTING BORING," SAID ROLAND, SITTING DOWN AT THE LONG table in Karp's office. The same gang sat around the periphery, called together after the day's work by Karp in response to what Marlene had told him after court.

"We'll try to make it interesting for you, Roland," said Karp. "We've had a break in the case. Marlene?"

Marlene said, "Yeah, well, what happened is that Aziz Nassif tried to move some funny coins to Sokoloff. We just arrested him. Harry here has just completed a warranted search of his restaurant and apartment—"

"A warrant?" Roland interrupted. His voice rose. "A warrant for the Ersoy killing?"

"No, of course, not, Roland," answered Marlene sweetly. "We would never do anything like that. How would it look if we went after a warrant for a crime in which we already had an indicted suspect? The defense would eat you up. No, the warrant was for the fraud. But, of course, objects in plain view associated with any other crimes are subject to warrantless seizure—"

"I know the doctrine, Marlene," said Roland sourly. "What'd he find?"

"Harry?" said Marlene.

Harry Bello reached into his cheap vinyl briefcase and pulled out several clear plastic evidence bags. "One, a ski mask. Matches the description given by the witnesses at the scene. Two, blue parka with red stripes, the same. Three, box of nine-mm Parabellum pistol ammo, half empty. A clip from a nine-mm pistol, empty. Ballistics says it's from a Kirrikale, a copy of a German gun made in Turkey."

"Not the gun itself?" asked Roland.

"No gun," said Bello, and continued with his inventory: "Four, a rental agreement from a National car rental in Maspeth for a '78 Ford Fairlane two-door, blue. The make and model identified at the scene. Rented March 12, returned March 13, the day of the murder, two hours later than the hit. Fifth and last, a card showing rental rates from a mini-storage locker at Boulevard Storage, also in Maspeth. I called them. They have a hundred-square-footer rented to Ahmet Djelal. That's it."

Everyone looked at Roland, who sat, working his jaw, saying nothing, as the seconds passed heavily by. Finally he observed, "You don't have much. No gun. The mask and parka don't mean a lot. Same with the car. And I thought Nassif had an alibi."

"Yeah, from the workers in his restaurant, who're scared shitless of him," said Bello. "They won't hold up once we start pushing, start yanking their phony green cards around."

Some more silence. Everybody there knew that Roland's case against Tomasian was not that much more impressive than the case against Nassif. At last Karp spoke up. "Guma, what's the story on the tape?"

"The deal is still set for Thursday, day after tomorrow," Guma replied. "Aside from that, nothing new."

"Why don't we give them something new? Goom, do you think

you could arrange to have Joey Castles learn that we picked up Nassif for fraud? If it comes through in the phone tap, then at least we'll know that we're talking about the same Turks."

"I think I could arrange it," said Guma.

"Do that. The next thing to do is to talk to Nassif. We've got him next door. V.T.? And . . ." Karp paused and looked at Roland. It was the critical moment, akin to the first time you sit down in a divorce lawyer's office with your erstwhile sweetie. Roland had every right to interrogate Nassif. It was his case, and he was arguably the best interrogator in the office. The question was, would he?

The expressions raced across Roland's face, and Karp thought he could read them like stock quotes on a tape. If he didn't go after Nassif, Karp would do it himself, and then, if it turned out that the Turks really had done it, Roland would look like a complete asshole. Whereas if Roland got a confession out of the Turk, he'd still be the man on a hot case, the TV lights would still shine on him. Of course, the Turk could be a dud too, but then he still had Tomasian.

"Okay, let's take a look at him," Roland said at last.

"Terrific," said V.T. "I'll be the nice guy."

The two men left the room. Frangi got up to go with them, but Karp gestured for him to remain. Marlene said, "I notice Roland didn't mention his jailhouse snitch. What about that?"

"Yeah, what about that?" said Karp. He stared at Frangi, who was down at the other end of the table, looking ill at ease.

Frangi shrugged. "Hey, all I know is, I got a call from the jail captain said this cell mate Medford, wanted to talk about Tomasian for a deal. I told Roland and we talked to the A.D.A. on the guy's check kiting and then we went and talked to Medford. That's all I know."

"Well, if we're right about Nassif," said Karp, "it looks like the guy's lying."

"Snitches lie," said Frangi.

"Yeah, they do, but it's hard to believe a mutt like Medford would've come up with a hoax like that on his own." Frangi started to protest, but Karp held up his hand and continued, "I don't mean it was you. Or Roland either."

"Who, then?" asked Marlene.

"I don't know, but it doesn't matter at this point," Karp said quickly, although he thought it did matter a lot. A suspicion was growing in his mind, but he couldn't do anything about it at present. It would have to wait. He said, "Thanks, Joe," and Frangi left, followed soon by Guma.

Karp said, "Djelal, guys. How do we get him?"

"Not a prayer," said Marlene, "unless his *cugine* rats him out, or unless you want to totally shit on the D.A. and harass Djelal's butt and start an international incident. Even then he's clean. We don't have anything on him we could put on a warrant. Renting a locker and buying a jeweler's furnace? Having a sleazy cousin? On the other hand, I'm dying to know what he has in that locker."

"Yeah, me too," said Karp, "but we're going to have to keep dying, because we got no way into it legally."

Marlene and Bello exchanged a look, so brief that no one else saw it, but one that compressed megabytes of data, like a satellite transmission.

As they walked out of the office together after the meeting, Harry said, "I got a delivery truck I can borrow, with a lift on it."

"Good," said Marlene. "Don't hurt your back."

Roland stopped by Karp's office at ten that night. Karp was on his cot, memorizing his summation notes for the next day.

"You look comfy," said Roland. "Comfy but lonely. Want me to send somebody up?"

"I'll survive. This is the last day. What did you get?"

"We got shit. Nassif wouldn't talk. I don't mean he wouldn't confess. I mean he wouldn't talk, literally. And he was scared too. I never saw anyone in that much terror. His teeth were actually chattering."

"Well, he does have the right to remain silent," said Karp. "I guess he took it seriously."

"No, he was waiting for us to start the tortures. Isn't that Turkey where they hang you upside down and beat your feet with sticks? Frangi and me were screaming at him and dancing up and down, and he must've thought we were the good cops."

"So you think they did it? The cousins?"

Roland frowned. "I didn't say that. I think they did something, but I got no reason to believe that Tomasian wasn't part of it."

Karp nodded. "Okay."

"Okay? That's it?"

"Yeah, Roland, that's it. It's your case, like I've always said. We'll see how things develop. Meanwhile, we'll book Nassif for the fraud and see how he likes jail, with his cousin running around free. Maybe he'll come around."

Karp shaved and took a whore's bath in the hall john that night. He was too tired to walk over to the jail; more than that, he didn't want to see Russell again, except in court.

The next morning, of course, he did. Russell did not look well: even older than his years and his cheap suit was loose around his neck. Perhaps Freeland was giving him lessons in appearing pathetic and harmless, or maybe the reality of his situation was finally coming home to him.

Freeland led off on summation, as tradition demanded. He spoke for twenty-two minutes, a shortish speech, but then he didn't have a lot to say. His own evidence was fairly weak: Tyler's it-wasn't-him and Ashakian's gymnastic feat and the Sister. He spent most of his time pointing out the various places where the authorities might have lied. If you believed in conspiracies, it was a good story.

Karp spoke for nearly three times as long, but then, he had a lot more material to cover. He started off with James Turnbull's testimony, the dramatic scene in the police station—Russell sitting there *without* his blue shirt and Turnbull leaping at him, accusing him with no prompting at all, the man who was physically the closest witness to the actual murder. *You swine!* This was the guy.

Then the chain of police testimony—Thornby's adventure in the stifling black basement, the hiding fugitive, the sales slip found. Then Jerry Shelton's identification—this was the man who had fled from the pursuing crowd.

Then the discovery of the purse and the knife and the shirt, and the identification of the shirt in the jail by the defendant himself.

He disposed of Tyler: a ridiculous witness—a one-second, impossible full-face glance at thirty, or was it forty-five, feet, compared to people—the Digbys, Shelton, Turnbull—who had positively and independently identified the defendant.

Karp walked over to the evidence table and picked up the sales slip from Bloomingdale's and walked back to stand in front of the jury box.

"Susan Weiner is dead, her life cut short on a summer's day at twenty-eight years of age. But in a way she is here in this courtroom right now. Because when she bought a pair of stockings at Bloomingdale's in one of the last acts of her young life, she did something that was very human. She might have been in a hurry to come home to have lunch with her husband, so when they gave her her charge slip at Bloomingdale's, she grabbed it and shoved it down among three bills, two ones and a five, that were in her purse.

"Hosie Russell murdered her for that seven dollars, but when he tore the wages of his crime out of her purse, he didn't notice the VISA receipt wrapped in the currency; he was in a hurry too. And Officer Thornby found it in his pocket."

Karp fluttered the little piece of white paper in front of the jury.

"This is Susan's last message to us all. It doesn't just say 'six-ninety-five plus tax.' It says, 'Hosie Russell murdered me on my doorstep for seven dollars.' It says, 'Give me justice!'

"Ladies and gentlemen of the jury, the evidence in this case is overwhelming and conclusive. It demonstrates beyond a resonable doubt, to a moral certainty, that Hosie Russell stabbed Susan Weiner to death in the course of a robbery. And so, in the name of the People of New York, I ask you to find Hosie Russell guilty of felony murder and guilty of intentional murder: guilty as charged."

Karp waited a few beats, looking at each face in turn, and then spun on his crutches, walked over to his seat, and sat down.

Martino charged the jury. It was a good, fair charge, but in the nature of things, as he went over the points of evidence, explaining how the law applied to each one, it was inevitable that he mentioned prosecution evidence more than that of the defense. Karp had no problem with the charge, but Freeland did. All of his motions were, however, denied, and the jury marched out to deliberate at 4:45.

"How did it go?" Marlene asked.

"The usual." They were in his office.

"You were brilliant and the other guy was an asshole?"

Karp laughed. "Needless to say."

"What do you think?"

"I think we'll get felony murder. It's a toss-up if they'll go for intentional murder on the second count. Man one's more likely. The poor scumbag probably really didn't want her dead—he just wanted the purse."

"Will they be out long?"

Karp considered this. It was an endless topic of debate among lawyers whether a short or a long deliberation had anything to do with the outcome, and on that topic, at least, the jury was still out. He said, "Not an all-nighter. I think five, six hours." He paused and smiled. "Then I'll get someone to drive me home. I'll honk and you can hoist me to heaven like a side of beef."

"Oh, cripes, that's right, you'll be home," said Marlene.

Karp noticed her expression and gave her a quizzical look. "Where'd you think I'd be? Look, you got plenty of warning. Just enough time to whip off a quick one and kiss him good-bye."

"Oh, don't be a jerk," said Marlene, too quickly. "It's just . . . well, I guess I was thinking I should've prepared some sort of official homecoming celebration."

"Just don't let the winch slip this time," said Karp, wondering what his wife was up to now.

■　　■　　■

They came back at 8:50. Karp straightened his tie in the reflection of a bookcase and heaved himself down to Part 52 for the orgasm.

He had judged rightly. The jury found Hosie Russell guilty of felony murder and guilty of manslaughter in the first degree. Martino thanked the jury, set a date for sentencing, and the courtroom cleared.

Karp sat in his chair and watched them take Russell away. Their eyes met for a moment, and Russell seemed about to say something, but the moment passed, and the convict shuffled out between two court officers, head bowed at the traditional angle.

Susan Weiner did not spring miraculously to life after this transaction, and Karp felt the familiar quasi-post-coital letdown.

"Christ, I hope I get dealt a better hand next time."

Karp looked up. It was Freeland, smiling, extending his hand for a collegial handshake. Karp ignored the hand. He stared silently at the other man until he dropped his hand and shrugged.

Freeland said, "Hey, the schmuck admitted that blue shirt—what could I do?"

"You could have refrained from suborning perjury," said Karp quietly. "You could have refrained from dragging the sister up there for no goddamn reason."

"Hey, just a minute there, Karp! Suborning . . . ?"

"Uh-huh. Or the next thing to it. The old fart never saw anything, and you know it. That's why you didn't take a statement off him when he waltzed in. You worked him until he gave you a story."

Freeland smiled coldly. "Believe what you want. I thought it was worth a shot. I mean, the jerk admitted he did it. I wasn't going to put him on the stand to make me look like shit, so all I had was the other-guy defense." He looked at his watch. "Well, it's been a joy, Counselor—"

"Wait a minute!" Karp snapped. "Hosie *told* you he did it?"

"Sure." Freeland smiled again, as at a joke. "You're not going to tell me that only the innocent are entitled to representation?"

"No, I was going to tell you you're a real scumbag, Freeland.

And I'm going to give you a piece of advice. You got two jobs here. One is cutting pleas, cranking the system. The other is keeping the cops and the D.A.'s honest. The way you do that is the way Tom Pagano did it—by being squeaky clean yourself. You want to play cute tricks, go private. Because if I ever catch you again doing something like you did on this one, I'm going to put your cute white ass in jail."

A brief staring and jaw-clenching contest then ensued, with no clear winner. Freeland turned and stalked away. Karp sighed. A nasty, faintly crooked Legal Aid director was just what he needed. It made a matched set with his nasty, faintly crooked boss, Sanford Bloom.

Karp went back to his office and placed the case file in the glass bookcase and closed the door on *People* v. *Russell*. He sat there in the dark for he did not know how long, listening to the distant sounds of late traffic and the hum of the building itself. Centre Street never slept; night court would be going on, and the complaint room, and babies just out of law school would be scurrying through the halls, learning how to cop felonies to misdemeanors with dispatch.

The phone rang. Karp waited for whoever it was to go away. At the eighth ring he picked it up.

"Karp."

"This Russell. Hosie."

"Yeah, Hosie, what is it?"

"Trial's over."

"I'm aware. What can I do for you?"

"Song like that, trial's over, all my trials." There was a pause. Then Russell cleared his throat noisily. "I can talk to you now, can't I?"

"Yeah, Hosie, talk away. What's on your mind?"

"They's a dude here, name of Medford? Talkin' about gettin' loose on account of he snitched out this fella supposed to've killed some big shot over by the U.N. Said he heard this guy admit it."

Karp felt a tingling in his belly. "Go on, what about him?"

"It's bullshit, that's what about it. Medford in a cell with me, not this other guy 'Arasium, somethin' like that."

"Tomasian. Aram Tomasian."

"Yeah! That's the dude. Anyway, Medford, he ain't nowhere near this guy. Guy in some other cell. He tol' me, like he some sharp motherfucker, this big shot from the D.A. set the whole thing up. He rat on Tomasian, he get to walk. Then they move him out, put him in the right cell, with Tomasian. And he calls the cops. Cops don't know nothin' till he tells them. It was all set up before by the D.A."

"Um, did Medford give you a name for this big shot?"

"Yeah, he ack like this motherfucker was his own cousin. Name Wharton."

Karp got the night-duty driver to take him home to Crosby Street. He mounted the absurd contraption and rode upward in the warm, dark shaft. Mercifully the winch did not slip, and he arrived safely in the bosom of his family.

"So, tell me!" said Marlene.

"It went the way I thought."

"My hero! You don't seem very hyped by it. When I saw your face, I thought maybe they walked him. What's wrong?"

"I don't know. I'm pissed off generally. I got into a stupid cat fight with fucking Freeland after the trial. And Roland came by and told me he didn't get anything out of Nassif. And I got this thing on my leg. The usual."

He clumped across the loft and collapsed on the red couch.

"And the whip cream on the charlotte russe was I got a call from my old buddy Hosie Russell. He told me who worked the scam on Tomasian. The jailhouse witness."

"You made a deal with Russell?"

"No, that's the weird part. He just called me up after the trial and spat the whole thing out. For free."

"Why'd he do something like that?"

"I don't know. I gave him a stupid lecture once about trying to just do something because it was right. I guess it sank in. Miracles happen, or maybe it was just an extra clever scam because I will do something for him after all. I'll make sure he gets old in some nice medium-security joint. There's no point in putting him in Attica. He's not violent unless he's loaded, and he's not a runner. I think he likes prison, as a matter of fact."

"Don't we all, each in our own way. So who was it?"

"Wharton, who else?" said Karp dully.

"Shit! What're you going to do?"

He rubbed his face. "I don't know. But he's gone—out of the office, that's for sure. I'll go to Bloom. He'll do the right thing once he knows the story. I mean, he likes Conrad, but not nearly as much as he likes himself. It'll be quiet and quick."

"What'll happen to him, not that I give a shit?"

Karp laughed bitterly. "They'll probably make him a judge." He fell back against the cushions and closed his eyes. Marlene looked at him with some alarm. She had never seen him so wan and diminished.

She said, "Poor baby! Did you eat?"

"No. You know I never eat when the jury's out. Why? Are you going to cook me something?"

"I might open you a can," said Marlene.

Which she did, a can of Progresso black bean soup with cheese ground thickly on top and a plate of olives and salami and provolone and egg tomatoes with olive oil on it and a chunk of warm, fresh bread rubbed with olive oil and garlic. He ate it like a wolf. Marlene drank black coffee and watched him eat.

He mopped up the soup with the last of his bread and leaned back in his chair, regarding his wife with an appraising eye. Matter-of-factly he asked, "So, Marlene, what's in the crate?"

"The crate?"

"Yeah, that big wooden crate in the corner with all the old cartons near your speed bag. With the drop cloth on it."

"Oh, that crate. Well, you know, to be perfectly honest, I don't know what's in it because I haven't opened it yet."

"Uh-huh. You don't think it has caviar in it? I'm just guessing that that's what it says on the top of the crate."

"Nope. I doubt the caviar."

"And how did this object come to be in our domicile, if I may ask?"

"Harry brought it up last night. Don't give me a lot of shit on this, Butchie. I only did—"

He held up a hand to stop her. "No, I don't want to know about it. And the reason for that is, when you're indicted for, let's see, misfeasance, grand larceny, burglary, and tampering with physical evidence, and maybe you have to go upstate for a while, I'll be able to say that I was not an accomplice after the fact. I'm thinking of the kid, here."

"Yes, good point," said Marlene. "Although I think I could make a good showing that I acted to save a priceless cultural relic from certain destruction. Harry said the furnace was all unloaded and set to go, in the locker."

"Mmm, there's that, although I think you're supposed to make said showing to a judge *before* you conduct a raid. You're supposed to have one of those pieces of paper—what's the word I'm looking for—begins with a *W* . . . ?"

"I hate it when you get sarcastic like this."

"Not to mention that, having done this bag job, you've destroyed the evidentiary value of whatever's in that crate. Which may mean never being able to prove that Djelal and Nassif did the murder."

Karp was groggy with the aftereffects of the trial. At such times he needed to sleep, to purge his mind of the accumulated memorized facts, the precedents, the points of law that had stuffed every available brain cell for weeks. He was not capable of a closely reasoned argument with his wife, nor was he capable of making the next logical connection: that there was an object worth thirty million dollars in his home, an object of interest to at least one Turkish murderer. And the mob.

He sighed and looked at her, his eyes bleary. Marlene did not respond to his last comment, so he said, "Well, whatever. You're a nut. I love you. I married you. I can't think about it right now. I'm going to crash. You coming?"

"Yeah, I'll just clean up here. Look, don't worry, okay? It'll be all right. About the crate."

"What crate? I din see no stinkin' crate," said Karp, and clumped his way slowly to bed.

Ahmet Djelal parked the black Cadillac Sedan de Ville on Crosby Street and looked up at the loft building he had come to burgle. He didn't much like using an embassy car, but his little sports car was too small to carry what he had to carry away. He also didn't like the idea of hauling the crate down five flights of stairs, but there didn't seem to be a choice. He had cased the building earlier that day, found out that his target was on the fifth floor, and learned that there wasn't an elevator.

He got out of the car, stretched, and checked the pistol in his shoulder holster. He was a large man, well over six feet tall and burly. He had a close-cropped head, a thick neck, and a dark flowing mustache. He looked like a Turkish policeman, which he was.

Djelal had no doubt that he could manage the crate by himself. Rolled up in his pocket was a furniture mover's strap. He would carry it down the stairs on his back.

Djelal also had no doubt that he could deal with whoever had stolen his property. After the first moment of panic when he had arrived at the storage place and found the thing missing, he had made a careful search of the area and found a crumpled MasterCharge slip with a name and a telephone number, obviously dropped by the thief. It was not hard to find the address from this information. He was, after all, a policeman.

The thief had an Italian name, which suggested that the people to whom he had planned to sell the gold and jewels might have arranged the theft. He knew who Marlene Ciampi was from her visit to the embassy. Obviously she was corrupt and had somehow learned where the mask was from that idiot Nassif and told her relatives. Djelal was not particularly worried that Nassif had been arrested. It had perhaps been a mistake to involve Nassif, a mere merchant, not a warrior, as he himself was, but one had to depend on family. And at least Nassif was a real Turk. He would not betray his cousin.

Djelal picked the lock of the downstairs door with ease. He put away his lock picks and turned on a pencil-beam flashlight. Slowly he mounted the steep, dark stairs.

At the fifth-floor landing he paused and listened. There was no sound from the other side of the door. He dropped to his knees and directed his light at the lock. He had just inserted his pick when Harry Bello came up silently behind him from the shadows of the landing and hit him across the back of the head with a braided leather sap.

"He's coming around," said Marlene.

A skylight and a colored glass lamp swam into Djelal's view and then a woman's face in the center of a cloud of black hair. He was lying on his back, his hands uncomfortably constrained behind him. His head hurt and he felt the bite of handcuffs on his wrists.

The dark, fuzzy edges of his vision cleared, and Djelal could see that he was in a large room with three people, the woman, a stocky man with a gray face, and a very tall man with a cast on his leg. The stocky man held a revolver in his hand.

The woman said, "Mr. Djelal, I'm Marlene Ciampi, an assistant district attorney, and this man here is Harry Bello, a police officer. You're under arrest for the murder of Mehmet Ersoy." Then she told him that he had the right to remain silent and the right to a lawyer, and that if he couldn't afford a lawyer, one would be provided for him. She asked him if he understood those rights.

He said, "*Bir kelime bile anlamiyorum. Bir tercüman bulabilir minisiz?*"

Marlene turned to Harry. "He's useless. Take him out and shoot him and throw the body in the river."

Involuntarily, sweat started out of Djelal's brow, and he gasped. Marlene looked at him sharply. "Yes, I think you understand English well enough. Now, do you understand your rights?"

Djelal said, "Yes."

"Good. Are you willing to make a voluntary statement at this time?"

"This is an outrage. I am an official of the Turkish government. I have diplomatic status."

"Yeah, but we're not talking about a parking ticket, are we?"

She pulled up a straight chair and sat down just a few inches from the couch on which he lay. Her knees almost touched his shoulder. She was wearing a blue bathrobe, and he thought she might be nearly naked underneath it. He could smell her body. He thought he was going insane; women did not do this to men, question them while they lay bound and helpless. The other way around was correct, as he himself had done many times when he was an intelligence officer with the military. It was like a nightmare in which you found yourself with a saddle on your back and a horse riding you.

"You're a very stupid man," she said. "I think maybe Ersoy was the brains of this operation. After you killed him, the two of you have been stumbling around like a pair of idiots. Once we knew about the art theft and forgery ring, it was no problem finding you. And nailing you. You understand that expression, 'nailing'? You're nailed.

"You had a nice little operation going, but the Mask of Gregory was too big for you. Too much cash involved. You figured, why split three ways when you could have half each? So you killed Ersoy, probably with that pistol you brought along tonight. . . ."

She gestured toward a low table, where his gun sat in a clear plastic bag. His mouth sagged.

"Yeah, I figured. It's the same gun. Dumb. Bone stupid. You thought you were smart pinning it on the Armenians, but it turns out that was really stupid. That's what got us started on the trail that led to the art scam. If you'd've just shot him on a dark street and lifted his watch and wallet, nobody would have asked any questions.

"But that's not the stupidest thing you did. No, the stupidest thing was to think that half of what you were going to get from Joey Castles for the gold and jewels from the mask was more than a third of what Kerbussyan would've paid for the mask itself. The two of you outsmarted yourselves out of about ten million dollars." She laughed in his face.

He broke. Djelal jerked himself upright and roared and lunged at Marlene with his teeth, his mouth throwing ropes of spit. She kicked her chair backward to avoid him, and instantly Harry Bello was between them with his pistol pressed hard against Djelal's skull and his arm locked around his neck.

"It was not the money, whore!" the Turk shrieked. "*Piç!* It was the Armeniy! Ersoy was going to sell the filthy saint to the Armenians! We were going to cheat them, like they cheated us. But he said, no, Kerbussyan would not be fooled. We can get more if we sell it. But we are real Turks. How could we give this filthy thing to our enemies, for them to glory in it and defame us more? Melt it, I said. But no, he wouldn't. He was corrupt, a politician! So we had men to steal it and we . . ."

"You killed him."

"He deserved death. He was a traitor."

Marlene said, "Wrap him up, Harry. We can get a statement from him in the morning. Did you get all that, Butch?"

Karp was no shorthand expert, but he could write like blazes when necessary; few who can't get through law school. He finished his scribbling and said, "Yeah, I think so. Except he said something like 'peach' at the start. Right after 'whore.'"

"I bet it was something nasty, right, Ahmet?"

But Djelal had sunk into morose silence. He did not resist when Bello led him out of the loft.

"That was quite a performance," said Karp. "Did you plan that whole thing? Like, how did he know to come here?"

"Harry planted a charge slip at the storage locker. I got the idea from the Russell case. Funny, isn't it? It was patriotism, not greed, that killed Ersoy. God protect us all from noble motives."

"Look who's talking," said Karp. He got up from the table and hopped over to the wall phone.

"Who are you calling? It's two A.M."

"Roland. I'm going to get him out of bed and get him down to Centre Street to spring Tomasian and write up Djelal."

"Oooh, nasty!"

"No, it's his case. He should handle it."

"You think he'll ever forgive you?"

"Roland isn't into grudges. Tomorrow there'll be a check in an envelope on my desk, and he'll never mention it again and neither will I."

Karp made his call, which was terse. He hung up and went back to the couch. Marlene put a kettle on to boil. She made tea, and they sat down at the porcelain-topped table in the kitchen to drink it.

"I've been thinking," Karp said. "All's well that ends well, but did you ever think that our guy might not have come alone? What if old Ahmet there'd brought three guys with machine guns along? Harry didn't have any cops backing him up, did he?"

"Not cops," said Marlene carefully. "Not as such. But there's backup, and more than three guys with machine guns."

"Kerbussyan! You tipped the Armenians this was going down. But that means . . ."

She sipped from her mug and waited.

"You're going to give the thing to Kerbussyan?"

"What thing is that, Butchie?" asked Marlene, giving him a hooded look, of just the kind that some ancestress of hers might have produced in the aftermath of an affair of poisoned daggers at the Palermo court of Robert the Devil.

Kerbussyan arrived ten minutes later in the company of two silent, mustached men, the same ones Karp had seen at the house above the Hudson many months ago. They wore field jackets, though it was a warm night. They clanked with weapons.

The old man embraced Marlene warmly and kissed her hand.

"My dear, I have no words—"

"No problem, Mr. K.," said Marlene, "but before we get all excited, let's check what's in the box."

Kebussyan's two shadows followed her back through the loft and returned bearing the crate. She gave one of them a short wrecking bar, and he took the top off the crate. Inside, in a nest of straw, was a package wrapped in padded cotton, secured with rigger's tape. One of the shadows drew it out and placed it on the dining room table. It was about the size and shape of a loveseat cushion, but obviously very heavy. The man grunted with the effort.

Kerbussyan approached the thing and studied it, as if he could see through the wrappings, through the centuries. He was pale and white around the nostrils. Marlene handed him scissors. Carefully and slowly he cut the tape and unwrapped layer after layer of gray padding.

Gold glinted as the last of the wrapping fell away.

"It is. It *is!*" cried the old man.

The cloth was swept aside and it stood there, a golden block the size of an atlas and as thick as an unabridged dictionary. On the closed doors of the reliquary triptych were embossed the figures of a man and a woman in Byzantine imperial regalia. They stood out, grave and holy, from a background studded with pearls and small diamonds.

"The emperor Zeno and the empress Ariadne," breathed Kerbussyan. "The donors." His fingers fumbled at the central catch, and then he threw open the doors of the reliquary.

Numen flooded off it like water off a broaching whale, filling the room with emotional power, like light for the deeper feelings. The door on the left was inscribed with a gold and enamel-work martyrdom of St. Hrip'sime, and on the right was St. Gregory preaching to the Armenian nobles, assisted by angels. In the center, the golden face of the Illuminator stared out, terrible and marvelous, his eyes great sapphires, alive with blue flames.

The three Armenians fell to their knees and crossed themselves, and there was a chorused prayer in the ancient tongue. Marlene felt her own knees dip involuntarily, and her hand twitched to make the cross. Karp, the Jewish pagan, just watched, fascinated in spite of himself.

After some time, they shut the doors and wrapped up the soul of Armenia in its padding. Kerbussyan was nearly speechless with gratitude.

"Please," he said, "what can I do for you? You must let me give you some—anything . . . anything I have."

"Thank you, Mr. Kerbussyan, but I can't accept anything. It's just my job. We return stolen property, and the fact that it was stolen a long time ago doesn't enter. I'm glad you got it back."

She walked them to the door. They were going to go to Centre Street to pick up Aram Tomasian. Marlene was thinking, naturally enough, about roots, about lost homelands, and a thought flashed into her mind.

"Ah, there is one small favor, if you could," she said hesitantly.

"Ask."

"You're in the real estate business. Do you know a guy named Morton Lepkowitz?"

"The name is familiar. What about him?"

Marlene explained their condo-conversion predicament.

"I'll take care of it," he said.

"How?"

"My dear, don't worry about it. What you have done is worth a bracelet of buildings like this one. As long as there are Armenians you will never want for a home. That is the same as forever." He gave her a flash of his shark's smile and left, flanked by his minions, bearing treasure.

Marlene walked back to the mattress. She felt light-headed, wired, and exhausted at the same time. Karp was waiting for her there, propped up on pillows, his hands behind his head. "Well," he said, "did you get your bribe?"

"It's not a bribe. I just asked him to see if he could convince Lepkowitz to go easy on us, and he said he'd do it."

"I bet. Has it occurred to you what's going to happen when all this comes out at the trial?"

Marlene got into bed and looked at him. "Trial? Who, Djelal? He'll never go to trial. He'll plead to the top count."

"What makes you so sure, Counselor?"

"Because if he doesn't, we'll deport his ass to Turkey, and they'll try him for stealing national treasures."

"He won't get much for that."

"It's a death sentence. How long do you think an ex-cop will last in a Turkish jail? A week? Especially the kind of cop Djelal was. And especially a Turkish jail. No, he'll do his twenty to life in Attica and be glad about it, and he'll give us Nassif too. What's the matter? You look like you swallowed a frog."

Karp blew air out, puffing his cheeks. "The bad guys are punished, the good guy is out—why don't I feel right?"

She put an arm around his shoulder and drew him close. "Because," she said, "you're basically honest, and you believe in the system, and I'm basically a crook, and I only believe in the system when it comes out the way I want. I believe in myself. How'd that Dylan line go? 'To live outside the law you must be honest . . .' Whatever that means, that's Marlene."

Karp said, as Bogart, "Don't be silly, you're taking the fall."

Marlene laughed. "Yeah, I know. You notice that Bogie doesn't marry Mary Astor and live happily ever after in that one. One of these days you'll turn my ass in. Why *did* we get married anyway?"

Karp reached for her. "Because you knew that someday you're going to need a good lawyer."